Jesse's kiss lingered in her cupped palm. Then his hand stole up to her waist and he tugged her toward his lap.

"No don't—not again," Abbie begged even as he eased her down expertly.

"Why not?" he whispered as his strong hands closed over her shoulders and turned her toward his chest.

"Because we hate each—" He stopped her words with his open lips, claiming her mouth until she broke away, protesting. "This is crazy, we must not—" But he pulled her mouth to his once more, and she thought, *I am crazy* and let him go on kissing her until his hands were on her back again, then at her waist.

"Don't fight it, Abbie," he murmured. "For once, don't fight it. . . ."

HUMMINGBIRD "will leave you breathless with wonder at the majesty of a master storyteller at her ver best ... a story that will remain as a monument to love, not just for today, but for always."
—*AFFAIRE DE COEUR*

HUMMINGBIRD

by LaVyrle Spencer,
author of **THE FULFILLMENT,**
THE ENDEARMENT,
and **TWICE LOVED**

Hummingbird

LaVyrle Spencer

A JOVE BOOK

HUMMINGBIRD

A Jove Book / published by arrangement with
the author

PRINTING HISTORY
Jove edition / May 1983
Second printing / June 1983
Third printing / January 1985

ISBN: 0-515-08373-9

Jove books are published by The Berkley Publishing Group,
200 Madison Avenue, New York, N.Y. 10016.
The words "A JOVE BOOK" and the "J" with sunburst
are trademarks belonging to Jove Publications, Inc.

PRINTED IN THE UNITED STATES OF AMERICA

With love to Mom and Pat.

And thanks to Janis Ian,
whose poignant love song
"Jesse" inspired me
to write this story.

Chapter 1

WHEN THE 9:50 pulled into Stuart's Junction, it always attracted a crowd, for the train was still a novelty which the whole town anticipated daily. Barefoot children squatted like quail in the sand reed and needlegrass just outside town till the loud, gaseous monstrosity flushed them up and raced them the last quarter-mile toward the gabled depot. Ernie Turner, the town drunk, came each day to meet it, too. Belching and weaving his way out of the saloon, he would settle on a bench by the depot porch and sleep it off till the afternoon train sent him back for his evening round. Down at the smithy, Spud Swedeen laid down his maul, let loose of his bellows, and came to stand in the gaping door with black arms crossed upon blacker apron. And when the ringing of Spud's iron ceased, all the ears of Stuart's Junction, Colorado, perked up. Then along the short expanse of Front Street shopkeepers stepped from their doorways onto the weather-bleached planks of the boardwalk.

That early June morning in 1879 was no different. When Spud stopped his clanging, the barber chair emptied, bank clerks left their cages, and scales in the assay office swung empty while everybody stepped outside to face northeast and watch for the arrival of the 9:50.

But the 9:50 didn't come.

Before long, fingers nervously toyed with watch fobs; timepieces were pulled out, opened, and snapped shut before dubious glances were exchanged. Murmurs of speculation were eventually replaced by restlessness as one by one the townsfolk returned to their shops to peer out occasionally through their windows and wonder at the train's delay.

Time crawled while every ear was cocked for the moan of that whistle, which didn't come and didn't come. An hour, and the stillness over Stuart's Junction became a hush of reverence, as if someone had died, but nobody knew who.

At 11:06 heads lifted, one by one. The first, then the second merchant stepped to his doorsill once again as the livening summer wind lifted the incoming steam whistle on its heated breath.

"That's her! But she's comin' in too fast!"

"If that's Tuck Holloway drivin' her, he's settin' to put 'er right through the depot! Stand back—she might jump the rails!"

The cowcatcher came on in a blur of speed while steam and dust wafted away behind it, and a red plaid arm flailed from the open window of the cab. It was Tuck Holloway, all right, whose words were lost in the slamming of iron and the hiss of steam as the engine overshot the depot by a hundred yards—still miraculously on both tracks. But Tuck's hoarse voice could not be heard above the babbling crowd who'd surged toward the depot. Then a single gunshot made every head turn and every jaw stop as Max Smith, the newly appointed station agent, stood with a pistol still smoking in his hand.

"Where's Doc Dougherty?" Tuck bellowed into the lull. "Better get him fast 'cause the train got held up about twenty miles north of here and we got two injured men aboard. One of 'em's bad shot, for sure."

"Who are they?" Max asked.

"Didn't stop to ask for names. Both of 'em's strangers to me. The one tried to rob my train and the other one saved it. Got hisself shot while he was doin' it, though. I need a couple men to tote 'em off."

Within minutes, two limp bodies were borne from the depths of the train, down its steps, into the waiting arms of bank clerk, hostler, assayer, and blacksmith.

"Someone get a wagon!"

Through the crowd came a buckboard, and onto it the motionless bodies were placed, while from around the saloon corner Doctor Cleveland Dougherty came panting and snorting, his black bag whacking his overweight calves as he ran. A moment later he knelt beside the first stranger, whose face was chalky and unnaturally pacified.

"He's alive," Doc pronounced. "Just barely." The second man was likewise checked. "Can't tell about this one. Get 'em to my place quick, and Spud, you make damn sure you miss every rock and pothole on the street between here and there!"

All who came to town that day lingered. The saloon did a roadhouse business. Down at the livery, Gem Perkins ran out of stalls. The floor beneath the cuspidors in the hotel lobby was well stained long before midafternoon, while underneath the beech trees in Doc's front yard townspeople sat with their eyes trained on his door, waiting now as they'd earlier waited for the arrival of the 9:50. Waiting to hear the fate of the two who'd ridden it in on their backs.

Miss Abigail McKenzie heaved a sigh that lifted her breasts beneath the pleated bodice of her proper Victorian blouse. She ran one small, efficient finger around the inside of the lace-edged choker collar to free it from her sticky skin. She made a quarter-turn to the left, blue eyes glancing askance into the mirror, and placed the back side of one hand beneath her jaw—just so—lifting the skin there to test it for tautness.

Yes, the skin was still firm, still young, she assured herself soberly.

Then she quickly slipped the oversized filigreed hatpin from the crown of her daisy-trimmed hat, placed the hat carefully upon her sternly backswept brown hair, rammed the pin home, and picked up her pristine white gloves from the seat of the huge umbrella stand—a thronelike affair with a mirror on its backrest and umbrellas and canes threaded through holes in its outsized arms.

She considered her gloves a moment, looked out front through the screen door at the shimmering heat ripples radiating skyward, laid the gloves down, hesitated, then resolutely picked them up again, dutifully drawing them over her slim hands. The heat is no excuse to go over town improperly dressed, she scolded herself.

She walked to the rear of her house, rechecking each shade

on each south window, assuring herself they were all drawn low against the harsh sun. She glanced in a full circle around her kitchen, but nothing needed straightening, putting away, or taking out. Her house was kept as fastidiously as was her clothing. Indeed, everything in Miss Abigail McKenzie's life was always as orderly and precise and correct as it could possibly be.

She sighed again, crossed the straight shot from kitchen to dining room to front parlor, and stepped onto the porch. But abruptly she reentered, checking the doorstop fussily, in the way of those who manufacture worry because their lives contain too little of the genuine article.

"No sense risking your lovely oval window," she said aloud to the door. That window was her pride and joy. Satisfied that the door was secure, out she went, closing the screen as gently as if it had feelings. She crossed the porch, walked down the path, and nodded hello to her well-tended roses beside the pickets.

She walked erectly, chin parallel to the earth, as a lady of propriety ought. Let it never be said that Miss Abigail stooped, slouched, or slogged when she walked over town. Oh, never! Her carriage was utterly proper at all times. Her sensible shoes scarcely peeked from beneath her skirts, for she never hurried—rushing was most undignified!

She had things on her mind, Miss Abigail did, which didn't rest lightly there. Her errand was not one she relished. But one would never guess from perusing her as she strode down Front Street that there could be the slightest thing amiss with Miss Abigail McKenzie, if indeed one ever could.

Coming along past the houses and yards, her eye was caught by the unusual scene up ahead. Doc Dougherty's lawn was crowded with people, while across the street the benches of the boardwalk were hidden behind solid skirts and men sat on its high ledge while children scuffled in the dirt and horses waited at the hitching rails.

One could always rely upon Miss Abigail to keep her nose out of other people's business. Seeing the crowd, she swung left, walked the short block over to Main, and finished her trek over town along its all but deserted length. Thus Miss Abigail avoided what was probably some sordid spectacle at Doc Dougherty's. That kind of thing attracted riffraff, and she was not about to be one of their number!

Miss Abigail thought it truly lamentable to have to do what she was about to do. Oh, not that there was anything wrong with Louis Culpepper's establishment. He ran a neat and orderly eatery—she'd give him that. But waiting tables was truly a last resort—oh, truly a last! It was not at all the kind of thing she'd choose to do, had she the choice. But Miss Abigail had no choice. It was either Louis Culpepper's place or starve. And Abigail McKenzie was too ornery to starve.

Sensible black squat heels aclicking, she entered beneath the sign hailing, THE CRITERION—FINE FOOD AND DRINKS, LOUIS CULPEPPER, PROP. As she carefully closed the door, she ran a hand over her blouse front, making sure it was tightly tucked into her skirtband, then, turning, she again sighed. But the place looked deserted. There was a faint odor of yesterday's cabbage adrift in the air, but nothing resembling the aroma of meats stewing for the supper clientele, who wouldn't be long in coming. Why, one would have thought Louis to be better organized than this!

"Hello?" she called, cocking her head, listening.

From somewhere in the rear came a tiny, tinny sound. She walked toward the kitchen to find the alley door open and a hot breeze buffeting the saucepans that hung above the wood range. The place *was* abandoned.

"Well, I declare!" Miss Abigail exclaimed to no one at all. Then, glancing in a circle, repeated, "Well, I *do* declare!"

It had taken her some weeks to finally decide she must speak to Louis. To find his restaurant empty was most disconcerting. Wiping an errant bead of perspiration from her forehead with a single finger of her pristine glove, Miss Abigail chafed at this unexpected turn of events. Inspecting the fingertip, she found it dampened by her own sweat and knew she could not put herself through this a second time. She must find Louis now, today!

Adjusting her already well placed hat, she again took to Main Street, then over one block to Front, on which both she and Doc lived, some two blocks apart. Rounding the corner, she found herself part of the throng that filled Doc Dougherty's yard and the surrounding area. Doc himself was standing under his beech trees, sleeves rolled up, speaking loudly so everyone could hear.

". . . lost a lot of blood and I had to operate to clean up the hole and shut it up. It's too early to tell if he'll make it yet. But you all know it's my duty to do whatever I can to keep him alive, no matter what he's done."

A distracted murmur passed among the townspeople while Miss Abigail glanced around hopefully, looking for Louis Culpepper. Spying a towheaded youth who lived next door to her, she whispered, "Good day, Robert."

"Howdy, Miss Abigail."

"Have you seen Mr. Culpepper, Robert?"

But the boy's neck was stretched and his ears tuned to Doc again as he grunted, "Un-uh."

"Who is Doctor Dougherty talking about?"

"Don't rightly know. Some strangers got themselves shot on the train."

Relieved that it was none of the town's own, Miss Abigail was nonetheless forced to give up her cause as fruitless until the crowd dispersed, so turned her attention to the doctor.

"The other one's not in as bad of a shape, but he'll be out of commission for a few days. Between the two of 'em, I'll have my hands full. You know Gertie's gone off to her cousin's wedding in Fairplay and I'm caught shorthanded here. There's plenty of you'll be hollering for me, and I just plain can't be in more than one place at a time. So if there's anybody that'd volunteer to give me a hand looking after these two, well, I'd be obliged."

From somewhere in the crowd a woman's voice spoke what many were thinking. "I'd like to know why we should feel obliged to take care of some outlaw tried his hardest to do us dirt! Robbing our train that way and shooting that innocent young man in there. Why, what if it'd been Tuck he shot?"

Doc raised his hands to quiet the swell of agreement.

"Now, hold on! I got two men in here, and granted, the one done wrong and the other done right, but they're both in need of help. Would you people have me tend the one that's hurt less and turn out the one that's nearly dead?"

Some of them had the grace to drop their eyes, but still they demurred.

Doc continued while he had 'em feeling guilty. "Well, a man can do just so much alone, and that's all he can do. I need help and I'm leaving it up to you to find it for me. The problem isn't just mine—it's all of ours. Now, we all wanted the Rocky Mountain Railroad to put their spur line through here, didn't we? And sure enough we got it! 'Course, we only banked on it hauling our quartz and copper and silver out of here and bringing our conveniences in from the East. But now that we get a little trouble hauled in too, we're not so all-fired anxious to stand up and pay the price, are we?

Still nobody volunteered.

What Doc said was undeniably true. The railroad was an asset from which they all benefited. Having a spur line run into a hidden mountain town like Stuart's Junction opened it up to both East and West, bringing the town commerce, transportation, and a stable future that it had lacked before the R.M.R. laid tracks up here.

The citizens chose to forget all that now, though, leaving Doc Dougherty to plead his case, and leaving Miss Abigail somehow inexplicably angry at their heartlessness.

"I could pay anyone that took on to help me—the same as I pay Gertie when she's here," Doc offered hopefully.

Miss Abigail glanced around. Her mouth puckered.

"Hell, Doc," someone hollered, "Gertie's the only nurse this town's ever saw or prob'ly ever will. You ain't gonna find nobody to take her place nohow."

"Well, maybe not anybody as qualified as Gertie, but anybody that's willing is qualified enough to suit me. Now what do you say?"

The sweat broke out upon Miss Abigail's upper lip. What she was considering was too sudden, too unprecedented, yet she had no time for rumination. And the smug attitudes surrounding her made her unutterably angry! The thought of tending two injured men in the privacy of her own home seemed far, far preferable to carrying stew and soup to the lot of them. Furthermore, she was almost as skilled as Gertie Burtson. Her pulse thrummed a little behind her proper, tight collar, but her chin was high as ever as she stepped forward, squelching her misgivings, putting those around her in their proper place.

"I believe, Doctor Dougherty, that I would qualify," Miss Abigail stated in her ladylike way. But since a lady does not shout, Doc didn't quite hear her. Nobody believed what they were seeing as Miss Abigail raised a meticulous white glove.

"Miss Abigail, is that you?" he called; somehow the crowd had silenced.

"Yes, Doctor Dougherty, it is. I should like very much to volunteer."

Before he could check his reaction, Doc Dougherty raised his brows, ran a grizzled hand over his balding head, and blurted out, "Well, I'll be damned!"

Excusing herself, Miss Abigail made her way to Doc's side. She parted the crowd almost as Moses parted the Red Sea, still with that level chin and that all-fired dignity she always maintained. As she passed, men actually reached as if to doff hats they weren't wearing.

"G'day, Miss Abigail."

"How do, Miss Abigail."

"Howdy, Miss Abigail."

The ladies greeted her with silent, smiling nods, most of them awed by her cool, flowing presence as she glided toward Doc in her customary, pure-bred way while they fanned themselves and raised their arms to let the breeze at their wet armpits. Moving through their midst, Miss Abigail somehow managed to make them all feel gross and lardy and—worse— small, for the help they'd stubbornly refused.

"Come inside, Miss Abigail," Doc said, then raised his voice to the crowd. "You might as well go home now. I'll leave word up at the station with Max if there's any change." Then, solicitously taking Miss Abigail's elbow, he led her inside.

His widower's house was a mishmash of flotsam, collected and never discarded. The big front room looked like a willful child had messed it up in retaliation for being spanked, except that the strewn articles obviously were an adult's. Doc Dougherty removed a stack of journals and newspapers from an armchair, kicked aside a pair of forlorn house slippers, and said, "Sit down, Miss Abigail, sit down."

"Thank you," she replied, sitting in the cleared spot as if it were the dais in a throneroom.

While she gave the impression that none of the debris around her infiltrated her superb hauteur, Miss Abigail noticed all right. Old Doc Dougherty meant well enough, but since his Emma died the place had become slovenly. Doc kept absurd hours, running to anyone who needed him at any hour of the day or night, but leaving himself little time for such refinements as housecleaning. Gertie Burtson was hired as his nurse, not as his housekeeper. That was all too evident by the looks of the room.

Doc Dougherty sat down on the arm of an old lumpy horsehair sofa, spread his old lumpy knees, and covered them with his old lumpy hands. As his rump came into contact with the overstuffed arm, Miss Abigail saw a puff of dust emanate from the horsehair and overcast the air around him. He studied the floor a minute before speaking.

"Miss Abigail, I appreciate your offer." He didn't know exactly how to say this. "But you know, Miss Abigail, I hardly thought you'd be the one to step forward and volunteer. This is probably a job somebody else is better suited for."

Irritation pricked her. Crisply, she asked, "Are you refusing my help, Doctor Dougherty?"

"I . . . I'd hate to say I'm refusing. I'm asking you to consider what you're getting into."

"I believe I have considered it. As a result, I've offered my services. If there is some inexplicable reason why I shan't do, then we are both wasting our time." When Miss Abigail was piqued, her voice became curt and she tended to get eloquently wordy. She rose, looking down her nose as she tugged her gloves more securely on her hands.

He moved quickly to press her back into her chair, his dust cloud swirling with him. She looked up at him from under her hat brim, inwardly gratified that he'd seen her pique. Fine time for him to get choosy!

"Hold on now, don't get yourself all in a huff."

"In a huff, Doctor Dougherty? I hardly would describe myself as being in a huff." She arched one brow and tipped her head.

Doc Dougherty stood above her, smiling, peering at her upturned face under its crisp bonnet of daisies. "No, Miss Abigail, I doubt you've ever been in a huff in your life. What I'm trying to make you see is that you might be if I agree to let you nurse those two."

"Pray tell why, Doctor?"

"Well, the truth is . . . because you're a . . . a maiden lady."

The phrase echoed cruelly through Miss Abigail McKenzie's thirty-three-year-old head, and within her fast-tripping, lonely heart.

"A maiden lady?" she repeated, mouth puckered a little tighter.

"Yes, Miss Abigail."

"And what possible bearing does my being a . . . a

maiden lady—as you so kindly put it—have upon my being capable of helping you?"

"You must understand that I hoped for a married woman to volunteer."

"Why?" she asked.

Doc Dougherty turned his back and walked away, searching for a delicate way to phrase it. He cleared his throat. "You'd be exposed to parts of these men that you'd probably rather not be and asked to perform duties that would be—to say the least—unpalatable to a lady of your—" But his words faltered. He found himself unwilling to embarrass her further.

Miss Abigail finished for him. "Tender sensibilities, Doctor?" Then with a little false laugh asked, "Were you about to expound upon my being a lady of tender sensibilities?"

"Yes, you might put it that way." He turned once again to face her.

"Are you forgetting, Doctor, about the years I cared for my father while he was ill?"

"No, Miss Abigail, I'm not. But he was your father, not some gunshot stranger."

"Posh, Mister Dougherty," she said, giving the impression she'd spit out the words when they'd come out with calculated control, along with the word *Mister* instead of *Doctor*. "Give me one good reason why I should not care for these two gentlemen."

He flung his hands out in frustration. "Gentlemen! How do you know they're gentlemen? And what if they're not? What'll you do when I'm fourteen miles out in the country and you're wishing I weren't? One of those *gentlemen* just tried to rob a train and I'm willing to treat him, but that doesn't mean I'll trust him. Suppose he tries to overpower you and escape?"

"A moment ago you advised me not to get into a huff. May I now advise you the same, Doctor? You've been shouting."

"I'm sorry, Miss Abigail. I guess I was. But it's my responsibility to make you see the risk involved."

"You've done your duty then, Doctor Dougherty. But since I see your plea for help did not raise a plethora of willing volunteers, I hardly see that you have a choice but to accept my offer."

Doc shook his head at the threadbare carpet, wondering what her father would have said. Abbie had always been the apple of the old man's eye.

Miss Abigail looked up at him, so prim and erect from her spot on the forlorn old armchair, her mind made up.

"I have a strong stomach, a hand full of common sense, and a nearly empty bank account, Doctor," she stated. "And you have two wounded men who need looking after. I suspect that neither of them is healthy enough right now to either harm me or escape from me, so shall we get on with it?"

She knew she had him with that reference to her bank account.

"You're sure one smooth talker, Miss Abigail, and I'm up a crick, I'll grant you that. But I can't pay you much, you know. Thirty dollars for the week is about it. It's as much as I pay Gertie."

"Thirty dollars will do nicely . . . oh, and one thing more," she added, easing to the edge of her chair.

"Yes?"

"What do you propose to do with them when your patients arrive tomorrow morning?"

Miss Abigail's eyes had not scanned the room; they didn't have to for Doc to know that his place wasn't exactly her idea of a suitable hospital. He had no delusions regarding the condition of his house. What could be seen from their present vantage point was a sorry mess at best. They both knew what she'd find if she were to peruse the upstairs or—worse—the kitchen. They both knew, too, that she had a penchant for cleanliness. And so when Doc finally finished eyeballing the room, he was totally aware of the place's shortcomings.

"I don't suppose we could put 'em upstairs?" he asked fruitlessly.

"I don't suppose that would be the most convenient place. I propose that we remove them to my house as soon as you think that would be possible. It would be infinitely easier for me to care for them were I to have my own kitchen at my disposal."

"You're right," Doc agreed, and abruptly Miss Abigail got to her feet.

"Now, may I see our patients?"

"Of course. One's on the surgery table and the other on the sofa in the waiting room, but they're both out cold for the time being. Tomorrow'll be time enough for you to take charge of them."

They walked through an archway into Doc Dougherty's waiting room, which was only slightly tidier than the parlor.

On a sagging sofa beneath a triple window a man lay unmoving. He wore a city suit, its vest and jacket unbuttoned. One of his feet, brown-stockinged, stuck out from a pant leg while the other sported a bandage covering the forefoot but leaving the heel bare where it rested on a pillow. His face, in repose, was pleasant. His hair was nondescript brown and fell away from his forehead in boyish waves. His ears were flat and his nails clean. And that was good enough for Miss Abigail.

"This is the man who robbed the train?" she asked.

"No. The other one robbed the train. This one—Melcher's his name—apparently interrupted the proceedings. The way Tuck tells it, Melcher here took a stray bullet from that one's gun." Doc thumbed over his shoulder in the direction of the surgery. "Must've been some kind of scuffle involving a bunch of passengers because by the time Tuck got the train stopped and got back there to see what was going on, everybody was telling the story a different way and these two were lying there bleeding. One of the shots took Melcher's big toe clean off his right foot."

"His big toe!" she exclcaimed, pressing her fingers to her lips to hide the smile.

"Could've been worse if the shot had been higher. On the other hand, it could've been little or nothing if he'd had a sensible pair of boots on instead o' them flimsy city shoes he was wearing."

Miss Abigail looked to where Doc Dougherty pointed, and there on the floor sat a single stylish brown shoe of fine, soft leather.

"Had to cut the other one off him," Doc informed her. "Wasn't any good anyway, with the end shot off like it was."

Miss Abigail had to smile in spite of herself. First at Doc's keeping the single shoe, which was no good without its mate, and secondly at the absurdity of the town's first hero saving the day by getting his big toe shot off!

"Is something funny, Miss Abigail?" She sobered at once, chagrined at being caught in a state of levity at this unfortunate man's expense.

"No . . . no, forgive me, Doctor. Tell me, is the loss of a toe a serious injury? I mean, is his life in danger?"

"No, hardly. The toe came off real clean, and there was no lead shavings or powder left on him once the bullet went through that shoe. He was in awful shock and lost some blood, but I put him to sleep and stitched him up and he'll be good as new in no time. When he wakes up, that toe is gonna throb like a bitch in heat, though . . ." Doc suddenly seemed to realize to whom he was talking. "Oh . . . forgive me, Miss Abigail. I forgot myself."

Miss Abigail colored deeply, stammering, "I . . . oh, I shall certainly sympathize with poor Mr. Melcher."

"Yes . . . well . . ." Doctor Dougherty cleared his throat. "Mr Melcher will undoubtedly find himself walking with a limp from now on, but that should be the worst of it. We'll keep the foot propped up, keep it bandaged for a couple of days, and I'll give you some salve for it. But mostly time and air will have to heal the stitches. You're right—Mr. Melcher will need good old-fashioned sympathy most of all."

"So much for the damage done here. And what about the other?" Miss Abigail asked, relieved that her composure was returning.

Turning toward the surgery door, the doctor walked a step or two toward it. "The other bullet, I fear, did far more damage. This scoundrel will undoubtedly rue the day he set foot on that R.M.R. train . . . if he lives long enough."

They came to the doorway and Miss Abigail preceded him into its cream-colored depths. Here at last was cleanliness, although she devoted not even the quickest glance to it. Her eyes were drawn to the rectangular table where a sheet shrouded an inert figure. The table faced the doorway, so all that was visible was the sole of a left foot—a very long left foot, thought Miss Abigail—and the rise of sheet covering an updrawn right knee and leg.

"This one is lucky to be alive. He lost plenty of blood from the gunshot and more when I had to clean the wound out. He'd have been better off if the bullet had stayed in him. As it was, it came out the other side and blew a hole in him twenty times bigger than the one it made going in. Left a pretty big mess on its way through, too."

"Will he die?" Miss Abigail whispered, staring at that long foot that made her insides jitter. She'd never seen a man's bare foot before, other than her father's.

"No need to whisper. He's dead to the world and he's going to stay that way for a while, or I miss my guess. But as to whether or not the poor son of a b—the poor fool will die, that I can't say yet. Looked to be healthy as a horse before this

happened to him." Doc Dougherty had walked farther than
Miss Abigail into the room and now stood beside the man on
the surgery table. "Come and have a look at him."

Miss Abigail experienced a sudden stab of reluctance but
ventured far enough to see bare shoulders with the sheet slicing
them at armpit level. Above was a chest shadowed with dark,
curled hair, broad, tanned shoulders, and the bottom of a dark-
skinned face that sported an evil-looking moustache. She
couldn't see any of the features above the moustache from this
angle, only the nostrils, which were shaped like half hearts,
and the lower lip, which suddenly twitched as she looked at it.
His chin wore only a trace of the day's growth of whiskers, and
she suddenly found herself thinking that for a train robber he
certainly kept himself up, if the clean foot and the recent shave
were any indication.

The sheet covered him from biceps to ankle, giving no
indication of where he was injured or how seriously. From here
he looked as if he might have stretched out for a nap, one knee
slung up haphazardly as he serenely dozed.

"He was shot in the groin," Doc said, and Miss Abigail
suddenly blanched and felt her stomach go weightless.

"In . . . in the—" she stammered, then halted.

"Not quite . . . but very close. Do you still want the
job?"

She didn't know. Frantically she thought of everyone in town
hearing the reason she had changed her mind. She stood there
considering a man coming to such an end. Whether she still
wanted to care for him or not, she felt somehow sorry for the
unconscious fellow.

"A train robber might expect to come to a bad end, yet
nobody should come to this."

"No, Miss Abigail. It's not a pretty sight, but it could've
been worse. A few inches difference and he could've lost
. . . well, he could have been dead."

Miss Abigail blushed again but nevertheless looked resolutely at Doc Dougherty. Nobody else had come forward but
herself. Even a hapless train robber deserved human consideration.

"I quite understand, Doctor, what the man's dilemma might
have been, but don't you agree that even a robber deserves our
sympathies, in his present state?"

"My sympathies he's got, Miss Abigail, and plenty of them.

He'll get every bit of care I can give him, but I got to warn you, I'm no miracle worker. If he lives it'll be just that—a dad-blamed miracle."

"What am I to do for him, Doctor?" she asked, suddenly deciding that a man this age—he looked to be thirty-five or so—was much too young to die.

"You're sure about this? Very sure?"

"Just tell me what to do." The look in her eyes, just like years ago when she'd taken on the care of her father, told Doc Dougherty she meant business.

"You'll keep the knee raised, keep the thigh up, so the air can get at the underside as well as the top. I managed to staunch the flow of blood, but if it starts up again, you'll have to apply alum to try to stop it. Keep the wound clean—I'll tell you what to disinfect it with. Watch for any putrefaction and if you see any, come runnin' like a cat with her tail on fire the minute you see any sign of it. We'll have to try to keep his fever down. For the pain there's not much we can do. Keep him still. Try to get him to eat. Do you think you can handle that, Miss Abigail?"

"Everything but setting my tail on fire," she replied drily, surprising Doc with her wit. He smiled.

"Good. You go home now and get a good night's rest because it'll probably be your last for a while. I'm expecting a run on the place in the morning and I'd like to have these two out of here before it starts. I 'spect everyone with so much as an ingrown hair will be in here hoping for a glimpse of either a genuine robber or a genuine hero."

"Ah well, I expect I'm the lucky one then, to have seen them both at close range." A brief smile tugged at the corner of Miss Abigail's mouth.

"I 'spect you are at that. How can I thank you?"

"I'll see you in the morning. Everything shall be in order for their arrival."

"I'm sure it will be, Miss Abigail. Knowing you, I'm sure it will be."

She turned to leave, but at the door turned back.

"What . . . what is his name, the robber's?"

"We don't know. Men in his profession don't carry calling cards like Mr. Melcher did."

"Oh . . . oh, of course not," she replied, then hesitated a moment longer to add, "but it would be a shame if he should die and we should not know whom to inform. He must have someone somewhere."

Doc Dougherty had scarcely had time to think of that yet.

"Only a woman with a heart would think of that at a time like this."

"Nonsense," Miss Abigail said briskly, then turned to leave.

But of course he was right, for her heart was doing monkeyshines as she walked home, remembering a bare long foot; a dark, furred chest; and the prospect of caring for a wound near the man's—

But Miss Abigail McKenzie not only avoided speaking such a word. She could not even think it!

Chapter 2

THE SUN WAS hotter than ever the following day as Doc approached the loiterers on the sagging veranda of Mitch Field's feedstore. They congregated there to drape on the feed sacks, spit and chew, and never give poor Mitch so much as a lick of business.

"All right, which of you lazy no-goods is gonna give me a hand," Doc challenged.

They even laughed lazily, then squinted at the sun, gauging the discomfort of exerting themselves against the chance of getting a gander at them two up at Doc's house. Old Bones Binley scratched his grizzled jaw with the dull edge of a whittling knife and drawled, "Reckon you can count me in, Doc."

It was Doc's turn to laugh. Bones had a yen for Miss Abigail and the whole town knew it. Bones looked just like his name, but along with some help from Mitch and Seth Carter, the transfer of patients was handled without mishap.

Miss Abigail was waiting at her front door and directed Doc and Mitch to place David Melcher in the southeast bedroom upstairs and the other man in the downstairs bedroom, since it was probably inadvisable to carry him up the steps.

The train robber was too long for the mattress, and his feet hung beyond the footrail, so the sheet covered him only up to the waist. Bones and Seth watched Miss Abigail's face as she came around the doorway and saw that bare, hairy chest lying there, but she barely gave it a glance before turning to the pair and dismissing them coolly and unquestionably. "Thank you, gentlemen. I'm sure you have pressing business down at the feedstore."

"Why, uh, yes . . . yes we do, Mizz Abigail." Bones grinned while Seth elbowed him in the ribs to get him moving.

Outside, Seth said, "It might be ninety-nine degrees everywhere else, but a body could freeze to death anywhere within fifteen feet o' Miss Abigail McKenzie."

"Ain't she somethin', though?" Bones gulped, his Adam's apple protruding.

"Whole town knows she can twist you around her finger, but that sugary voice of hers don't fool me none. Underneath that sugar is mostly vinegar!"

"You really think so, Seth?"

"Why, sheee-oot, I know so. Why, lookit how she just excused us, like we was clutterin' up her bedroom or somethin'."

"Yeah, but she took in that there train robber, didn't she?"

"Did it for the money, the way I heard tell. It's prob'ly the only way she could get a man in her bed. And that one that's in it now will be sorry he didn't die when he comes to and finds hisself bein' nursed by the likes of her."

There were those in town, like Seth, who considered Miss Abigail just a touch above herself. Granted, she was always soft-spoken, but she had that way, just the same, of elevating herself and acting lofty.

When Doc had settled the patients and told her to send Rob Nelson if she needed anything, he promised to check in again that evening, then left with Mitch in tow.

She thought Mr. Melcher was asleep when she crept to the door of his room, for his arm lay over his forehead and his eyes were closed. Though his beard had grown overnight, he had a very nice mouth. It reminded her of Grandfather McKenzie's mouth, which had always smiled readily. Mr. Melcher looked to be perhaps in his late twenties—it was hard to tell with his eyes closed. Glancing around, she spied his suitcase under the Phyfe library table near the window and tiptoed across to open it and find his nightshirt. When she turned, she found that Mr. Melcher had been watching her.

"Ah, you're awake," she said gaily, disconcerted at being caught searching through his personal belongings.

"Yes. You must be Miss McKenzie. Doc Dougherty said you'd volunteered. It was very good of you."

"Not really. I live alone and have the time that Doctor Dougherty doesn't." She looked at his foot then, asking, "How does it feel this morning?"

"It's throbbing some," he answered honestly, and she immediately colored and fussed with the nightshirt.

"Yes, well . . . we'll see if we can't relieve it somewhat. But first I believe we'd best get you out of your suit. It looks as if it could stand a flour bath." The brown wool worsted was indeed wrinkled but Miss Abigail had grave misgivings about how to gracefully get him out of it.

"A flour bath?"

"Yes, a dredging in clean flour to absorb the soil and freshen it. I'll take care of it for you."

Although he moved his arm off his forehead and smiled, he was smitten with discomfort at the thought of undressing before a lady.

"Are you able to sit up, Mr. Melcher?"

"I don't know. I think so." He raised his head but grunted, so she crossed the room quickly and touched his lapel, saying, "Save your energy for now. I shall be right back." She returned shortly, bearing pitcher and bowl, towel and wash-cloth, and a bar of soap balanced across a glass of bubbling water. When she had set things down, she stood beside him, saying, "Now, let's get your jacket off."

The whole thing was done so slickly that David Melcher later wondered how she'd accomplished it. She managed to remove his jacket, vest, and shirt and wash his upper half with a minimum of embarrassment to either of them. She held the bowl while he rinsed his mouth with the soda water, then she helped him don his nightshirt before removing his trousers from beneath it. All the while she chatted, putting them both at ease. She said she would rub flour into his suit jacket and let it sit for a few hours, and by the time she hung it on the line and beat the flour from it with her rug-beater, it would be as fresh as a daisy. He'd never heard of such a thing! Furthermore, he wasn't used to a woman fussing over him this way. Her voice flowed sweetly while she attended him, easing him through what would otherwise have been a sticky situation had she been less talkative or less efficient.

"It seems you have become something of a local hero, Mr. Melcher," she noted, giving him only the beginnings of a smile.

"I don't feel much like a hero. I feel like a fool, ending up stretched out here with a toe shot off."

"The townspeople have a great interest in our new railroad and wouldn't like to see it jeopardized in any way. You've saved it from its first serious mishap. That's nothing to feel foolish about. It is also something which the town won't forget soon, Mr. Melcher."

"My name is David." But when he would have caught her eye she averted hers.

"Well, I'm pleased to meet you, though I regret the circumstances, on your behalf. From where do you hail, Mr. Melcher?"

When she used his surname he felt put in his place and colored slightly. "I'm from back East." He watched her precise movements and suddenly asked, "Are you a nurse, Miss Abigail?"

"No, sir, I'm not."

"Well, you should be. You're very efficient and gentle."

At last she beamed. "Why, thank you, Mr. Melcher. I take that as one of the nicest things you could say, under the circumstances. Are you hungry?"

"Yes, I don't remember when I ate last."

"You've been through an ordeal, I'm sure, that you'll be long in forgetting. Perhaps the right food will make your stay here seem shorter and your bad memories disappear the faster."

Her speech was as refined as her manners, he thought, watching her move about the room gathering his discarded clothing, stacking the toilet articles to carry away. He felt secure and cared for as she saw to his needs, and he wondered if this was how it felt to be a husband.

"I'll see to your suit after I prepare your breakfast. Oh! I forgot to comb your hair." She had stopped halfway out the door.

"I can do that myself."

"Have you a comb?"

"Not that I can reach."

"Then take the one from my apron pocket."

She came back and raised her laden arms so he could get at the comb. His hesitation before reaching to take it told her things about him that a thousand words could not tell. David Melcher, she could see, was a gentleman. Everything about him pleased her, and she later found herself inexplicably buoyant and humming while she worked in the kitchen preparing his meal. Perhaps she even felt the slightest bit wifely as she delivered the tray of bacon, eggs, and coffee, and wished she could stay and visit. But she had yet another patient needing her attention.

At the bedroom doorway downstairs, she hesitated, gazing at the stranger on her bed. Just the fact that he was a criminal was disquieting, though he remained unconscious, unable to harm her in any way. His beard was coal black, as were his moustache and hair, but his skin, since last night, had taken on the color of tallow. Coming fully into the room, she studied him more closely. There was a sheen of sweat on his bare chest and arms, and she reached out tentatively to touch him, finding his body radiating an unhealthy inner heat.

Quickly she fetched a bowl of vinegar water and sponged his face, neck, arms, and chest, as far as his waist, where the sheet stopped, then left the cool compresses on his brow in an effort to bring down his fever. She knew she must check his wound, but at the thought her palms went damp. She held her breath and gingerly lifted a corner of the sheet. Flames shot through her body at the sight of his nakedness. Her years of caring for an incontinent father had done nothing to prepare her for this! With a shaky hand she lay the sheet at an angle across his stomach, his genitals, and left leg, then fetched two firm bolsters to boost up his right knee. She snipped away the gauze bindings, but the bandages stuck to his skin, so next she mixed vinegar water with saltpeter and applied the dripping compresses to loosen the cotton from his wounds. The shot had hit him very high on the inner thigh, which had been firm before the bullet did its dirty work. But now, when the bangage fell free, she saw that the wound had begun bleeding again. One look and she knew she had her work cut out if he wasn't to bleed to death.

Back in the kitchen she spooned alum into an iron frying pan, shaking it over the hot range until it smoked and darkened. She sprinkled the burnt alum liberally onto a fresh piece of gauze, but when she hurried back to the bedroom with the poultice, she stood horrified, gaping at the blood of this nameless train robber as it welled in the bullet hole then ran the short distance into the shallow valley of his groin, where coarse hair caught and held it.

How long she stood staring at the raw wound and the collecting blood she did not know. But suddenly it was as if someone had shot her instead of him. Her body jerked as if from the recoil, and once again she was frantically bathing, staunching, praying. In the hours which followed, she fought against time as a mortal enemy. Realizing that he must soon eat . . . or die . . . she beat a piece of steak with a mallet and put it into salt water to steep into beef tea. But he kept bleeding and she began to doubt that he'd live to drink it. Remembering her Grandmother McKenzie saying they'd packed arrow wounds with dried ergot, she next made a poultice of the powdery rye fungus and applied it. Feeling the man's dark, wide brow, she realized it had not cooled, so she swabbed him with alcohol. But when she stopped sponging, he immediately grew hot again. The fever, she realized, must be fought from within rather than without. She scoured her mind and found yet another possibility.

Wild gingerroot tea!

But when she brought the ginger tea back to him, he lay as still as death, and the first spoonful dribbled from his lips, rolled past his ear, and stained the pillowcase a weak brown. She tried again to force another spoonful into his mouth, succeeding only in making him cough.

"Drink it! Drink it!" she willed the unconscious man almost in an angry whisper. But it was no use; he'd choke if she forced the tea into his mouth this way.

She pressed her knuckles to her teeth, despairing, near tears. Suddenly she had an inspiration and ran through her house like a demented being, flew out the back door, and found Rob Nelson playing in his backyard next door.

"Robert!" she bellowed, and Rob jumped to stand at attention. Never in his life had he seen Miss Abigail look so bedeviled or raise her voice that way.

"Yes, ma'am?" he gulped, wide-eyed.

Miss Abigail grabbed him by the shoulders so tight she like to break his bones. "Robert, run fast up to the livery stable and ask Mr. Perkins for a handful of straw. Clean straw, do you understand? And run like your tail's on fire!'' Then she gave Rob a push that nearly put him on his nose.

"Yes, ma'am,'' the amazed boy called, scuttling away as fast as his legs would carry him.

It seemed to Miss Abigail that hours passed while she paced feverishly, waiting. When Rob returned, she grabbed the straw without so much as a thank you, ran into her house, and slammed the screen in the boy's face.

Leaning over the robber's dark face, she tipped up his chin and forced two fingers into his mouth. His tongue was ominously hot and dry. But the straw was too flimsy, she could see after several unsuccessful attempts to get it down his throat. Harried, she scoured her mind, wasting precious minutes until she found an answer. Cattails! She plucked one from a dried bouquet in the parlor, reamed the pith from its center with a knitting needle, and—hardening her resolve—lifted the dark chin again, pried open his mouth with her fingers, and rammed the cattail down his throat, half gagging herself at what she was doing to him.

But it worked! It was a small success, but it made her hopeful: the ginger tea went down smoothly. With not a thought for delicacy, Miss Abigail filled her mouth again and again, and shot the tea into him, but as she was removing the straw from his mouth, some refleex in him decided to work and he swallowed, clamping down unknowingly upon her two fingers. She yelped and straightened up in a pained, arching snap, pulling her fingers free to find the skin broken between the first and second knuckles of both. Immediately she stuck them in her mouth and sucked, only to find a trace of his saliva on them. An outlaw! she thought, and yanked a clean handkerchief from within her sleeve, fastidiously wiping her tongue and fingers dry. But staring at his unconscious face, she felt her own flood with heat and her heart thrum from something she did not understand.

Realizing it was near noon, she left the man to prepare David Melcher's tray. When she brought it to his doorway, Melcher's jaw dropped.

"Miss Abigail! What's happened to you?"

She looked down to find flecks of blood strewn across her breasts from beating the steak, maybe even some from the body of the man downstairs. Raising a hand to her hair, she

found it scattered like wind-whipped grass. As her arm went
up, a large wet ring of sweat came into view beneath the
underarm of the trim blue blouse which had looked so
impeccable this morning. Too, there were those two bloody
tooth marks on her fingers, but those she hid in the folds of her
skirt.

Gracious! she thought, I hadn't realized! I simply hadn't
realized!

"Miss Abigail, are you all right?"

"I'm quite all right, really, Mr. Melcher. I've been trying to
save a man's life, and believe me, at this point I think I'd be
grateful to see him with enough strength to try to harm me."

Melcher's face went hard. "He's still alive, then?"

"Just barely."

It was all David Melcher could do to refrain from snapping,
"Too bad!"

Miss Abigail sensed his disapproval, but saw how he made
an effort to submerge his anger, which was altogether justifi-
able, considering the man downstairs had done Mr. Melcher
out of a big toe. "Just don't overdo it. I don't think you're used
to such hard work. I shouldn't want you becoming ill over the
care of a common thief."

An undeniable warmth came at his words, and she replied,
"Don't worry about me, Mr. Melcher. I am here to worry about
you."

Which is just what she did when he'd finished eating. She
brought his shaving gear and held the mirror for him while he
performed the ritual. She studied him surreptitiously, the gentle
mouth and straight nose, strong chin with no cleft, no dimples.
But it was his eyes she liked best. They were pale brown and
very boyish, especially when he smiled. He looked up and she
dropped her eyes. But when he tended his chore again,
swiveling his head this way and that, his jaw jutting forward
and the cords of his neck standing out, it made the pulse beat
low in her stomach. Without warning came the memory of the
robber's sharper features, thicker neck and longer, darker face.
Forbidding countenance, she thought, compared to the inviting
face of David Melcher.

"The robber wears a moustache," she observed.

All the gentleness left David Melcher's face. "Typical!" he
snapped.

"Is it?"

"It certainly is! The most infamous outlaws in history wore them!"

She lowered the mirror, rose, and twisted her hands together, sorry to have angered him.

"I can see that you don't like to speak of him, so why don't you just forget he's down there and think about getting yourself better? Doctor Dougherty said I should change the bandage on your foot and apply some ointment if it gives you pain."

"It's feeling better all the time. Don't bother."

Rebuffed, she turned quickly to leave, sorry to have riled him by talking about the robber, especially after Mr. Melcher had been so complimentary over the fried steak and potatoes and the fresh linen napkin on the tray. She could see there was going to be friction in this house if the criminal managed to live. Yet she'd taken on the job of nursing him, and she was bound to give it her best.

Returning to the downstairs bedroom, she found he'd moved his right hand—it now lay across his stomach. She studied its long, lean fingers, curled slightly, the shading of hair upon its narrows, and saw what appeared to be a smear of dirt on it. Edging closer, she looked again. What she had taken for dirt was actually a black and blue mark in the distinct shape of a boot heel. Carefully picking up the injured hand by the wrist, she laid it back down at his side. But when it touched the sheet, he rolled slightly, protectively cradling it in his good left hand as if it pained him. Instinctively she pressed him onto his back, her hands seeming ridiculously minuscule upon his powerful chest. But he fell back as before, subdued and still again.

It was hard to tell if the hand was broken, but just in case, she padded a small piece of wood, fit it into his palm, and bound it, winding gauze strips up and around his hairy wrist, crossing them over the thumb until any broken bones could not easily be shifted. She noticed as she worked that his hands were clean, the nails well tended, the palms callused.

Checking his forehead again, she found it somewhat cooled but still hotter than it should be. Thinking back wearily to yesterday when she'd set out for town and a job at Culpepper's, she thought how little she'd suspected she'd end up with a job like this instead. Perhaps Culpepper's would have been preferable after all, she thought tiredly, slogging back to the kitchen for cotton and alcohol again. She looked around in dismay at the room: pieces of torn rags and gauze everywhere;

used wet lumps of cotton in bowls; vinegar cruet, salt bowl, herb bags, scissors, dirty dishes everywhere; blood splatters on the wall and the highboy, and the stench of burnt alum hanging sickeningly over everything.

Turning on her heel, she uncharacteristically disregarded it all and returned to her bedroom.

Dear God! He'd turned over . . . and onto his right leg!

Pushing and grunting, struggling with his limp weight, she managed to get him onto his back again, then fell across his stomach, panting. But she knew even before she looked what she'd find: the wound was bleeding profusely again.

So, sighing heavily, almost stumbling now, she fought the entire battle once more: cleansing the wound, burning the alum, staunching the blood, applying ergot, and praying to see the flow stop. He seemed to be rousing more often as the afternoon wore on. Each time he moved a limb, she poured her strength on him, holding him flat if need be, willing him to lie still, badgering him aloud, sweating with the effort, but wiping the sweat from his fevered body rather than from her own. Toward evening when he still hadn't gained consciousness, she gave up hoping for him to awaken fully enough to drink the beef tea and force-fed him again.

Sometime later she was standing staring trancelike at his exposed white hip, counting the minutes since the bleeding had stopped, when Doc Dougherty's knock brought her from her reverie. "Come in." But she barely had the strength left to call out.

Doc had had a tough day himself, but he took one look at her and demanded, "Miss Abigail, what in tarnation did you do to yourself?" She looked ghastly! Her eyes were red-rimmed and for a moment he thought she might start crying.

"I never knew before how hard it is to save a life," she said hoarsely. Doc led her by the arm into her disastrous kitchen. She laughed a little madly as he forced her into a chair. "And now I know why your house looks the way it does, too."

Rather than feel insulted, he snorted laughingly. She'd been initiated then, he thought, as we all must be at first.

"You need a good dose of coffee, Miss Abigail, and a bigger dose of sleep."

"The coffee I'll accept, but the sleep must wait until after he revives and I know he'll make it."

Doc poured her a cup of coffee and left her to check the

patients, but as he walked from the kitchen he saw Miss Abigail's back wilt against her chair and knew he was lucky it was she who'd offered to help. Yet, entering the room where the robber lay, he wondered again if she wasn't too delicate to handle wounds like this. At first he'd considered only her sense of propriety, but seeing her so whipped, he wondered if the physcial strain wasn't too much for her.

But one look at her handiwork and he marveled at her ingenuity and tenacity. What he found when he checked the wound genuinely surprised him. The man doesn't know how lucky he is that he ended up where he did, Doc thought. The wound looked good, the fever was low, no bleeding, no gangrene. She'd done as much as Doc himself could have.

Upstairs, he said, "Mr. Melcher, I think you're in good hands with Miss Abigail dancing attendance on you. However, I thought I'd lend my meager medical assistance just the same."

"Ah, Doctor Dougherty, I'm happy to see you." Melcher looked fit as a fiddle.

"Foot giving you much pain?"

"No more than I can handle. It throbs now and then, but the salve you gave Miss Abigail helps immensely."

"Laundanum salve, my man. Laudanum salve applied by Miss Abigail—a very effective combination, don't you agree?"

Melcher smiled. "She is wonderful, isn't she? I want to thank you for . . . well, I'm very happy I'm here in her house."

"I didn't have much to do with it, Melcher. She volunteered! And even though she's being paid, I think she puts out more than the money will compensate her for. The two of you are a real handful for her."

At the reminder of the other patient, Melcher's face soured. "Tell me . . . how is he?"

"He's alive and not bleeding, and both facts seem to be more than believable. I don't know what Miss Abigail did for him, but whatever it was, it worked." Then, noting the expression on Melcher's face, Doc thumped the man's good leg. "Cheer up, my man! You won't need to be here under the same roof with the scoundrel too much longer. This toe is looking up. Shouldn't hold you up here for long at all."

"Thank you," Melcher offered, but his face remained untouched by warmth as he said it.

"My advice to you is to forget he's down there if it bothers you so much," Doc said, preparing to leave.

"How can I forget it when Miss Abigail has to be down there too . . . and caring for him!"

Ah, so that's the way the wind blows, thought Doc. "Sounds like Miss Abigail has made quite an impression on you."

"I dare say she has," admitted Melcher.

Doc laughed shortly, then said, "Don't worry about Miss Abigail. She can take care of herself. I'll be around again soon. Meanwhile, move that foot and use it as much as you want, as long as you feel comfortable doing it. It's doing well." But Doc was smiling at this unexpected turn of events as he headed downstairs.

The coffee had revived Miss Abigail somewhat.

"Got a cup for me?" Doc asked, returning to the kitchen. "Naw, don't get up. Cups in here? I'll pour my own." As he did, he continued visiting. "Miss Abigail, I'm sorry I doubted you yesterday, I can see what kind of fool I was to do so. You've not only done a proper job of nursing those two . . . it seems you've made a devotee of Mr. Melcher."

"A devotee?" She looked up, startled, over her cup.

Doc Dougherty leaned back against the edge of her sideboard as he sipped, his eyes alight.

Flustered, she looked into her cup. "Nonsense, Doctor, he's simply grateful for a clean bed and hot food."

"As you say, Miss Abigail . . . as you say." But still Doc's eyes were mischievous. Then abruptly he changed the subject. "Word came in by telegraph that the railroad wants us to keep that stranger here till they can send someone up here to question him."

"Ah, if he lives to talk." Once again he could see the weariness in her, could hear the dread in her voice.

"He'll live. I examined the wounds and they look real good, Miss Abigail, real good. What in blazes have you got on those poultices?"

"Powdered ergot. It healed the wounds from Indian arrows. I figured it might heal his."

"Why didn't you call me when he got bad?"

Her eyes looked incredulous. "I didn't think of it, I guess."

He chuckled and shook his head. "You planning to run me a

little competition in the healing business, are you?'' he asked, eyes twinkling.

"No, Doctor. It's far too hard on a maiden lady. When these men are fit, I shall give up my life in medicine, and gladly."

"Well, don't give it up yet, Miss Abigail, please. You're doing one damn fine job for me."

Too tired to even object to his language, she only answered, "Why, thank you, Doctor." And he could have sworn she beamed, there in her evening kitchen amidst the mess and the smell that was so unlike her usual tidiness. He knew she'd be okay then; she had qualities in her that most women didn't. Also, she was experiencing the first fledgling joy afforded to those who beat the odds against death.

On his way to the door, Doc turned. "Oh, I forgot to mention, the railroad said they'll foot the bill for as long as it takes to get these two healthy. I think they mean to pacify Melcher and keep him from kicking up a fuss about getting shot while on board one of the R.M.R. trains. As for the other one . . . he must be wanted for more than just one holdup for them to be that interested. I don't mean to scare you, just wanted you to rest easy about the money. Are you afraid, being here alone with him?"

She almost laughed. "No, I'm not afraid. I've never been afraid of anything in my life. Not even when I thought I was running out of money. Things have a way of working out. Yesterday I was facing penury and tonight here I am with a railroad supporting me. Isn't that handy?"

He patted her arm and chuckled. "That's more like it, Miss Abigail. Now see that you get some sleep so you can stay this way."

As he opened the screen door, she stopped him momentarily, asking, "Doctor, did the telegram say what that man's name is? It seems strange always referring to him as 'that man' or 'that . . . robber.' "

"No, it didn't. Just said they want him kept here and no question about it. They want to get their hands on him pretty bad."

"How can they possibly know if he's wanted for other charges when they haven't seen him?"

"We sent out a description. Somebody along the line must have recognized him by it."

"But suppose the man does die? It wouldn't seem proper for a man to die where not a soul even knew his name."

"It's happened before," Doc stated truthfully.

Her shoulders squared, and a look of pure resolve came over her face. "Yes, but it shan't this time. I will make it my goal, a sort of talisman if you like, to see that he revives sufficiently to state his name. If he can do that, perhaps he can recuperate fully. As you see, Doctor, I intend to be a tenacious healer." She gave Doc a wry grin. "Now hurry along. I have a kitchen to see to and a supper to prepare." Doc was chuckling as she whisked him away. It took more than weariness to defeat Abigail McKenzie!

She hadn't time to worry about her own appearance while she prepared David Melcher's supper tray, yet her heart was light as she pondered Doc's words. A devotee. David Melcher was her devotee. A delicious sense of expectation rippled through Miss Abigail at the thought. She took extra care with his meal and paused to tuck a few stray wisps of hair into place before stepping into his room. He was lying quietly, facing the window with its view of the apricot sky. As she paused in the doorway, he sensed her there and turned with a smile. Her heart flitted gaily, filling her with some new sense of herself.

"I've brought your supper," she said softly.

"Please sit with me while I eat it and keep me company," he invited. She wanted to . . . oh, how she wanted to, but it simply wasn't proper.

"I'm afraid I have things to do downstairs," was her excuse. His face registered disappointment. But he was afraid to be too insistent; she'd done so much already. The room grew silent, and from outside came the wistful cry of a mourning dove. Miss Abigail set the tray on his lap, then offered brightly, "But I've brought you something to read if you'd care to, after you've finished your supper." From her pocket she pulled a book of sonnets.

"Ah, sonnets! Do you enjoy sonnets too? I might have guessed you would."

At his smile of approval she grew flustered and raised her eyes to the cotton candy clouds beyond the window. Again came the call of the mourning dove, singing its question, "Who? Who? Who?" It suddenly seemed to Miss Abigail that the question was being asked of her. It was a question she'd asked herself more times than she cared to remember. Who would there ever be to brighten her life? To give her reason for living?

Lost in reverie, Miss Abigail said rather dreamily, "I find the evening a particularly appropriate time of day for sonnets—rather the softest time of day, don't you think?"

"I couldn't agree more," came his gentle reply. "It seems we have something in common."

"Yes, we do." She became suddenly aware of how she looked, and touched her lower lip with the tips of her fingers. She still wore her stained, sweaty dress that she'd worn all day, and her hair was terribly untidy. Yet even as she fled the room, she realized he'd smiled sweetly and spoken almost tenderly. Was it true, what Doc had said? Abigail McKenzie, you're so tired you're getting fanciful!

But tired or not, her day was not over.

Dusk had fallen and in the gloom of her downstairs bedroom its occupant looked darker than ever. She found herself comparing him to Mr. Melcher. The whiskers on his chin had nearly doubled in length, and she decided that tomorrow she would shave him. She had never like dark-whiskered men anyway. And moustaches! Well, if dark chin whiskers were sinister, black moustaches were positively forbidding! This one—she stepped closer—bordered his upper lip like thick, drooping bat's wings. She shuddered as she studied it and crossed her arms protectively. Vile! she thought. Why would any man want to wear a bristly, unattractive thing like that on his very face?

But suddenly Miss Abigail's grip on her upper arms loosened. She had a dim recollection of—but no, it couldn't have been, could it? She frowned, remembering the feel of that moustache when she'd fed him, and in her memory it was not bristly, but soft.

Surely I'm mistaken, she thought, shaking herself a little. How could it be soft when it looks so prickly? Yet she was suddenly sure it had been. She glanced warily behind her, but of course nobody was there. It was simply silly to have looked! But she checked again, stealthily, before reaching out a tentative finger to touch the thick black hair beneath the robber's nose. It came as a near shock to find it almost silky! She felt his warm breath on her finger, and quickly, guiltily, recrossed her arms. The softness was disconcerting. Suddenly feeling sheepish, she spoke aloud. "Moustache or not, thief or not, I'm going to make you tell me your name, do you understand? You are not going to die on me, sir, because I simply shan't allow it! We shall take it one step at a time, and the first shall be getting your name out of you. It's best if you understand at the onset that I am not accustomed to being crossed up!"

He didn't move a muscle.

"Oh, just look at you, you're a mess. I'd better comb your hair for you. There's little else I can do right now."

She got her own comb from the dresser and ran it through his thick hair, experiencing a queer thrill at the thought that he was a robber of trains yet she was seeing to his intimate needs. "I can't say I've ever combed the hair of an outlaw before," she told him. "The only reason I'm doing so now is that, just in case you can hear me, you'll know you're not allowed to just . . . just lie there without fighting. This hair is dirty, and if you want it washed, you shall simply have to come around."

Suddenly his arm jerked and a small sound came from him. He tossed his head to one side and would have rolled over, but she prevented it by holding him down with restraining hands. "You've got to lie flat. I insist! Doctor Dougherty says you must!" He seemed to acquiesce then. She felt his forehead and found it cool. But just in case, she brought a sewing rocker from the living room—an armless, tiny thing offering little comfort—and sat down for only a moment, only until she was sure he wouldn't thrash around anymore and hurt himself.

In no time at all her head lolled and her thoughts grew dim as she faded into a dream world where the stranger awakened and smiled at her from behind his soft black moustache. His wide chest moved near and she pressed it with her hands. She avoided his tempting lips, arguing that he was a thief, but he only laughed deep in his throat and agreed that he was, and wanted to steal something from her now. But I don't know your name, she sighed like the night wind. He smiled and teased, Ah, but you know more of me than my name. And she saw again his naked body—soft, curled, intimate—and felt again the wondrous shame of sensuousness. And upon the tiny sewing rocker her sleeping body jerked.

His flailing limbs awakened her and she jumped up and flattened him, using her own body to keep him on his back and still. The strange, forbidden dream was strong in her as she felt the flesh of this man beneath her own. She should not think such thoughts, or touch him so.

Yet she stayed beside him, guarding him through the night. Time and again he tossed, and she ordered, "Stay on your back . . . keep that knee up . . . tell me your name . . ." until she could fight him no longer. In the deep of night she fumbled into the dark kitchen, found a roll of gauze, and tied his left ankle to the brass footboard, his left wrist to the headboard. Blurred by sleep, she again sat on the armless rocker. But sometime during the night she arose insensibly, clambered over the footboard, and fell asleep near the end of the bed with her lips near his hip.

Chapter 3

SLOWLY . . . HAZILY . . . HE became aware of a great, steady heat on his face. And he could tell by its constancy that it was sun.

Mistily . . . lazily . . . he became aware of a soft, lush heat against his side. And he could tell by its curves that it was woman.

Progressively . . . painfully . . . he became aware of raw, gnawing heat in his flesh. But this he could not identify, knew only that it pained in a way nothing ever had before. His eyeballs rolled behind closed lids, refusing yet to give up their private dark, hemming him in with the three heats that melded to scorch his very fiber. He wondered, if he opened his eyes, would he rouse from this dream? Or was it real? Was he alive? Was he in hell? His eyes grated open but he stared up at a ceiling, not the roof of a tent. His body ached in many places. Sweet Jesus, he thought, and his eyes faded closed to leave him wondering where he was and who lay down there near the foot of his bed. He tried to swallow but couldn't, lifted drugged lids again and gritted his teeth till his jaw popped, then raised his head with a painful effort.

A female satyr of some kind was braced on its elbows, gaping at him with wide eyes.

He had only one conscious thought: I must be slipping. This one's a hag and she had to tie me up to get me to stay.

Then he slipped once more into blackness. But he took with him the image of the ugly hag, her hair strewn like vile straw around a face that seemed to have fallen into collapsing folds from her eyes downward. In his insensibility he dreamed she harped at him, commanding him to do feats of which he was incapable. She insisted that he speak, roll over, don't roll over, answer her, be still. Sometimes he dreamed her voice had turned to honey, but then it intruded, thorny-like again, until he finally escaped her altogether and slept dreamlessly.

Miss Abigail despaired when his head fell back and he was lost in oblivion before she could wrest his name from him. All she knew that she hadn't known before was that his near-black eyes held a faint touch of hazel. She'd expected they'd be jet, hueless, as foreboding as the rest of him. But the hazel flecks saved them from all that.

Groaning, she pulled herself off the bed.

Never in her life had Miss Abigail looked into a morning mirror and seen a sight like that which confronted her today. The night had taken its toll, seemingly having shrunken the skin above her eyes and stretched that below. Plum-colored shadings accentuated her too-wide, distraught eyes while elongated lines parenthesized her lips. Tangled, devastated hair set it all off with cruel truthfulness.

She studied her reflection and felt very old indeed.

The thought of David Melcher brought her out of her maunderings.

She bathed in the kitchen and brushed her hair, coiling it neatly at the base of her neck, then donned a soft, cream-colored blouse much like that she'd worn yesterday and a brown broadcloth skirt. On an impulse she applied the tiniest bit of attar of roses to her wrists.

"Miss Abigail, don't you look lovely this morning!" David Melcher exclaimed appreciatively when she stepped to his doorway with a breakfast tray.

"And aren't you chipper, Mr. Melcher!"

Again he invited her to stay while he ate, and this time she accepted, though propriety demanded she stay only briefly. But he praised her cooking, the coddled eggs, toast, and apple butter, teasing, "Why, Miss Abigail, I'll be plain spoiled by the time you throw me out of here."

His appreciation ruffled her ego in a gentle, stirring way, like a low breeze can lift the fine hair at the back of one's neck and create delicious shivers.

"I would not, as you say, throw you out of here, Mr. Melcher. You are free to stay as long as you need."

"That, Miss Abigail, is truly a dangerous offer. I may take you at your word and never leave." His eyes held just the right amount of mischief to make the comment thoroughly proper. Yet that tickle stirred the back of her neck again. But she'd stayed as long as it was prudent.

"I'd like to visit longer, but I do have work I should like to complete while the morning coolness prevails."

"Why, Miss Abigail, you made that sound just like a sonnet. You have such an eloquent way of speaking." Then he cleared his throat and added, in a more formal manner, "I'd like to read through the sonnets again today, if you don't mind."

"Not at all. Perhaps you'd enjoy some others I have also."

"Yes . . . yes, I'm sure I would."

As she rose from her chair and ran her hands down her sleeves to free them of any nonexistent wrinkles, he thought of how delicate the high collar and long sleeves made her look and of how she smelled like roses and of what a perfect little lady she was.

She fed the robber warm broth through the cattail again. Now, nearing him, her pulse did strange, forbidden things, and as if to get even with him, she scolded the unconscious man, "When will you make up your mind to awaken and tell me your name and take some decent nourishment? You're being an awful lot of trouble, you know, lying there like a great hibernating grizzly! You've put me to the task of feeding you as I did yesterday. I know it seems a vicious method, but it's the only way I can think of . . . and believe me, sir, it's no more palatable to me than it is to you, especially with that moustache."

The feeding finished, she brought out the shaving gear and intrepidly set out to clean him up, not at all sure how well she'd do. She lay thick towels beneath his jaw, lathered him up, and set to work with the blade, all the while puzzling over that moustache.

Should she or shouldn't she?

It truly was a dirty, ominous-looking feature. And maybe if

David Melcher hadn't pointed out how typical the moustache
was of outlaws, and maybe if it hadn't been so alarmingly soft,
and maybe if her heart hadn't betrayed her when she touched it,
she wouldn't have shaved it off.

But in the end she did.

When it was half gone she had a pang of guilt. But it was too
late now. After she had finished, she stood back to evaluate the
face without the moustache and found, to her chagrin, that
she'd spoiled it completely! The moustache belonged on him
just as surely as did his thick black eyebrows and his swarthy
coloring. Suppose when he awoke he thought the same thing?
The thought did little to calm her misgivings, and the next task
did even less. It was time to give him a bath.

She set about doing so, a section at a time, first lightly
soaping an arm, then rinsing it and wiping it dry. His armpit
was a bed of straight, thick black hair—unnerving. So she
concentrated on his shoulder and tried not to look at it. The far
arm presented a problem, for the bed was pushed up into a
corner of the room. She tried pulling the bed out to get at him
from that side, but he was too heavy and it wouldn't budge.
She ended up climbing once again onto the bed with him to
facilitate matters.

His upper half was done . . .

She gulped, then remembered he was, after all, unconscious.

Slipping the oilcloth beneath his right leg, she washed it
carefully, avoiding the damaged thigh. His foot was long, and
it evoked a queer exhilaration as she washed the sole, then
between the toes, which were shaded with hair between the
knuckles. She admitted now that what Doctor Dougherty said
was true: it was infinitely more disconcerting tending the
intimate needs of a stranger than those of a father. The sheet
still shrouded his private parts. She managed to keep them
covered while doing his other leg. *That part* of him she did not
wash.

But she had seen it once, and couldn't get the picture from
her mind.

As the day progressed, his eyes moved more often, though
they remained closed. Now and then she saw muscles flex, and
he tossed repeatedly, so she kept him safely tied to the bedrails.

* * *

While Miss Abigail freshened up David's room that morning, she learned he was a shoe salesman out of Philadelphia. Then he surprised her by announcing, "When I get back, I'll be sure to send you a pair of our best."

She placed one small hand on the high collar of her blouse, fingers spreading delicately over her neck as if to hide a pulsebeat there.

"Oh, Mr. Melcher . . . it wouldn't do at all, I'm afraid, much as I'd love a fine pair of city-made shoes."

"Wouldn't do? But why?"

Miss Abigail dropped her eyes. "A lady simply does not accept such a personal gift from a gentleman unless he's . . ."

"Unless he's what, Miss Abigail?" he asked softly.

She felt herself color and stared at her hem. "Why, Mr. Melcher, it simply wouldn't be proper." She looked up to find his brown eyes on her. "But I thank you anyway," she added wistfully.

She thought the issue was settled, but at noon Mr. Melcher announced he felt good enough to come downstairs to eat his dinner, but apologized for having nothing to put on his feet.

"I believe I can find a pair of Father's slippers here somewhere."

She brought them and knelt before him.

Such a feeling welled up inside David Melcher, watching her. She was genteel, soft-spoken, refined, and each favor she did for him made David Melcher revere her more. He got up shakily, hopping on one foot to catch his balance, and she whisked an arm around his waist while his came about her shoulder.

"The floor is slippery, so hold the banister," she warned.

They started down, one step at a time, and each time he leaned on her, his face came close to her temple. Again she smelled of roses.

Her free hand was on his shirtfront and she felt his chest muscles flex each time he braced on the banister.

"What color would you like, Miss Abigail?" he asked, between jumps.

"Color?" They stopped and she looked up into his face, only inches from hers.

"What color shoes shall I pick for you?" They took one more step.

"Don't be silly, Mr. Melcher." Again they'd stopped, but now she was afraid to raise her eyes to his.

"How about a pale dun-colored kid leather?" He lightly squeezed her shoulder, sending her heart battering around wildly. "They'd look grand with what you're wearing now. Imagine the leather with this soft lace." He touched the lace of her cuff.

"Come . . . take another step, Mr. Melcher."

"I'd be honored if you'd accept the shoes."

She kept her eyes averted, her hand still upon his chest. "I'd have no place to wear them."

"That I cannot believe. A fine-looking woman like you."

"No . . . I'd have no place. Please . . . our dinner is ready." She nudged him, but he resisted, and beneath her hand she felt his heart drumming as rapidly as her own.

"Don't be surprised if a pair of shoes arrives one day for you. Then you'll know I've been thinking of you." His voice was scarcely above a whisper as he murmured, "Miss Abigail . . ."

At last she looked up to find a multitude of feelings expressed in his eyes. Then his arm tightened upon her shoulder, he squeezed the soft sleeve, the arm beneath. She saw him swallow, and the breath caught in her throat as his pale brown eyes held hers. As his soft lips touched her she again felt the commotion beneath the palm on his chest. His gentle kiss was as light as a sigh upon her lips before he drew back and looked into her liquid gaze. Her heart thrilled, her knees weakened, and for a moment she feared she might tumble headlong down the stairs, so dizzy was she. But then she dropped her lashes demurely, and they continued on their halting, heart-bound way to the kitchen.

It had been years since David Melcher had lived in a house with a kitchen like this. The tabletop was covered with a starched yellow gingham to match the window curtains that lifted in a whispering wind. Dishes and silver had been precisely laid, and a clean linen napkin lay folded atop his plate. His eyes followed Abigail McKenzie as she brought simple, fragrant foods—three puffed, golden biscuits were dropped on his plate, then she returned with a blue-speckled kettle and spooned thick chunks of chicken and gravy over the top.

"How long has it been since you were home, Mr. Melcher?"

"You might say I have no home. When I go back to Philadelphia, I take a room at the Elysian Club. Believe me, it's nothing at all like this."

"Then you . . . you have no family?"

"None." Their eyes met, then parted. Birds chittered from somewhere in the shade-dappled yard, and the heady scent of nasturtiums drifted in. He thought he never wanted to leave, and wondered if she might be feeling the nesting urge as strongly as he.

The black-haired, clean-shaven man became aware of the smells around him this time much as he'd become aware of the heat once before. With his eyes still closed, he caught the scent of something sweet, like flowers. There was, too, the starchy, agreeable smell of laundry soap in fresh linens. Now and then came the tantalizing aroma of chicken cooking. He opened his eyes and his lashes brushed against some fancy, knotted stitchery on a pillow slip. So . . . this wasn't a dream. The sweet smell came from a bouquet of orange things over there on a low table near a bay window. The window seat had yellow-flowered cushions that matched the curtains.

He shut his eyes, trying to recall whose bedroom it was. Obviously a woman's, for there were more yellow flowers over the papered walls and a dressing table with hinged mirrors.

He had not moved—nothing more than the opening and closing of his eyelids. His left hand was tingling, it prickled as if no blood ran through it. When he flexed the fingers they closed around a cylinder of metal, and he realized with a shock that he was tied onto a bed.

So that hag was no nightmare! Who else could have tied him up? He was no stranger to caution. Stealthily he tested the bindings to see if he could break them. But they were tight on both hand and foot.

He lifted his lids to a brown skirt, smack in front of him, standing beside the bed. He assessed it warily, wondering if he should use his right hand to knock her off her feet with one surprise punch in the gut. He let his eyelids droop shut again, pretending to go back under so he could get a look at her face through a veil of near-closed lashes.

But he couldn't tell much. She had both hands clasped over her face, forming a steeple above her nose as if she was in joy, distress, or praying. From what he could tell, he'd never laid

eyes on her before. There wasn't much to her, and from the
stark hairdo she wore he knew she was no saloon girl. Her long
sleeves and high collar were no dance hall getup either. At last,
surmising he was safe from her, he opened his eyes fully.

Immediately she withdrew her hands and leaned close to lay
one—ah, so cool—along his cheek.

She didn't smell like a saloon girl either.

"Your name . . . tell me your name," she said with a note
of intense appeal.

He wondered why the hell she wouldn't know his name if
she was supposed to, so he didn't say a thing.

"Please," she implored again. "Please, just tell me your
name."

But suddenly he writhed, twisted at his bindings, and looked
frantically around the room in search of something.

"My camera!" he tried to croak, but his voice was a
pathetic, grating thing, and pain assailed him everywhere. At
his wild thrashing, she became big-eyed and jumped back a
step, her eyes riveted on his lips as he mouthed again, "My
camera." The attempt to utter his first words shot a searing
pain through his throat. He tried again, but all that came of it
was a thick rasp. But she read his lips and that was all she
needed to make her suddenly vibrant.

"Cameron," she whispered in disbelief.

He wanted to correct her but couldn't.

"Mike Cameron," she said louder, as if the words were
some kind of miracle. "Cameron . . . just imagine that!"
Then she beamed and clasped her hands joyfully before her,
saying, "Thank God, Mr. Cameron. I knew you could do it!"

Was she zany or what? She resembled the witch he'd
imagined in the bed beside him, only she was neat and clean
and easy on the eye. Still, she acted as if she didn't exactly
have all her marbles, and he thought maybe he *should* have
punched her one broadside when he'd had the chance, to bring
her out of a spell.

She whirled now, facing the bay window, and from behind it
looked like she was wiping her eyes. But why the hell would
she be crying over him?

When she faced him again, he tried to say, "My name's not
Cameron," but once more the pain shot through his throat, and
the sound was unrecognizable.

"Don't try to speak, Mr. Cameron. You've had some foreign

objects in your mouth and throat, that's why it hurts so badly. Please lie still.''

He attempted to sit up, but she came immediately and pressed those cool hands of hers on his chest to stay him. "Please, Mr. Cameron," she pleaded, "please don't. You're in no condition to move yet. If you promise you won't try to get up, I will remove these gauze bindings." She peered into his stark eyes that were lined with dark suspicion of her.

He had a damn good look at her then, and she looked about as strong as a ten-year-old boy, but her eyes told him she'd give it her best shot at subduing him if need be. So far, every time he'd moved, some muscle pained him like a blue bitch. He felt disinclined to tussle with even such a hummingbird as her. He scowled, gave her the merest nod, then there was a snipping sound above his head and again at his foot and she came away holding the gauze strips, freeing him to move limbs that somehow now refused to do his bidding. "Dear me, Mr. Cameron, you can see what a weakened condition you're in." She lowered his dead arm and began rubbing it deftly, massaging the muscles. "Give the blood a chance to get back. . . . It'll be all right in a minute. You mustn't move, though, please. I have to leave you alone for a bit while I prepare you some food. You've been unconscious for two days."

But suddenly the blood came racing back like a spring cataract, pounding through his arm, shooting needles of hot ice everywhere. He gasped and arched. But gasping hurt his throat and arching hurt everything else. He tried to swear but that hurt worse, so with a drooping of eyelids he subsided, fighting the giddy sensation that his skin was trying to explode. She clasped the inert hand under her armpit while he lay there listening to the deft sound of her beating the blood back into his prickling limb; it sounded like she was making a meat patty for his dinner. He felt nothing of her and a moment later opened his eyes to find his hand again on the sheet at his side, the woman gone from the room.

His right knee was raised. When he flexed its muscles a film of sweat erupted from his forehead and armpits. What the hell! he thought. He looked down his bare torso. A white patch decorated his right thigh. Automatically lifting his right hand to explore the bandage, a new pain gripped him, this time centered in the hand. It felt as if some giant paw were doling out a grisly handshake. He used his left hand instead, exploring damp, clinging cloths that guarded some secret near his groin. It told him nothing. Feeling around, he found a sheet drawn across his left leg, covering his privates, and folded back across his navel. To wake up naked in a woman's bed didn't surprise him at all, but to wake up in one belonging to a woman like this sure as hell did!

His eyes wandered while he listened to clinking, domestic sounds from around the doorway, and he wondered how long it had been since he'd been in a place like this. The room looked like some old maid's flower garden—flowers everywhere! He had no doubt it was her room, that like a hummingbird she'd fit into it. He saw a pair of portraits beside the bouquet, in a hinged, oval frame, and an open book on the bay window seat, with the tail end of a crocheted bookmark trailing from its pages. There was a small rocker with a needlepoint cushion, and a basket of sewing things on the floor beside it. A chifforobe stood against one wall, the dressing table against another.

Through the doorway he saw a green velvet settee in what must be her parlor. A little table beside it, and an oil lamp with globes of opaque white glass painted with roses. God, more flowers! he thought. A corner of a lace-curtained window with fringed, tassled shades. The parlor of a goody twoshoes, he thought, and wondered, as his eyes slid shut, how the hell he had gotten here.

"Here we are, Mr. Cameron." His eyes flew open; he jumped and winced. "I've prepared a light broth and some tea. It's not much, but we'll have to cater to your throat rather than your appetite for a short while." She held a carved wooden tray, white triangles of linen falling over its edges.

Lordy, he thought, would you look at that! Probably handstitched those edges herself. Bracing the tray against her midriff, she cleared a space on the bedside table. He was surprised to see the tray pull her blouse against a pair of healthy, resilient breasts—she dressed like a woman who didn't want the world to suspect she had any! But if there was one thing he knew how to find, it was a pair of healthy breasts. His eyes followed while she crossed to the chifforobe and found a pillow. When she came to mound it up beneath his head, he again caught the drift of that starchy, fresh smell, both from her and the pillow, and he thought of many nights sleeping on the floor of a wet canvas tent with a musty blanket over him as the only comfort. As she cupped the back of his head and lifted it, ripples of pain undulated from muscles far down his body. Automatically his eyes sank shut and he sucked in a sharp breath. When his pain had subsided, her voice came again.

"I've brought something to freshen your mouth. It's just soda water." A cloth pressed his jowl and a glass touched his lips, then he pulled the salty solution into his mouth. "Hold it a minute and let it bubble around. The effervescence is very refreshing." He was too weak to argue, but watched her covertly as she brought the bowl for him to spit into. When dribbles wet his chin, she immediately applied a warm, damp cloth, then proceeded to wash his entire face as if he were a schoolboy. He tried to jerk aside, but it hurt, so he submitted. Next she placed a napkin under his chin and dipped the spoon, cupping her hand beneath it on its way to his mouth.

She wondered why he scowled so, and talked because his near-black eyes were frightening. "You're a lucky man, Mr. Cameron. You were critically shot and nearly bled to death. Luckily Doctor Dougherty . . ."

She rambled on but he heard little beyond the statement that he'd been shot. He tried to lift his right hand, remembered how it hurt, used his left instead to stop the spoon. But he bumped her hand and the soup spilled on his chin, running down his neck. Goddamnit! he thought, and tried to say it—unsuccessfully—while she dabbed, wiped, and sponged fussily.

"Behave yourself, Mr. Cameron. See the mess you've made here!"

She knew perfectly well that any man who'd just found out he'd been shot would want to know who did it! Did he have to ask, with this inflamed throat of his! She dabbed away at the stupid soup, and this time when he grabbed, he got her by the wrist, catching the washcloth, too, under his grip, bringing her startled eyes wide.

"Who shot me?" he tried, but the pain assaulted his throat from every angle, so he mouthed the words broadly, *oooo . . . shawt . . . mee?* She stared at him as if struck dumb, knotted her fist, and twisted it beneath his fingers until she felt the birdlike bones straining to be free.

"It wasn't I, Mr. Cameron," she snapped, "so you've no need to accost me!" His grip loosened and she wrenched free, amazed at how strong he was in his anger. "I fear I untied you

too hastily," she said down her nose, rubbing her fingers over
the redness where the stiff lace had scratched her wrist.

He could tell from her face that she wasn't used to being
manhandled. He really hadn't meant to scare her, but he wanted
some answers. She'd had plenty of time to fill him in while
flitting around getting that pillow and washing his face. He
reached for her wrist again but she flinched away. But he only
touched it to make her look at his lips. Who shot me? he
mouthed once more.

She stiffened her face and snapped, "I don't know!" then
jammed the spoon into his mouth, clacking it against his teeth.

The spoon kept coming faster and faster, barely giving him
time to swallow between each thrust. The bitch is going to
drown me, damn her! he cursed silently. This time he grabbed
the spoon in midair and sent chicken broth spraying all over the
front of her spotless blouse. She recoiled, sucked in her belly,
and closed her eyes as if beseeching the gods for patience. Her
nostrils flared as she glared hatred at him. He jerked his chin at
the soup bowl, glowering furiously until she picked it up and
held it near his chin. He'd discovered while eating the broth
that he was nearly starved. But with his left hand he was
clumsy, so after a few inept attempts, he flung the spoon aside,
grabbed the bowl, and slurped directly from it, taking perverse
pleasure in shocking her.

A barbarian! she thought. I have been fighting to save the
life of a barbarian! Like some slobbering beast, he went on till
the bowl was empty. But as her thumb curled over it, he jerked
it back, mouthing, "Who shot me?" She jerked the bowl
stubbornly again, but with a painful lunge he yanked it from
her, flung it across the room, where it shattered against the base
of the window seat. He pierced her with eyes which knew no
end of rage. His face went livid as he was forced to use the
voice that cut his throat to ribbons.

"Goddamn you, bitch! Was it you!" he croaked.

Oh, the pain! The pain! He clutched his throat as she jumped
back, squeezing both hands before her while two spots of color
appeared in her cheeks. Never in her life had anyone spoken to
Miss Abigail McKenzie in such a manner. To think she had
nursed this . . . this baboon and struggled to get him to
awaken, to speak, only to be cursed at, called a bitch, and
accused of being the one who shot him! She drew her mouth
into a disdainful pucker, but before she could say anything

more, the alarmed voice of David Melcher rang through the house.

"Miss Abigail! Miss Abigail! Are you all right down there?"

"Who's that!" the rasping voice demanded.

It gave her immense pleasure to answer him at last. "That, sir, is the man who shot you!"

Before her answer could sink in, the voice came again. "Did that animal try to harm you?"

She scurried out, presumably to the bottom of the steps. "I'm fine, Mr. Melcher, now go back to bed. I just had an accident with a soup bowl."

Melcher? Who the hell was this Melcher to call him an animal? And why did she lie about the soup bowl?

She came back in and knelt to pick up the broken pieces. He longed to hurl questions at her, to jump up and shake her, make her fill in the blanks, but he hurt everywhere now from throwing the damn bowl. All he could do was glare at her while she came to stand beside the bed with a supercilious attitude.

"Cursing, Mr. Cameron, is a crutch for the dim-witted. Furthermore, I am not a bitch, but if I were, perhaps I *would* shoot you to put you out of your own self-inflicted misery and to be rid of you. I, unlike you, am civilized, thus I shall only stand back and hope that you will choke to death!" She punctuated this statement by dropping the broken china on the tray with a clatter. But before she left, she plagued him further by dropping one last morsel, just enough to rouse a thousand unaskable questions.

"You were shot, Mr. Cameron, while attempting to hold up a train . . ." She arched a brow, then added, "As if you didn't know." And with that she was gone.

Chapter 4

HE CLENCHED HIS good fist. Oh, she was some smug bitch! What train? I'm no goddamn train robber! And who is this Melcher anyway? Obviously not her husband. Her protector? Ha! She needs protecting like a tarantula needs protecting.

Miss Abigail stood in her kitchen quaking like an aspen, looking at the broken fragments of china, wondering why she hadn't heeded Doctor Dougherty's warning. Never in her life had she been spoken to this way! She would have him out of here—out!—before this day ended, that much she promised herself. Pressing a hand to her throbbing forehead, she considered running down to Doctor Dougherty's and pleading illness, but if she did that he would certainly remove Mr. Melcher, too. Then she remembered how desperately she needed the money and steeled herself for a long day ahead.

In the bedroom, he longed to raise his voice and bellow like a bull moose until somebody told him what the hell was going on around here. He lay instead sweating profusely, having writhed far more than he should have. His leg, hip, and lower stomach had turned to fire. Resting the back of a hand across his eyes, he gritted his teeth at the pain. That was how she found him.

"It has been two days since . . ."

He jumped and another pain grabbed him. Damn her! Did she have to pussyfoot around like that all the time?

Very collectedly now, she began again, with exaggerated control. "I thought you might have to relieve yourself." But she looked at the knob on the headboard while she said it.

Eyeing her mistrustfully, he knew she had him over a barrel. He did have to relieve himself, but he knew he wasn't going anywhere to do it. So just what did she have in mind?

With a voice like ice, she issued orders. "Don't try to speak or strain your leg in any way. I shall help you roll onto your side first." And coming to the side of the bed, she removed the bolsters from under his knee, lowered it with surprising gentleness, then snapped the ends of the under sheet loose from their moorings and rolled him with it until he faced the wall, still covered by the top sheet. She laid a flat porcelain pan next to him and without another word left the room, closing the door with not so much as a click of the latch.

What kind of woman was she anyway? She sashayed in here carrying that bedpan as if she had no idea that he was the one who'd only minutes before shattered her china soup bowl and called her a bitch. Most women would have refused any further services on spite alone . . . but not her. Why should that aggravate him too? Maybe because she looked frail enough to cow with a savage glare. Maybe because he'd tried it and it didn't work.

She came to collect the bedpan with the same silent poker face as before. They needn't have spoken anyway to tell each other they'd met their matches.

She had the perfect revenge for his insufferable attitude this morning: she left him alone. Miss Abigail knew perfectly well he was lying there with a hundred unasked questions eating him up. Well, good! Let them eat him up! It's no more than he deserves.

In the flowery bedroom that's exactly what was happening. Bitch! he thought time and again, unable to shout, to ask anything he wanted now worse than ever to know. He seethed for the remainder of the day, caught like some damn fool bumblebee in a glass jar, in that insufferable yellow flower garden she'd trapped him in. Once he even heard her humming out there in what seemed to be the kitchen, and it made him all the madder. She was out there humming while he couldn't make so much as a squeak without paying dearly.

Much later he heard her go upstairs, then the two of them come down to supper. Snatches of their conversation drifted through the quiet house, and he heard enough to know they were feeling pretty cozy with each other.

"Oh, Miss Abigail, nasturtiums on the table!"

"Ah, how pleasant it is to find a man who can actually identify a nasturtium."

"How pleasant it is to find a woman who still grows them." The eavesdropper in the bedroom rolled his eyes.

"Perhaps tomorrow you'll feel well enough to sit in the backyard while I do some weeding."

"I'd love that, Miss Abigail, I truly would."

"Then you shall do it, Mr. Melcher," she promised before inquiring, "Do you like fresh lemonade?"

"I wish you'd call me David. Yes, I love lemonade."

"We'll have some, tomorrow . . . in the garden?"

"I'll look forward to it."

She helped him back to bed. The man downstairs heard them go up and a silence that followed and thought to himself, no it couldn't be. But indeed it could be, and David Melcher kissed Miss Abigail adoringly, then watched her go all peach-colored and fluttery.

She came back downstairs from her pleasant interlude to face the horrifying prospect of feeding that black brute again. She'd like to let him starve to death. Furthermore, she was afraid to go near him, and more afraid that it might show. She prepared milk toast for him, and entered the bedroom armed with it, ready to fling it on him and scald him should he make a grab for her again.

"I've brought you milk toast," she informed him. He thought she looked like it had soured in her mouth.

"Bah!" was all he could get out to let her know just what he thought of milk toast. "I'm starving!" he mouthed.

"I wish you were," she said, all honey-voiced, and rammed a napkin under his chin. "Hold still and eat."

The hot milk nearly gagged him, the lumps of slimy bread slithered down his throat, disgustingly. Even so, every swallow was torture. He wondered just what had been in his mouth to make it hurt this way, but it appeared she was still in a snit and wasn't going to tell him anything.

They eyed each other menacingly. He, waiting for the chance to ask questions, she, ready to spring to safety at the first sign of brutality. She could hardly stand the sight of him and thought the only good thing about feeding him was that he couldn't speak. And since he looked in no way ready to carry on a dignified conversation, she left him to stew. She put her kitchen back in order and found herself exhausted. Alas, all of her night things were in her bedroom and the last thing she wanted was to go in there again. So she dreamed up an excuse: a gargle.

Before entering, she tiptoed to the doorway, peeped in, gathering her courage. He faced the window, jaw muscles tensing repeatedly. Ah, so he is still angry, she thought. His beard had grown again, darkening his entire face. Studying the lip, which she had willfully denuded, she trembled to think about what would happen when he discovered his moustache gone. She willed it to please . . . please, hurry up and grow back!

She tread soundlessly across the threshold, her insides ascatter with apprehension.

"Are you ready to act civil?" she asked. His head snapped around and his good fist clenched. Then he grimaced in pain.

Damn that pussyfooting! he thought. "Are you trying to kill me with neglect?" he whispered stridently and pressed a hand to his abdomen, "or just let that slimy milk toast do the job for you?"

The thought of David Melcher's warm compliments made her voice all the more frigid as she replied, "I attempted to teach you a lesson, but apparently I failed." She turned to leave.

"No . . . wait!" he grated hoarsely.

"Wait, Mr. Cameron? For what? To be insulted and cursed at and to have my possessions shattered as repayment for bringing you food?"

"You call that slop food? I'm half starved and you bring me broth and milk toast, then hustle your fanny out of here without so much as a fare-thee-well! I've been laying here waiting for some answers for who the hell knows how long, so just keep your bones where they are, missus!"

Appalled by his rude outburst, she attempted to level him with a little cool, sarcastic superiority.

"My! What an extensive vocabulary you harbor, Mr. Cameron. Slop . . . fanny . . . bones . . . spoken like a true scholar." She threw him a disparaging look, then stiffened her spine and tried to give the impression she was taking command, although she felt far less cocksure than she sounded.

"If you want answers to any questions, quit your cursing, *sir*, treat me with respect, and stop issuing orders! I shall issue orders if any are to be issued, is that understood? You have fallen under my care and—despicable as you are—I am committed to giving it to you. But I do not—repeat, *do not*—have to accept your grossness or your abuse. Now, shall I leave or will you comply?"

He jerked his chin once, gave her a withering look, and whispered something that sounded like, "Sheece!" Then in a guttering voice he obliged, "Enter, Goody Twoshoes, and I'll try to hold my temper."

"You had better do more than try, *sir*." She could say sir in the most cutting way he's ever heard, considering that sweet little voice she had.

"Yes, *ma'am*," he countered, giving her a dose of her own hot tongue.

"Very well. I've made a gargle to ease your throat. If you use it, I'm sure it will offer some relief by morning." But she hesitated, just beyond his reach, as if still unsure of him. He considered winking at her just to see her jump, but nodded instead, agreeing to lay off the rough stuff.

She came nearer. "Here, just gargle, don't swallow." She helped him sip sideways. He pulled half the contents into his mouth, but it flew out again in a flume.

"What kind of piss is this!"

"*Missster* Cameron!" she hissed, pulling her blouse from her skin.

He really hadn't meant to spray her that time. After all, he wanted his questions answered, even if he had to toe the line to get his way.

"Sorry," he whispered insincerely.

It seemed to appease her momentarily, for she shoved the cup in his direction and he grimaced, gulped, and gargled while she took vast pleasure in informing him, "It's an old remedy of my grandmother's—vinegar, salt, and red pepper."

This time he hit the bowl, but he couldn't help gagging.

"Rinse!" she ordered imperiously, handing him a glass. He eyed it suspiciously, finally taking it. But it was only water this time.

"What the hell happened to my throat?" he guttered.

"As I said, it had some foreign objects in it while you were unconscious. It should feel better by tomorrow. I'd appreciate it if you would keep your crudities to yourself."

"It's not enough I get shot . . . I have to get choked, too. That would make any man cuss. And what's the matter with this hand?"

"Your gun hand?" she inquired sweetly, intimating a gross guilt upon him with that single arched eyebrow of hers.

He scowled, causing forbidding creases to line his forehead.

"I assume somebody trounced on it in the scuffle, since it has the perfect imprint of a boot heel on its back."

"It hurts like hell."

"Yes, it should, from the looks of it. But then you brought it all on yourself by robbing that train."

"I didn't rob any goddamn train!" he whispered fiercely. Across the room, where she'd been taking things out of a dresser, her back stiffened like a ramrod. It was obvious to Miss Abigail that cursing flowed from his lips more readily than blood from his wound. She would be hard put trying to keep a civil tongue in his head. But there were other barbs with which to admonish him.

"Then why is Mr. Melcher lying upstairs at this very moment, wounded by you, and why has he sworn out a legal complaint against you for the damage you've done?"

"Who is this Melcher anyway?"

"The man you shot . . . and who shot you."

"What!"

"The two of you were carried off the train here at Stuart's Junction, and there was a car full of witnesses to prove you attempted to rob the R.M.R. passengers and he attempted to stop you. In the tussle, the two of you shot each other."

He couldn't believe it, but apparently she did, and a few others in this town, too, by the sound of it. At least he knew where he was now.

"So, I'm in Stuart's Junction."

"Yes."

"And I'm the villain?"

"Of course," she agreed with that uppity look.

"And this Melcher's the town hero, I presume."

This she declined to answer.

"And why did you get the honor of caring for us . . . *Miss* Abigail, is it?"

She disregarded his sarcastic tone to answer, "I volunteered. The R.M.R. is paying me and I need the money."

"The *R.M.R.* is paying *you*?"

"That's right."

"Hasn't this town got a doctor?"

"Yes, Doctor Dougherty. And you'll probably see him again tomorrow. He didn't come by today, so I expect he was called out to the country. You may save the rest of your questions for him. I am extremely fatigued. Good night, Mr. Cameron." She sallied out with her head up like a giraffe, cutting off the rest of his queries, and he got mad all over again. He'd seen some cold-hearted women in his day, but this one beat them all. And stiff! She was so stiff he figured she'd go lean herself in the corner out there someplace and go to sleep for the night. Good night, Mr. Cameron, my eye! My name's not Cameron, but you didn't give me a chance to say so. Just come strutting in here throwing orders around like some pinched-up shrew who takes pleasure from paining a man just because he is one. Oh, I've seen your kind before—bound up so tight with corset stays that you've got permanent indigestion.

Still, from what he'd heard of the conversation between her and this Melcher, he wondered if Melcher had miraculously made some of her juices flow. Then, glancing down at his own bare hip, he wondered what the old shrew's reaction had been to him sprawled out naked in her bed. If it wouldn't have hurt so bad, he would've laughed. No, he decided, she's as cold as frog's blood, that one. He fell to plotting how he might get even with her for shutting him off like this.

In the darkness, a light rustling sounded. He supposed she was changing clothes out in the parlor. He half expected to hear an explosion when those corset stays came undone.

There were spare bedrooms upstairs, of course. But somehow Miss Abigail thought it would be less than appropriate for her to go up there to sleep, now that she and David Melcher were getting along so well. It would be far better for her to stay down here on the parlor settee. True, the formidable Mr. Cameron was just around the other side of the wall, but their antagonism made this arrangement acceptable. After all, by now she had ceased caring whether he lived or died.

* * *

She awakened and shivered and stretched her neck taut, aware that something had roused her. It was deep night—no bird sounds came through the windows, only a chill damp, coming in on the dew-laden air.

"Miss Abigail . . ."

She heard her name whispered hoarsely and knew it was he calling her, and unconsciously she checked the buttons up the neck of her nightie.

"Miss Abigail?" he whispered again, and this time she didn't hesitate, not even long enough to light a lamp. She walked surely through the dark, familiar house to the side of the bed.

"Miss Abigail?" he rasped weakly.

"Yes, I'm here, Mr. Cameron."

"It's . . . it's worse. Can you help me?"

"I shall have a look." Something told her he was not feigning, and she lit the lamp quickly to find his eyes closed, the covering sheet kicked completely off him. She flickered it in place and bent to remove the bindings and poultice.

"Oh, dear God," she breathed when the odor assaulted her nostrils. "Dear God, no." The edge of the bullet hole had turned a dirty gray, and the stench of putrefaction all but knocked her from her feet. "I must get Doctor Dougherty," she cried in a choked voice, then hurried out.

Barefoot she ran, the always proper, always fastidious Miss Abigail McKenzie, heedless of the dew that wet the hem of her nightie, made her feet slip on the sharp gravel. Hair flying wildly, she took the length of Front Street to Doc's house. But she knew even as she mauled his front door that he wasn't home. He hadn't come to see the men tonight, which meant he could be sleeping in some forlorn barn with a sick horse or delivering a baby in a country home any number of miles away. Running back home, she alternately cursed herself and prayed, scanning her mind for answers to questions she'd never asked Doc Dougherty, never believing she'd have to know. Never should she have allowed anger to overcome common sense. But that's just what she'd done today. That man had made her so irate that she couldn't bear the thought of checking those poultices to see if they needed repacking. Oh, why hadn't she done it, even in spite of her anger? Her mother had always said, "Anger serves no purpose but its own," and now she knew exactly what that meant.

She leaped the front porch steps, night skirts lifted above the knees, and panted to a halt at the foot of her bed. He lay upon it with eyes closed, breath too shallow and sweet to be healthy. Forgotten now was her anger at him, her fear of him. All she knew was that she must do all she could to save his life. She dropped to her knees to scramble through a cedar chest at the foot of the bed, searching for a much-used book that had crossed the prairies in a conestoga wagon years before with her grandparents. It contained cures for humans and animals alike, and she desperately hoped it held answers for her now.

He moved restlessly as her frantic fingers scanned the pages. "Where's the doc?" he whispered hoarsely. She flew to his side.

"Shh . . ." she soothed. Eyes dark, hair ascatter, she flopped the pages, reading snatches aloud before finally finding the remedy. Then she lurched toward the door, cast the book aside, muttering, "Charcoal and yeast, charcoal and yeast," like a litany.

He drifted for a long time in a kind of peaceful reverie from which he was curiously removed yet somehow aware of his surroundings. He heard the stove lids clang, heard her exclaim, "Ouch!" and he smiled, wondering what she'd done to hurt herself, such a careful woman like her. Some glassy, tinkly sounds, fabric ripping, water being poured. She seemed to float in, arms and hands laden. But he was smacked from his blissful nether state when she began cleaning his wound.

"I'm sorry, Mr. Cameron, but I've got to do this."

He reached down to combat her hands.

"Please don't fight me," she pleaded. "Please. I don't have time to tie you again." He groaned, deep and long and raspy, and she gritted her teeth and bit on her inner cheek. He clasped the sheet with his one good hand while the other tapped listlessly against the mattress. She removed the useless, dead flesh, swallowing the gorge in the back of her throat, wiping at her forehead with the back of a hand.

Tears formed in her eyes, leaked down the corners while she bathed the wounds with disinfectant, then whispered, "I'm almost done, Mr. Cameron." She felt his hand grope at her chest and thought stupidly how he was using his battered hand and that he shouldn't be. Still, she let him grab a weak handful of the front of her nightgown and pull her up close to his mouth.

"My name's not Cameron. It's Jesse," he croaked.

"Jesse what?" she whispered.

But he drifted into oblivion then, his grip falling slack, his lips grown still, close beneath hers.

It became a personal thing then, refusing to let him die. She mixed warm, damp yeast with the remnants of charcoal, forming the mixture she hoped would keep him alive, all the while feeling for the second time that obdurate will to prevent the death of another human being. What he was and how he had treated her became insignificant against the fact that he was flesh and blood. Stubbornly she vowed that he would live.

If the night before had been difficult, the remainder of this one was a horror.

The book said to keep the poultices warm, so she made two, running to the kitchen to reheat them. The fire flagged and she slogged outside for more wood. Still the poultices cooled too fast, so she topped them with mustard plasters, the only thing she knew that would retain heat. But they needed frequent changing, so rather than bind them, she propped the bottom one and held the top one lightly in place with her hand. He often jerked spasmodically or tossed wildly, and when his moans brought her flying back from the kitchen, she wet his lips with a damp cloth, squeezing a drizzle of water into his mouth, massaging his throat, trying to make him swallow. Sometimes she said his name, the new name—Jesse—encouraging him to fight with her.

"Come on, Jesse," she whispered fiercely. "Come on, help me!"

She knew not if he heard her.

"Don't die on me now, Jesse, not now that we've come this far." He tossed, wild with delirium, and she fought him, throwing what she thought was the last of her strength on him to keep him flat. He muttered insensibly.

She argued with intense urgency, "Fight with me, Jesse. I know what a fighter you are. Fight with me now!"

But she herself could fight just so long. She fought long after she knew what she was saying or who she was or who he was or where they were.

When unconsciousness overtook her she never knew it.

Chapter 5

MR. MELCHER WAS truly on top on the world the next morning. His toe gave him nearly no pain at all, so he decided to surprise Miss Abigail by going down to breakfast unaided. The house was abnormally quiet as he limped downstairs. From the bottom step he eyed the bedroom doorway leading off the parlor. He was repelled by the thought of that felon sleeping under the same roof as himself and Miss Abigail, but he had an urge to sneak a small peak at the man nevertheless. It would be something to tell the boys back at the Elysian Club just what that robber looked like after he'd laid him low.

But he hadn't expected the shocking sight that greeted him when he stuck his carefully groomed head around the door-frame!

There was the wounded robber all right, but the man had absolutely not a stitch of clothing on, save his bandages. He lay stark naked and hairy, one leg draped over a pair of bolsters, the other sprawled lasciviously sideways, riding the curve of a woman's stomach. She occupied the lower half of the bed, her gown scrunched up to mid-thigh, feet dangling, along with his, between the footrails. Her face was nearly at his hip, but buried beneath a mop of plical-looking hair in which the man's fingers were twined. But most lurid of all: the harlot had one arm stretched out across the brute's hairy thighs, her palm precariously near the man's genitals!

From the looks of her, none of this was surprising. The slut was a mess. The soles of her feet were filthy, her gown the same, smirched with ocher and gray stains; the lace cuffs were grimy. Her hands looked no better than the rest of her, fingernails encrusted, knuckles long in need of scrubbing, those of her left hand wrapped in a piece of dirty gauze, as if she'd been in a saloon brawl.

How the man had managed to get the woman in here was a mystery, but Miss Abigail would be shocked to her very core to witness such a spectacle!

At that moment the man twitched restlessly and mumbled something incoherent. The woman came out of her deep sleep just enough to sigh, grope toward the bandage, and mumble, "Be still, Jesse." Then her hand fell away limply across his knee as she slumbrously snuggled against his long, bare leg, turning her face.

"Is that you, Abbie?" he mumbled, eyes still closed.

"Yes, Jesse, it's me, now go back to sleep."

He sighed, then a gentle snore sounded as his hand relaxed in her hair. And soon her rhythmic breathing joined his while a horrified David Melcher crept soundlessly back to his room.

The scene remained fixed in his memory during the awful days that followed, during the bittersweet afternoons in Miss Abigail's garden, when he longed to ask her for explanations but feared there were no good ones. His jealousy grew, for she spent most of her time with the outlaw, who recovered at a snail's pace. There were times when David paused, passing the room, and looked inside, nursing his hatred for the man who had not only maimed him but stolen the greatest joy from his life. David's limp seemed permanent now, and it undermined his self-esteem, making him believe no woman could possibly find him attractive. He watched the care with which Miss Abigail attended the man, though he was drugged now with laudanum for his own good, and each minute she spent in that downstairs bedroom was a minute of which David felt robbed of her attention.

Miss Abigail puzzled over his withdrawal. She longed for him to kiss her again, to buoy her tired spirits at the end of an arduous day, but he didn't. David's toe seemed completely healed and she dreaded the thought that he might leave without ever again pressing his suit. When she tried to please him with small favors, he thanked her considerately, but his old compliments were part of the past.

After Doc finally gave the orders to drop the laudanum, Jesse awoke one sunny morning, weak, but hungry as a bear, and amazed to find himself still alive. He flexed his muscles, found them stiff and sore from disuse, but those grinding pains had faded. He heard voices from the kitchen and remembered the man who'd put him here, wondered how many days he'd lain unconscious.

He heard not so much as a footstep, yet somehow knew she was standing there in the doorway. He turned from his study of the trees outside the window to find her watching him with all traces of her former antagonism gone.

She looked as crisp as a spring leaf in a skirt of forest green and a white lawn blouse, her brown hair knotted in its careful coil at the base of her neck, her skin fresh and peachy. And he saw for the first time how a smile could transform her face.

"So you've made it," she said quietly.

He studied her for a moment. "So I have." Softly, he added, "Come over here."

She paused uncertainly, then drifted slowly to the side of the bed.

"You been busy?" He smiled up at her crookedly.

"A little," came her mellow reply.

He flopped an arm out, gathered her in by her forest green skirts, and boldly caressed her buttocks, saying, "I guess I owe you." It was nothing Jesse hadn't done to a hundred women a hundred times, but it was just Miss Abigail's luck he chose that precise moment to do it to her, for the sound of their voices had brought David Melcher to the doorway.

The blood flooded his face before he remarked dryly, "Well, well . . ."

Miss Abigail froze, horrified, helpless. It had happened so fast. She squirmed, but Jesse only held tight and drawled with a lopsided grin, "Mr. Melcher, our avenging hero, I presume?"

"Have you no decency!" David hissed.

Undaunted, Jesse only turned his grin up at Abbie as she struggled to break his hold. "None whatever, have I, Abbie?"

"Abbie, is it?" returned the outraged David while she at last managed to struggle out of Jesse's hold, her eyes on the man in the doorway.

"This . . . this is not what it seems," she implored David.

"Yes it is," Jesse teased, enjoying Melcher's discomfort intensely, but Miss Abigail whirled on Jesse, all her venom returned in full force.

"Shut up!" she spit, little hands clenched into angry balls.

David gave the pair a scathing look. "This is the second time I've found you with him in wh . . . what I'd term a c . . . compromising position," he accused.

"The second time! What are you talking about? Why, I've never—"

"I *saw* you, Miss Abigail, curled up beside him with your hand on—" But he pursed his mouth suddenly, unable to go on.

"You're a liar!" Miss Abigail exclaimed, her hands now on her hips.

"Now, Abbie," put in Jesse, "there were those couple nights—" She whirled on him, sparks seeming to fly from her eyes.

"I'll thank you to shut your despicable mouth, Mr. . . . whatever your name is!"

"You called him Jesse in your sleep," David declared.

"In my—" She didn't understand. Jesse just smiled, enjoying it all.

"I thought you were such a lady. What a fool I was," Melcher disdained.

"I have never done any of what you've intimated. Never!"

"Oh? Then where had you been that night if not out romping in the grass? Your gown, your feet, your hands . . ."

She remembered them all too clearly, the knuckles bound because she'd burned herself on a live coal as she dug for charcoal, her feet and gown soiled by running to Doc's house.

"He was unconscious, and gangrene had set in. I went to fetch Doctor Dougherty."

"Oh? I don't seem to remember the doctor coming that night."

"Well, he didn't . . . I mean, he wasn't home, so I had to treat Jesse—Mr. Cameron, I mean, as best I could."

"You seem to have treated him to more than a mustard poultice," David accused.

"But I—"

"Save your explanations for someone who'll buy them, *Miss* McKenzie."

She was as pale as a sheet by this time and clutching her hands together to stop their trembling.

"I think you had better go, Mr. Melcher," she said quietly. A muscle worked in his jaw as he looked at her standing so still and erect beside the smirking man.

"Yes, I think I had," he agreed, quietly now too, and turned from the room. He went upstairs to gather his things together with a heavy heart. When he returned downstairs she stood clear across the parlor, the pain in her heart well hidden as she faced him.

"I have no shoes," he said forlornly.

"You may wear Father's slippers and have someone return them when they come for your valise." Her hands were clutched as their eyes locked, then parted.

"Miss Abigail, I . . ." He swallowed. "Perhaps I was hasty."

"Yes, perhaps you were," she said in clipped tones, too hurt to soften.

He limped to the screen door and each step crushed a petal of some fragile flower which had blossomed within her since he'd come here. He pushed the door open, and her hand instinctively reached toward him. "You . . ." He turned and she retracted the guilty hand. "You may take one of Father's canes. There's no need to return it."

He took one from the umbrella stand, looked balefully across at her, and said, "I'm ever so sorry." She longed to cross the room, draw an arm through his, and say, "It's all a big mistake. Stay and we'll set it straight. Stay and we'll have lemonade in the garden. I too am sorry." But pride kept her aloof. He turned and limped away.

She watched him until he turned a corner and was lost to her. He was a gentle man and a gentleman, and both attributes had lifted Miss Abigail's waning spinster hopes, but those hopes were firmly dashed now. There would be no lemonade in the garden, no soft, kid city shoes arriving to tell her he was thinking of her. There would be only her quiet afternoons of weeding and her twilights spent with the sonnets. What have I done to deserve this? she thought painfully. I've done nothing but save an outlaw's life.

As if on cue, his voice came, clear and resonant. "Abbie?"

Impossible to believe how a single word could make one so angry.

"There's no one here by that name!" she exploded, swiping at an errant tear.

"Abbie, come on," he wheedled, louder this time.

She wished she could ram a fork down his throat and incapacitate it again! She ignored him and went to do her morning chores in the kitchen.

"Abbie!" he called after several minutes, his voice growing stronger and more impatient. But she went on with her tasks, drawing extreme pleasure now from disregarding him. Hate lodged in her throat like a fishbone.

"Goddamnit, Abbie! Get in here!"

She cringed at the profanity but vowed it would never put her at a disadvantage again. Two could play this wily game, and she wasn't above trying to get even for what he'd done. She calmly ignored his calls until finally, in a voice filled with rage, he bellowed.

"Miss Abigail, if you don't get in here this minute, I'm going to piss all over your lily white bed!"

Appalled, blushing, but believing every word he said, she grabbed the bedpan and ran. "You just try it!" she shouted, and flung the bedpan from the doorway. It came down on his good knee with a resounding *twin-n-n-g*, but she was gone before the reverberations ended. In her wake she heard him hiss something about a vicious asp.

Horrified and shaking, she knew she'd made it worse, for she'd have to go back in there and collect the thing and—oh! he'd been so angry again! Maybe she shouldn't have flung it at him, but he deserved it, and worse. He'd have deserved it had it been full! She pressed her hands to her cheeks. What am I thinking? He's turning me into the same sort of uncouth barbarian he is. I must get control of myself, pull myself together. I'll get rid of him as soon as I can, but until I do, I'll level my temper, like Mother always warned me I must, and somehow squelch this urge for revenge. She was in careful control by the time she reentered his room and spoke with cold disdain.

"I suggest, sir, that for the duration of your convalescence we draw a truce. I should like to see you well and on your way again, but I simply cannot brook your hostility."

"My hostility! I deserve a fit of hostility! First I got shot by that . . . that *fool* for something I didn't do, then tortured by a woman who whacks me in the teeth with her spoon, refuses to tell me where I am or why, calls me by somebody else's name, ties me to the bedpost, and holds out on me when I need a bedpan! Lady, you talk about hostility, I've got plenty, and more where that came from!"

His shouting shattered her nerves, but she carefully hid it, purring, "I see you've regained full use of your vocal chords."

Her high and mighty attitude made him bellow all the louder. "You're goddamn right I have!" Her eyes actually twitched.

"I do not allow profanity in this house," she gritted.

"Like hell you say!" he roared.

"How brave you are when you shout like a madman." And finally he started to simmer down. Using her finest diction, her quietest tones, and her explicit vocabulary, she laid down the law while she had him feeling sheepish. "At the onset, sir, you must understand that I shall not accept your calling me by such familiar and disparaging terms as Abigail, Abbie or . . . or *lady*. You shall call me Miss Abigail, and I will call you by your surname if you will kindly give it to me."

"Like hell I will."

How easily he could rout the importance of etiquette and make her feel the one in error.

"What's the matter with calling me Jesse?" he asked now. "It's my name. You were so anxious for me to tell you what it was when you thought I might not make it."

"Yes, for your tombstone," she said smugly.

Unexpectedly, he smirked. "Now I'll never tell you the rest of it." She turned away quickly, fearing she might smile.

"Please, can't we quit this bantering and resolve our dispute?"

"Damn right we can. Just call me Jesse, *Miss* Abigail." Once he'd said it, she wished he hadn't—not that way! He was the most irritating man she'd ever met.

"Very well, if you won't tell me your last name, I'll continue to call you Mr. Cameron. I've grown used to it, in any case. However, if you persist in using crudities as you did earlier, we won't get along at all. I'd appreciate it if you'd temper your tongue."

"My tongue doesn't take to tempering too readily. Most of the places I go it doesn't have to."

"That has become very obvious already. However, I think

neither of us likes being cast together this way, but seeing that we are, shall we make the best of it?"

Again he considered her words, analyzing her highfalutin way of speaking and that cocky eyebrow that constantly prickled his desire to irritate her.

"Are you going to poison me with any more of your potions you concoct for naughty gunslingers?" he queried mischievously.

"You have proven this morning, without a doubt, that you don't need it," she replied, her ears still ringing from his tirade.

"In that case, I accept your truce, Miss Abigail." And with that, the tension seemed to ease somewhat.

She went to the bay window and opened it to the morning air. "This room smells foul. It and you need a thorough airing and cleaning. You have grown as rank as your bedclothes," she finished, her back to him as she flung the curtains up over their rods.

"Tut-tut, Miss Abigail, now who's goading?"

That "tut-tut" sounded preposterous coming from a man like him. She wasn't sure if she could handle his newfound sense of humor.

"I only meant to say I thought you might appreciate a bath, sir. If you would rather lie in your own effluvia, I will thankfully let you." By now he knew that she cut loose with her high-class words whenever she got flustered. It was fun seeing her color up that way, so he went on teasing.

"Are you proposing to give me a bath while I lay naked in this bed?" He gasped in mock chagrin and pulled the sheet up like some timid virgin.

Turning, she had all she could do to keep from laughing at him in that ridiculous pose. She cast him a look of pure challenge and stated in no uncertain terms, "I did it before . . . I can do it again."

His thick black eyebrows shot up in surprise. "You did it before!" He pushed the sheet back down, just below his navel. "Well, then . . ." He drawled, relaxing back with his good hand cradling his head.

When she spun from the room he lay there smiling, wondering if she'd really give him a *thorough* cleaning. His smile grew broader. Hell, I'm willing if you are, Abbie, he thought, and lay in the best fit of humor he'd enjoyed since falling into this flower bed of hers.

When she returned, he watched her roll up her sleeves, thinking, ah, the lady bares her wrists to me at last. He knew he had her pegged right. She was virtuous to the point of fanaticism, and he couldn't figure out how she was going to handle this situation and come out as innocent as she went in. He enjoyed himself immensely, potent buck that he was, lying back waiting for her discomfort to begin.

She had very delicate hands that looked incapable of managing the job. But some minutes later she had an oilcloth under him so fast, he didn't remember raising up to have it slid into place. He submitted complacently, raising his chin, turning his head, lifting his arm upon command. He had to hand it to her, she really knew how to give a man a decent bed bath. It felt damn good. He couldn't believe it when she climbed up next to him to get at his left side. But she did it, by Jove! She did it! And raised a new grudging respect in him.

"Now that we've drawn a truce, maybe you'll tell me why you started calling me Cameron," he said while she lathered away.

"I thought you were awake and sensible that first time you spoke. I asked you your name and you said 'Mike Cameron.' I heard it, or rather saw it, distinctly."

He remembered back and suddenly laughed. "I didn't say Mike Cameron, I said 'my camera,' but at the time it felt like somebody was drying their green rawhide around my neck, so it might not have come out too clear." He looked around. "By the way, where is it?"

"Where is what?" She kept on ascrubbing, kneeling there beside him.

"My camera."

"Camera?" She glanced up dubiously. "You've actually lost a camera and you think *I* know where it is?"

He raised a sardonic eyebrow. "Well, don't you?"

She'd been washing his side. The cloth in her hand rested nearly on his hip now, the sheet still covering him from there down. She looked at him and said dryly, "Believe me, Mr. Cameron, I have not come upon a camera on you . . . any-place." It was out before she could control it, and Miss Abigail was immediately chagrined at what she'd said. Her startled eyes found his, then veered away as she set to work with renewed intensity.

"Why, Miss Abigail, shame on you," he drawled, grinning at the rising color in her cheeks. But he was sincerely worried about his equipment. "A camera and plates take up one hell of a lot of space. What could have happened to them?" he asked. "And my grip was with my photographic gear. Where is it?"

"I'm sure I don't know what you're talking about. You were brought to me just as you are, sir, and nobody said anything about any camera or plates. Do you think I'm hiding them from you? Put your arm up, please."

Up went his arm while she scrubbed the length of it, including his armpit.

"Well, they've got to be someplace. Didn't anybody get them off the train?" She started rinsing the soap off the arm.

"The only things they carried off that train were you, Mr. Melcher, and his valise. I'm sure nobody expected a thief to be carrying a camera." The little upward tilt of her eyebrow told him just how preposterous she thought his little fable. "Tell me, sir, what an outlaw does with a camera." She looked him square in the eye, wondering what lie he'd concoct.

He couldn't resist. "Take pictures of his dead victims for his scrapbook." His evil grin met her appalled look.

"That, Mr. Cameron, isn't even remotely funny!" she snapped, suddenly scrubbing too hard.

"Ouch! Take it easy! I'm a convalescent, you know."

"Please don't remind me," she said sourly.

His tone became conversational. "You wouldn't believe me anyway, about my camera, so I won't bother to tell you. You'd rather think I was merrily robbing trains, then you can feel justified in . . ." his voice raised a few decibals as he yanked away ". . . . tanning my hide instead of just scrubbing it! Ouch, I said! Don't you know what ouch means, woman?" He nursed his knuckles. But he could almost hear the bones snap in her neck, she stiffened up so fast.

"Don't call me woman, I said!"

She snatched his hand back and began drying it roughly.

"Why? Aren't you?" Her hands fell still, for he had taken hold of her hand, towel and all, and was holding it prisoner in his long, dark fingers. Panic knifed through her at the flutter of her heart. She looked up at his dark eyes, probing with an intensity that alarmed her.

"Not to you," she answered starchily, and pulled her hand free, then quickly clambered off the bed.

Something indefinable had changed between them in that instant when he grasped her hand. They were now quiet while she proceeded with the washing of his right leg. She soaped the length of it, working gingerly at the area near the wound. Once he arched his chest high and dug his head back into the pillow with a swift sucking breath of pain.

"It's healing, no matter what it might feel like."

But she was still upset about his earlier comments. She was briskly working her way toward his foot with fresh lather when he looked down his chest at her and asked quietly, "Are you to old Melcher?"

Her head snapped up. "What?"

"A woman. Are you a woman to old Melcher?"

But his timing was ill chosen. She had him by the bad leg and was none too gentle about slamming it back down, suds and all. He gritted his teeth and gasped, but she stood there with an outraged expression on her face, hands jammed on the hips of her wet-spotted apron, eyes glaring.

"Haven't you done enough damage where Mr. Melcher is concerned without pushing my nose in it? He's a gentleman . . . but then you wouldn't know anything about gentlemen, would you? Does it satisfy your ego to know you've managed to lose him for me, too?"

His leg hurt like hell now and a white line appeared around his lips, but she had little sympathy. How much more could she take from him?

"If he's such a gentleman, why did you throw him out?" Jesse retorted.

Her mouth puckered and she flung the cloth into the bowl, sending water splattering onto his face, the floor, and pillow. He recoiled, hollering after her retreating figure, "Hey, where are you going? You haven't finished yet!"

"You have one good hand, sir. Use it!" And her skirts disappeared around the door. He looked down at his soapy foot.

"But what'll I do with the soap?"

"Why don't you try washing your mouth out with it, which your mother should have done years ago!"

The soap was beginning to itch. "Don't you leave this soap on me!"

"Feel lucky I've conceded to wash as much of you as I have!"

He drove his good fist into the mattress and shouted at the top of his lungs, "Get back here, you viper!"

But she didn't return, and the soap stayed until the itching became unbearable and he was forced to lean painfully to remove most of it, then dry his foot and calf with the sheets.

As Miss Abigail left the house, she whacked the screen door shut harder than she'd ever done in her life. She pounded down the back steps like a Hessian soldier, thinking, *I have to get out of the same house with that monster!* Nobody she'd ever known had managed to anger her like he had. Standing in the shade of the linden tree, gazing at the garden, she longed for a return of tranquility to her life. But not even the peaceful, nodding heads of her flax flowers could calm her today. She wondered how she would ever endure that odious man until he was well enough to walk out of here on his own. He was the crudest creature she'd ever encountered. She almost had to laugh now at the memory of Doc worrying about her "tender sensibilities." If only he knew how those sensibilities had been outraged by the man she'd freely allowed into her house.

Miss Abigail's mother and father had been people with faultless manners. Cursing and raging had been foreign to her life. She had always been taught to hide anger because it was not a genteel emotion. But Mr. Cameron had managed to elicit more than just her anger. She was smitten by guilt at all she'd done—withheld a bedpan from an invalid, then thrown it at him, then abused his leg, causing him intentional pain, and slamming out of the house like a petulant child. Why, she'd even made one unforgivalbe ribald comment! The memory of it scalded her cheeks even now.

But the one who had precipitated it all would not allow her escape, not even out here in her garden. His voice riveted through the still summer air, abrading her once more.

"Miss Abigail, what's the railroad paying you for, half a job? Where's my breakfast?" he needled.

Oh, the gall of that man to make demands on her! She wanted nothing so badly as to starve him out of here. Loathsome creature! But she was caught in a trap of her own making. All she could do was gather her ladyhood around her like a mantle while she returned to the kitchen to prepare his meal.

* * *

When she came in with the tray, the first thing he noticed was that there was no linen napkin lining it like before.

"What? Don't I get flowers like old Melcher did?"

"How did you know . . ." she said before she could think. He laughed.

"Sounds carry in your house. Is that a real blush I see on the woman's cheek? My, my, I wonder if old Melcher knew he had what it takes to put it there. He certainly didn't look as if he did." The way he said "old Melcher" made her want to smack him!

"Remember our truce, *sir?*" she said stiffly.

"I only wondered why I don't get equal consideration around here," she complained in mock dismay.

"You wanted food, sir. I've brought you food. Do you wish to lie there and blather all morning or to eat it?"

"That depends on what you've chosen to poison me with this time."

It didn't help her temper any to recall all the warm, appreciative comments Mr. Melcher had made about her cooking. She brought a pillow to boost up that black devil's head, wishing she could use it instead to smother him. The thought must have been reflected in her face, for he eyed her warily as she spread a cloth on his chest and picked up the spoon. The glimmer in his eye warned her she'd better look out for those precious, sparkling teeth of his!

"Would you rather do it yourself?" she asked brittlely.

"No, it doesn't work when I have to lie so flat. Besides, I know how you enjoy doing it for me, *Miss* Abigail." A slow grin began at the corner of his mouth. "What is this stuff?"

"This . . . *stuff* . . . is beef broth."

"Are you determined to starve me?" he asked in that horrible, teasing tone she found more offensive than his belligerent one.

"At dinner time tonight you may have something heavier, but for now, it's only broth and a coddled egg."

"Terrific." He grimaced.

"You may consider it terrific when you taste what will follow your breakfast."

"And what's that?"

"I'll prepare a decoction of balm of Gilead, and while you may find it quite bitter, rest assured it's very fortifying for one of your debility." He considered this while she poked a few more spoons of broth into him, carefully avoiding his teeth.

"Do you ever talk like other people, Miss Abigail?" he asked then.

Immediately she knew he was trying to rile her again. "Is there something wrong with the way I speak?"

"There's nothing wrong with it. That's what's wrong with it. Don't you ever talk plain, like—'I mixed up some medicine and it'll make you stronger'?"

She could not help remembering how David Melcher had likened her speech to a sonnet. A light flush came to her face at this newest unfair criticism. She had always prided herself on her literacy and began to turn away to cover the hurt at being criticized for it now. But he grabbed her wrist.

"Hey, Miss Abigail, why don't you just bend a little sometime?" he asked, and for once the teasing seemed absent from his voice.

"You've seen me as . . . as . . . *bent* as you ever shall, Mr. Cameron. You have managed to anger me, make me lose my patience, shout like a fishwife, and more. I assure you it is not my way at all. I am a civilized person and my manner of speech reflects it, I hope. You have goaded me in countless ways, but I find no reason for this newest assault. Do you intend to wring that spoon from my wrist again?"

"No . . . no, I don't," he answered quietly, but neither did he release it. Instead, he held it loosely, very narrow and fine within the circle of his wide, dark fingers while his hazel-flecked eyes looked from her hand to her eyes and back again. He shook it gently; the hand flopped, telling him that she was not about to try to resist his superior strength. "But you're more believable when you're angry and impatient and shouting. Why don't you get that way more often? I won't mind."

Surprised, she slipped easily from his grasp.

"Eat your eggs." He opened his mouth and she put a spoonful in.

"These things are slimy."

"Yes, aren't they?" she agreed, as if overjoyed. "But they'll build your strength, and the faster you get strong, the sooner I shall be rid of you, so I intend to take excellent care of you from now on. When you've finished your breakfast, I shall walk over town to Mr. Field's feedstore to buy flax seed for a poultice. Flax seed will heal that wound as fast as anything can, but never too fast to suit me."

"How about something for this sore hand, too? Must be something broken in there because it hurts like hell." She gave him a sharp look. "Well, it does. Don't get me wrong, Miss Abigail. I positively glow at your doting, but with two good hands I might have one free for you to hold."

"Save your ill-advised wit for someone who'll appreciate it."

Jesse was beginning to appreciate her more and more. She had a caustic tongue, which he liked, and whether she knew it or not, she didn't have such a bad sense of humor. If he could just get her to bend that ramrod back and those ranrod ideals just a little she might be almost human, he thought. Breakfast really hadn't been so bad after all.

"Oh," he said, "One more thing before you leave. How about a shave?"

She looked like she'd just swallowed a junebug.

"There's no . . . no hurry, is there?" She acted suddenly fidgety. "I mean, it's been growing ever since you've been unconscious. What will a few more hours matter?" He rubbed his chin and she held her breath, feeling suddenly nauseous. But she was given a temporary reprieve, for his hand stopped its investigation before getting to his upper lip. Suddenly she seemed eager to leave the house. "I'll make you the decoction of balm of Gilead, then go up to the feedstore, and you can . . . well, you can rest while I'm gone . . . and . . ."

"Go . . . go, if you want." He motioned her toward the door, puzzled by her sudden nervousness, which was so unlike her. When she returned a minute later with the balm of Gilead, he opened wide and gulped it down. It was vile.

"Bluhhh . . ." he grunted, closing his eyes, shivering once, sticking out his tongue. Normally his grimace of displeasure would have been all it took to make Miss Abigail happy, but she was too worried about his missing moustache to gloat.

She worried about it all the way over town.

The bay window faced south, with east and west facets. He saw her as she passed along the road, striaght and proper, and he couldn't believe she'd donned a hat and gloves on a hot June day like this. She was something, Miss Abigail was. The woman had starch in everything from her bloomers to her backbone, and it was amusing trying to make it crackle. She passed out of his limited range of vision and he thought of other things.

He wondered if they'd found his camera and gear down in Rockwell, at the end of the line. If it had stayed on the train, the crew in Rockwell more than likely had it by now and had let Jim Hudson know it had arrived without Jesse. Jim would get word to him sooner or later.

A knock on the door disturbed Jesse from his thoughts. "Come in!" he called. The man who came was stubby, short of hair and of breath, but long on smiles. He raised his bag by way of introduction.

"Cleveland Dougherty's the name, better known as just plain Doc around here. How you doing, boy? You look more alive than I ever thought to see you again."

Jesse liked him instantly. "That woman's too stubborn to let me die."

Doc howled in laughter, already sensing that the man had sized up Miss Abigail quite accurately. "Abigail? Aw, Abigail's all right. You were damn lucky she took you in. Nobody else in town would, you know."

"So I gathered."

"You were in some shape when we got you off that train. All that's left of your stuff is this shirt and boots. We had to cut the pants off you, o' course. And I guess this belongs to you, too." Doc lifted a pistol, weighing it in his hand while he peered over lowered brows at the man on the bed. " 'Course it's empty," Doc said pointedly. Then, as if that subject were totally cut and dried, Doc tossed the gun onto the bed.

"I guess you can put my boots and shirt under the bed," Jesse said. "That way we won't clutter up Miss Abigail's house."

"Sounds like you already know her ways, eh? Where is she anyway?"

"She went 'over town' to the feedstore." He managed to say it just like she would have.

"I see you've had the full lash of Miss Abigail's tongue," Doc said, chuckling again. "What in thunderation is she doing there?"

"She said she was going to get flax seed for a poultice."

"That sounds like Miss Abigail all right. Got more cures up

her sleeve than a chicken's got lice. Let's see here what she's done to you." He lifted the sheet and found the wound looking surprisingly healthy. "I'd have sworn the best you'd come out of this was losing the leg to gangrene, the way it looked. But she made up a mixture of charcoal and yeast that purified it and kept working the matter to the surface. It seems to have saved your life, boy, or the very least your leg."

"But I hear you did surgery first. I guess I owe you for taking me on when they dragged me off that train. They said I was robbing it and that might've made some men hesitate to patch me up."

"Some men, maybe. Even some men around here. But we're not all that way. Ah . . . what the hell's your name anyway?" Jesse liked the man's down-to-earth language and the fact that he seemed not to care whether it was a train robber or someone else whom he saved.

"Just call me Jesse."

"Well, Jesse, I figure a man'a got a right to medical treatment first and a trial second."

"A trial?"

"Well, there's talk around. 'Course, there's bound to be, the way you came in."

"Raised an uproar, did I?"

"Uproar isn't the word for it. Whole damn town congregated on my lawn to raise objections to me taking you on as a patient. Riled me up something fierce, let me tell you! Still, it's natural folks were a mite jumpy about having you under their roofs, considering the circumstances. You can hardly blame them in some ways."

"Still, Miss Abigail braved it?"

"She sure did. Marched right down there in the middle of that crowd, cool as a cucumber salad, and told the whole damn town she was willing to take you in—the pair of you yet! Left everybody feeling a little sheepish, being what she is and all."

"And what's that, Doc?"

"You mean you don't know?"

"Well, I've got a pretty fair idea, but I'd like to hear your version."

"I can tell you, but it's nothing you don't know after spending any time with her at all. I'm sure you've divined she's no floozy. Miss Abigail is more or less the town yardstick." Doc scratched his head thoughtfully, puzzling out a way to

describe how everybody felt about her. "I mean, if you want to
see just what a proper lady ought to be, you measure her
against Miss Abigail, cause she's the damnedest most proper
lady this town's ever seen. You want to know what a devoted
daughter should act like, you measure her up against Miss
Abigail, after the way she saw to her old man in his last years.
There's a few women in this town could take a lesson from her
on keeping their noses out of other folks' business, too. Oh,
she's exactly what she appears, make no mistake about that—
every inch a lady. I guess that's why the townspeople were
pretty surprised that she'd take in a gunslinger like she did."
The word might have rankled, but Doc had a way of saying it,
offhand, as if it didn't matter to him.

"Has she ever been married?" Jesse asked.

"Miss Abigail? No . . ." Then, recalling back, Doc
added, "Now wait a minute. She almost did once. A rounder
he was, never could see the two of them together. But, as I
recall, he courted her right up until the time her father got bad.
Seems he wasn't willing to take on a bedridden old man along
with his bride, so he left her high and dry. You know, over the
years a person forgets those things. She was different then, of
course. But it's hard to think of Miss Abigail as anything but a
maiden lady. Guess that's why we were all so surprised when
she took you in." Doc looked up. "How's she bearing up?"

"Staunch as a midwife."

"That'd be typical of her too. She's that way, you know.
When she takes on a responsibility she's prepared to see it
through, come hell or high water. She gave up the better part of
her youth seeing after her father, and by the time he died, we all
kind of took for granted that she'd become the town's resident
old maid. Some folks thought she got a little uppity, but then
you can't blame her. Hell, who wouldn't, being so young when
all your neighbors labeled you a spinster? Ah well, in any case,
we'd all appreciate it if you gave her her due respect."

"You've got my word on it. Oh, and Doc, could you check
this hand of mine?"

Doc pronounced the hand only brusied, then summed up his
findings. "Well, you're healing fast, thanks to her, but don't
push it. Take 'er slow and easy. Try sitting up tomorrow, but no
more than that. I'd say, by the looks of you, you'll be
managing a slow shuffle by the end of the week anyway. Just
don't overdo it."

Jesse smiled and nodded, liking the man more than ever as Doc prepared to leave.

"Doc?"

"Yup?"

"What's up with that Melcher fellow?"

"Wondered when you'd ask about him." Doc could see the first hard lines in Jesse's face since he'd walked in the room. "Seems he's leaving town today. Went to the depot and bought himself a ticket for Denver on the afternoon train. Did you know you shot his toe off?"

"I heard."

"He probably will limp for the rest of his life. Plenty of grounds for a lawsuit, huh?"

"You'll pardon me if I'm not overcome by guilt," Jesse said with a bitter edge to his voice. "Look what he nearly did to me!"

"Around here that's not going to count for much, I don't think. You see, you're the villain—he's the hero."

Strange, but even at those frank words, Jesse felt no criticism from Doc. As the two eyed each other, it was with mutual silent approval.

"Tell Miss Abigail I'll try to be around if she needs me again, but I don't think she will."

"Thanks, Doc."

Doc stopped in the doorway, turned one last time, saying, "Thank Miss Abigail. She's the one that kept you alive." Then he was gone.

Jesse lay thinking of all Doc had told him, trying to imagine a young and vibrant Miss Abigail courted by an ardent suitor, but the picture wouldn't gel. The image of her taking care of a sickly father seemed far more believable. He wondered just how old she was, guessing her to be thirty or thereabouts. But her bearing and actions made her seem far older, stodgy, and fusty. To picture her with a husband and children seemed ludicrous. She would seem miscast in that role, with a child's sticky fingers pulling at her spotless apron or admiring a mud pie brought for her approval. Neither could he imagine her moaning in ecstasy beneath a man.

But like the change of cards in a stereoscope came the picture of Miss Abigail as she'd been that night fighting for his life, hair and gown and skin a mess, leaning over him, pleading, urging him to fight with her. How intense she'd been then, all fire and dedication, so different from the primness which she usually exuded. The two just didn't go together. But according to Doc Dougherty, he owed his life to her. He felt a prickle of discomfort, thinking about how she'd been jilted by that other man so many years ago just because she'd accepted the responsibility of caring for a sick man, and now the same thing had happened again and it was his fault. Guilt was a new thing to Jesse. Still, he decided he owed her something and would temper his tongue because she'd lost her boyfriend on his account.

But I'll surely miss teasing her, he thought. Yup, I'll surely miss it.

Chapter 6

ALL THE WAY home Miss Abigail knew she couldn't avoid shaving him any longer. He was bound to find out sooner or later that she'd shorn him, if he hadn't already! She'd intended to get the ordeal over with at the same time as his bath, but he'd riled her so that she simply couldn't face it. Oh, if only it were all over. He was simply going to explode when he found that moustache gone, and now that she knew how volatile he was, the thought made her quaver.

"I'm home," she announced from the bedroom doorway, surprising him, as usual. How a woman could move through a house without making a sound that way beat him.

"Aha."

With a half sigh of relief that he still hadn't made the discovery, she came into the room, pulling the white gloves from her hands on her way to the mirror. He was surprised to find himself glad she was back.

"And have you brought your flax seed?" he asked, eyeing her in semiprofile as she raised her arms above her head and removed the ornate, filigreed hatpin. He noticed again that she had generous breasts. Her usual starch-fronted blouses concealed the fact, but from this angle, and with her arms raised that way, they jutted forward, giving themselves away.

"Indeed I have," she said, turning now. "And some fresh lemons for a cool drink."

He bit back a cute remark about Melcher and asked instead, "Did you bring a beer for me?"

She soured up. "Your days of ebriosity are recessed temporarily. Lemonade will have to do while you're here." He understood her now, the way his teasing made her pluck some pretentious word from her ample store of them and use it to bring him down. Ebriosity! But again his newfound agreeability stopped him from teasing, and he agreed pleasantly, "Actually, lemonade will do quite nicely, Miss Abigail."

She stood there in the center of the room, ill at ease for some reason she couldn't define, and the shifting breeze from the open window caught her skirt, billowing it out before her. She took her hat and used it to flatten the skirt down again, the gesture very youthful and enchanting, making him wonder again what she'd been like as a young girl.

"I . . . . I'll shave you now, if you like." Her eyes avoided his, and she fussed distractedly with the daisies on her hat. He rubbed his jaw while her heart jumped into her throat.

"I probably look like a grizzly bear," he ventured, smiling.

"Yes," she agreed rather weakly, thinking, and you'll probably act like one in a minute, too. "I'll go heat water and gather the necessary things."

She left the room to stoke up the fire, then found clean cloths and her father's old cup and brush. She was reaching for the basin when his voice roared from the other room.

"Miss Abigail, get your ass in here and fast!" She straightened up as if the toe of his boot had given her a little impetus, then closed her eyes to count to ten, but before she finished, he was yelling again. "Miss Abigail . . . now!"

He had completely forgotten his promise to be nice to her. She came in holding the washbasin like a shield before her.

"Yes, Mr. Cameron?" she almost whispered.

"Don't you 'yes Mr. Cameron' me!" he roared. "Where the hell is my moustache?"

"It's gone," she squeaked.

"I've just now discovered the fact. And who is responsible?"

"Responsible? I don't see why you put it that—"

"I'll put it any way I damn well please, you interfering—" He was so angry he didn't trust himself to call her a name, not knowing what might come out. "Who in the hell gave you permission to shave me?"

"I didn't need permission. I am being paid to see after you."

"You call this seeing after me!" His black, piercing eyes held no softening hazel flecks now. "I suppose you figured as long as you were changing everything around here—sheets, bedpans, bandages—you might as well keep right on changing. Well, you changed just one thing too many, do you hear me, woman! Just one thing too many!"

Though she quailed before his wrath, she was unwilling to be spoken to this way. "You're shouting at me and I don't like it. Please lower your voice." But her very control seemed only to raise his temperature and his volume.

"Oh God," he implored the ceiling, "save me from this female!" Then he glared at her. "What did you do, decide the big bad train robber needed his fingers slapped, is that it? I suppose you picked this way to do it. Or did you shave it off just for spite because it's masculine? Oh, I've got you pegged, *Miss* Abigail. I've seen your kind before. Anything male is a threat to you, isn't it? Anything that smacks of virility dries you up till you squeak when you walk. Well, you've picked the wrong man to wreak your puritanical vengeance on, do you hear me, woman? You'll pay for this and dearly!"

Miss Abigail stood red-faced, horrified that he'd struck so near the truth.

"I am paying for this, just standing still for your abuse and your name calling, which I do not deserve."

"You want to talk about deserving? Did I deserve this?" He made a disgusted gesture near his wounded leg. "Or this?" He next pointed to his upper lip. She was again struck by the fact that he looked very naked and unnatural without the facial hair.

"I may have acted hastily," she began, still trembling but willing to compromise now with a sort of apology, if only to silence him. He let out a derisive snort and lay there glaring at the ceiling. "If it makes you feel any better," she said, "I'm sorry I did it."

"Believe it or not, it doesn't make me feel a damn bit better." Then he went on in an injured tone, "Just why the hell did you do it? Was it bothering you?"

"It looked dirty and gave you the appearance of a typical outlaw." Then her voice brightened noticeably. "Why, don't you know that some of the most famous outlaws in history had moustaches?"

"Oh?" He raised his head a little to peer at her. "And how many of us have you met?"

"You're the only one," she answered lamely.

"I'm the only one."

"Yes," she said very meekly.

"And you shaved me so I wouldn't look like the others, huh?"

Miss Abigail, who always had such control, came very close to blubbering. "Actually n . . . no. Well, not . . . I mean, it is very much trouble when . . . well, when you're eating. I mean . . . well, it tickled."

His head came up off the pillow. "It what!"

"Nothing!" she snapped. "Nothing!"

"It tickled?"

Mortified by her traitorous tongue, she was forced to expound. "Yes, when I was feeding you." That brought his head up even further.

"Would you care to explain that, Miss Abigail?" But she had turned so red he could almost smell the starch scorching in her collar as she spun from the room. While she gathered his shaving things, he lay considering. A crazy notion took hold of him, and being very much a ladies' man, it swelled his considerable ego and cooled his anger somewhat. But common sense told him it couldn't be true—not of the ramrod-spined Miss Abigail! Still, the notion gained credence when she returned, for she was skittish as a cat at howling time, fussing around with that shaving stuff, avoiding his eyes, and obviously very uncomfortable.

She felt his eyes following her with a feral glint, but steeled herself and approached, poured some hot water into the cup, and worked up a lather. But when she made a move toward his face, his black eyes snapped warningly.

"I'll do it myself," he protested, and grabbed the soapy brush from her hand. "Just hold the mirror," he ordered. But once he got an eyeful of his naked face in it, he grew disgusted again. "Damnit, Abbie, you might as well have changed the shape of my nose. A moustache is part of a man he doesn't feel the same without." He managed to sound quite wounded now. Looking into the mirror, he shook his head woefully at his own reflection, then started lathering as if to cover up what he saw.

As the black whiskers became covered with white he looked less fearsome, so she admitted, "I knew that as soon as I did it. I'm sorry." She sounded genuinely contrite, so he stopped brushing the soap on his jaws and turned to study her. She kept her eyes on the mirror but said, "I . . . I found that I'd liked you far better with it." Fearing she'd again said the wrong thing and given him ammunition, she ventured a peek at him. But his scowl was gone and, surprisingly, so was much of the anger from his voice.

"It'll grow back."

Something told her that the worst was over, that he was trying, really trying, to control himself for her.

Pleased, she offered, "Yes, your beard grows exceedingly fast." They assessed each other for a few seconds, and in that time he realized she'd studied him in his sleep long enough or hard enough to mark the speed with which his beard grew.

"How observant you are, Miss Abigail," he said quietly. And damn if she didn't blush. "Here, you can take over." He handed her the brush. "I'm not too coordinated with my left hand."

"Are you sure you trust me?" Her one fine eyebrow was hoisted higher than the other, but still he smiled.

"No, should I?"

"Mr. Melcher did," she lied, not knowing why she should want this man to think she had shaved David Melcher.

"He didn't look like he had enough man in him to grow a beard. Are you sure there was hair on his face when you started?"

"Hold still or I may cut your nose off yet." She poised the blade above his cheek. "And, unlike your moustache, it shan't grow back."

"Just stay away from my upper lip," he warned, then pulled his mouth muscles to tighten them and could feel the blade as she scraped around none too proficiently. He reached up to stop her so he could talk without getting cut.

"Shape it down around here—"

"I remember the shape well enough, sir," she interrupted, "and you have me by the wrist again." An interminable moment charged past while his brown fingers circled her little wrist.

"So I do," he grinned. "I shall take the razor from you and slit it if you take off one more hair than I think you should." He released her and shut his eyes while she finished. She was getting better at it as she went along. So, he thought, she remembers the shape well enough, does she? For some reason that vastly pleased him.

"Miss Abigail?" She turned from rinsing the razor to find his black eyes filled with wicked amusement as they smiled from his freshly shaved face. "I shall spend time thinking of a way to get even with you for the loss of my moustache."

"I'm sure you shall, sir. Meanwhile, we'll drink lemonade together as if we were the best of friends, shan't we?"

When she brought the lemonade, he had a difficult time drinking from the glass.

"Here, try this," she said, handing him something that looked like a willow twig.

"What's this?"

"A piece of cattail which I reamed out with a knitting needle. You may drink your lemonade through it." He tried it and it worked.

"How ingenious of you. Why didn't you bring it for the broth this morning? Were you so anxious to spoon-feed me?"

"I simply did not think of it."

"Ah," he said knowingly, his expression saying only a fool would believe that.

"I have things to do," she said abruptly, deciding not to stay and drink her lemonade after all, not if he was going to tease again.

"Aren't you having any lemonade? Bring it in here and let's talk a minute."

"I grow weary of your talk. I almost wish your voice hadn't come back."

"How cruel of you to deny me the use of my voice when it's one of the few parts of me that's working right." Before she could decide if he meant the remark to be suggestive, he encouraged, "Don't go. I just want to talk awhile."

She hesitated, then perched on the sewing rocker, wondering why she stayed in the room with him. She sipped daintily while he pulled thirstily at the fresh drink through the piece of cattail, then growled, "Ahhhh, that's almost as good as beer."

"I wouldn't know." No, he supposed she wouldn't.

"Doc Dougherty was here while you were gone."

"And how did he find your condition?"

"Much better than expected." She lifted her glass but not

her eyes. "He told me I ought to thank you for saving my life."

"And are you?" she challenged.

"I'm not sure yet," he answered. "Just what all did you have to do to save it? I'm curious."

"Not much. A poultice here and a compress there."

"Why so modest, Miss Abigail? I know it took more than a pat on the head to bring me around. I have a natural curiosity about what you did to keep my carcass from rotting."

Unconsciously, Miss Abigail studied her two bitten fingers, rubbing her thumb over the small scabs which had formed, unaware that his eyes followed hers.

"There was very little for me to do. You were strong and healthy and the bullet couldn't do you in, that's all."

"Doc and I are both wondering as to how you fed me. I heard you say I ate—more than once today you referred to it. How can an unconscious man eat?"

"Very well, I'll tell you. I force-fed you, using that piece of cattail you're drinking through. I had to insert it into your throat. That's why it hurt so severely when you first awakened." Again he noted her preoccupation with the marks between her knuckles and began putting two and two together.

"Are you saying you spooned medicine and food through this little hole?" She was growing very uncomfortable under this line of questioning, then suddenly realized his eyes were on the knuckles she'd been nursing and hid them in her skirt.

"I did not spoon it. I blew it," she admitted impatiently.

"With your mouth, Miss Abigail?" he asked in surprise.

"With my mouth, Mr. Cameron." But she would not meet his eyes.

"Well I'll be damned."

"Yes, you probably already are, but please refrain from saying so in my presence."

"Is that how you got tickled by my moustache? By this little bitty short straw here? It sure seems to me like it could have been cut a little longer."

Feeling her face heat up, she shot out of the rocker but he was too quick. He grabbed and got her by the back of her hand. He looked at her exposed fingers, then up at her face, with a mischievous smile creasing one side of his mouth.

"And these . . ." he said, studying the fingers, "what are these?"

"Turn my hand loose, sir!"

"As soon as I'm satisfied about what took place here while I was not coherent. Could these be my tooth marks?"

"Yes!"

He held the hand in a viselike grip while she struggled to pull it free. "What were your fingers doing in my mouth?"

"Holding it open and forcing your tongue down while I inserted the straw into your throat."

"And you call that *nothing much*?"

She glared at him silently, red to the ears now.

"To feed a common thief, mouth to mouth, to put your fingers into his mouth and suffer him to bite them until he broke the skin, and to take broth into your own mouth and blow it into his? That is much more than *nothing much*. That is dedication, Miss Abigail. That is stalwart, admirable dedication, isn't it? It seems I do owe you my gratitude."

"You owe me nothing . . . Let my—"

"I owe you my gratitude. How shall I express it?"

"Just let my hand go and that will be quite enough."

"Ah no, Miss Abigail. Surely that won't do. After all, you've been forced into some unorthodox—not to mention intimate—methods of caring for me. I would be ungrateful to let your generosity pass without notice." With his thumb he gently stroked the tooth marks on her fingers. Their sparring eyes met while a queer thrill grabbed her stomach and she strained to pull free of his grasp. "Since I have no more ticklish moustache to offend you with, allow me . . . by way of apology for this . . ." Then in slow motion he pulled her fingers to his lips and kissed the small scars. He felt the change when she stopped fighting and let him take the fingers to his mouth. Then he turned the hand over, kissed the palm with a light, lingering touch, and lightly ran his tongue out to wet her skin. She jerked then and grabbed the stricken hand with her other.

"I must have been out of my mind to bring you into my house!" she spit.

"I only meant to apologize for biting you. Don't worry, it won't happen again."

"And is this . . . this form of apology your way of getting even for my having shaved your moustache?"

"Oh, that. No, never, Miss Abigail. When I choose the time and the method of getting even, you'll well know it."

His implication was plain, and all Miss Abigail could do was scuttle out, escaping those casually smiling lips and eyes which were so much more of a threat in his newfound good humor than they'd ever been in his anger.

She kept as far away from that bedroom door as she possibly could for the remainder of the day, telling herself that each time she remembered his kiss and her stomach trembled, it was from anger.

At noon she was forced to go to him with his dinner. She made the thickest stew she could manage and uncermoniously plopped the bowl on his chest.

He'd been dozing and awoke with a start. All he had time to say was, "Boy, the service is really going downhill around this place." But she was gone again. She didn't care how he managed or failed to manage eating that stew. Furthermore, she hoped it was thick enough to tear his gut out!

"Got any more of that stew out there?" he hollered a few minutes later.

I should have guessed that a goat like him would eat everything in the house and never be bothered by it at all! She slapped more stew into his bowl and again plopped it wordlessly onto his chest while he lay there grinning as if he knew something she didn't.

In the afternoon she went up to clean Mr. Melcher's room, only to find the book of sonnets lying like a love letter from a lost beau. In a lifetime of much loneliness, she remembered how for those few treasured days he had been an harbinger of something better to come. But he was gone from her life as suddenly as he'd entered it.

A timid knock on the downstairs door brought Miss Abigail from her brown study. Coming down the steps she recognized the fabric of David Melcher's suit sleeve, which was all she could see of him. It brought a flutter to her heart as, crossing the parlor, she paused, put a hand to her breathless lips, then smoothed her blouse front, her waistband, then touched a hand to the coil of hair at the nape of her neck. She didn't realize that from the bedroom Jesse saw it all.

She moved beyond his range of vision, but every word was audible, and even from the bedroom he could detect her breathlessness.

"Why, Mr. Melcher, it's you."

"Yes . . . ahem . . . I came to return your father's slippers."

"Yes . . . yes, of course. Thank you." The screen door
spring went twinnng, and a long silence followed.

"I'm afraid I've been a lot of trouble to you."

"No, no, you've been no trouble at all."

Melcher seemed to be having some trouble with his throat.
He cleared it several times, followed by a second lengthy
silence. When they spoke again, it was simultaneously.

"Miss Abigail, I may have jumped to . . ."

"Mr. Melcher, this morning was . . ."

Silence again while the man in the bedroom cocked his ear.

"You were within your rights to get angry with me this
morning."

"No, Mr. Melcher. I don't know what came over me."

"You had good cause, though. I never should have said
those things."

"Well, it really doesn't matter, does it, since you're leaving
Stuart's Junction on the train within an hour?"

"I want you to know what it meant to me, this time I've
spent in your lovely house while you cared for me. You did far
more than was expected of you."

"Nonsense, Mr. Melcher . . ." Conscious now of the man
in the bedroom, she realized he could hear every word, but
there was nowhere else she could take David Melcher. The
front porch was too public, the kitchen too private.

"No, it's not, Miss Abigail. Why, your . . . your nasturtiums and the sonnets and your tasteful way of doing
things . . . I mean, I'm not used to such treatment. And all
that delicious food and your fine care—"

"All in the line of duty."

"Was it?" he asked. "I'd hoped . . ." But this he didn't
finish, and Miss Abigail toyed with the lace edging of her high,
stiff collar.

"Hopes can be very hurtful things, Mr. Melcher," she said
quietly.

"Yes . . . well . . ."

"I see you have purchased yourself a pair of new shoes."

"Yes. Not quite as fine as those I sell, but . . ." Once
again his words trailed away.

"Feel welcome to keep Father's cane. I have no use for it
since he's gone."

"Are you sure?"

She suddenly wanted very badly for him to take it, for him to carry away some small thing from her house which would always remind him of her.

"I shan't miss it, but you might, if you had to go without it."

"Yes . . . well . . . thank you again, Miss Abigail."

It grew silent again and Jesse pictured the two of them, both probably gaping at the old man's cane. The spring on the screen door sang again.

"If I ever get back through here, I'll return the cane to you."

"You needn't bother."

"Ah . . . I see," he said, rather forlornly.

"I didn't mean . . ." But her words, too, trailed away.

"I will always think of this place when I smell the scent of nasturtiums."

She swallowed, her heart threatening to explode, her eyes to flood.

"Goodbye, Miss Abigail," he said, backing away slowly.

"Goodbye, Mr. Melcher."

It grew so quiet then that Jesse could hear each and every one of Melcher's irregular steps shuffling off down the road. He saw the limping figure through the east facet of the bay window, below the half-drawn shade, and thought, damn fool should've used his head on that train and he wouldn't be limping now. It was the first time Jesse was able to think of Melcher without getting frustrated and angry at his own incapacity. He heard the footsteps of Miss Abigail go back upstairs long, long after Melcher limped away. She must have watched him out of sight, Jesse thought. He couldn't help recalling all that Doc had told him about the other man who'd walked out on her once before, couldn't help comparing now to then. And he could not stop the irritating twitch of conscience that prickled him.

From an upstairs window Miss Abigail watched the puffs of smoke as the afternoon train pulled in. Its whistle swooned through the stillness as she held the lace curtains aside. She pictured Mr. Melcher limping aboard the train. Her heart called to him not to forget her. A puffy cloud lifted above the roof of the depot and the steam whistle cried mournfully once more, bearing David Melcher out of her life. Her eyes stung as she turned to put fresh sheets on his bed.

She fully expected to be teased again after everything the man in her house had overheard. She came to his doorway to find him sound asleep. It gave her a moment of perverse pleasure to disturb him.

"I found some wild weeds that will help your hand," she said loudly, businesslike.

He roused at her words, clenched his good hand, and gave one of those shivering, all-over stretches. It was slow, masculine, and she averted her eyes, remembering how he'd earlier said that anything masculine threatened her. He growled lazily, deep in his throat, twisting and yawing. At last he opened his eyes and drawled, "Howdy, Miss Abigail. Have you been there long?"

"I just . . ." But she had. She'd been watching those muscles twisting and turning.

"Studying my beard grow again?"

"You flatter yourself, sir. I'd as soon watch grass grow."

He smiled, again slowly and lazily.

"I came to put a fomentation on that bruised hand. The sooner it heals, the sooner I'll be excused from wringing out your shaving cloths."

He laughed. He seemed for once to be in a halfway human mood. "Spoken like a true adversary, Miss Abigail. Come on in. I can use the company now that I've been so rudely awakened anyway. I expect you can too, now that Melcher is gone."

"Leave Mr. Melcher out of this, if you please," she said acidly. "Do you want the compress on your hand or not?"

"By all means. After all, it's my gun hand, isn't it?" He extended it toward her and she came to unwrap the old gauze strips and pad. As she unwound the pieces, he added, "And my loving hand, too." She automatically halted all movement, realized her mistake, continued unwrapping while he went on. "Hard for a right-handed man to make love with only one good hand and that his left."

She could already feel the color creeping up behind her choker collar.

"How indelicate of you to say so."

The hand was free now and he flexed it only a little, at the same time moving it toward her face. She jerked back.

"And how indelicate of you to flinch, Miss Abigail, as if I

had designs on you. After all, a hand like this is in no shape for loving or shooting, either one. When it is, you'll know it."

Rattled now, she turned her back on him, and her voice was almost pleading. "What do I have to do to keep you from teasing me this way? I am unused to it, thus I have no defense against it. I'm sure the women you've known in the past were quick with rebuttal, but I am simply tongue-tied, time and again, and deeply embarrassed. I realize this is precisely the outcome you hope to achieve with me, so it must pleasure you endlessly to hear me finally admit it. But I lay my soul bare to you and admit that these taunts are disconcerting. I ask you to make my job easier by treating me fairly and honorably."

"Do you want me to beseech you to put fresh nasturtiums in my room?"

When she spoke her voice was exceedingly quiet, almost defeated. "I want absolutely nothing from you except to be treated like a lady, as I was by Mr. Melcher. But then you obviously disdain Mr. Melcher. His qualities of kindness and consideration are foreign to you, I know, but you only make yourself more offensive by making fun of him."

"Old Melcher got to you, did he?"

With an effort she kept her voice calm. "Mr. Melcher knows how to treat a lady, how to make her feel valued and appreciated, how to eke a bit of the sublime out of the everyday tedium. These things may seem soft and weak to you, but it is because you have never learned the strengths to be found in the beautiful and gentle things of this life. Strength to you is only . . . only . . . anger and cursing and goading and making others do what you want by the force of these things. I pity you, Mr. Cameron, for you've somehow been denied the knowledge that such well-worn attributes as politeness, respect, patience, forbearance, even gratitude, have a pecular strengthening quality all their own."

"And you've practiced these virtues all your life?"

"I've tried." He saw her shoulder blades draw erect proudly as she admitted it.

"And what good did it do you? Here you are, polite and bitter, and left with me and deserted by Melcher."

Still with her back to him, she cried, "You have no right, Mr. Cameron! No right at all! *You* are the reason he is lost to me, you and your teasing tongue. I'm sure you feel supremely self-satisfied that he is gone and that with him went my last chance for . . . for . . ." But at last Miss Abigail broke down, lowered her face into her hands and sobbed, her small shoulders shaking as Jesse had never thought to see them. The last woman he'd caused to cry had been his mother, the last time he'd left New Orleans to come back out West again. Seeing Miss Abigail cry now was equally as disturbing. It made him feel exactly as she had many times said he was: callous and coarse. And this feeling was something new and disturbing. He wanted suddenly to make up for the hurt he'd caused, but before he could say more, she gulped, "Excuse me, sir," and fled the room.

It struck him that even in her discomposure she clung to her impeccable manners as tightly as possible.

Miss Abigail was aghast at her own actions. Never in her life had she cried before a man. Strength came from many sources, but crying, she believed, was not one of them. Still, it was peculiar how purged she felt when she finished. All the bitterness and waste of her life, all the given years, all the unexperienced joys, all the foregone pleasures which she had never before begrudged her father or Richard . . . ah Richard . . . it was a blissful relief to even think his name again . . . welled now in a great, crushing hurt which she allowed herself to explore. All the pent-up frustrations which a lady never shows felt like a blessed release after years in prison.

She stood in her shaded backyard and cried at last for the loss of Richard, of her father, of David Melcher, of children and warmth and companionship. And for the first time ever she rued those years she had sacrificed to her father.

And her breakdown before Jesse made her something which she had never seemed to him before: vulnerable.

And his having caused it made him something she could hardly have suspected him capable of being: contrite.

And so it was that in the late afternoon, when she came to him next, there was a first hint of harmony between them. She came with the same self-assured dignity as before her outburst, as if it had never taken place. The only residual of her tears was a faint puffiness beneath her eyelids. Her face held neither challenge nor rebuke as she stood in the doorway, saying, "It seems I've neglected your hand again."

"My fault," he said simply. He seemed agreeable, no hint of teasing showed in his face.

"I'll take care of it now?" she asked more than stated.

"Come in," he replied. "What have you got this time?"

"The trappings for a fomentation. May I put it on?" What she was really asking was if she could come in without being tortured again by his tongue. He nodded, fully understanding. She entered, took his bruised hand, and began working over it. A grudging admiration once again overtook him. Time and again she came to him, no matter what he did or what he said. There seemed no end to her tenacity in the face of duty.

"How is it feeling?" she asked, studying the hand.

"Not good."

"Do you think any bones are broken?"

"Doc says no, but it hurts every time I move it."

"It would be surprising if none were broken," she said. The bruise was by now a ghastly yellowish-green. She picked up a small, filled cloth bag from a steaming cup.

"What's that?" he asked suspiciously.

"Be still." Holding it gingerly between two fingers, she blew on it.

"Are you punishing me with that thing?" But she only squeezed it against the side of the cup and laid it on the colorful bruise. It didn't quite burn him, but was mighty uncomfortable. "I guess I deserve it," he ventured while she only concentrated on wrapping the hand. "What have you put in that?"

"Something that will take away the aching, heal the bruise."

"Well, is it a secret or what?"

"No, it's no secret. It's just a weed."

"A weed? What weed?"

"A weed called arsesmart."

"Arsesmart! Are you serious?" It was all he could do to keep from making choice remarks about that, but he resolutely refrained.

Meanwhile Miss Abigail thought, Is there nothing we can say to each other that hasn't some ulterior meaning? He was, of course, wearing a grin, which she ignored. To cover her discomfort, she lectured.

"My grandmother taught my mother, and she taught me the value of arsesmart. It can dissolve congealed blood, which is why I'm using it on your hand. My grandmother used it for everything. She even used it on a small mole she had on her chin right here." At last Miss Abigail looked into Jesse's eyes, touching her own chin. Lamely, she finished, "But as far as I can recall, that mole never disappeared. She never . . ." Her words trailed off as she looked into Jesse's dark face, still painfully aware of the tears he had seen her shed earlier, wondering if he would mention them. But he said nothing and now looked deep in thought.

She gathered up the roll of gauze. "I believe that by morning you'll find those muscles noticeably relieved." Her eyes slid to his hand. Now, she thought, now he will taunt me. But instead he only held out the hand, shook his head as if scolding himself.

"Well, that puts one pistol hand out of commission. But it feels much better."

It was not a thank you, but it was close, and Miss Abigail thought about it all the while she fixed his supper tray. An apology was too much to hope for—he had probably never apologized for anything in his life. Still, her outburst of tears had mollified him somewhat, and to let him know she would not be faulted for a genteel life style, she picked a small nosegay of nasturtiums and put them in a delicate cut glass ewer on his tray, which was again spread with a spotless linen liner.

When he saw the neat tray and fresh flowers, he quirked an eyebrow questioningly but took it all as a peace offering and decided he'd accept.

"Is it these things that smell so sweet?" He flicked a petal.

"It is."

"Nasturtiums, I presume?"

"They are."

They eyed one another like two bighorns deciding whether to butt or back off.

"With this hand I won't be able to handle a knife." And with those words her olive branch was accepted.

"I'll handle the knife," she offered. Then added, "I hope you like liver, Mr. Cameron. It was simply too warm a day to keep the range stoked for long. Liver and onions was the fastest thing I could think of."

At her words he felt a curious swelling at the base of his tongue, warning him not to open his mouth for any liver. But there she sat on the sewing rocker beside his bed, cutting the meat, extending it to his mouth, some sort of unspoken, rocky truce at last between them. So he took it, chewed slowly, and swallowed, willing himself not to gag, not to displease her again as he seemed to do so easily. But oh! how he despised liver!

She kept it coming and coming and finally he had to think of something. "What's in the cup?" he asked.

"Coffee."

"Where's your straw?"

"Right here." She produced it from under the linen napkin on the tray.

"I'll have a drink of that." He was in too much of a hurry and burned his mouth, opened it wide, exclaiming, "Waugh!"

"Oops," she said innocently. "I guess I should have warned you it might be too hot."

But by this time he was too concerned about finishing that liver to ride her about scalding him with coffee. She wanted peace and she would have it, by God! He steeled himself for more liver and never uttered a word, but ate dutifully until the plate was empty.

Meanwhile she rambled on, talking about the many home cures and remedies she'd learned from her mother and grandmother, telling him about the book where she'd found the yeast and charcoal remedy that had saved his life.

And all the while his stomach rebelled.

At last she said, "By morning your hand could be so much improved that you might be slicing your own liver . . . I mean, slicing the liver by yourself."

But he was lying with closed eyes, curiously impassive. Please, no, he was thinking. Anything but liver. Unaware of his roiling stomach, she left with the tray, gratified for the first time at how docile and obedient he had been.

Halfway through the dishes she heard him weakly call, "Miss Abigail?" She cocked an ear, smiled, pleased that he at last was calling her Miss Abigail without his usual annoying tone, yet wondering at the same time what trick he might be up to now.

"Miss Abigail . . . bring me a bucket, please—quick!"

Was that *please* she heard? Then suddenly she realized he'd asked for a bucket. His silence during supper, his closed eyes

right afterward, his uncharacteristic passivity . . . oh no!
"I'm coming!" she bellowed at the top of her lungs.

The bucket had no more than hit the floor beside the bed
when he groaned, struggling to roll over toward it. She
whipped the bolsters from under his leg, reached across, and
grabbed him—sheet and all—by the buttocks and rolled him to
the edge of the bed just in time. He upchucked every bit of her
fried liver, onions, coffee, green beans, and even the cherry
cobbler. He lay sweating, face down over the edge of the bed,
his eyes closed.

At last he took a fortifying gulp of air, then said to the floor,
"Has it occurred to you, Miss Abigail, that perhaps we're fated
to aggravate each other without even trying?"

"Here, roll over," she ordered. "You must not lie on your
wounded leg that way." She helped him onto his back again
and saw his chalky complexion beneath the black, black
whiskers. "Perhaps I'd better check your wound again."

He flung an arm across his forehead and eyes. "It's got
nothing to do with my wound. I just detest liver, that's all."

"What?" she gasped. "And still you ate it all anyway?"

"Well, I tried," he managed with a rueful laugh. "I tried,
but it didn't work. I was bound and determined not to
antagonize you again, especially when I saw how you'd done
up that tray. But it seems I can't keep peace even when I try."
He flopped his arm weakly away from his eyes to find Miss
Abigail McKenzie in a state of suspended humor, her wide
smile hidden behind both hands, and he couldn't help his own
sheepish grin from spreading across his face. And then Miss
Abigail did the most amazing thing! She collapsed onto the
rocker, sending it rolling backward while she laughed and
laughed, clutching her waist and letting her merriment fill the
room. It was the last thing in the world Jesse had expected her
to do. Forward she came, then back again, forgetting herself
for once, lifting her feet as a child pumps on a swing, a flash of
petticoat lace accompanying her libration. And, oh, how
enchanting she looked limp and laughing that way.

"I'm sorry I can't join you," he said, "but it hurts to laugh
right after you've just heaved your guts out." But his smile
was there just the same while he continued thinking how
surprisingly beguiling she looked with her guard down.

"Oh, Mr. Cameron," she sighed at last, "perhaps you're
right and we are fated, you and I. Even when you try to do my

cooking justice it backfires." She laughed once more, gaily.

"Backfires? For once you've chosen the perfect word," he said, chuckling in spite of his sore stomach muscles. "Oh God, don't make me laugh . . . please." He hugged himself.

"You deserve it after the way you have just insulted my cooking."

"Who insulted whom? You're the one who poked that liver down me without bothering to ask if I liked it or not. It was more than an insult to have to eat it. Believe me, lady, it was a lethal weapon."

By now she was so amused that she forgot to take offense at either his profanity or the way he'd laughingly called her *lady*. She only lolled back in the rocker while he enjoyed just watching her.

"One by one I'm discovering the chinks in your armor," she said, coasting to a stop, with her head tilted back lazily. "And one of them is liver." She was relaxed as he'd never seen her before, hands lying palms-up in her lap. The golden evening sun came through the west window, lighting her hair, her chin, her high collar, the tips of her earlobes and eyelashes, turning them all to gilt.

He wondered again how old she was, for she looked suddenly young, leaning back on the chair that way, and he experienced again a momentary flash of regret for what he'd said earlier about how she'd been deserted by Melcher. He wanted the air cleared of that, thought that maybe now when she was relaxed and affable they might talk about it and exorcise the lingering bad feelings it had caused.

"How old are you?" he asked.

"Too old for it to be any business of yours."

"Too old to let a good prospect like Melcher get away?"

"You're despicable," she said, but without much fight, still easy in that chair. She rolled her head toward him, met his eyes, and a faint smile limned her lips.

"Maybe," he admitted, smiling too. "And you're worried."

"What am I worried about?"

"About getting old and having no man. But there are more where Melcher came from."

"Not in Stuart's Junction there aren't," she said resignedly.

"So . . . I fixed it good between you and Melcher and he was the last prospect around, huh?"

She didn't reply, but then she didn't need to. He studied her appreciatively as she looked into the sun's rays through slitted eyes, as if playing some game with them.

"Should I apologize for that, Miss Abigail?"

She quit playing with the sunbeams and rolled her head his way, quiet for the moment, considering. "If you must ask, it counts for naught," she said softly.

"Does it?" Then after a moment, "Anyway, it would be a bit of a letdown to have apologies between us now, wouldn't it? After all, we started out fighting like alley cats. You'd miss it if I suddenly became meek."

"And it would pain you to apologize, wouldn't it?" she countered.

"Pain me? Why, you do me an injustice, Miss Abigail. I'm as capable of apologies as anyone." But still he didn't say he was sorry.

"I apologized about your moustache, didn't I?"

"Out of fear, I think."

She rolled her head away, back toward the light that poured through the window, and shrugged her shoulders. "An apology is a move denoting strength—not strength of body, which I'm sure you've always had, but strength of character such as Mr. Melcher has."

His mellow mood was suddenly soured by her words. He was getting sick and tired of being compared unfavorably to that man. His ego was definitely singed. He didn't like being found lacking, even by such a sexless woman as her, and certainly not when put up against a milktoast like Melcher. If it took an apology to sate the woman's eternal appetite for mitigation, well she'd have it, by God!

"I'm sorry, Miss Abigail. Does that make you feel better?"

She didn't even turn his way, just sat intent upon that sunlight. But she heard the defensiveness in his voice, making the apology less than sincere.

"No, not really. It's supposed to make *you* feel better. Did it?"

He felt the blood leap to his face, scourged by her refusal to gracefully accept his apology after it had taken much soul-searching to bring it out. Never in his life had he lowered himself to apologize to any woman, and now that he had, look what had come of it. Suddenly angered, he laughed once, harshly and short.

"Tell you what'd make me feel better—if you'd just get out of here and take your liver and all your rosy pictures of Melcher with you!"

Turning, she found his face suffused with irritability. Her amused eyes remained upon his hard ones. She could see that he thought she should have blithely accepted his apology; it did not occur to him that it had been given for all the wrong reasons, making it totally without contrition. The color was back in his face again, and the bite of his words suddenly sowed a seed of suspicion within Miss Abigail. Why, he's jealous of David Melcher! Unbelievable as it was, it had to be true. What other reason could there possibly be for him to react as he had? He glared at her while she, wearing a secret cozening smile, rose and sweetly wished him good night.

It was her smug attitude and that sugary good night that drove him to call after her, "I now owe you two! One for the moustache and one for the liver!"

When she had gone upstairs for the night, he lay awake a long time, puzzling over how she could manage to anger him this way. What was it about Abigail McKenzie that got under his skin? He reviewed all the obvious irritations she'd caused—the moustache and the bedpan and such—but none of these was really the crux of his anger. It stemmed from the way she'd managed to make him feel guilty about scaring Melcher off. Why, he'd had women from New Orleans to the Great Divide, any one of whom would make Abigail McKenzie look like a sorry scarecrow, and here she was, mooning over that pantywaist Melcher, flinching from so much as a finger twitched her way by himself. And when she had finally wheedled an apology out of him, what had she done? Thrown it back in his face, that's what! For a while there tonight, while she sat in that rocker laughing, he wondered if she could be human, with impulses like other women had. Well, he thought, we'll soon find out if that female has impulses or not. If she wants to moon around making me feel guilty about Melcher, always reminding me what a gentleman he is and what a despicable cad I am, even when I'm trying to apologize, I'll give her something to back it up, by God! And maybe next time she forces an apology from me—if that day ever comes— she'll show some of that impeccable breeding she's always throwing in my face and accept it like the lady she claims to be!

Chapter 7

HE HEARD HER creeping softly down the stairs before dawn had fully blossomed in the sky. She flashed past the area he could view from his bed, and he heard the front door open. After a stretch of silence he heard her humming ever so faintly. Off in the unseen distance a rooster crowed. He imagined her standing there at the east door, looking out at the dawn, listening to it. She passed his door on catfeet.

"Taking in the dawn, Miss Abigail?" he asked. And her head popped back around the doorsill. She still had her nightie on, so hid behind the wall.

"Why, Mr. Cameron, you're awake, and you're sitting up!"

"Doc Dougherty said I could."

"And how does it feel?"

"Like I ought to be out there with you watching the sun come up. I'm used to watching it rise over the roughlands, but I haven't seen it for a while. What's it like today?"

She gazed toward the front door, still shielding herself behind the doorframe, but he could see the mere tip of her nose. "It is a myriad of pinks today—striated feathers of color, from deepest murrey to palest primrose, with the spaces between each color as deep and clear as the thoughts of sages."

He laughed, not unpleasantly, and said, "Well put, Miss Abigail. But all I understood was pink."

She felt foolish for having been carried away by the beauty of the dawn, but he would, of course, not be the kind to apprecite it in the same way she did.

"I . . . I need some things for today. May I come in and get them?"

"It's your room. Why the sudden request for permission?"

"I . . . I forgot my robe last night. Would you please look away while I come in?"

From around the doorway came the healthiest laugh she'd ever heard.

"Unless I miss my guess, Miss Abigail, you're swathed in white cotton down to your wrists, up to your ears, and down again to your heels. Am I right?"

"Mr. Cameron!"

"Yes ma'am," he drawled, "yes ma'am, you can come in. You're safe from me." Naturally he sat there leaning against the head of the bed, watching her boldly as she gathered up fresh clothing for the day. She saw his smile from the corner of her eye, and once he had the audacity to ask, "What's that?" She tucked the undergarment out of sight, assuring herself that she would not again forget to get her things out of here while he was sleeping.

"The leg feels fine today," he said conversationally, "and so does the hand. The only thing that hurts is my stomach after the liver you flushed it out with last night. I'm so hungry I could eat a horse and chase the rider!"

She almost laughed out loud. Sometimes it happened so easily that she couldn't control herself, for usually she did not want to be amused by him. But now she replied, "If I see any coming this way, I'll be sure to warn them off. I somehow don't doubt that you'd do it!"

"Feisty this morning, Miss Abigail?"

"I might ask you the same thing, Mr. Cameron," she rejoined, making for the door with her cumulate riggings.

"Abbie?" The shortened name brought her up short.

"*Miss* Abigail," she corrected, raising her chin and turning toward him.

And it was then that she saw the gun.

It was black, oiled, sleek, and he held it loosely in his left hand. She had not the slightest doubt that he could use it accurately at this range, left-handed or not.

All he said was "Abbie" again, reiterating much more than the name. There followed a vast silence while he let the significance of the gun and the shortened name sink in. Then he said in a casual, mellow voice, "You know, I am feeling a bit feisty this morning after all." A sinister half smile played upon his generous lips, beneath the shadowed skin to which she'd once taken a blade.

She stared at that lip, then back at the gun as he hefted it in his hand carelessly, making her clutch the articles of clothing tightly against her chest.

"Wh . . . where did you get that . . . that thing?" she asked in a quivering voice, her eyes riveted to it.

"I'm a train robber, am I not? How can I rob trains without a gun?"

"B . . . but where did you get it?"

"Never mind that now." But there was little else she could mind. Her eyes were like moons while he took perverse pleasure in the fearful way she gawked at it.

"Abbie?" he repeated. She didn't move, just gaped at the gun while he used the end of it to point at the floor at her feet.

"Drop the duds," he ordered, almost mildly.

"Th . . . the duds?" she choked.

"The ones in your arms." It took some time before the words seemed to get through to her. When they did, she released the clothes in slow motion, letting sleeves, stockings, underwear trail regrettably down to the floor at her bare feet.

"Come here," he ordered quietly. She swallowed but didn't budge. "I said come here," he repeated, lifting the pistol now to point it directly at her, and she began slowly inching around the foot of the bed.

"What did I do?" she managed to squeak.

"Nothing . . . yet." His left eyebrow arched provocatively. "But the day is young."

"Why are you doing this?"

"I'm going to teach you a couple of lessons today." Her eyes, like a cornered rabbit's, didn't even blink. "Do you know what I'm going to teach you?" he asked, and her head moved dumbly on her neck. "Number one . . ." he went on, "I'm going to teach you never to shave the moustache off an unsuspecting outlaw. I said come here and I meant it." She moved nearer but still not near enough for him to reach from where he sat leaning leisurely against the brass headboard. He swung the pistol slowly her way.

"Here," he ordered, pointing with it to the floor directly beside him.

"Wh . . . why are you threatening me?"

"Have I made any threats?"

"The gun is a threat, Mr. Cameron!"

"*Jesse!*" he spit suddenly, and she jumped. "Call me Jesse!"

"Jesse," she repeated meekly.

"That's better." Once again his voice went quiet, almost silky. "Lesson number two, Abbie, is what happens when you wheedle an apology out of a man then use it to slap him in the face with."

"I did not wheed—"

"You wheedled, Abbie, you wheedled," he wheedled. "You got me to the point where I was actually sorry I'd made old Melcher run off like a scared chipmunk. Did you know you got me to that point, Abbie?"

She shook her head, staring blindly.

"And when I apologized, what did you say?"

"I don't remember."

"I mean to make you remember, Abbie, so you'll never do it again."

"I won't," she promised, "just put your gun away."

"I will . . . after I've taught you your lesson. What you said was that my apology should make *me* feel good, only it didn't . . . because you wouldn't let it. But I aim to feel good—real good, real soon."

She clutched her arms tightly over her breasts, gripping the sleeves of her batiste nightgown.

"Put your arms down, Abbie." She stared into his black, amused eyes, unable to make her muscles move.

"What?" she gulped.

"You heard me." At last she did as ordered, but again in slow motion. "Since I scared Melcher away and you declined to accept my apology for it, I figured the least I could do is make up for what you missed, huh?"

Here it comes, she thought in panic, and her eyes slid closed while she quaked all over.

"But I'm stuck in this bed, so you'll have to come to me,

Abbie . . . come on." He made a beckoning motion with the tip of the gun. When she stood directly beside and above him, he pointed the pistol at her, not even looking up as he did so. "You were so all-fired breathless with Melcher, there were times when I heard your heart pitty-patting clear in here. But if old Melcher had any spine, he'd have hung around at least for a little billing and cooing. You know what I mean? Since the big, bad train robber chased him off, the least he can do now is stand in for old Melcher, right?" When she only stood quaking, saying nothing, his silky voice continued. "I know you get the picture, Abbie, so kiss me. I'm waiting."

"No . . . no. I won't," she answered, wondering where she got the air to speak—her chest felt crushed by fear. He moved the pistol then and even through her nightie she could feel the cold metal barrel against her hip. He still didn't even look up, just nudged her hip with the gun. She slowly leaned over and, with eyes wide open, touched his lips quickly with hers.

"You call that a kiss?" he scoffed when she jumped away again. "That felt like some dry, old lizard whipped her tail across my lips. Try it again, like you would if I were Melcher."

"Why are you doing this—" she began, but he cut her off.

"Again, Abbie! And shut your eyes this time. Only a lizard keeps her eyes open while she's kissing."

She lowered her face to his, seeing his black, amused eyes close before her as she dropped her eyelids and kissed him again. The new growth of moustache was like the stem of a wild rose bush.

"Getting better," he said when she again leaped away. "Now give me some tongue."

"Dear God . . ." she moaned, mortified.

"He's not going to help you now, Abbie, so get down here and do as I say."

"Please . . ." she whispered.

"Please, Jesse!" he corrected.

"Please, Jesse . . . I've never . . . I haven't . . ."

"Quit stalling and get to it," he ordered. "And sit down here. I'm getting dizzy watching you bounce up and down."

With her insides trembling, she sat down gingerly on the edge of the bed, hating every black whisker that shadowed his skin, every hair that surrounded his hatefully handsome face.

"What is it you want of me? Please get it over with," she begged.

"I want a responsive, wet female kiss out of you. Haven't you ever kissed a man before, Abbie? I have nothing but time while you practice. What are you afraid of?" When her eyes refused to lower to the gun at her side, he chuckled. "Let's get back to the lesson at hand. You were going to give me some tongue. It's called french kissing and everybody does it that way, probably even lizards." He lounged there insolently, and when she sat stiffly he had to put the gun to her again, this time beneath her right jaw. "Wet!" was all he said, then cocked the gun, making her jump at the metallic click.

She closed her eyes and resigned herself. He didn't quite close his, saw hers pinched tightly shut beneath woven eyebrows, saw her brows twitch as the tip of her tongue touched his upper lip and his tongue came out to meet it. Against her lips he said, "Relax, Abbie," and he lowered the gun and put an arm around her shoulders, pulling her against his bare chest, turning his mouth sideways on hers. "Put your arms around me," he said as he felt her elbows digging against him in resistance. "Come on, Abbie, unless you want to be here all day." And one of her arms crept up around his neck, the other around his bare side. She felt the gun, still in the hand which he used to press the back of her head, forcing their mouths so tightly together. His lips opened farther; the inside of his mouth was hot. He pushed his tongue into the secret crevices of her mouth, withdrew it again, then lightly bit her tongue making her fearfully push against his chest. But he somehow wrestled her arms away, pulling her against him, squashing her breasts flat against his skin, combating her every move while his mouth retained its hold on hers. He broke away then, sliding his lips down, taking her lower lip gently between his teeth. "Jesse!" he ordered in a fierce whisper, ". . . say it."

"Jesse," she whimpered before his mouth slid onto hers again, warm and wet and melting some of her resistance.

"Jesse . . . again," he demanded, feeling her thundering heartbeat through the thin batiste nightgown upon his chest.

"Jesse," she whispered while he rubbed the back of her neck with his fingers and the butt of the gun: warm and cold together. Then he silenced the word again, kissing her with that same intercourse of tongues as before, compounding fear and delight, sensuality and shame, refusal and acceptance all within her confused body.

"Ab . . ." he whispered then, Ab . . ." Her lips were free to correct him but the thought never entered her head, for some strange languor had befallen her. Then, using his hands and mouth, he pushed her abruptly away, stunning her by asking, "Did it tickle that time?"

She could not look at him. Her head hung down and she felt suddenly filthy, violated in some way she could not comprehend. Not by him but by herself, because she'd stopped fighting him sometime while his tongue moved within her mouth, because she'd begun liking the wet, warm touch of it, the feel of his broad, muscled shoulders beneath her hand, her racing heart upon his chest.

"Today's lesson is over," he said dismissingly, the satisfied smile once again about his eyes. "I told you, when I set out to get even you'd know it."

"And I told you that force is not strength. Gentleness is strength."

"Force is damn effective, though, isn't it, Abbie?"

Once free of him, off the bed, her courage returned. "I want you out of here, do you hear? Immediately!"

"Don't forget who holds the gun, Abbie. Besides, I can't walk yet. What reason will you give all your inquisitive neighbors when they ask why you threw a helpless man out of your house? Will you tell them it was because he taught you how to kiss properly?"

"They won't ask. None of them was willing to take you in in the first place. They won't find fault with me for putting you out now."

"I've been meaning to talk to you about that, Abbie. Doc Dougherty said you were the only one who stood up and spoke for me out of this whole town. I've been meaning to thank you for that."

His words brought her blood to the boiling point. Oh, the nerve of the conceited fool to sit there thanking her after what he'd just done! "Your thanks are not essential, nor are they wanted anymore. The railroad is paying me to keep you until they can get their hands on you. It's all the thanks I need!"

He reared back and laughed. "Have you thought of why they want me, Abbie?" he asked, with a knowing look in his eyes.

"What a question from a *train robber*!" She longed to smack the disgusting smirk from his face. "I shall go to the depot today and wire whomever it is that wants you next to come and get you! The railroad can have you, wound, moustache, and all!"

"You'll miss the money you could make off me during my recuperation."

"I will miss nothing of you, you filthy, conceited goat!" she all but shrieked.

"Enough!" he suddenly roared. "Get out of here and get yourself dressed and make me some breakfast before I decide to get even with you for feeding me that liver last night. How long can a man live without decent food?"

She stomped to the pile of clothing at the foot of his bed, flailing the air with each piece before hooking it in the crook of an arm and stamping her way out. Her lips were pursed so tightly that her teeth were dry from sucking wind. When she was gone, Jesse's head arched back and his body bounced with great gasps of silent laughter. Then he dug his dirty shirt out from under the sheet near his feet, wrapped the empty gun in it, and put it back under the mattress.

She had absolutely no intention of cooking him one morsel of food. She made a fire, bathed, dressed, and all the while he periodically bellyached for his breakfast.

"What the hell's taking you so long out there?"

"I'm starving, woman!"

"Where's my food?"

She kept her eye on the clock, anxious for it to reach a proper hour so she could go over town and send the wire. But in the midst of her extreme pleasure in starving the goat in the other room, he informed her, "I don't smell anything cooking out there. I have this gun trained at the wall where I think you are. Should I try for a lucky shot?"

His answer was the loud, tinny whack of a kettle as she smacked it onto the range. She'd fill him up to shut him up, but she'd be blinkered if she'd feed him anything remotely delectable! Cornmeal was the fastest, cheapest, least appetizing thing she could think of. He kept up the needling while she cooked.

"What are you doing now, butchering the hog for bacon? . . . I smell something cooking. What is it? . . . If you're thinking of wasting time bringing me the pitcher and bowl, forget it, unless they're filled with food. A man could starve here and go unnoticed while he's doing it!''

On and on he yammered until by the time she took his tray in she was livid.

"Ah, I see you heard me at last," he said, with a stupid grin on his face. She looked for the gun but it was nowhere in sight.

"The people clear over town heard, I'm sure."

"Good! Maybe somebody will take pity on me and bring me some hardtack and jerky to store under my mattress. It would sure beat the cooking around here—not to mention the service. You didn't bring me any more of your slimy eggs, did you?''

"You are insufferable! Despicable!'' she spit venomously.

He only smiled broader than before. "You too, Miss Abigail, you too.'' He sounded downright jovial. "Now stand back and let me at this Epicurean delight of the week. Ahhh, cornmeal. Takes a skilled hand to make cornmeal.''

The only thing she could think of at the moment was, "Even animals wash before they eat.''

"Oh yeah? Name me one," he said through a mouthful of cornmeal. She looked aside in distaste.

"A racoon.''

"Coons wash their food, not their faces. Besides, they can afford the time. Nobody makes them throw up then leaves them to starve all night.''

It was beyond her why she spoke to him at all. But just once she'd like to get the best of him. But there was no dealing with a swine. Irritated, she flounced out. In a ridiculously short time he called for more cornmeal mush.

"I could use another bowl of that Epicurean cornmeal," he informed her loudly. She took the kettle right in there and plopped a now-cold gob of the stuff in his bowl. It had, in the ensuing time, acquired the look and texture of dried adobe.

"When you get rid of me, why don't you get a job slinging hash?'' He grinned devilishly. "You've got a real knack for it.'' He chopped the cornmeal brick into smaller pellets that sat like islands sticking out of the lake of cream he poured over them. As she turned on her heel, he was smiling crookedly and digging in again.

Why in the world did I ever think that taking care of him would be preferable to "slinging hash" at Louis Culpepper's,

she wondered. I would work for Louis now . . . and gladly
. . . if only I could!

By the time he'd filled that empty leg of his he'd cleaned up
enough cornmeal to stuff a flock of geese. All he said by way
of appreciation was, "We could use you in camp, Abbie." It
crossed her mind that any woman foolish enough to be found in
a bandit's camp would undoubtedly find herself used, all right!

Next he raised his voice and shouted, "What does a man
have to do to get a pot of hot water around here? I need to wash
up and shave. Do you hear me, Abbie?"

She had no source of comparison by which to measure the
man's capacity for being overbearing and rude, but surely he
must set the world's record, she thought. She delivered the
water and as stinging an insult as she could manage. "Wash
yourself . . . if you've ever learned how!"

He only laughed and observed, "Witty little chit this
morning, aren't you?"

He made a real sideshow out of his washing. Even from the
kitchen she knew every single thing he was doing. He sang out
loud, splashed, exclaimed how good this felt, and that felt. It
was disgusting. She had no idea how he was coping with one
hand, but she didn't care. Several times she became angrier
because he almost made her smile. Finally he called, "I'm as
fresh as a blinkin' nasturtium. Come and smell!"

Even in the kitchen she blushed. Never in her life had she
been so worked up. He had to threaten her with the gun again
to get her to bring the shaving gear. When she carried it in, she
cast her eyes down her nose at an angle suggesting that perhaps
she was trying to outstare a fly on its end. "Shall we proceed?"
she asked acidly. Half expecting him to be buck naked, she was
at least relieved to see he'd covered himself with the sheet.

"We?"

She stood with strained patience, awaiting his newest
objection, wishing she could take the blade and scrape every
hair off his entire head.

Maybe the look in her eye told him to beware, for he finally
said, "Keep away from my beard, woman. You made me wash
up by myself—just why so anxious to help me shave? As if I
didn't know. I've got one and a half good hands and I can sit up
now. I'll manage without your help." Then, as she turned to
leave, he added, ". . . Delila."

Her back stiffened, and he began his shave. He was damned

if he was going to let her near his moustache again after what he'd done to her this morning. He smiled, remembering it. But shaving turned out to be more difficult than he'd planned, being only slightly better than one-handed. The mirror was one of hers. Damn female gizmo! he thought. He tried to hold the long handle between his knees while he pulled at one cheek, used the other hand to work the blade, but the useless thing slipped down or turned sideways, refusing to stay where he wanted it. He finally gave up in frustration and called, "Miss Abigail, I can't manage the mirror. Come and hold it for me." She only began singing as if she hadn't heard a word he said. But his voice was deep and strong again, and there was no way it could be missed. "Did somebody step on a cat's tail out there? Seems I have to shout to be heard above the caterwauling! Come and hold the mirror!"

"You have one and a half good hands and can sit up again. Hold it yourself!" She listened, heard him sigh disgustedly. Then—lo and behold!—out came the magic word.

"Please?" That brought an enormous smile to Miss Abigail's lips.

"I'm sorry, did you say something, Mr. Cameron?" she called, the smile growing wider.

"I said please, and you know damn well I did, so quit basking in self-righteousness and get in here."

"I'm coming," she sang. She was fast learning what exquisite joy it could be to be snide. From the doorway she said pleasantly, "How can I refuse a man with such sterling manners?" She eyed his foamy face, which spoke for itself. "What would you have me do?" His eyes, like chunks of coal in a snowman, were stark and snapping.

"Just hold the damn mirror, Your Highness!"

Taking it, she noted, "You're obviously in more than one kind of a lather. If you'd like, I'll shave it for you. My hand is undoubtedly steadier anyway—see the way you're shaking?" He ignored her and peered at himself sideways in the mirror, scraping a cheek, circumscribing a black, thick sideburn, outlining one side of his precious moustache.

She raised a little finger. "Ah, be careful of the moustache," she warned, watching the lather come away black-speckled while his scowl was revealed beneath it.

"Just hold the thing still so I can see." He drew his top lip down, curling it against his teeth, shaping the moustache. "It's damn hard to follow . . . a shape . . . that isn't there anymore."

"I think you should have etched it a bit more deeply along this side," she advised, lowering her brows as if seriously studying the fault.

"Damnit, Abigail, shut up! You were easier to put up with before you found your sense of humor. You moved the mirror again!"

"Oops, sorry." She settled back and watched him finish. It was surprisingly enjoyable. Amazing, she thought, how fast the man's beard grows. When he finished his shave, the moustache stood out blackly again. Funny thing, she thought, but the fool actually looks better with it.

"Intriguing?" he asked. She jumped, abashed at being caught regarding him that way. "You can feel it any time you want. The pleasure will be mine."

"I'd as soon feel the whiskers of a billy goat!" she snapped.

"You're excused," he laughed, as she headed for the door. On second thought, added, "But just be good."

It seemed to take forever until it was late enough to go over town while she wondered just what "be good" meant. Would he try to stop her with that gun again? She tiptoed to the back door, knowing she could not cross the open bedroom doorway without being seen. But the spring gave her away, and his voice told her he knew exactly what she was up to.

"While you're gone, see if they have any meat in this town besides liver, will you? Nobody's going to come for me tomorrow. It's Sunday."

She gave into some deep, deep need and slammed the screen door until it whacked against the frame and bounced halfway open again before settling shut. Naturally he laughed.

Chapter 8

"I can't send no such wire on your say-so," Max insisted.

"Why ever not?" Miss Abigail bristled.

"Got to be the sheriff does 'at," Max said importantly. "You go over and see Sam about it, then he'll send the wire. He knows who's the right person to sent it to anyways. I don't."

Stymied, Miss Abigail stood, stiff-backed and upset, at a loss now. She didn't want to traipse all over town letting the entire citizenry know she was anxious to have that man out of her house. What rankled was that he was partially right. She was afraid that if she ran all over saying "I want him out," people would wonder why. And then what would she say? That he'd drawn a gun on her and made her kiss him? No power on earth could make her confess such a thing. Could she say he drew a gun on her to make her fix him his breakfast? Hardly. After all, she was being paid by the railroad to do those things for him. How would it look if she admitted she'd tried to starve him out of her house? What if she said he'd forced her at gunpoint to help him shave? The implications became worse all the time. Oh, why did that fool Maxwell Smith have to get all uppity with her? One quiet telegram is all it would have taken. Against her better judgment she went to Sheriff Samuel Harris next.

"Sorry, Miss Abigail," Sheriff Harris said. "Got to have a release from Doc Dougherty first. It's the law. Any prisoner under a doctor's care has got to be released officially by the doc before he can be transferred from one jail to the next—oh, begging your pardon ma'am, that's not to say your house is a jail. You know what I mean, Miss Abigail."

"Yes, of course, Mr. Harris," she condescended. "I shall speak to Doctor Dougherty then."

But Doc Dougherty wasn't home, so she went back to Main Street again, headed for the butcher shop, thoroughly disgusted now.

"Howdy, Miss Abigail," Bill Tilden greeted, coming out of his barbershop.

"Good day, Mr. Tilden."

"Hot, ain't it?" he observed, glancing at her unhatted hair. She nodded briskly, moving on. "Going over to Culpepper's for dinner," he called after her conversationally just as Frank Adney hung up his sign next door that said OUT TO LUNCH.

"How do, Miss Abigail," he greeted.

"Mr. Adney," she acknowledged.

"Some scorcher, huh?

"Indeed." She headed on up the boardwalk thinking how limited the range of conversation was in Stuart's Junction. Behind her, Bill Tilden asked Frank Adney, "You ever seen Miss Abigail uptown without her hat and gloves before?"

"Come to think of it, I ain't."

"Well, wonders never cease!" they turned to watch Miss Abigail as she entered the door of Porter's Meat Market, shaking their heads in disbelief.

"Howdy, Miss Abigail," Gabe Porter said.

"Good day, Mr. Porter."

"Heard tell you took in that train robber up to your house."

"Indeed?"

Gabe stood with his ham-sized arms crossed over his mammoth, aproned stomach, the flies buzzing around the blood stains there, one occasionally landing on the fly paper that hung coiled from the ceiling. "Shucks, everybody knows about it. He ain't giving you no trouble, now, is he?"

"No, he's not, Mr. Porter."

"Heard 'at other city dude cleared out on the train yesterday, huh?"

"Yes, he did."

"Ain't it a little risky, you bein' up there all alone with 'at other one?"

"Do I look as if I'm in jeopardy, Mr. Porter?"

"No, no indeed you don't, Miss Abigail. Folks is just wonderin' is all."

"Well, folks may cease their wondering, Mr. Porter. The gravest danger I'm in is that of being eaten out of house and home."

Then Gabe jumped, realizing she was waiting to buy some meat. "Ah . . . right! And what'll it be today?"

"How are your pork chops today? Are they fresh and lean?"

"Oh both, ma'am. Fresh cut today and kept on ice for as long as I can keep it from melting."

"Very well, Mr. Porter. I shall have three of them."

"Yup, coming right up!"

"On second thought, perhaps I shall need, four—no, five."

"Five? These ain't gonna keep till tomorrow, Miss Abigail, even down the well."

"I nevertheless shall take five, and a length of smoked sausage, oh, say—this long." She held up her palms six inches apart, then lengthened the span to ten or so and said, "No, this long."

"What in Hades you feedin' up there, Miss Abigail, a gorilla?"

It was all she could do to keep from replying, "Exactly!" Instead she thrust poor Gabe into total dismay by requesting, "I should like one pig's bladder added to my order."

"One . . . pig's bladder, Miss Abigail?" Gabe asked, bug-eyed.

"You just butchered, did you not? Where are the entrails?"

"Oh, I got 'em. I mean, they ain't been buried yet, but what—"

"Just wrap up one bladder, if you please," she ordered imperiously, and he finally gave up and did as she requested. When she was gone Gabe muttered to the flies, ". . . a pig's bladder . . . now what in the hell is she gonna do with that?"

When Miss Abigail reached her house again there were fresh buggy tracks in the fine, dry dust out front, and she realized she'd missed Doctor Dougherty again. What dismal luck to have missed him when she needed his help to get that man out of here.

In her customary way, she stopped to peak at her reflection in

the mirror of the umbrella stand. There was no hat to remove,
so she smoothed her hair, her sleeves, her waistband, then
quickly tested the tautness of the skin beneath her chin with the
back of her hand.

"Is it firm?" a deep voice asked, and she whirled and
jumped a foot off the floor, pressing a hand to her heart.

"What are you doing up?" He was standing just this side of
the kitchen archway, leaning on crutches, his dark chest,
calves, and feet sticking out of a sheet he had wound around
himself.

"I asked first," he said.

"What?" All she could think of was, what if that sheet
dropped off!

"Is it firm? It should be, the way you point that saucy little
chin at the ceiling all the time." As if to verify it, up went her
chin.

"If you are up, you are strong enough to get out of here.
How heartening!"

"Doc brought me the crutches and I needed to go out back
after he left, so I decided to give it a go. But I'm not as strong
as I thought."

"You traipsed clear across the backyard dressed in that
sheet?" she gasped. "What if someone saw you?"

"What if they did?"

"I have a reputation to uphold, sir!"

"Don't flatter yourself, Miss Abigail," he smirked. She
stood there with the blood cascading into her face, until even
her ears felt hot. "You know, I'm getting a bit lightheaded," he
said.

"Lightheaded? Don't you dare pass out wrapped in that
sheet! Get back into bed, do you hear? I should never be able to
budge you if you collapsed on the floor!"

He stumped his way across the far end of the parlor and all
went well until he came to a hooked rug that lay in the bedroom
doorway. One crutch caught in it and he began to waver. She
hurried across, grabbed him around his middle to keep him
from tipping over, and when he was steadied, went down on
one knee to remove the rug. But the crutch was still planted on
it, holding it down. "I can't pick it up. Can you move the
crutch?" she asked, looking up the long length of him. It was a
long, long way indeed to the top of that length, and she

warned, "Mr. Cameron, if you tip over on top of me I'll never forgive you."

"There'd be nothing left to forgive with. You'd be one . . . squashed . . . hummingbird." He swayed against the doorjamb as one crutch crashed to the floor.

"Quickly, get to bed," she ordered, taking his arm over her shoulders. He was as tall as a barn door and nearly as broad at the shoulder, but they made it to the bed all right and sat down on the edge side by side. She quickly unwound his arm from her shoulder and rose.

"I'll thank you to use some common sense from now on. First of all, if you intend to parade around, you shall do so in pajamas and a robe. Secondly, you shall tend to necessities and not stand around yammering while you make a hazard of your big self in my house. If a . . . a gorilla like you ever fell, how would I ever get you up?"

In spite of his haziness, he asked, "Did you send your telegram, Miss Abigail?"

"Yes!" she lied, "and they cannot come too soon to get you off my hands."

"If you want to get rid of me, you'd better start feeding me better. I'm as weak as a mosquito. Did you buy some decent meat?"

"Yes! I bought something perfectly suited to you!"

He awakened from a dream that there was rain spattering on the canvas of his tent, but it was the pork chops splattering away on top of Miss Abigail's kitchen range. He stretched, feeling the skin of his right leg tight but healing and hurting less all the time. Something smelled so good his stomach lurched over, his mouth salivated, and a rumble sounded somewhere deep inside of him. By the time she brought the tray in he was ravenous.

"Mmm . . . it smells like pork chops. Is it some real meat at last?" He brightened as she set the tray on his lap. She had even considerately covered the plate with an upturned bowl to keep it hot.

"Yes, real meat," she confirmed, all smiles.

"Could it be you have a heart after all?"

"Decide for yourself," she replied saucily as the bowl came up in her hands, revealing the raw pig's bladder. She simply had to stay long enough to see the expression on his face. It was a black, shaking visage of anger while a spate of filth poured from him. At some time while he cursed, he asked what the hell it was on the plate.

"Real meat. Isn't that what you wanted?" she asked innocently, enjoying every minute of this. "As a matter of fact, it is pork. A pig's bladder . . . simply perfect for a goat like you."

He glared at her venomously and roared, "I smell pork chops, Abbie! Don't tell me I don't! Now do I get some or do I walk uptown in my sheet and tell them that the hussy Abigail McKenzie refuses to feed me as she's being paid to?"

She was in a fine fury, little fists clenched into tight balls, eyes bright with vindication as she stamped her foot.

"It is *my* turn to teach *you* a lesson, *sir*! I have pork chops, potatoes, gravy, vegetables, everything to sate your fool appetite and get you strong and out of here. All I want from you in return is some decent treatment. You give me that filthy gun!"

"Bring me my pork chops!" he shouted, glowering at her.

"Give me the gun!"

"Like hell I will!"

"Then you shan't have pork chops!" But the gun appeared so quickly she'd have sworn it was there in his hand all the time. It shut her up like a sprung trap.

"Give . . . me . . . my . . . pork . . . chops," he growled.

She stammered, "Keep th . . . that filthy thing out of m . . . my sight!"

"I'll put it away when you bring me the pork chops you're being paid to give me!"

"Please!" she bellowed now.

"PLEASE!" he bellowed back.

Then silence crashed around them, and for one self-conscious moment they both felt foolish, glaring at each other that way.

He got his pork chops all right. And by that time, Miss Abigail was in a state! She admitted that it was a blame good thing tomorrow was Sunday. She was definitely in need of divine guidance after all the transgressions she'd been committing lately. Anger, spite, vengeance, lying, even promiscuity. Yes, she even admitted that what had happened during that kiss had been undeniably promiscuous—well, it had ended that way, anyway. But if she was guilty of all this, think of what he had to ask forgiveness for—not that he ever would. Besides his own, he'd caused every single one of her sins!

The pig's bladder had mysteriously disappeared. She didn't know where it had gone and didn't ask. Being the goat that he is, she thought, he probably ate the thing and enjoyed every bite!

"I've brought you some bed clothes of my father's. Put them on and leave them on. I'm sick and tired of looking at your hairy legs and chest."

"So you say." He puffed out the chest in question and rubbed its furred surface as if it were spun gold. She ignored his conceit, moving away, but then she spied the bladder soaking in the water bowl. She reached two fingers in to pick up the smelly thing and take it away, but he ordered, "Leave it where it is."

"What!"

"I said leave it where is it."

"But it stinks!" She made a face at the offensive innard which had left a residue of scum on the surface of the water.

"Leave it!" he repeated, "and leave the pajamas and get out."

She dropped the gut back in its swampy water and left, thankfully.

It was Saturday afternoon and she spent it cleaning the house for Sunday, as she'd done all her life. When she had cleaned everything else, she came near the door to his room, calling first, "Are you decent now, Mr. Cameron?"

"Does a snake have armpits?" came the reply.

She grabbed her cheeks to keep from laughing. How could that infernal man make her laugh so easily when she was thoroughly disgusted with him?

"I'm covered, if that's what you're asking, but I'll never be decent, hopefully."

She took one look at him and had to work diligently to prevent her face from smiling again. He looked utterly ridiculous. The pajama legs stopped halfway down his hairy calves.

"Well, what are you smirking at?" he grumbled.

"Nothing."

"The hell you say. Keep it up and I'll take these idiotic things off. I feel like a damn coolie in them anyway . . . or at least I would if they were long enough. Your old man must've been a midget!"

"They'll just have to do. I have none that are longer." But in spite of herself she stood there smiling openly now at the hairy calves and feet sticking out of the drawers.

"All right! Get to your cleaning if that's what you came in here for because if you stand there smirking one minute longer I'll take these damn things off!"

"You have the vilest tongue of any man I've ever known. I'm tempted to fix it with the cattail again."

"Just get on with the cleaning and quit hassling me."

Their constant bickering had come to have a pattern. When they were angry their tongues cut sharp and deep with words they seldom meant. And when it went too far they reverted to sarcasm or teasing, scrimmaging verbally in a way which even Miss Abigail had come to enjoy. Cleaning the room, she felt his eyes on her all the while. He moved to the window seat while she changed his sheets and dustmopped under the bed. Kneeling, she saw his boots pushed deeply beneath it, and the lump of what must be his shirt with the gun wrapped in it, between the mattress and the open wire spring. The only way it could have gotten there was if Doc Dougherty had brought it to him, but she couldn't believe the man's idiocy to do such a thing. She didn't mention the gun again, but made as if she hadn't seen it there, then went on to her featherdusting, and finally to clean the tabletop where the pitcher and bowl sat.

"May I ask what you propose to keep this filthy thing for?" She looked distastefully at the bladder.

"Never mind," was all he'd say. "Just leave it."

Supper passed uneventfully, except that he let her know he hated those bloody-looking beets.

The bladder still lay in the bowl. And a plan was forming in Miss Abigail's head.

Evening came and Jesse grew bored and listless. It was funny how he'd grown used to her coming and going. The minute it grew quiet and he was left alone, he almost wished she'd come in, even if only to argue. Like a child who's fought with a playmate, he found he preferred her aggravation to her absence. He heard her making a lot of watery noises and got up with the crutches and came to find her leaning over the back step, washing her hair. He opened the screen door and tapped it against her head twice, softly, just enough to vex her. "This is a hell of a place to wash your hair. You're directly in the path between bedroom and outhouse.''

"Get that screen door off my head!'' she exclaimed from under her sopping hair. 'I'll wash my hair anywhere I like. It just so happens I do it here because it makes less mess to clean up than in the kitchen.''

He stood looking down at her, kneeling on the earth with her head over the basin. The hollow at the nape of her neck held some soap suds, and he found it hard to take his eyes off it. He opened the screen door enough to get out, causing her to sidestep on her knees. She felt vulnerable, knowing he stood above her, watching her.

The way he stood, right foot hanging conveniently before him, it was easy to reach out and put his big toe right there in that little hollow that held the shampoo captive at the back of her neck.

"Getting rid of all the nasty *effluvia* so you're all polished and shined for church tomorrow?'' he teased, using the pretentious word she'd once used on him. She swatted blindly at the foot, but he'd swung on down the yard, wearing only those short pajama pants, calling back, "Whose redemption are you going to pray for, Miss Abigail, yours or mine?''

And from the yard next door Rob Nelson heard and saw it all and ran into his house, hollering, "Maw! Maw! Guess what I just seen!''

She was gone, pan and all, when he came back to the house. He felt weak again and went straight to his bed, making up his mind that he must continue to work up his strength by staying up longer each time with the crutches. He sank down on the edge of the bed and ran a hand through his hair. It itched. In spite of his teasing, that shampoo had looked mighty inviting.

"Miss Abigail?'' he called, but the house was quiet. "Can you hear me?''

No answer.

"Don't I get a shampoo?''

There still was no answer but he heard a floorboard creak above him.

"Hey, I could use one myself, you know.'' He didn't really expect an answer, neither was she about to give one. To himself, he said, "She keeps typical old maid's hours. Closeted in her bedroom before eight o'clock on a Saturday night.'' He was bored to death and wished she'd come down

and keep him company. If she could just hold that sharp tongue
of hers, he'd try to do the same, just for somebody to talk to for
a while. The sounds of light revelry drifted from the direction
of town, and he longed for a beer and a little company, maybe
even a woman on his knee.

Miss Abigail was drying her hair at an open upstairs
window, fluffing it with a thick towel, wondering when she
would find her first gray hair. He called something again, but
she ignored him, thinking of how he'd touched the back of her
neck with his toe, secretly smiling. He could be so exasperat-
ing and so funny at the same time. She thought of what she'd
wear for church in the morning; this time she'd gathered all her
things from his room. She thought of the gun beneath his bed.
She thought of his kiss, but pushed the thought aside because it
did funny things to her stomach. The air was so still you could
hear every sound from the saloon, but then it was nearly July
and the summer heat did that. How many Saturday nights had
she washed her hair and combed it dry, gone to bed early, and
wished to be doing something else? Something with a man.
Now she was thrown together with a man who might have been
company had he not turned out to be the height of loath-
someness. How much longer would she be stuck with him?
She heard him call, saying he wanted a shampoo too.
Nonsense! He couldn't stand up long enough to have his hair
washed. How many days had it been since he'd had his hair
washed? Nine? Ten? She remembered how she'd promised
when he was unconscious that she'd wash it for him. She was
stuck with him until the railroad took him off her hands. At
least if he was clean he would be that much less offensive, she
told herself, not wanting to admit that she was lonely, that even
his company was preferable to none.

When she stepped into his room and saw what he held, she
asked in disgust, "Whatever are you doing with that vile
thing?"

The pig bladder was scraped clean, blown up, and tied with
yarn from her sewing basket. He clenched it in his right hand,
squeezing repeatedly, then relaxing time and again. The action
was as suggestive as the licking of lips, and he smiled as he
drawled, "Exercising my *gun* hand."

Mortified, her eyes could not seem to leave the dark, supple
fingers as they squeezed, squeezed, squeezed. Her lips fell
open and her stomach went light and fluttery. Should she turn

and escape? And let him have the satisfaction of humiliating her once again? Though her cheeks blazed, she ordered, "Put that horrible thing away if you want me to help you with your hair."

He gave it several more slow, suggestive squeezes before tossing it aside negligently, with that same knowing smile on his lips. Well, well, he thought, the queen descendeth! And in her nightie and wrapper, no less!

"You're too weak to stand or lean over long enough to shampoo your hair with water, so I'll give you the next best thing, an oatmeal shampoo. It's not as fragrant, but it works."

"No offense, Abbie, but do you know what you're doing?"

"Precisely, but you'll have to lie down."

"Oatmeal?" he asked skeptically, making no move to lie down yet.

"Exactly," she said crisply. "Do you want the dry treatment or none at all?" Too late she realized what she'd said. The smile was already sneaking around the outer edges of his eyes, and by the time it made it to his lips she was the color of cinnamon.

He stretched out full length and drawled, "By all means, give it to me dry."

Flustered beyond belief, she fussed with her bowl of dry oatmeal, a towel, and three clothespins while he eyed them inquisitively. "The towel goes *under* your head," she said testily, as if he were truly a dolt.

"Oh yes, how stupid of me." He grinned, lifting his head while she arranged the towel under it. Then, to his amazement, she dumped half of the bowl of oatmeal on his hair and started working it in as if it were soap and water.

"Serves double duty, huh?" he quipped. "Tomorrow you can cook it for my breakfast instead of cornmeal." She was caught unaware and let out a huff of laughter while he peeked up at her prankishly. Finally he shut his eyes and let himself enjoy the feeling of her hands in his hair—a Saturday night feeling remembered from childhood. He believed he could nearly smell the fresh shoe blacking on all the shoes of his sisters and brothers, lined up at the bottom of the stairs awaiting Sunday morning. How long since he'd been in a house where Saturday was set aside for those get-ready things?

"Up!" she ordered, interrupting his reverie. "I must shake this. Hold still till I come back." She took the towel gingerly by its four corners and went away with the soiled oatmeal. She repeated the process once again, only this time when she had the clean oatmeal in his hair, she bound the towel up turban-style and secured it with the clothespins. "The oatmeal will absorb the oils. We'll leave it on for a while," she said, and went to the bowl to wash her own hands. But the water was still there from the pig bladder. With a grimace she took it away to dump.

When she returned, he was exercising his hand with that *thing* again, but he invited, "Stay while I soak."

She glanced at the flexing hand, back up at him skeptically.

"What can I do bound up like a sheik with the fleas?" he asked, rolling his eyes upward. Unconsciously she tightened the ends of her tie belt that held the wrapper. Finally, he tossed the thing aside and said cajolingly, "Hey, it's Saturday night, Abbie, the social hour . . . remember? I've been in this bed for almost two week now and, truthfully, I'm getting a little stir crazy. All I want is a little talk."

She sighed and perched on the trunk at the foot of the bed. "If you're growing restless you must be healing."

"I'm not used to sitting still for so long."

"What are you used to?" She wasn't really sure if she wanted any sordid details about his robber's life, yet the prospect of hearing about it was strangely alluring. He, meanwhile, was wondering whether she'd believe him if he told her the truth.

"I'm not used to a place like this, that's for sure, or spending time with a woman like you. I travel around a lot."

"Yes, I supposed you did, in your occupation. Doesn't it grow tiresome?"

"Sometimes, but I have to do it, so I do."

She looked him dead in the eye—Miss Goody Twoshoes giving her reformer's pitch. "Nobody has to live that kind of life. Why don't you give it up and find a wholesome occupation?"

"Believe it or not, being a photographer isn't far from wholesome."

"Oh, come now, you can't think I believed your story about the camera you left on the train?"

"No, a woman like you wouldn't believe it, I guess."

"What is it that you claim you photograph?" she asked, making it clear that this was all too farfetched.

"The building of the railroads," he said, with that half smile on his face. "The grandeur of history in the making," he emoted, raising his arms dramatically. "The spanning of our land by twin iron rails, capturing it forever for our posterity to share." But then he dropped his arms and his dramatizing and fell thoughtful, introspective. "You know, it'll never happen again just like it's happening now. It's been something to see, Abbie." He sighed, entwined his fingers behind his head, and studied the ceiling. And for a moment she almost believed him, he sounded so sincere.

"I'm sure you would like me to believe you, Mr. Cameron."

"Would it hurt you to call me Jesse? It would make it more pleasant while we talk this way."

"I thought I'd made you understand that I live by rules of propriety."

"There's nobody here but you and me. I won't tell," he teased mischievously.

"No, you won't, because I shan't call you Jesse . . . ever. Now quit changing the subject and tell me about your occupation. Try to convince me that you are not a robber of trains."

He laughed, then said, "All right. I work for the railroad, photographing every phase of its construction, just like I said. I have free passage as long as I work for them, and I travel to the railhead—wherever that may be—to take most of my photographs. I live in camps and on trains most of the time. There's not much more to tell."

"Except why, if you have a decent job, you chose to steal from the very hand that feeds you."

"That was a mistake, Abbie."

"Miss Abigail," she corrected.

"Very well, Miss Abigail, then. Have you ever seen a railroad camp?"

"Hardly."

"No, you wouldn't have. Well, it's no Abigail McKenzie's house, I'll tell you that. It's wild out in the middle of nowhere, and the men who work there are not exactly parlor fare."

"Like you?" she couldn't resist saying. Again he laughed lightly, letting her think what she would.

"I'm a veritable goldmine of manners compared to the navvies who build the railroads. Their life is rough, their language is rougher, and anybody who crosses anybody else can expect a bullet between the eyes. There's no law where they live, none at all. They settle their disputes with guns and fists and sometimes even with hammers—anything that's convenient. There not only is no law at the end of a railroad line, there's no town. No houses, stores, churches, depots—in other words, no shelter of any kind. A man who lives in the wilds like that won't survive long without a gun. There are bobcats in the mountains, wolves on the prairies, and everything that grows teeth in between. Naturally they all go to water, which is usually where bridges and trestles go up. About this time of day the animals always come to drink.''

"What's your point, Mr. Cameron?''

"My point is that I carry a gun like every other smart fellow who expects to tame the West and live to see it. I'm not denying I had a gun on me on that train. I am denying I used it to pull a holdup.''

"You're forgetting you were caught red-handed.''

"Doing what? I had just taken it out, thinking I'd clean it, but before I got it unloaded, some nervous old biddy was screaming, and I found myself on the floor, shot, and the next thing I knew I woke up here in your house. That's all I know.''

"A likely story. You would make a fine actor, Mr. Cameron.''

"I don't need to be a fine actor—I'm a fine photographer. When I get my plates back, you'll see.''

"You seem very confident about that.''

"I am, wait and see.''

"Oh, I shall wait, but I doubt that there will be anything to see.''

"You're a hard woman to convince.''

"I'm a woman who recognizes the truth when it's staring her in the face.''

"But that's what I do as a photographer. Recognize the truth and record it permanently in pictures.''

"The truth?''

He considered for a moment, then cocked his head to the side as if studying her. "Well, take last night for instance. You'd have made a very fetching subject last night when you sat in that rocker there, laughing. The light fell on you at precisely the right angle to take all of the affected hardness away from your face and lend it a natural quality it was meant to reflect. Call it unpretentiousness, if you will. In that brief moment, if I'd had my camera I might have captured you as you really are, not as you pretend to be. I might have exposed you as a charlatan."

Faintly smarting at his words, denial sprang instantly to her lips. "I am no charlatan." Rather than argue, he studied her with cocked head, as if he could see into her depths and knew exactly what he was talking about. "If there is any charlatan here it is you. You have proven it by your own words. Any photographer knows that a subject could not be photographed rocking in a rocking chair. Even I know that subjects must be stiff, sometimes even braced into place in order to take successful photographs."

"You've missed my point completely, but on purpose, I think. However, if that's how you want it, it's all right with me. Let me only say that if you want stiff, braced-looking results, they're easy to obtain. My photographs lack such artifice. It's why I do what I do for the railroad. They want their history photographed as it happens, not as some fools see fit to pose and posture the real thing. It can be the same with people. Someday I'll take your picture and it will prove to you what I meant. It will show you what the real Abbie is like."

It was easy to tell from her expression that she had censured out of his words all she chose to disbelieve. "The real me is inutterably weary," she said, rising from the trunk. "But not weary enough to fall for such a story as yours. I still believe you're a finer actor than either train robber or photographer."

"Have it your way, Miss Abigail," he said. "Charlatans usually do."

"You should know," she replied, but his eyes caught and held hers, making her wonder just what he'd meant by all he'd said. At last she glanced at his turbaned head and said, "I believe we can remove the oatmeal now." She went to the dressing table to get her brush.

"I can brush it myself," he offered, but she waved away his hand, removed the clothespins, stretched out the towel, and began brushing.

"You'd have it all over everything and oatmeal attracts mice," she said. "They are not as opposed to eating it secondhand as you are."

He closed his eyes and rolled his head this way and that when she told him to. What a Saturday night, he thought, getting oatmeal brushed out of my hair by a woman who dislikes me and mice. "I can't reach the back. Could you sit up and lean over the edge of the bed?" He sat up, hunched forward, elbows to knees, and she spread the towel carefully on the floor between his feet. He watched the oatmeal dust drifting down as she brushed from the nape of his neck forward in deft strokes. There were times when she could be quite appealing, like last night in the rocker, and now, doing a common thing like brushing his hair. It was seldom, though, that she did anything in a common way. She preferred, for some reason, to pose herself, taut, rigid, as inflexible as the everlasting restrictions she put upon her behavior. It was beyond him why he should try to make her see herself truthfully. If she was happy with the artifice, let her be, he thought. Still, it was hard for him to understand why anyone would set such a mold for themselves.

The brushing made goose pimples shiver up his arms. It was deliciously relaxing. In his drowsy thoughts he wondered about Abigail McKenzie, thought of other things he might say to her, but then he realized the brushing had stopped; she had gone as silently as she'd come, leaving the brush lying bristles-down on the back of his neck.

Chapter 9

_____

SHE HAD LEFT him relaxed and drowsy and lay now listening to the muffled sounds below. She heard the bedsprings twang beneath his weight, then the muted chiming of the brass headboard as he pulled against it. She visualized him turning on his side, sighing and falling asleep while she waited patiently. She fought drowsiness, listening to the occasional sounds from town petering out until all was as still as eternity. A dog barked, once, far away and lonely, but it made her flinch awake and sit up straighter, resisting slumber.

After an interminably long time she arose, quickly and lightly, creating only one little twank that was then gone. Again she waited, patient as a cat on the stalk, and when she moved, it was to the accompaniment of sheer soundlessness. She took the stairs barefoot, in a swift, gliding descent, knowing she risked less sound going that way than if she hesitated on each step. But once at the bottom, she waited again. She could hear his breathing in the stillness—long, rhythmic, somnolent. And she moved again, stopping not at the bedroom door, or the foot of his bed or to peer down to make sure he was sleeping; any of these hesitations, especially the last, might key some instinctual reaction and arouse him. Instead, surefooted and silent, she

glided to the side of the bed and lay down on the floor half
under it.

He breathed on as before while her breath came in short,
scared spurts.

The shirt-wrapped gun was close to the outer edge of the
mattress, where he could get at it without having to reach too
far underneath. She touched it, exploring the fabric of the shirt,
the hard lump inside, the ridges of the cartridge chamber, the
sharp, crooked hammer, the butt, the barrel. She shivered. If
she were to try to pull it through the rectangular spaces
between the wires of the spring, it would undoubtedly get
caught, for the gun was bigger than the holes. Instead, she
studied the shape as a blind person might: using her fingertips,
determining that it was so near the edge that no more than the
slightest upward pressure on the mattress would free the gun so
she could slip it out sideways.

The problem was raising the mattress an inch or so.

She would simply have to wait until he decided to roll over.
Maybe when the springs squeaked she could yank the gun out
quickly and he'd never know the difference. The floor grew as
hard as an anvil. She grew chilled and needed badly to fidget,
and still he slept on peacefully. She heard the dog again, far
off, and the answering call of a wolf even farther, and in spite
of the hard floor, began to get sleepy. To keep awake she
reached out a hand and it touched something cold and fleshy.
She recoiled in fear, then realized it was only the pig bladder.
The memory of his long, strong fingers squeezing it came back
to haunt her, and she pinched her eyes shut to blot out the
picture. But just then Jesse snuffled, sighed, and shifted onto
his side, causing the bedsprings to creak. At that exact
moment, she pushed with one hand through the open spaces of
the bedspring while with her other she pulled the shirt free, gun
and all. It landed in the small of her chest, thudding heavily,
and she checked the impulse to gasp at the weight of it.

She lay absolutely motionless, repulsed by the thing weighing her down. But she had the ominous weapon at last! Slowly
she unwrapped it. The shirt lay upon her stomach and breasts
and she could smell the smell of him in it. She shuddered.
Then she slowly rolled the shirt into a tight ball, making sure
not so much as a button clicked on the floor. While she waited
with the cold steel upon her chest, she imagined what kind of a
person it took to draw it, raise it, and aim it at another human

being. She saw herself at the other end of it as she'd been this morning, and once again told herself it would take an animal to do such a thing.

He was breathing evenly again. She held her breath, shivering at the thought of getting caught. But the hardest part was done—the rest was easy. Be patient, be patient, she admonished herself. He was snoring lightly now. With the gun in one hand and his shirt in the other she sat up, alert, poised to spring should he move, almost startled to see how near she'd actually been to his head all this time. He faced the wall so she raised herself further, soundlessly as ever, and the moment her soles touched the floor she hit for safety.

She had taken less than one full step when an arm lashed out, caught her, and flipped her over backward, somersaulting her across a lumpy hipbone till her toes cracked high against the wall. As she slithered down into a heap, a horrible weight settled upon her chest. In the next moment she was sure she was dying, for he'd knocked the wind out of her. The small of her back where it had bumped across him felt like there were two boulders beneath it and she reached to knead the pain, but just that fast he pinned the arm beneath him and pinioned the other one against the mattress over her head, the gun still tight in her grasp.

"All right, lady, you want to sneak around under my bed, this is what you get!" he snarled. "Give me the goddamn gun! Now!" He pushed her wrist into the mattress, trying to wrest the pistol from her fingers. But it was useless. They were clenched in a death-grip, locked in mid-motion when he'd flattened the breath from her. The pain in her chest grew to a choking, hammering, crushing insistence while she struggled for air that refused her. He pummeled her wrist against the bed, leaning on her, adding stress to her lungs until she felt her eyes would pop from their sockets.

"Give me the gun, you asinine woman! Did you think I was fool enough to let you get away with it?" Still no breath came and her fear swelled and swelled and she panicked, unable to tell him what was wrong. And just when she knew more certainly than ever that she was starting to die, a rattling issued from her throat and her hand went lax, loosing the gun. He heard the hissing and gasping as she fought for breath. Then suddenly her knees pulled up fetally.

He jumped off her chest, exclaiming, "Christ, Abbie!" She

curled up like an armadillo, half crying, half gasping, and rolled from side to side, grasping her knees. He tried to make her straighten out so the air could get in, but she only curled tighter.

Finally he flung her onto her belly like a rag doll, the gun flying to the wall, then clunking to the floor in the corner behind the bed. With her forehead now screwing itself into the mattress, she clutched her stomach, writhing, her hind side hoisted up by nature trying to renew her life force. Jesse got her by the hips, his giant hands holding her up, trying to help her breathe again.

"I didn't mean to knock the wind out of you." Still her breath came hoarse and rasping. She could feel her posterior shimmed up against something warm. "Abbie, are you okay?" But his thumb pressed a spot that had been brusied by his hipbone. Heaving, gasping, crying all at once, she tried to break free.

"Put me . . ." But her voice wasn't working yet and he held her in that ignominious position against his pajama-clad body.

"Don't try to talk yet," he ordered, "let your breath come back first."

Then finally it came. Blessed, pure, giant puffs of air flowing into her lungs and fortifying her. "Put . . . me . . . down," she managed while her fists still gripped the sheet and she flailed one foot dissolutely. He released her at last and she slumped flat. She felt her weight roll as he moved to kneel beside her.

"Hurt?" he asked, and she felt his hand rubbing the small of her back while she lay there limp, panting, waiting for her near-bursting heart to ease.

"Get . . . your . . . filthy . . . hands . . . off . . . me," she sputtered into the mattress between gasps of air.

"It's your own fault," he said, ignoring her order, still rubbing, warmer now and in longer sweeps. "Just what were you trying to do, shoot me?"

"Nothing would pleasure me more," she puffed.

"That goes to show what you know," he said, and purposely ran his long, lean fingers—one swipe—down her spine where its hollow widened, then narrowed. She jumped like a jackrabbit in a desperate leap toward the corner of the bed, lunging for the gun. But her head hit the corner wall with a resounding crack! The bedsprings twanged and he grabbed her by the calves and dragged her backward, her fingers never touching the pistol, her nightgown shinnying up in a roll beneath her. She reached for it desperately, but just then he flew and landed full-length on top of her, reaching easily with one long arm to retrieve the gun from the floor. His chest pushed her face into the bed, then the weight was gone, settled farther down as he straddled her like a cowboy on a bronc, holding her arms pinned to her sides by his knees.

But now he was panting too, gritting his teeth while he pressed a hand to his throbbing wound. He rocked a time or two, suddenly angry because of the pain.

"All right, Miss High-And-Mighty, so you want to play guns, do you? Okay, I'll play." Through the ringing in her head she heard his ragged breathing. Then he swung off her hips and she heard the gun click by her ear. "Roll over," he ordered.

She struggled with the nightgown, but as she tugged, the gun barrel skewered it to the center of her back, holding it where it was.

"Roll over," he repeated, tight and hard now, and nudged her a little harder with the barrel. She rolled fearfully away from him, shivering near the wall. "Why is it that every time I wake up you seem to be in my bed?" he accused.

She clutched her head, which was aching uncontrollably now, closed her eyes while his unctuous voice flowed. "Is this why you took me into your house, Abbie? So you could weasel your way into a gunslinger's bed? Why didn't you just say so instead of pretending to be the gracious nurse? Nurse . . . ha! Do you know what all you've done to me under the guise of nursing? Let me recount every one so you'll know what I'm about to get even with here. First you shaved off my moustache for no apparant reason at all. You made me lie in need until I thought my bladder would burst. Then you threw the bedpan at me. Then you pushed branches down my throat until it was practically useless to me, then claimed afterward that it was for my own good you had to starve me. Next, you proceeded to calmly poison me with liver until I puked like a buzzard. Then, you presented me with a raw pig's bladder while I groaned for a square meal. And now—last but not least—you try to shoot me!"

"I did not try to shoot you!"

"You, Miss Abigail, were caught red-handed. Are those familiar words? Do you remember hearing them recently?"

"You shot Mr. Melcher and he has a toe gone to prove it. I shot nobody. I was only after the gun."

"You shot nobody because I was faster than you. What's the matter, your head hurt now?"

"I hit it on the wall."

"As you also said to me once, it's your own fault. You brought it on yourself when you came sneaking in here. you pulled your pussyfooting act just once too often."

"I saved your life, you ingrate!" she spit, and was going to call his bluff, thinking he wouldn't really harm her. But her shoulders got no more than a hand's width off the mattress before she found herself pushed flat again, his knuckles prying into the bones of her chest.

"Ingrate?" he chuckled wickedly. "Yes, perhaps I have been an ingrate. Perhaps I haven't shown the proper gratitude for all you've done for me. Maybe I'd better do it now . . . in kind. Pay you back for all you've done to me, is that what you want?"

"N . . . no, I didn't mean it."

"But of course you meant it. Let's just call it payment for services rendered."

"Don't . . ." She crossed her arms protectively over her chest.

"Let's see how you like having your mouth invaded, Abbie." He moved so swiftly she had no chance to fight. The next moment one of her arms was imprisoned between the mattress and his body, the other wrist pressed against a rail of the brass headboard while he held it there with a powerful hand. His mouth swooped down but she rolled her face aside and he missed. He tried again but she rolled the other way.

"So you still want to play games, huh?" She struggled while he yanked her arm down. But he rolled her easily to her side, forcing the arm up behind her back before her own weight and his rendered it useless. His newly freed hand came to the back of her neck, long fingers trailing up through her freshly washed hair, controlling her as he lowered his mouth to hers again and ran his tongue across her bared teeth. She gasped and bucked, but pain shot into her arm so she fell still, realizing she was no match for his strength. He lightened his hold on her lips, teasing now with his tongue, running it to the corners of her mouth, torturing her with its sleek, wet insinuation. Unable to combat him, her only recourse was to lay limp and submissive, determined to show neither fight nor fear.

He sensed what she was doing and slid his lips down to the hollow beneath her jaw, whispered near her ear, "I'm going to pay you back for every single thing you did to me, Abbie." Then he nuzzled his way back to the corner of her mouth, his full lips closing upon it leisurely while she resolutely kept her jaws clamped shut. He chuckled low in his throat and she felt him smile against her lips. "How do you like it, Abbie?" Her heart danced to her throat and her eyelids trembled as she held them tightly shut. He moved to catch the side of one nostril as a stallion nips a mare, leaving her skin damp as he moved on, bending lower. He took her small pointed chin in his mouth, sucking gently, sending shafts of heat darting through her body. And far down the bed she felt him grow harder and harder against the back of her captured hand. Wanting to die, yet feeling more alive than ever before in her life, Abbie absorbed the feeling of it all. Held prisoner, she suddenly felt as if she soared free.

His hand slid away from her hair and he ran only the outer edges of its little finger down the valley between her breasts, to her waist. Then, hooking each button with that single finger, he flicked them open on his leisurely way back up. "Hey," he whispered against her neck, "did you think you were going to get away with my shirt tonight? You steal mine . . . I steal yours." Then slowly he pushed aside the bodice of her gown, opening first the left side, then the right, still using only that little finger, but sailing its back side against the surface of her breasts, over each smooth mound to each erect nipple, skimming them like warm wind and creating uninvited goose bumps upon her skin.

"You know what you do to me, Abbie? You rub me in a hundred wrong ways. Let me show you the one right way." His palm cupped her bare breast and her eyes flew open. She saw his dark moustache so close to her face, felt his breath on her mouth, his hot hardness against the back of her hand. And all the while he kneaded her breast with its unforgivable taut nipple, he caressed her ribs and stomach with his forearm. Her eyelids slid closed, the breath which he'd earlier knocked from her caught now in her helpless throat.

"How about a bed bath, Abbie? I owe you one." Her senses

fled to one central spot as he fondled one breast while leaning
to circle the other with his warm, wet tongue, slowly and
painstakingly bathing it, from rigid crest to softest perimeter.
She felt the forbidden lick of grain upon smoothness, made
sleek by moisture. His teeth, open, gently sliced, their edges
unhurting, knowing. Between tongue and upper teeth he took
the ruby crown of her breast, lightly, lightly, stroking, tugging
until her shoulder strained off the mattress. He lowered his
mouth to the soft cay where breast met rib and there washed
her with warmth before continuing downward while her body
reached its dewpoint. He dipped his tongue into the cupule of
her navel as a bee dips into the chalice of a flower for honey.
His warm tongue disappeared, then he kissed her lightly a little
lower, raised his face to ask, "Should I do a thorough job or
leave you half-finished like you did me?"

"Please . . ." she begged in a ragged whisper.

"Please what? Please finish or please stop?"

"Please stop." Tears seemed to have gathered in her eyes,
her throat, and between her legs.

"Not yet. Not till I bring some life to these limbs like you
did to mine. Remember, Abbie? Remember how you massaged
the life back into me and made my blood beat again after you
tied me up?" She could no longer tell if this was torture or
treat. It seemed her heart beat in every pore of her body as once
again, in that slow, slow motion, he did what he wanted with
her, sliding his arms along the lengths of her own, catching one
up high above her head, sealing the other beneath them. He
stretched his length out upon her, holding her now from behind
while her wrist was clamped against brass which chimed a
muted knell each time he pulled, grinding his tumescent body
against her aroused one. Her lips fell open as her traitorous
body responded. Her breath beat fast and warm upon his face.
She'd made no sound, yet he heard her whimper all the same.
Whimper for all the fear mingled with this new sensual
turbulence so suddenly awakened in her, the pulsing void that
seemed to cry for fulfillment.

Suddenly he stilled, looking down into her shadowed face
with its closed, trembling eyes, its open, trembling lips. He
touched the crest of her cheek softly. "How old are you,
Abbie? You lied to me, didn't you? You said you're old
because it's a shield you hide behind, afraid of what life is all

about. But what do you fear now, living with this or without this?"

A sob caught in her throat. "I am thirty-three and I hate you," she whispered. "I shall hate you till my dying day." Her fear of him was gone, replaced by fear of a new and different kind: a fear of herself. A fear of the muscle and blood that had responded too plainly to all he'd said and done.

How long had her hands been free? They rested inanimately, curled in limp abandon, commanded now only by the air, for he was smoothing the hair back from her brow—too gently, too gently. He had claimed his victory over her, true, but somehow it left him hollow and beaten himself. As she lay beneath him, disheveled and defeated, he suddenly wished he had the old Abbie back, all starch and spitfire.

"Hey, what started this anyway?" She heard the change in his voice and it did nothing to calm the riotous vibrations of her flesh. She swallowed the tears in her throat, but her voice was thick, the back of her wrist falling across her eyes.

"If I remember correctly, somebody brought a train robber into my house and he wore a moustache."

"Abbie . . ." he said tentatively, as if there were so much more unsaid. But she pushed him off her and struggled to the edge of the bed, leaving him sorry he'd done as much as he had, sorrier still that he hadn't done more. But as she slid across the rumpled sheets her hand touched cold steel, abandoned in their struggle which had ceased to be a struggle. Her fingers closed over it as she moved off silently in the dark.

Chapter 10

———

IT WAS A fine Sunday, bright and fresh, the sky as blue as a robin's egg. But all through services Miss Abigail found it difficult to pay attention. Even while praying to be forgiven for the responses she'd been unable to control last night, she felt her skin ripple sweetly in remembrance. Standing to join in a hymn, her lips parted to form the words, but the memory of his tongue between them scorched her with shame and a tingling, forbidden want. Putting a hand to the nape of her neck to smooth her hair, the memory of his hand there made her hang her head in shame. But as she did she looked down the lace-covered bodice of her proper, high-necked dress only to know that within it her nipples were puckered up like gumdrops. And within her pristine soul Abigail McKenzie knew that she was truly damned now, yet all through no real fault of her own. She had lived a demure life, one in which—granted—little temptation of last night's sort had been put in her way. But she had not deserved to be treated so ruthlessly.

While Miss Abigail contemplated all this she occasionally caught herself eyeing the back of Doc Dougherty's bald head, wishing she could take the butt of that gun and rap some sense into it!

When the service was over she lost track of how many times

she was asked how everything was going up at her house, how many times she was forced to lie and answer, "Fine, fine." She was asked everything from how the outlaw's wounds were healing to what in the world she wanted with that pig bladder! To the latter she again replied with the half lie that the train robber used it to strengthen his bruised hand—true enough, but hardly the reason she'd bought it. When she finally got Doc Dougherty off to one side, she was upset not only with him but with everyone who'd asked her what was none of their business.

Doc was his usual congenial self as he greeted, "How-do, Miss Abigail."

"Doctor, I must talk to you."

"Something wrong with our patient? What's his name again? Jesse, isn't it? Has he been up getting some exercise?"

"Yes he has, but—"

"Fine! Fine! That limb will stiffen up like an uncured pelt if he doesn't move it. Feed him good and see that he gets up and around, maybe even out of the house."

"Out of the house! Why the man has no clothes. He went to the outhouse yesterday wrapped in nothing more than a sheet!"

Doc laughed, his belly hefting jovially. "Never thought about that when I brought his stuff back the other day. Guess we'll have to buy him some clothes, eh? The railroad'll pay for—"

Impatiently, she interrupted, "Doctor, whatever were you thinking to return his gun to him? He . . . he threatened me with it, after all I've done for him."

Doc scowled worriedly. "Threatened you?"

"Shh!" She looked quickly around, then lied again. "It was nothing too serious. He just wanted some fried pork chops for his dinner."

Suddenly Doc suspected just what sort of rivalry might have sprung up between two such willful people, and a telltale sparkle lit his eyes as he inquired, "And did he get them?"

She colored, fussed about pulling her glove on tighter, and stammered, "Why . . . I . . . he . . . yes, he did."

Doc reached into a breast pocket, found a cigar, bit off the end, and gazed off across the distance reflectively. Then he spit the cigar end into the dirt and smiled. "Pretty crafty of him, considering the gun had no bullets."

Miss Abigail felt like somebody had just opened her chemise and poured ice water inside.

"Bullets?" she snapped, her jaw so tight she could have bitten one in half just then.

"Bullets, Miss Abigail. You didn't think I'd turn his gun over to him with a cylinder full of bullets, did you?"

"I . . . I . . ." But she realized how very stupid she must appear to Doc Dougherty, admitting that she'd been duped by a felon with an empty pistol. "I had not thought the gun might be empty. I . . . I . . . should have known."

"Of course you should have. But I'm sorry he pulled it on you anyway. Sounds like you've had your trials with him. Is everything else all right?"

Miss Abigail could not, would not admit to a living soul how extremely unright everything was. She could never again face a person in this town if people found out what she had suffered at the hands of that scoundrel up at her house. She prided herself on control, good breeding, fine manners, and the town respected her for those things. She would not give them any reason to raise eyebrows at her now. Not at this late date!

"I assure you that everything is all right, Doctor Dougherty. The man has harmed me in no way whatsoever. But he is a loutish brute, crude-mannered and vain, and I have grown thoroughly sick of having him in my house. The sooner he gets out, the better. I should like it if you would sign a release immediately so that Sheriff Harris may wire the railroad authorities to come and get him."

"Sure enough! I'll do it first thing in the morning. He should be well enough to travel soon."

"Just how long do you think it will be before they come and get him?"

Doc scratched his chin. "That's hard to say, but it shouldn't be too long, and I'll be up every day. You can count on that, Miss Abigail. As soon as I see he's able to travel, we'll have him out of there and off your hands for you. Anything else I can do for you?"

"Yes. You may purchase some britches for him. If he is to be traipsing around on those crutches I insist he dress properly."

"Sure thing. I'll have 'em up there first thing."

"The earlier the better," she suggested, none too placatingly. Then with that little upward nudge of chin she wished him good day and turned toward home, angrier than she ever remembered being in her life. To think that she'd been duped, gulled, toyed with in such a manner by that . . . that *dog* she'd taken in off the streets when nobody else in town would so much as throw their table scraps to him! He had victimized her not once, but *twice* . . . and with an empty gun yet! The thought had her positively sizzling by the time she reached the house.

Jesse heard the loud Clack! Clack! Clack! of her heels on the steps as she went noisily upstairs. A moment later she came down again, marching loudly, regularly, as if some band accompanied her parade. The uncharacteristic noise surprised him; before church she'd been pussyfooting again. She flashed past his door, went to the kitchen, and opened the pantry door. He heard her pouring something, then here she came again, still marching. Around the bedroom doorway she swished. Up to the bed she hiked, and before he could say a word, wound up, hauled off, and smacked him across the face so hard that his cheek reverberated off the headboard. The brass sang out like she'd slammed it with a ball peen hammer. While he was still stunned senseless, she crossed calmly to the water pitcher, dumped a cupful of something into it, then held his pistol over it, using thumb and forefinger only.

"Never again will you threaten me with this distasteful object you once called a gun," she said, all eloquent and self-righteous, before releasing the gun with a plop! into the water. "Neither *with* nor *without* bullets!" Still too surprised to move, he heard burbles from within the pitcher as water gurgled its way into the barrel. When it finally struck him what she'd done, he leaped from the bed and hobbled to the pitcher. He was about to plunge his hand in after the gun when she coolly advised, "I wouldn't try dunking for it unless you want your hand dissolved, too, by the lye." She had retreated a safe distance.

He hopped around, swinging awkwardly to face her, but jostling the table in the process. "You daughter of a snake! Get that gun out of there or I'll dump the whole thing on the floor, I swear!"

"My tabletop!" she exclaimed, as the lye water puddled on the varnish. She lurched a few steps toward it, but stopped uncertainly.

"Get it out!" he roared. They glowered at each other, his

jaws grinding, her mouth pinched and quivering. Like feral animals they poised, wary, tensile, cautious. In a scarcely controlled fit, from between clenched teeth he spoke, punctuating his words with grand, empty gaps: "Get . . . it . . . out!"

And she knew she'd better get it out.

With a toss of shoulders and thrusting out of ribs, she carried the pitcher away, out the back screen door. He heard it slam, then the slosh as she emptied the whole mess into the yard. She came running back with a rag to wipe off her precious tabletop. While she dabbed at it, Jesse collapsed into the rocker, burying his face in his hands, muttering disgustedly, "What did you do a goddamn thing like that for?"

In a voice oozing sarcasm, she began, "Your foray into the prolix is truly impressive—"

"Just don't start in on me with your three-dollar words," he barked, "because we both know that every damn time you do it, it's because you're running scared! I'll say anything I want, any way I want to!"

"So will I! You may have thought you bested me last night, but Miss Abigail McKenzie shall not be bested, do you hear!" She scrubbed at the tabletop with violent motions. "I take you into my house—You! A common train robber!—and keep your rotting hulk alive, and for what! To be criticized for my cooking, my language, my manners, even the flowers I grow in my garden! To be pawed and degraded in repayment for my care!"

"Care?" He laughed harshly. "You never cared about anything in your entire, dismal life! Your blood is as cold as a frog's. And just like a frog, you live on your lonely lily pad, jumping in and hiding whenever anything resembling life comes anywhere near you! So you found out the gun wasn't loaded, huh? And that's why you marched in here and smacked me clear into next week, then dropped my gun into lye? Is it?"

"Yes!" she screeched, whirling on him, tears seeping to her eyes now.

"Like hell it is *Miss* Abigail McKenzie! The reason you did it is because you knew that gun wasn't even pointed at you anymore when you turned to jelly beneath me, isn't it? Because what you felt last night had absolutely nothing to do with a gun. You've lived your whole life in this godforsaken old maid's house, scared to death to show any emotion whatever, until I came along. Me! A common train robber! A man your warped sense of decency has told you to beware of since the first minute I was hauled in here. Only you can't admit to yourself that you're human, that you could be lit up by the likes of me, that you could lie there on that bed and find that bare skin can be something less than sordid, in spite of who it's touching, in spite of what you've forced yourself to believe all these years. You've also learned that a little fight now and then can be pretty invigorating, not to mention downright sexually stimulating. Only it's not supposed to be, is it? Since I've been here you've experienced every emotion that's been forbidden to you your entire life. And the truth is, you blame me because you like them all and you don't think you're supposed to."

"Lies!" she argued. "You lie to defend yourself when you know that what you did last night was low and cruel and immoral!"

"Low? Cruel? Immoral?" Again he laughed harshly. "Why, if you had any sense, Abbie, you'd be thanking me for showing you last night that there's hope for you after all. The way you've been pussyfooting your life away with your clean white gloves and your fastidiously clean thoughts, I'm surprised you didn't ask the congregation to stone you as a martyr this morning. Admit it, Abbie. You're sore because you enjoyed rolling around on that bed with me last night!"

"Stop it! Stop it!" she shrieked. Then she whirled and threw the lye-soaked rag at him. It landed across his lower face, a sodden end cloying like a rat's tail around his jaw and neck. Instantly his skin began to burn and his eyes grew wide. He clawed at the rag wildly as she realized, horrified, what she'd done. The next moment she was reacting as her life had programmed her to react, grabbing a dry towel from the washstand, lunging to wrap his face. Their hands worked together frantically to dry his skin before any damage was done. He saw her eyes widen with fear, telling him she knew she'd gone one step too far.

"You . . ." she choked out, scrubbing at his skin harder than she had at the tabletop. "You laugh at all I do for you and de . . . deride me for everything that is your fault. Never once since you've been here have you ap . . . appreciated a single thing you've done for you. Instead, you criticize and berate and slander. Well, if I'm so cold-blooded and straight-laced and undesirable, why did you start what you did on that bed last night? Why?" Stricken, on the verge of breaking down, she met his eyes nevertheless. "Do you think that I don't know the reason you turned me loose? Do you think I'm so naive that I couldn't tell you ended up in self-defeat by liking it yourself?" Her hands had fallen still on the towel, which trailed away behind his shoulders. It covered his mouth, but his moustache appeared blacker than ever, contrasted against its whiteness. They faced each other now in silent standoff. His black eyes bored into hers, which dropped to his bronze chest. Her hands fluttered from the towel as her eyes had from his relentless, knowing gaze. She suddenly wished she could reclaim her words. In slowest motion his swarthy fingers pulled the towel free from his mouth. His words, when at last they came, were the most fearsome yet, for they were spoken in a hushed, confused voice.

"And what if I did, Abbie? What if I did?"

Stricken anew, she felt her nerves gathering into wary knots, the skin at the back of her neck prickle, while confusion sluiced through her. He was a player of games, a law breaker, her enemy. He could not be trusted. Still she looked up at his disconcerting train robber's eyes and they skewered her to the spot as no gun ever could. He neither smiled nor frowned, but looked at her with an expression of intense sincerity.

"I did not ask for it," she managed in a choked whisper.

"Neither did I," he said low.

Quickly she turned from him, asking, "Is your skin burned?" But his strong hand came out to stay her in a firm grip just above her elbow.

"Did you really want to burn me?" he asked, studying the taut cords of her neck as she arched sharply away from him and swallowed.

"I . . . no . . . I don't know what I wanted." Her voice was timorous and uncertain. "I don't know how to survive around you. You make me so angry when I don't want to be. I want . . ." But she sighed to a halt, unable to finish. All she wanted was peace, not this hammering heart, this threatening desire for a person like him.

"You make me angry too," he said most gently, squeezing the flesh beneath his sinewed fingers.

He watched the profile of her right breast lift as she drew in a great, shuddering breath. He saw her eyelashes drift down upon her pinkened cheek.

"Let my arm go," she begged shakily. "I don't want to be touched by you."

"I think you're too late, Abbie," he said. "I think you already are." He shook her arm gently. "Hey, look at me."

When she wouldn't, he gripped her narrow shoulders and forced her to face him. She studied the floor at his feet while his hands burned a trail down her limp arms to her elbows and on to her wrists. He took her hands loosely in his while she fought the compulsion to raise her gaze to those dark, dark eyes.

"It's Sunday, Abbie. Should we just be friends for one day and see how it works?"

"I'd . . . ." She swallowed. Her heart clamored in her throat and she braved raising her eyes as far as his chin. He had shaved while she was gone, and he smelled of soap. His moustache was thick and black, but she would not raise her eyes farther. Suddenly he sighed and dropped back down into the rocker again, still holding her hands, doing something soft and wonderful to the backs of them, rubbing them slowly with his thumbs, from cuff to knuckle, while she stood in confusion, telling herself to pull her hands free from his, yet absorbing the very niceness of the touch, so different from how he'd ever touched her before. This was gentle, tender in a way she would have sworn this man could never be. She stared at their joined hands and knew fully what he was doing, but she let him go about it.

Slowly he turned a palm to his mouth, and his eyes closed as warm lips and soft moustache grew lost in it. Her fingers lay curled beneath his chin and she stood like a statue feeling the touch of a magic wand, suddenly imbued with life-giving current while his kiss lingered in her cupped hand. Then his hand stole up to her waist and he tugged her toward his lap.

"No, don't—not again," she begged even as he eased her down expertly.

"Why not?" he whispered as strong hands closed over her shoulders and turned her inexorably toward his chest.

"Because we hate each—" He stopped her words with his open lips while his hands went aroving up and down her back. His moustache was soft now, almost as soft as before she'd shaved it, and his warm tongue came seeking, thrilling, inviting with supple sensuousness before she broke away, claiming, "This is crazy, we must not—" But his long palms spanned her cheeks and he had his way with her again. He pulled her mouth to his, then found her arms and placed them behind his neck, holding them in place until he felt her acquiesce and curl them around his head.

And she thought, I am crazy, and let him go on kissing her until his hands were on her back again, running up and down, up and down. Then at her waist, pressing firmly at her sides, down low, just above her belt line.

He whispered things into her mouth. "Don't fight it, Abbie . . . for once, don't fight it," and the words were blurred from his tongue moving against hers as he spoke. His hands moved lower, to her hips, swiveling them around until she half lay, half sat on his lap. He stiffened his body in the very small chair, lifting and shifting her until she no longer controlled where she was or how she rested upon him. With chest and waist arched away from the chair, Jesse manipulated her until she lay upon him. He was one smooth, hard plane of flesh upon which she settled while both of his arms circled her waist, holding her very still, allowing her to know the feel of him through flounced petticoats.

And he was long . . . and hard . . . and somehow very good.

Sense intruded and she broke away, resisting. "No . . . you are a thief. You are my enemy."

"You are your own enemy, Abbie," he whispered. Then she felt his hands cup her beneath her arms while he raised her whole body, sliding it effortlessly upward until her breasts were over his face and he held her that way, breathing through the starched front of her proper dress, blowing hot life into her who fought against wanting it.

"Oh, please . . . please, put me down." She was almost in tears now, pain and pleasure intermingling in her breasts, her heart, her hands upon his hard shoulders . . . and the part of her that now rested against his chest.

"Abbie, let me," he said into her breasts, "let me."

"No, oh, no, please," she begged, her lips brushing against his soft hair as she spoke into it.

"Let me make a woman of you, Ab."

"No, don't," she gasped. "I . . . . I won't touch your gun or your moustache again. I promise. I'll feed you anything you want, only let me go, please."

"You don't want me to," he said, letting her slide back

down the length of him until her lips were at his again. But the towel had worked its way between their mouths somehow.

"Take the towel away, Abbie," he entreated, his arms firm and solid about her waist.

"No, Jesse, no," she breathed tremulously.

And hearing her utter his name, Jesse knew that she wanted him, too. He raised his chin, nudging the towel down with it, nuzzling her neck. "Let's be friends," he said against her high, stiff collar.

"Never," she denied as his lips eased back to hers. He pushed the rocker back and lay further horizontally, his hips plying hers, rocking a little bit, a little bit, each movement of the chair driving his hard body against hers. He knew it was truly beyond her to say yes to him, that the only way he'd ever have her would be nothing short of rape, for even if she gave in, she'd be doing so against her will. He had to hear her say yes or turn her loose. But he understood, too, that that one word—*yes*—was impossible for her to utter. When he released her, she'd be shamed even by what she'd done so far. But release her he must, and so, to make it easier on her, he quipped, "Say yes quick, Abbie, because my leg hurts like a bitch."

At his teasing she jumped back, too peeved for shame. "Oh, you! You are egotistical and insufferable!" To her dismay, he laughed, holding her down just a moment longer.

"But let's still be friends, for today anyway. I'm sick of the fighting too."

She struggled up from his lap, adjusting her clothing. "If you promise not to do anything like this again."

"Well, could I maybe just think about it?" His dark moustache curled above a teasing smile while Abby scarcely knew where to let her eyes light, she was so flustered. She headed for the kitchen and he followed on his crutches.

"Mind if I sit out here awhile?" he asked. "I'm getting pretty sick of that bedroom."

She wouldn't look at him, but allowed, "Do whatever you like as long as you stay out of my way."

He sat down nonchalantly beside the table, leaning the crutches on the floor beneath his legs. "I won't be any bother," he promised. However, it bothered her already, the way he sat there with his legs sprawled and those walking sticks resting against his crotch. It took a supreme effort to keep her eyes from straying to it, and she had no doubt he knew exactly what he was doing to her. But before he could fluster her further, Doc Dougherty's voice came from the front door.

"Hello in there. Can I come in?" And in he came, for the way Miss Abigail's house was designed he could see down the straight shot from front to back that they were both in the kitchen. "W-e-e-ll," he drawled at the sight of Jesse, "you're looking fit as a fiddle, sitting up on that kitchen chair. How do you feel?"

"Stronger every day, thanks to Miss Abigail," Jesse answered, pleased, as usual, to see the doc.

"So she told me at church earlier. Oh, Miss Abigail, I got those britches you asked me to get. Avery opened his store special. We figured pants for a real necessity, so he obliged. If they don't fit, it'll be too bad, because Avery already locked up again."

Miss Abigail gave the denims a scant glance, then continued with her dinner preparations again as Doc and Jesse retired to the bedroom to have a look at his leg. She could hear their muffled voices before Doc came back to repeat his order of earlier. "He's long past any danger and he can do whatever he feels strong enough to do—inside, outside, doesn't matter. A little fresh air and sunshine might do him good. Now that he's got decent clothes, it wouldn't hurt to take a ride in the country or sit in that garden of yours."

"I doubt that he'd enjoy either of those things."

"I already suggested it and he seemed real anxious to get out. Might not do you any harm either. Well, I better be off now. You need anything else, just holler."

She showed him to the front door, but halfway there Jesse came out of the bedroom, dressed now in blue denims and a pale blue cotton shirt, which hung open.

"Thanks for stopping, Doc, and for the clothes," he said, and went along to the front door as if the house were his own.

"It was Miss Abigail's idea," Doc informed him.

"Then maybe I should thank Miss Abigail," Jesse said, casting a brief grin her way. But Doc was away, out the door, down the porch steps, calling as he went, "See you tomorrow, you two!" The way he said it, lumping the two of them together that way, left a curious warm feeling almost like security in Abbie, standing there beside Jesse at the front door after having ushered Doc out together.

Unexpectedly, Jesse's voice beside her was polite and sincere as he said, "It feels good to have some clothes on that fit me again. Thanks, Abbie." It took her aback because she had grown so used to his teasing and criticism, she hardly knew how to handle politeness from him. She was acutely aware of the fact that while Doc was here Jesse had politely called her Miss Abigail, but as soon as he left, he reverted to the familiar Abbie again. She could feel him looking down at her, caught sight of that bare, black-haired chest, those long naked feet, and wondered what to say to him. But he turned then, lifted a crutch, and gestured politely for her to move ahead of him back to the kitchen. She felt his eyes branding her back as he thumped along behind her.

She returned to her cooking and he to his chair, but the room remained strained with silence until Jesse commented, "Doc gave me hell for pulling that gun on you."

She could not conceal her surprise. Out of the clear blue sky he said a thing like that. Then he added, "I was surprised you admitted it to him."

Sheepishly, she said, "I only told him you made demands regarding pork chops, nothing more."

"Ah," he returned, "is that all?"

She was disconcerted by his sitting behind her, probably staring at every move she made. At last she ventured a peek over her shoulder. The crutches were resting against the same distracting spot as before as he leaned an elbow on the table, scowling, running a forefinger repeatedly over his moustache as if deep in thought.

She turned her back on him before inquiring innocently, "Did he say anything else?"

Silence for a long moment, then, "He wanted to know why my chin and neck were red. I told him I'd been eating fresh strawberries from your garden and they make me break out. You'd better have some strawberries in that garden of yours . . ." From behind, he saw her hands fall idle.

Abbie could feel the coloring working its way up her neck. "You . . . you mean . . . you didn't tell him about the lye in the rag?"

"No." He watched her shoulders slump slighty in relief.

To the top of the range, she said, "Yes, I do have strawberries in my garden."

Behind her, he sat watching as she started whipping

something with a spoon. The motion stirred her skirts until they swayed about her narrow hips. Suddenly she stood very still, and said quietly, "Thank you."

A strange feeling gripped him. She had never spoken so nicely to him before. He cleared his throat and it sounded like thunder in the quiet room. "Have you got anything to put on it, though, Abbie? It's starting to sting pretty bad."

She whirled quickly, and he caught an unguarded look of concern on her face as she crossed the room to him. Her hand reached tentatively for his chin, withdrew, and their eyes met, each wondering why the other had softened the truth when Doc Dougherty had asked his questions.

"Buttermilk should help it." Her eyes dropped to the crutches.

"Have you got any?" he asked.

"Yes, outside in the well. I'll get it.'

He watched her walk down the yard and draw the bucket up and bring a fruit jar back into the house. All the while the frown stayed on his face. "I'll get some gauze to apply it with," she said when she returned. Bringing it, she stood hesitantly, somehow afraid to touch him now.

He reached out a hand, palm-up, saying, "I can do it myself. You're busy." When she was back at the stove he surprised her once more by asking, "Are your hands okay?"

"My hands?"

"From the lye. Are they okay, or do you need some buttermilk too?"

"Oh, they're all right. I barely got them damp."

When she collected the buttermilk and wet gauze to begin setting the table for their dinner, she stopped in the pantry door, looked across the room at him. "Do you like buttermilk?" she asked.

"Yes, I do."

"Do you want some with your dinner?"

"Sounds good."

She disappeared, returned with a glass of frothy white, and handed it to him. His fingers looked tawnier than ever against the milk.

"Thank you," he said to her for the second time that day.

At last she joined him at the table, extended a platter his way, asking politely, "Chicken?"

"Help yourself first," he suggested. And pretty soon—

unbelievably—their plates were filled and they were eating dinner across from each other without so much as one cross word between them.

"We used to have chicken every single Sunday when I was little," he recalled.

"Who is we?"

"We," he repeated. "My mom and dad and Rafe and June and Clare and Tommy Joe. My family."

"And where was that?"

"New Orleans."

Somehow the picture of him in a circle of brothers and sisters and parents seemed ludicrous. He was—she reminded herself—a consummate liar.

"You don't believe me, do you?" He smiled and took a bite of chicken.

"I don't know."

"Even train robbers have mothers and fathers. Some of us even have siblings." He was back to his customary teasing again, but somehow she didn't mind this time. The word *siblings* was a surprise, too, the kind he now and then tossed out unexpectedly. It was her kind of word, not his.

"And how many *siblings* did you have?"

"I had . . . *have* . . . four. Two brothers and two sisters."

"Indeed?" She raised an eyebrow dubiously.

He raised his buttermilked chin a little and laughed enjoyably. "I can hear the skepticism in your voice and I know why. Sorry if I don't fit your notion of where I should or shouldn't have come from, but I have two parents, still living in New Orleans, in a real house, still eating real chicken on Sundays— only Creole-style—and I have two older brothers and two younger sisters and last night when you washed my hair it reminded me of Saturday nights back there at home. We all washed our hair on Saturday nights, and Mom polished our shoes for Sunday."

She was unabashedly staring at him now. The truth was, she wanted to be convinced that it was all true. Could it possibly be? She reminded herself again that he was an accused felon, that the last thing she should do was believe him.

"Surprised?" he asked, smiling at her amazed expression. But she wasn't ready to believe it yet.

"If you had such a nice home, why did you leave it?"

"Oh, I didn't leave it permanently. I go back regularly and visit. I left my family because I was young and had my fortune to seek, and a good and loyal friend who wanted to seek his along with me. But I miss them sometimes."

"And so you left New Orleans together?"

"We did."

"And did you find your fortunes?"

"We did. On the railroads—together."

"Ahhh, the railroads again," she crooned knowingly.

"What can I say?" He threw his hands out guiltily. "I was caught red-handed."

His blithe, devil-may-care attitude puzzled her, but she smiled at his affability, wondering if it was all true about New Orleans and his family.

"And what about you?" He had finished eating and leaned back relaxedly in his chair, one elbow slung on the table. "Any brothers or sisters?"

She immediately gazed out the screen door, faraway things in her expression as she answered, "None."

"I gathered as much from Doc. I left my family when I was twenty. He said you stayed with yours."

"Yes." She picked away a nonexistent thread from her skirt.

"Not by choice?"

She looked up sharply. It would not do to admit such a thing, no matter what the truth. A good daughter simply would not begrudge a father anything, would she? Jesse was absently toying with his moustache again, rested his forefinger beneath his nose as he continued. "Doc told me once that you gave up your youth to care for an ailing father. I find that commendable." She glanced to his eyes to see if he was teasing again, but they were serious. "How long ago was that?"

She swallowed, weighing the risks of telling him things she never talked about. Finally she admitted, "Thirteen years."

"When you were twenty?"

"Yes." Her eyes dropped to her lap again.

"What a waste," he commented quietly, making the skin at the back of her neck prickle. She didn't know what to reply or where to look or what to do with her hands. "It's not everyone who'd do a thing like that, Abbie. Do you regret it now?"

The fact that she did not deny her regret was the closest she had ever come to admitting it.

"When did he die?" Jesse went on.

"A year ago."

"Twelve years you gave him?" Only silence answered him while she demurely looked at her hands. "Twelve years, and all that time you learned how to do all the things you do so well, all the things it takes to make a house run smoothly, and a family . . . yet you never had one. Why?"

She was startled and embarrassed by his question. She'd thought they had come to a silent agreement not to intentionally hurt each other anymore. But some shred of pride kept her eyes from tearing as she replied, "I believe that's obvious, isn't it?"

"You mean you had little choice in the matter?"

She swallowed, and her face became mottled. I should have known better than to confide in him, she thought, her heart near bursting with bitter pain.

"Until Melcher came along and I took the choice away from you by scaring him away."

She could not tolerate his barbs anymore. She flew from her chair to run, but he stopped her with a hand on her arm. "I see now I was wrong," he said quietly, making her eyes fly to his. It was the last thing she had expected him to say. It wilted her resolve to hate him, yet she was now afraid of what would take hate's place should she relinquish it.

"Do we have to talk about this?" she asked the tan hand upon her sleeve.

"I'm trying to apologize, Abbie," he said. "I haven't done it many times in my life." She looked up, startled, to find utter sincerity in his eyes, and her heart set up a flurry of wingbeats at the somber look he wore.

Knowing that once she said it she would be on even more precarious footing, she said anyway, "Apology accepted." His dark fingers squeezed her arm once, then slid away. But it felt as if he had branded her with that touch while he spoke the words she had never thought to hear from him.

Chapter 11

————————

MISS ABIGAIL KEPT her gardens just as fastidiously as she kept everything else, Jesse thought as he lounged against a tree, hands laced on his stomach, watching her. There was a predominance of blues, but being a man, he could not identify bachelor buttons, canterbury bells, or forget-me-nots, though he did know a morning glory. He squinted as Abbie flitted to explore them where they climbed a white trellis against the wall of the house. He almost expected her to dip and sip from one, he had thought of her as a hummingbird for so long. Lazy and sated, he watched her move from flower to flower. She leaned to pull an errant weed and he smiled privately as her derriere pointed his way. The backs of her calves came into view beneath her skirt. He closed one eye, leaving the other open as if taking a bead on her. When she seemed about to turn around, he pretended to be asleep. Then, in a moment, he carefully peered out at her again. Once more he assessed her slim ankles, realizing that she was a damn fine-looking woman. Let that tight knot of hair down, unbutton a couple buttons, teach her it's all right to laugh, and she'd make some man sit up and take notice. Realizing what he was thinking, he shut his eyes completely and thought, *That hummingbird's not for you, Jess*. But then why had they goaded and fought with each other like they had? It had all the earmarks of a mating ritual and he knew it. Didn't the stallion bite the mare before mounting her? And the she-cat—how she screamed and growled and spit at the tom before he jumped her. Even the gentle rabbits became vicious beforehand, the doe using her powerful back legs to box and kick the buck as if repulsed by him.

He studied Abigail McKenzie through scarcely opened eyelids. She picked some yellow thing and raised it to her nose. She had a cute little turned up nose.

He considered the hummingbird. Even its disposition turned pugnacious at mating time, both male and female becoming quarrelsome and snappish in their own avian way. He'd seen hummingbirds countless times in the woods, feeding from honey trees sweet with blossoms. Each male marked his feeding territory, defending it against all comers who sought to sip the nectar of his chosen flowers. He fought off all invaders until one special female arrived to tempt him. Together they would flit through the air flirting, toward and away from the prized flowers. Then, at the last, the female stilled her wings and hesitated just long enough for the male to mate with her, thus paying for the taste of his flowers before sipping quickly and caroming away too fast for the eye to follow.

He recalled how Abbie had withheld food from him, trying to starve him out of her house. He remembered all the teasing, the fighting, the baiting they'd each done.

She straightened and wiped her forehead with the back of a hand, her breast thrown into sharp relief against the mass of blue flowers behind her.

Damnit, Jess, get your carcass healed and out of here! he thought, and sat up quickly.

"What do you say we go for that ride?" he asked, needing some distraction.

She turned. "I thought you were asleep."

"I've slept so much in the last couple of weeks I don't care if I never do again." He wore a faint scowl as he looked away at the mountains.

"How is your skin?" she asked.

"Sour, I think. This buttermilk was soothing but I think it'd better come off before the neighbors start complaining." An amused smile lifted her lips and she wiped the back of her forehead again.

"I'll get some water." Soon she returned with a basin of cold water, a cloth, and a bar of soap, placing them on the ground near him.

"Pew! You do stink!" she exclaimed, backing away.

"If you think it smells bad from over there, you should smell it from over here." Again she laughed, then sat down a proper distance away, tucking both feet to one side beneath her skirts, watching him draw the basin between his legs and lean over to bathe his face. He lathered his hands instead of the cloth, raised his chin, running the soap back around his jaw and neck. He rinsed, opened his eyes, and caught her watching him, and she quickly glanced off across the flats to where the mountains rose, blue-hued and hazy, even in the high daytime sun.

"It'd be nice to take a buggy ride out there," he said.

"But I don't own a buggy or a horse," she explained.

"Hasn't this town got a livery stable?"

"Yes. Mr. Perkins runs it, but I don't think it's a good idea."

"But Doc said it's okay. I've been up a lot. I was up all the while you were gone. I even washed my hair with soap and water, didn't you notice?"

Oh, she'd noticed all right. She could still remember the smell of it while he breathed into her breasts on the rocker this morning.

"Being up is different than riding along in a bumpy buggy." But she looked wistfully at the road, lifting smoothly out of the valley into the foothills that gently inclined toward the ridges above the town.

"Are you afraid to go for a ride with me?"

Startled because he'd guessed the truth, she was forced to lie. "Why . . . why no. No, why should I be?"

"I'm a wanted man."

"You're an injured man, and in spite of what Doc Dougherty says, I refuse to believe it could do you any good to go riding on a hard buggy seat."

"When's the last time you saw my wound, Abbie? Doc's been the one looking at it and he says buggy riding's okay."

"It's not a good idea," she repeated lamely, picking a blade of grass.

"It's not me you don't think should go off in a buggy, it's you. Admit it."

"Me!"

He squinted up at the mountains, while her eyes strayed to

the black hairs on the tops of his bare toes. "I mean," he drawled, biting on a piece of grass now himself, "it would probably look petty queer, Miss Abigail McKenzie renting a rig to take her train robber off to who know where on a Sunday afternoon."

"You are not *my* train robber, Mr. Cameron, and I'd appreciate it if you'd not refer to yourself as such."

"Oh, pardon," he said with a lopsided smile, "then the town's train robber." He could see her weakening—damnit, but she was getting to look more appealing by the minute—and he wondered if he should stay put.

"Why are you after me like this again? You promised you would behave."

"I'm behaving, aren't I? All I want to do is get out of here for awhile. Furthermore, I promised Doc I wouldn't harm you or try to escape. It's Sunday, everybody in town's relaxing and doing exactly as they please, and here you sit, gazing at the mountains from your hot backyard while we could be up where it's cooler, riding along and enjoying the day."

"I'm enjoying it right here—at least I was until you started with this preposterous idea." But she tucked a slim forefinger into the high, tight band of her collar and worked it back and forth.

He wondered if ever in her life she'd taken a buggy ride with a man. Maybe with that one thirteen years ago, she had. He found himself again trying to picture how she'd looked and acted when being courted.

"I wouldn't bite you, Abbie. What do you say?"

Her blue eyes seemed to appeal to him not to convince her this way, yet as her finger slid out of her collar her lips parted expectantly and she glanced once more at the mountains. Her cheeks took on a delicate pink color of her own primorses. Then she dropped her eyes to her lap as she spoke. "You would have to button up your shirt and put your boots on."

All was silent but for the chirp of a katydid. She raised her eyes to his and he thought, what the hell are you up to, Jess? He suddenly felt like some damn fool bumblebee sitting in her garden while she poised a glass jar above him, ready to slam it down and clap the cover on. But, against his better judgment, he smiled and said, "Agreed."

* * *

"Why, howdy, Miss Abigail," Gem Perkins said, answering her knock, trying hard not to show his surprise. Never before had she come to his door, but here she was, decked out flawlessly in white hat and gloves.

"Good afternoon, Mr. Perkins. I should like to rent a horse and buggy with a well-sprung seat. One that will jostle as little as possible."

"A buggy, Miss Abigail?" Gem asked, as if she'd requested instead a saddled gila monster.

"Do you or do you not rent buggies, Mr. Perkins?" she asked dryly.

"Why, o' course I do, you know that, Miss Abigail. I just never knew you to take one out before."

"And I wouldn't be now, except that Dr. Dougherty wants that invalid up at my place to grow accustomed to riding again so that he may be packed off on the train as soon as possible. However, we shall need an upholstered seat with lithe springs."

"Why, sure thing, Miss Abigail, upholstered seat and what was that other again?" He led the way to the livery, still surprised at her showing up here this way.

"Springy springs, Mr. Perkins," she stated again, wondering how long it would take for the news to spread to every resident of town what she was doing.

Jesse chuckled, watching her drive the rig up the street. He could see she didn't know the first thing about handling a horse. The mare threw her head and nickered in objection to the cut of the bit in Abbie's too-cautious hands. She pulled up in front of the pickets and he watched her carefully dismount, then swish up the walk. No, he decided, she'd never done anything like this before in her life.

By the time she entered the parlor, he was waiting on her graceful settee. Miss Abigail resisted the urge to laugh at how ridiculous he looked there—the only discrepancy in her otherwise tidy room. No, she thought, he'll never make *parlor fare.*

'The leg's a little stiff," he said, "and so is the new denim. Could you help me with my boots?" She looked down at his bare toes, chagrined to feel a peculiar thrill at the sight of them, then quickly she knelt and held first his socks, then his boots. They were fine boots, she noticed for the first time, well oiled and made of heavy, expensive cowhide. She wondered if he'd robbed a train to pay for them and was again surprised that the thought did nothing to deter her from wanting to ride out with him.

When the boots were on she rose, carefully avoiding looking at his dark-skinned chest behind the gaping garment. "You promised you'd button up your shirt," she reminded him.

He looked down at himself. "Oh, yeah." Then he struggled to stand clumsily on one foot, buttoned the shirt, then turned his back to her and unceremoniously unbuttoned his fly and began stuffing his shirttails in. Her cheeks flared red yet she stood and watched the play of his shoulder muscles while he made the necessary adjustments. Finally realizing what she was doing, she spun from the room and went to wait for him on the porch.

He stumped his way out on his crutches and moved to the side of the buggy. The denims were indeed very stiff. It immediately became apparent that he'd have trouble boarding. There was only a single, small footrest high on the buggy, and after three attempts to lift his foot to it, she ordered, "Wait on the steps and I'll pull up near them."

He withdrew to the porch steps to watch her inexpertly drive the rig around the end of the picket fence.

"You're pulling too sharp!" he warned. "Ease off!" He held his breath for fear she'd overturn the thing before the mission even got under way. But the rig arrived safely at the porch and he poised on his crutches on the second step.

"Can you make it?" she asked, measuring the distance visually.

He grinned, quipping, "If I don't, just ship my bones back to New Orleans." Then he swung both feet toward the floor of the rig, dangling momentarily by his armpits on the crutches. But the rest of his body didn't come along with his feet, and he teetered precariously, on the verge of going over backward.

"No!" Miss Abigail exclaimed, reacting automatically, reaching to grab the only thing she could see to grab: the waistband of his new denims. It did the trick, all right, but she yanked a little too hard and he came plummeting like a felled tree, nearly wiping her clean out the other side of the buggy. The next moment she found herself squashed beneath him, one hand splayed on his hard chest, the other still delving into his waistband. Suddenly realizing where that hand was buried, she jerked it out. But not before his suggestive smile made her face flame. She pushed him away and fussily adjusted her hat, whisked at her skirt, and refused to look at him. But his smirk remained in her peripheral vision. He was up to his cute tricks again, naturally! Red to the ears and trying to pretend she wasn't, she stiffened her back while he took the reins, clicked, whistled, and the mare set off while Abbie sat like a lump of her own cornmeal being taken for a ride.

"Are you all right?" he asked. But she could hear that smirk still coloring his words.

"I'm perfectly fine!" she snapped.

"Then what are you snapping at me for?"

"You know perfectly well why I'm snapping at you!"

"What did I do now?" All innocence and light.

"You know perfectly well what you did! You and your shifty, suggestive eyes!"

He smiled sideways at her starchy, affronted pose. "Well, I wasn't going to mention it, but as long as you did, what's a man supposed to do when a woman's got her hand in his pants?"

"My hand was not in your pants!" she spit, really puckered now.

He laughed boldly. "Oh, a thousand pardons, Miss Abigail. I guess I was mistaken. It must have been some other woman's hand in my pants just now." He looked around as if searching for the culprit. He chuckled low in his throat once, assessing her mirthfully. She wasn't taking his teasing too well today. He liked it best when she gave him tit for tat. He grinned, casting sideward glances at her stern face, and relaxed back and started whistling some little ditty softly between his teeth, deciding he'd be nice for a while and see if he couldn't sweeten her up some.

They headed north on a double track that paralleled the railroad tracks toward the foothills. It was scorching, and Miss Abigail was grateful for even the sliver of shade afforded by her narrow hatbrim. The leg space was inadequate for his long limbs, so his knees sprawled sideways, brushing against her skirts, though she kept her feet primly together and her hands in her lap. She inched away as far as possible, but they hit a bump and his knee lolled over and thumped against her and his smiling eyes leisurely roved her way. When she sat stiff and silent, he finally glanced off at the scenery without saying a word.

As they neared the foothills the undergrowth thickened and Jesse raised an arm, silently pointing. She followed his finger to where a cottontail hit for cover, and without knowing it, she smiled. Her eyes stayed riveted to the spot until they reached and passed it, and Jesse furtively watched her search for more animal life. A hawk appeared, circling above him, and she lifted her face to follow it. The greenery hedged closer to the road, and she seemed enchanted by a flock of lark buntings flitting in and out, feeding upon piñon nuts. The rails swung right while the wagon track bore left, and once again they broke into an open space where spikes of blue lupines created a moving sea all about them, as if part of the sky had fallen into the peaceful mountainside. Her lips formed a silent "Ohhh," and he smiled appreciatively. Silently they swayed along, climbing higher and higher until the terrain became rockier, with outcroppings here and there holding a strangling yew. They passed a cluster of bright orange painted cups, and again her eyes strayed behind to linger on the flowers as long as possible.

He turned his slow gaze upon her. "Where does this go?"

She perched like a little chipping sparrow, on the edge of her seat, alert and taking everything in. "To Eagle Butte, then along the Cascade Creek to Great Pine Rock and over the ridge to Hicksville."

Again they fell silent, he smiling and she taking in everything, while the mare trotted along. Once Jesse wiped his forehead on his shirtsleeve. They entered a patch of quaking aspen and the trembling, dappled shade the trees created. Here and there was a fragrant evergreen—juniper or spruce—vying for sky as the branches formed a tunnel overhead. Soon they came to a flat, shapeless gray rock precipice.

"Is this Eagle Butte?"

She looked around in a full circle. "I think so. It's been a long time since I was up here."

He stopped the horse and they sat with the sun pelting them mercilessly as they gazed beyond the enormity of Eagle Butte to a similar ridge that rose across a chasm along which they'd been riding for some distance. Over there the firs were in deep shadow—a rich, lush haven of coolness, while on this side the afternoon sun still blazed. Studying the scene opposite, Jesse absently unbuttoned two buttons of his shirt and ran a hand inside. Minglingly with the scent of pine was that of ripe grass and the pleasantly fecund scent of the sweating horse.

"If you continue on, we should soon reach Cascade Creek and it should be much cooler there."

He clucked to the mare and they moved on. When they reached Cascade Creek it was, indeed, cool and inviting. brattling its way shallowly down a rocky bed between shady willows and alders.

The horse plodded to the water, dipped her head, and drank, then stood blinking slow. Both of the riders watched the animal for several long, silent minutes.

At last Jesse asked, "Would you like to get down for a while?"

She knew it would be best to keep this outing strictly to riding, but she cast a wishful glance at the water. Instead of waiting for an answer, Jesse flicked the reins and turned the horse, nudging her toward a low-hanging branch on a gnarled pine tree. He stood, grabbed the sturdy branch, and swung easily to the ground. He retrieved his crutches from the buggy while she concealed her surprise at his lithe agility—for someone as big as he was, he moved like a puma. He reached up a brown hand to help her down, and she glanced, startled, at it, quite unprepared for this civility.

"Don't bump your head," he said, indicating the branch above her.

His palm waited, callused and hard, becoming more of an issue the longer she delayed placing her own in it. But she recalled that she was wearing her white gloves, and at last placed one in his firm grip as he helped her jump to the ground. She moved ahead of him toward the inviting water, but she had those gloves on, and he was on crutches so neither of them touched it. Instead they watched it bubble away at their feet. After some time he pulled his shirttails completely free of his pants again and unbuttoned the shirt the rest of the way. She stood stiff and formal, yet. Jesse glanced around, and spied a comfortable-looking spot where the water had scooped away the bank to form a rude, but natural chair. He hobbled over, threw his crutches down, then settled himself with a sigh. The creek burbled. The birds spoke. The woods were redolent with pine spice and leaf mold. Jesse crossed his arms behind his head and leaned back, watching the woman who stood on the creek bank.

Her back was as straight as a ramrod: she never allowed herself to relax those infernal gentilities of hers. Now she stood as stiffly as the boles of the pine trees, although he knew she was hot, too, for she'd raised a white glove to touch her forehead, then again to brush at the nape of her neck. What was she thinking as she looked at the creek? What did she want to do that her silly manners would not allow? He wondered if she'd even sit down, if she'd touch the water, if she'd condescend to talk to him.

"The water looks nice and cool," he commented finally, watching her carefully to see what she'd do. When she neither replied nor moved, he added, "Tell me if it is. I can't reach."

Her hands remained as motionless as a watched clock for a long, long time. Finally she drew her gloves off. He could tell by the hesitant way she leaned to touch the water that she wished he weren't watching her. Even a simple, sensual gesture like that caused her second thoughts. For a moment he pitied her. The hem of her dress slipped a little bit and she hurriedly clutched it up, away from the surface of the stream.

And he thought, let if fall, Abbie, let it fall, then wallow in behind it and see how great it feels. But he knew, of course, that she never would.

"Bring me some," he called anyway, just to see what she'd do.

She turned a brief, quizzical glance over her shoulder. "But I have nothing to carry it in."

"So carry it in your hands."

Abruptly she stood up. "There is a ridiculous suggestion if I ever heard one."

"Not to a thirsty man."

"Don't be foolish, you can't drink from my hands."

"Why not?" he asked casually.

He could hear her thinking, as clearly as if she'd spoken the words aloud, "It is just not done!"

"If I could drink from your mouth while I was unconscious, why can't I drink from your hands now?"

Her shoulder blades snapped closer together and she said, still facing away from him, "You take very great pleasure in persecuting me, don't you?"

"All I want is some water," he said reasonably, still with his head hanging backward in the cradle of his two hands. Then he sighed, looked upstream, and muttered, ''Aw, what the hell, just forget it then,'' and laid his head back on the creekbank and closed his eyes.

He looked very harmless that way when she ventured to peek at him. Funny, but she really did not like being on the bad side of him, yet she never quite knew what he was up to. She glanced at his moustache—it was almost as thick as when she first saw him—then to the water, then back at him again. She looked around for something she could shape into a cone or vessel, but there was nothing. Never in her life had she done such a thing, but the thought of doing it caused an earthy sensation in the pit of her stomach. The water had felt deliciously cool. Even the horse had needed a long drink. And Jesse was obviously very hot. He'd unbuttoned that shirt again, and she remembered how he'd run his hand inside it earlier. She looked at him dozing peacefully. She looked at the water.

Jesse's eyes flew open as two large splats of water hit his bare chest. He jumped but then grinned: she was standing over him with cupped hands.

"Open up," she ordered.

Well I'll be damned, he thought, and opened his mouth like a communicant. She lowered her palms, created a split in their seam, but the water trailed away, down inside her cuffs, some hitting his chest and chin, but none reaching his lips. She half expected him to jump up and smack her hands aside, remembering the time she'd clacked the spoon against his teeth, but he surprised her by rubbing a hand over his dark chest, spreading the water wide.

"Ah, that's cool," he said appreciatively, then his eyes twinkled. "But I'd like a little in my mouth, too."

"Oh, I got my cuffs wet," she complained, pulling at them. But they stuck to her wrists and would not even slide on her skin.

"As long as they're already wet, may as well try again."

This time it worked better, for he reached to cup the backs of her hands and pour the water into his mouth from her fingertips as if they were the lip of a pitcher.

It was a decidedly sensuous thing, watching him drink from her fingertips. It made queer quivers start way down low in her stomach. After he swallowed, droplets were left upon his moustache. Fascinated, she watched his tongue run along its edge and lap them up. She realized suddenly that she'd been staring. Immediately her eyes flitted to some distant bush.

"Why don't you have some?"

She touched her throat just below her jaw. "N . . . No, I don't want any."

He knew it was not true, but understood—she'd already gone too far.

"Come on, sit down awhile. It's nice and cool here and really quite comfortable."

She glanced around as if someone might catch her at it if she dared. Reaching some sort of compromise with herself, she said, "I'll sit here," and perched on a rock near his feet.

"You've never been up here before?" he asked, studying her back as she faced the creek.

"When I was a girl, I was."

"Who brought you?"

"My father. He came to cut wood and I helped him load it."

"If I lived around here I'd come up here all the time. It's too flat and hot down in the valley to suit me." He laced his hands behind his head and looked up into the trees. "When my brothers and I were small, we spent hours and hours by the Gulf, catching sand crabs, playing in the surf, shell hunting. I miss the ocean."

"I've never seen the ocean," she said plaintively.

"It's no prettier than this, just pretty in a different way. Do you want to?"

"Want to?" She glanced back at him.

"See the ocean?"

"I don't know. Richard was—" But she stopped dead and quickly faced the creek.

"Richard? Who is Richard?"

"Nothing . . . nobody . . . I don't even know why I brought him up."

"He must be *somebody*, or you wouldn't have."

"Oh . . ." She circled her knees with her hands. "He was just someone I knew once who always said he wanted to live by the ocean."

"Did he make it?"

"I don't know."

"You lost touch with him?"

She sighed and shrugged. "What does it matter? It was a long time ago."

"How long ago?"

But she didn't answer. She was afraid to confide in him. Yet he urged her to speak of things which no other person had ever cared enough to ask about.

"Thirteen years ago?" he prompted. Still she didn't reply, and he thought long and hard before finally admitting, "I know about Richard, Abbie."

He heard her breath catch in her throat before she turned startled eyes to him. "How could you know about Richard?"

"Doc Dougherty told me."

Her nostrils distended and her lips tightened. "Doctor Dougherty talks too much for his own good."

"And you talk too little for yours."

She hugged herself and turned away. "I keep my private affairs to myself. That is exactly how it should be."

"Is it? Then why did you bring up Richard?"

"I don't know. His name slipped out inadvertently. I've never talked about him since he left and I assure you I am not about to start now."

"Why? Is he taboo, just like everything else?"

"You talk like a fool."

"No, I suspect somebody did that long before I came along, or you wouldn't be so tied up in knots over letting go a little bit."

"I don't even know why I listen to you—a completely impulsive person like you. You have no notion of restraint or self-control of any kind. You . . . you charge through life as if to give it a shock so it will remember you've been there. That may work well for you, but I assure you it is not my way. I live by strict standards."

"Has it occurred to you, Abbie, that maybe you set your standards too high, or that somebody else may have done it for you?"

"That is impossible for any living person to do."

"Then tell me why you're sitting out here five miles from civilization yet you wouldn't take your hat off if it grew tentacles or even unbutton the cuffs that are probably chafing you raw right now. But worst of all you won't talk about something that caused you pain, because some fool said a lady shouldn't? Nor does she show regret or anger, is that right? A lady just doesn't spill her guts. She sits instead with them all tied in neat, prim knots. Of course talking would make you human, and maybe you prefer to think you're above being human." He knew he was making her angry, but knew too that was the only time she truly opened up.

"I was taught, sir, that it is both ill-mannered and—yes—unladylike to wail out one's dissatisfactions with life. It simply is not done."

"Who said so, your mother?"

"Yes, if you must know!"

"Humph!" He could just about picture her mother. "The best thing in the world for you would be to come right out and say, 'I loved a man named Richard once but he jilted me and it makes me mad as hell.'"

Her fists knotted and she spun to face him, eyes dangerously glistening. "You have no right!"

"No, but you do, Abbie, don't you see?" He sat straighter, intense now.

"All I see is that I should never have come up here with you today. You have succeeded again in making me so angry that I should like to . . . to slap your hateful face!"

"It'd be the second time today you slapped my face for making you feel something. Is it that frightful to you to feel? If slapping me would make you feel good, why don't you come over here and do it? How mad do I have to make you before you'll break out? Why can't you just cuss or laugh or cry when something inside Abbie says she should?"

"What is it you want of me!"

"Just to teach you that what comes natural shouldn't be forbidden."

"Oh, certainly! Slapping, crying . . . and . . . and that . . . that little scene on the rocker this morning! Why, if you had your way you would turn me into a wanton!" Tears brimmed at the rims of her eyes.

"Those things aren't wanton, but you can't see it because of all the silly rules your mother made you live by."

"You leave my mother out of this! Ever since you came to my house you've been contrary and fault-finding. I will not let you attack my mother when your own could have taught you a few manners!"

"Listen to yourself, Abbie. Why is it you can call me names and get angry with me when the ones you really blame are your mother and father and Richard for what they did to you?"

"I said leave them out of this! What they were to me is none of your business!" Her eyes blazed as she jumped to her feet.

"Why so belligerent, Abbie? Because I hit on the truth? Because it's them you blame when you think you're not supposed to? Doc Dougherty didn't have to tell me much to fit the pieces together. Correct me if I'm wrong. Your mother taught you that a good daughter honors her father and mother, even if it means sacrificing her own joy. She taught you that virtue is natural and carnality isn't, when actually it's the other way around."

"How dare you sit there and pour acerbations on innocent people who wanted only the best for me?"

"They had no idea of what was best for you—all except Richard, I suspect, and he was smart enough to know he couldn't fight your dead mother's code of ethics, so he got out!"

"Oh! And you know what's best for me, I suppose!"

He assessed her dispassionately. "Maybe."

She assessed him passionately. "And maybe you'll sprout wings and fly away from the law when they come to get you!" She waggled a finger in the direction of town.

Comprehension dawned in his eyes. "Ah, now we're getting down to the truth here, aren't we?" He reached for his crutches without taking his menacing eyes from her. "It baffles you how some common, no-good train robber like me could possibly hit on the truth about you, doesn't it?"

"Exactly!" she spit, facing him, fists clenched angrily at her sides. "A common, no-good train robber!"

"Well, let this common, no-good train robber tell you a few things about yourself, Miss Abigail McKenzie, that you've been denying ever since you laid eyes on me." He struggled to his feet, advancing upon her. "It is precisely *because* I'm an outlaw that you have, on several occasions, ventured forth from your righteous ways and lost control. With me you did things you never dared do before—you sneaked a peek at life. And do you know why you tried it? Because afterward you could wipe your conscience clean and blame me for goading you into it. After all, I'm the bad one anyway, right?"

"You talk in circles!" she scoffed, quaking now because he'd hit upon the truth and that truth was too awful for her to admit.

"Are you denying that it's because I'm a . . . a criminal

that you dared to bend your holy bylaws around me a little?"
They were nose to nose now.

"I don't know what you're talking about," she said prissily,
and turned away, crossing her arms tightly across her breasts.

He reached out to grab her upper arm and try to make her
turn to face him. "Oh, pull your head out of the sand, Miss
Abigail Ostrich, and admit it!" She yanked herself free of his
grip, but he moved in close behind her, pursuing her with his
relentless accusations. "You slammed doors and threw bedpans and kissed me and hollered at me and even got yourself a
little sexually excited, and you found out it all felt pretty damn
fun at times. But you could blame all those forbidden things on
me, right? Because I'm the nasty one here, not you. But what
would happen to all your grand illusions if I turned out to be
something other than the brigand you think I am?" Again he
got her by the arm. "Come on, talk to me. Tell me all your
well-guarded secret guilts! You can tell me—what the hell, I'll
be gone soon enough and take them all with me!"

At last she spun on him, whacking his hand off her arm. "I
have no secret guilts!" she shouted angrily.

His eyes bored into hers as he shouted back, with ferocity
equal to hers, "Now *that's* what I've been trying to make you
see all this time!"

Silence fell like a hundred-year oak. Their eyes locked. She
struggled to understand what it was he was saying, and when
the truth came to her at last, she was stricken by her own
comprehension, and she turned away.

"Don't keep turning away from me, Abbie," he said,
making his way to her on the clumsy crutches, touching her
arm more gently now, trying to make her face him willingly,
which she stubbornly refused to do. "Do I have to say it for
you, Abbie?" he asked softly.

Tears began gathering in her throat.

"I . . . I don't know what it is you want me to . . . to
say."

In the quietest tones he had ever used with her, Jesse spoke.
"Why not start by admitting that Richard was a randy youth,
that something happened between you and him that made him
leave." Jesse paused a long moment, then added even softer,
while with his thumb he stroked the arm he still held, "That it
had nothing to do with your father."

"No, no . . . it's not true!" She covered her face with her palms. "Why do you goad me like this?"

"Because I think Richard was exactly like me and it's got you scared to death."

She whirled then and hit him once with her pathetic little fist in the center of his bare chest. It send him hobbling backward, but he didn't quite fall. "Wasn't he?" Jesse persisted.

She looked into his relentless eyes like a demented wood-land nymph, shaken, tears now streaming down her cheeks. "Leave me alone!" she begged miserably.

"Admit it, Abbie," he said softly.

"Damn you!" she cried, sobbing now, and raised a hand to strike him again. He did not cringe or back away as the blow, and another and another rained upon his shoulders and chest. "Damn you . . . R . . . Richard!" she choked, but Jesse stood sturdy as she hit the side of his neck and her nails scraped two red welts upon it.

He did not fight her, did not block her swing, only said very gently, "I'm not Richard, Abbie. I'm Jesse."

"I know . . . I kn . . . I know," she sobbed into her hands, ashamed now of having sunk to such depths.

He reached out and encircled her shaking shoulders, gathering her near, pulling her forehead against his hard chest. Her tears scalded his bare skin and brought some wholly new and disturbing stinging behind his eyes. A crutch dropped to the ground, but he steadied himself and let it fall. Her hat had gone askew and he reached to pull the pin from it.

Her hands flew up and she choked, "Wh . . . what are y . . . you doing?"

"Just something you woundn't do for yourself—taking your hat off. Nothing more, okay?" He stuck the filigreed pin through the straw, tossed it behind him onto the creek bank, then pulled her again into his arms, circling her neck with one large hand, rubbing a thumb across the hair pulled so prudishly taut behind her ear.

She cried against him with her elbows folded tightly between them, comforted more than she'd thought possible by the feel of his forearm spanning her narrow shoulders and his palm stroking her sleeve. He touched her soft earlobe. He laid his cheek against her hair, and she felt a queer sense of security, staying within his arms that way.

Abbie, Abbie, he thought, *my little hummingbird, what are you doing to me?*

He smelled different than her father—better. He felt different than David—harder. She reminded herself who he was, what he was, but for the moment it didn't matter. He was here, and warm, and real, and the beat of his heart was firm and sure beneath her cheek upon his chest. And she needed so terribly badly to talk about everything at last.

When her crying eased, he leaned back, taking her face in both hands, wiping at the wetness beneath her eyes with his thumbs.

"Come on, Abbie, let's sit down and talk. Don't you see you've got to talk about it?"

She nodded limply, then he drew her by the hand toward the creek bank, and she followed docilely, exhausted now from her fit of tears.

A blackbird sang in the willows. The creek rushed past with its whispered accompaniment as Abbie began to speak. Jesse did not touch her again, but let her talk it all out, drawing from her the truths which he'd guessed days ago. He pieced together the picture of a pathetic, retiring husband and the single child, both of whom the mother had wronged with her narrow version of love. A rigid woman of stern discipline who taught her daughter that duty was more important than the urgings of her own body. And Richard, the man who made Abbie aware of those urgings, but could not free her from the stringent laws laid down by her mother. And Abbie, hiding all these years behind the delusion that Richard had deserted her because of the invalid father.

But Jesse now saw the imprisoned Abbie escape, as the bullfrogs set up their late-day chorus. He watched the woman on the creek bank change into a mellow, human entity, with fears, misgivings, frailties, and regrets. And it was this transformed Abbie of whom Jesse knew he'd best be careful.

Things were infinitely different between them by the time they started back to town. The myths were shattered. The truth now rode like a passenger on the seat, intimately, between them. There was a disturbing ease, born of a deeper understanding, and far more threatening than the animosities which had earlier riddled their relationship.

For she had learned he could be kind.

And he had learned she could be human.

They rode in silence, aware of each brush of elbow and knee. White moths of evening came out and the song of the cicada ceased. The shadows of the trees grew to long-stretching tendrils then disappeared in the cease of sun. The leaves whispered their last hushed vespers. The mare quickened her step toward home, her voice the only one heard as she nickered to the growing twilight. Abbie's sleeve brushed Jesse's shoulder and he leaned forward, away from it, staring straight ahead, elbows to knees and the reins limp in his hands. He had helped her break down many barriers today, but he was still bound by propriety. She was not at all his kind of woman. Yet he looked back over his shoulder and caught her watching him, her eyes quite the color of the evening sky, her piquant little face showing signs of confusion, but her hands again in white gloves, glowing almost purple now as dusk came on.

Her eyes strayed, then came back to meet his, and she knew the swift, intimidating yearning of the woman who feels herself drawn to the wrong man. The wheels hushed along, the riders rocked in unison, their eyes locked. At last her troubled gaze drifted aside, as did his. She thought of a gun in his hand on that train and her eyes slid shut, not wanting to picture it yet unable to keep the image at bay. She opened her eyes again and studied his broad shoulders with blue cotton pulled taut against rippling muscle, black hair curling down over his collar, thick sideburns curving low on a crisp jaw, sleeves rolled to elbows upon arms limned with dark hair, the limp wrist, those long fingers. She remembered them upon her, then looked away, distracted.

God help me, she thought, I want him.

Town approached. Jesse shifted the reins to one hand and, without saying a word, considerately buttoned up his shirt. In the gathering dusk she felt herself blush. He leaned back, their shoulders touched again, then her familiar white picket fence was beside them and he pulled up before the porch steps.

He handed her the reins. They were warm from his hands.

He spoke gently. "Don't turn her so sharp this time. I don't want you tipping over."

Something too good happened within her at his quiet admonition.

He stood in the twilight watching her again cut too sharply

around the pickets, holding his breath, releasing it only when she'd straightened the rig and was heading up the street. Then he clumped to the swing at the north end of the porch to wait for her. He braced his crutches in the corner and swung idly, surveying the porch, which was so typical of her. It was tidy, freshly painted, surrounded by a spooled rail that quit only where the wide steps gave onto the yard. At the opposite end was a pair of white wicker chairs with a matching table between them holding a sprawling fern. He thought of her while he swung, accompanied by the soft, jerking squeak of the ropes.

She rounded a corner down the street and he watched her come on, small and straight, and felt the strength of his healing muscles and knew he'd damn well better leave this place soon.

She started slightly when she saw him there in the shadows, one arm stretched carelessly along the back of the double seat. She wondered how it would feel to simply settle down in the lea of that arm and lean her head back against him and swing away companiably until full darkness fell and he should say, "It's time for bed now, Abbie."

But he was Jesse the ominous train robber, so she stood uncertainly at the top of the steps. Only, he did not look very ominous swinging away idly there. The ropes spoke a creaky complaint about his weight, and for a moment she remembered the awesomeness of it upon her. She dropped her eyes guiltily.

"Are you hungry?" she asked, unable to think of anything else to say.

"A little," he replied. He realized only too clearly what it was he was hungry for.

"Would cold chicken and bread be all right?"

"Sure. Why don't we eat it out here?"

"I don't think—" She cast a glance at the house next door, then seemed to change her mind. "All right. I'll get it." She left him swinging there, and when she returned with the tray he sensed her hesitation to approach him.

"Put it on the floor at our feet and come sit with me," he invited. "It's getting dark—nobody will see us." But her eyes skittered to the elbow slung along the back of the swing, and only when he lowered it did she set the tray down and perch beside him.

They nibbled silently, caught up by awareness, lashed into silence by the new tension which had sprung up between them.

They ate little. She told herself to take the tray back inside, but sat instead as if her legs had wills of their own.

He crossed his near ankle over his knee, dropped a dark hand over the boot to hold it there while each stroke of the swing now whispered his knee across Abbie's skirts. Her eyes were drawn to the sturdy thigh tight-wrapped in straining denim. She clenched her hand in the folds of her skirts to keep it from reaching out and resting upon that firm muscle which flexed repeatedly with each nudge of his heel upon the floor. She could almost feel how warm and hard that thigh would be, how sensual it would feel to run her palm along its long, inner side, to know the intimate shift of muscle as it moved with the swing. But she only stared at it while her unwieldy imagination did strange things to the low reaches of her stomach. A tightness tugged there, and queer trembles afflicted her most intimate parts. She sat there coveting that masculine thigh and becoming enamored with the mere touch of her own clothing against her skin.

He draped his wrist lazily over the back of the swing, never touching her, yet making her heart careen when she realized how close it hung to her shoulder.

"Well, I guess it's bedtime," he said quietly at last. Her pulses pounded and the blood beat its way up her cheeks. But he only removed his hand from the back of the swing and craned around for his crutches in the corner, then rose and positioned them, politely waiting for her to proceed him.

He managed the screen door, and when she passed before him into the parlor, asked behind her, "Do you want the inside door closed?"

She was afraid to look back at him, so continued toward the kitchen, answering, "No. It's a warm night, just hook the screen."

Jesse felt a sense of home, coming in with her this way, putting things in order for the night, and knew more than ever that it was time to move on. He shuffled through the dark in the direction of the kitchen.

"Where are the matches?" he asked.

Her voice came from someplace near the pantry door. "In the matchbox on the wall to the left of the stove."

He groped, found, struck a wooden tip and held it high. Abbie sprang into light, hovering in the pantryway with the tray pressed against her waist, and her eyes big and luminous in the lamplight. He put the chimney back on the lamp and looked across at her, tempted . . . oh so tempted.

For a minute neither knew what to say.

"I'll . . . I'll just set these dirty dishes in the pantry."

"Oh . . . oh, sure," he shrugged, looked around as if he'd lost something. "Guess I'll go out back then before bed." Resolutely, Jesse headed for the door, knowing he was doing the right thing. But as he was negotiating the dark steps he found her behind him holding the lantern aloft to illuminate his way. He swung around and looked up at her.

Unsmiling, she studied his face glowing red-gold below her, his hair blending with the backdrop of the night. The lantern caught the measureless depths of his eyes, like those of a cat impaled by a ray of direct light.

"Thanks, Abbie," he said quietly, ". . . good night." Then his arms flexed upon the crutches and he was gone, downyard, swallowed by the dark.

She put the pantry in order for the night, and still he hadn't come in. She went to the back screen and peered out. The moon had risen and she made out his shape by its pale white light, sitting in the backyard under the linden tree. His face was in lacy night shadow, but she made out his boots and the way one knee was raised with an arm slung over it.

"Jesse?" she called softly.

"Aha."

"Are you all right?"

"I'm find. Go to bed, Abbie."

When she did, she lay a long time listening, but never did hear him come back inside.

Chapter 12

THE FOLLOWING MORNING a grinning Bones Binley stood on Miss Abigail's front porch, looking like a jack-o'-lantern atop a knobby fence post, with his over-large head, gap-teeth, and protruding Adam's apple.

"Mornin', Mizz Abigail. Fine mornin'. Fine mornin'. This package . . . ah . . . come for you at the depot on yesterday's train, Mizz Abigail, but there wasn't nobody around to bring it on up, so Max he ast me to this morning."

"Thank you, Mr. Binley," she answered, opening the screen only enough to slip the package through, disappointing old Bones, who'd have given a half plug of tobacco to see just what was inside that box and the other half to see what that train robber was doing inside her house. But when Bones continued to grin at her through the screen, she added, "It was very obliging of you to deliver it to me, Mr. Binley."

She was the only person ever called him Mister that way.

"Sure thing, Mizz Abigail," Bones said almost reverently, nodding and shifting enormous feet while she wondered if she'd have to swat him off her porch with the screen door, like some pesky fly.

Once when they were younger Bones had bought Miss Abigail's basket at a Fourth of July picnic, and he'd never forgotten the taste of her sour cream cake and fried chicken, or her ladylike ways and the time she had him up to do a little repair work on the shingles and how she'd asked him in afterward for cake and coffee. But he could see now that he was no more going to get inside her house than any train robber was going to get inside her pants, which was after all what the whole town was buzzing about.

"How's that there robber feller doing?" he asked, lifting his battered hat and scratching his forehead.

"I'm not qualified to give a medical opinion on his state of health, Mr. Binley. If you want that information to pass around with your snuff down at the feedstore, I suggest you ask Doctor Dougherty."

Bones had just then worked up a good hock and was about to let 'er fly when Miss Abigail warned from her front door, "Do not leave your residue on my property, if you please, Mr. Binley!"

Well, by damn! thought old Bones, if she was talking about spit, why in tarnal didn't she just come right out and say spit? Maybe folks was right when they said she got a little uppity at times. But anyways, Bones waited till he got to the road before he laid a good gob. He wasn't gonna go messin' with her—nossir!—not old Bones. And unless he missed his guess, wasn't no man ever gonna mess with her, train robber or not!

The package was unmarked, except for a Denver postmark and her name and Stuart's Junction, Colorado. She did not recognize the handwriting. It was angular, tall, and made her heart race. In her entire life she might have gotten maybe three packages. There was one a long time ago that had brought the small picture frame she'd sent for, to hold her mother's and father's tintypes. Then there was the time she'd sent away for the bedpan when her father could no longer execute the walk to the backyard. This package now was Miss Abigail's third, and she wanted to savor its mystery as long as possible.

She shook it and it clunked like dried muffins in a pie safe. She saw Bones disappear down the street and on an impulse took the box back outside to the porch swing. She savored it for a long while before finally carefully removing the outside wrapper, keeping the paper in one piece to save away and treasure later. She shook the box again and even sniffed at it. But all it smelled like was the pages of an old book, papery and dry. She set it on her knees and ran a bemused hand over the lid and swung idly upon the swing, drawing out the delicious wonderment while curiosity welled beautifully in her throat. She took some moments to cherish the anticipatory feeling and file it away for future memory. Finally she lifted the lid and her breath caught in her throat. Nestled within, like two pieces of a jigsaw puzzle, was a pair of the most beautiful shoes she had ever seen. There was a folded note, but she reached for neither note nor shoes immediately, sat instead with her hand over her opened lips, remembering David Melcher's face as she had last seen it, stricken with regret.

At last she lifted the note in one hand and a single shoe in the other.

Oh my! she thought. Red! They are red! Whatever shall I do with a pair of red shoes?

But she examined the exquisite leather, soft as a gentian petal, so soft that she wondered how such supple stuff could possibly support a person's weight. They were buskin styled, with delicate lacets running from ankle to top and sporting heels shaped like the waists of fairies, concave and chic. Touching the chamois-soft texture, she knew without needing to be told that they were indeed made of kidskin, the finest money could buy. David, she thought, oh, David, thank you. And she pressed a shoe to her cheek, suddenly missing him and wishing he were here. She would have liked to put the shoes on while she read his note, but she could never put these scarlet shoes on where they might be seen. Oh, perhaps sometime in the privacy of her bedroom. But for now she laid the shoe back in the box beside its mate and read his note:

My Dear Miss Abigail,

I take the liberty—no, the honor—of sending the finest and newest pair of shoes from the shipment awaiting me when I arrived in Denver. It will please me to imagine them on your dainty feet as you snip nasturtiums and take them into your gracious home. I think of you in that setting and even now rue my rashness in speaking to you as I did. If you can find it in your heart to forgive me, know that I would have willed things to take a different course than they've taken.

> Yours in humility and gratitude,
> David Melcher

She'd thought thirteen years ago that she'd realized what a broken heart felt like, when she was spurned by the man she'd grown to love through all her growing years. But it felt now as if this sense of a thing lost before it was ever gained was sorrier than anything she'd suffered back then. Her heart stung at the thought that David Melcher pined for her—impossible as it seemed, herself being the age she was. Such a refined man, who was just what she'd been looking for for so many years, ever since Richard ran away. And now she had no way to reach him, to say, "Come back . . . I forgive you . . . let us begin from here." The shoebox told her nothing. It held no company name, no color or style markings. There was no clue as to whom he worked for. All she knew was that he'd mentioned Philadelphia and that this package had been posted in Denver. But they were big cities, Denver and Philadelphia, cities in which there were undoubtedly many shoe manufacturers, many hawkers. It would be impossible to find a man who did not even possess a permanent address. But at the thought of his lack of a residence, the words *Elysian Club* came back to her.

The Elysian Club! Phildelphia!

That was where he stayed when he went back there. With a leaping heart she knew she would write a thank you to him in care of the Elysian Club, Philadelphia, and just hope he would somehow receive it on one of his return trips, and maybe—just maybe—he would come back to Stuart's Junction some day and look her up.

"Abbie? What're you doing out there?" A tousled Jesse, fresh up, stood barefoot, bare-chested in the front door.

Excitement animated her voice as she bubbled, "Oh, Mr. Cameron, look at what has just arrived for me." She had eyes for nothing but the shoes, which he could not see yet. She brought the package into the front parlor, crossed, and laid it on the dining room table at the far end, the wrapping paper address-side-up so there could be no mistaking the shoes were meant for her.

Jesse hobbled over to see what it was. "Where did you order those from?" he asked, surprised when he saw the scarlet shoes, for they didn't seem at all the kind of thing she'd choose.

"I didn't order them. They are a gift from David Melcher."

Suddenly Jesse needed a second look, and after taking it,

decided he disliked the shoes wholeheartedly. "*David* Melcher? My, my, aren't we becoming informal all of a sudden? And shoes yet! How shocking, Miss Abigail."

"I find it rather endearing myself," she said, fingering the leather, her mind scarcely on what she was doing. "Not the kind of gift that just any man would choose."

Jesse could sense her excitement as she let her fingers flutter over the red leather, butterflylike, touching the laces, the tongue, the toes, almost reverently.

"You can wear 'em over town every time you need a pig's bladder from the butcher shop," he said testily, "or whenever you need to send a wire asking somebody to get rid of a gunslinger for you."

She was too happy to heed his attempt to snub the gift.

"Oh my, I fear I cannot wear them anyplace at all. They simply aren't—well, they're much too fine and elegant for Stuart's Junction."

A black scowl drew his eyebrows down. She was damn near fondling the red leather now, and her face wore a beatific expression while she raved on about the exquisite workmanship and the quality of the leather. He'd never seen her glow so before, or bubble this way. Her eyes were as blue and bright as her morning glories, and her lips were parted in a rare, pliant smile. Watching it, he wanted to smack those damn red shoes from her hands.

But suddenly Jesse realized that Abbie's hair was less than tidy and she was wearing an old, shapeless dark floral shirt with sleeves rolled up to her elbows and a dishtowel tied triangularly around her belly. She looked as ordinary as a scullery maid, and the effect was devastating. He found himself studying the knot of the dishtowel which rode the shallows of her spine.

"Oh, my heavens!" she said gaily, "you slept so late and here I stand gaping at these things while you're probably fit to starve." She plopped the cover back over the shoes and looked up to catch the dark frown on his face.

For a moment it seemed to Abbie that he'd grown taller overnight, but she suddenly realized why.

"Why, you're walking without crutches!" she exclaimed gladly. Then she thought, gracious, but he is tall! And immediately afterward, gracious, but he is only half-dressed! He was shirtless and barefoot, as usual, wearing nothing but the new dungarees. "Now, Doctor Dougherty said you must take it a little at a time," she scolded, to cover her flustration at the sight of his bare skin.

Her concern assuaged some of the nettlesome annoyance he'd felt over the shoes, and his anger faded.

"I'm starved. What time is it?" He rubbed his hard, flat belly, pleased to see her eyes skitter away.

"Approaching noon. You slept very late." She turned toward the kitchen and he followed.

"Did you miss me?" He gave the shoebox a last scathing look and eyed that knotted dishtowel as it lifted perkily, bustlelike, with each step she took. She had one of the trimmest backsides he'd ever seen.

"I hardly had time. I was busy doing the washing."

"Oh, so that's why you're dressed like a scullery maid. I don't mind saying it's a pleasant change."

Suddenly she became self-conscious and began unrolling one of her shirtsleeves, flicking the folds down to cover her exposed arms, and he wondered if she'd have left them rolled up were he David Melcher. The thought irritated him further.

"Dirty jobs do not magically get done," she said, all businessy again, efficiently buttoning up her cuffs, then reaching behind to untie her dishtowel. He was sorry to see it go as she set about preparing their noon dinner. There was no evidence of her having washed clothes in the kitchen, but outside he found lines strung now, holding bedding, dish-towels, and some skirts and blouses. Limping his way to the privy, he caught sight, too, of pantalets and chemises trimmed with eyelet, hidden as inconspicuously as possible behind the larger, more mundane pieces of laundry. The corset he'd imagined her in, giving her chronic gastric and emotional indigestion, was nowhere in evidence.

However, when he got back to the house he figured the reason it was not on the line was because it must be busily ↄinding her up in knots! Her waspish temperament had inexplicably returned. She started in on him the minute he walked in the door.

"I've asked you not to go about undressed that way, *sir!*" she stated tartly, obviously in a snit over a damn fool thing like that.

"Undressed!" He looked down at himself. "I'm not undressed!"

"Where is your shirt!"

"It's in the bedroom, for God's sake!"

"*Mister* Cameron, would you set aside your own offensive vernacular until you are once again in the sort of company that will appreciate it?"

"All right, all right, what bit you all of a sudden?"

"Nothing *bit* me, I just—" But she turned away without finishing.

"A minute ago you were all sloe-eyed over old Melcher's shoes and now—"

"I was *not* sloe-eyed!" She spun, eyes snapping, hands on hips.

"Huh!" he snorted, gripping the edge of the highboy behind him, tapping out a vexed rhythm with his fingertips. "He lit you up like a ball of swamp gas with those . . . those pieces of frippery!" He flung a disparaging hand toward the dining room.

Her eyebrows shot up. "Yesterday you were telling me to throw caution to the wind and feel things. Today you disparage me for a simple show of appreciation."

They stared at each other for a few crackling seconds before Jesse said the most absurd thing.

"But they're red!"

"They're what?" she asked, baffled.

"I said, they're red!" he roared. "The goddamn shoes are red!"

"Well, so what?"

"So . . . so they're red, that's all." He started pacing around in the corner by the pantry door, feeling silly. "What the hell kind of woman wears red shoes?" he squawked, forgetting that he'd just been admiring the way that dishtowel made her look like precisely the kind of woman who might wear red shoes.

"Did I say I wanted to wear them?"

"You didn't have to say it. The look on your face said it for you."

She pointed out the back door. "While I am trying to preserve some decorum around here, you limp out to the outhouse, naked as a savage, then have the audacity to scold me for thinking I should like to wear red shoes!"

"Let's get the issue straight here, *Miss* Abigail. You're not mad about me going out in the open without a shirt and shoes.

You're mad because I caught you looking sloe-eyed over those insufferable shoes!''

"And you're not mad because the shoes are red, you're mad because they're from David Melcher!''

"David Melcher!'' he squawked disbelievingly, almost in her ear as she thundered past him into the pantry. "Don't make me laugh!'' He followed right behind her, nose first, like a bloodhound. "If you think I'm jealous of a pantywaist like that—'' But just then she swung around and stepped on his bare toe. "Ouch!'' he yelped, while she didn't even slow down or say excuse me.

"You wouldn't get stepped on if you'd dress properly.'' She clapped some dishes on the table.

"The hell you say! You did that on purpose!''

"Maybe I did.'' She sounded pleased.

He nursed his toe against his calf. "Over nothing. I didn't do a damn thing this time!''

But she whirled on him, pointing an outraged finger at the backyard. "Nothing, you say? How dare you, sir, walk across my yard dressed like *that* and gape at my underthings in front of the whole town!''

His eyebrows shot up and a slow smile crept across his countenance, lifting one corner of his moustache before it lit up his mischievous eyes and he started laughing deep in his throat, then louder and louder until at last he collapsed onto a chair.

"Oh you . . . you . . . just . . . just shut up!'' she spluttered. "Do you want the whole town to hear you?'' She clapped herself down on the chair opposite and created a gross breach of etiquette for Miss Abigail McKenzie, serving herself without waiting for him. She whacked the serving spoon against her plate, splatting potatoes onto it while he sat there snickering. Finally she shoved a bowl in his direction and grunted, "Eat!''

He loaded his plate in between maddening chuckles while she felt like kicking his bad leg under the table. Finally he braced an elbow on the corner of the table, leaned near, and whispered very loudly, "Is it better if I whisper? This way the neighbors won't hear me.'' Even staring at her plate she could see that insufferable moustache right by her cheek. "Hey, Abbie, you know what I was looking for out there? Corsets. I wanted to see just how much rigging I'd have to get through before I hit skin.''

She dropped her fork and knife with a clatter and left her chair as if ejected from it, but he made a grab and caught her by the back of her skirt.

"Let me go!" She yanked at the skirt, but he hauled away and pulled her back between his spraddled thighs while her arms flailed ineffectually.

"How many layers are under there, Abbie?" he teased, trying to get an arm around her waist and pull her down to his lap. She yanked and slapped and tried to free her skirt but he hauled it in like lanyard, all the while chortling deep in his throat.

"Get away!" she barked while he got her up against his lap like a schooner against a piling. She battled frantically, then luffed around till she could push against his shoulder, still trying to control her skirt with the other hand.

His smile was wicked, his hands deadly, as he breathed hard in her ear, "Don't you wear petticoats, Abbie? Come on, let's see." They were a dervish of arms and hands and elbows and petticoats and knees by this time. He gained and she struggled. He captured and she flapped. He fended off a misaimed slap, feinting back expertly while she rapidly lost ground.

"You maniac!" she bellowed, clawing his fingers loose from her wrist.

"Come on, Ab, quit teasin'." He got her wrist again, tighter than before.

"Me! Let me go!" she squawked. But somehow he had her turned around facing him. He pulled her up against his crotch, her thigh against his vitals while she fell upon his stone-hard chest. But once more she yanked loose, spun in a half turn till his hands got her by the hips and took her into port again.

"God, can you scrap for such a hummingbird," he puffed. And as if to prove it she almost got away. But his powerful arm caught her waist and she felt her backside hauled unceremoniously against his lap. "Ugh!" he grunted when she hit his sore leg, but his grip held at her waist.

"Good!" she spit, "I hope I hurt you! Get your hand down! Leave my buttons alone!"

He had her from behind, cinched the arm tight around her little middle, grappling for the buttons at her throat with his other hand. He managed to get one undone while she struggled to snatch his hand away and contend with the other that snaked up her midriff to her breast.

"Come on, Abbie, I won't hurt you." Her struggle only seemed to amuse him further while the skirmish at her blouse front went on.

"I'll hurt you any way I can!" she vowed—a mosquito threatening a rhinocerous. "I warn you!" She struggled valiantly, breathless now, but he kept her pinned so tightly she couldn't get far enough away to do any damage.

"God, how I like you in this old faded shirt," he panted, and somehow managed to spirit a second button free while she tried to seize both of his hands and gain her freedom at the same time.

"You filthy louse . . . I hope they . . . hang you!" she grunted.

"If I hang . . ." he grunted back, "at least give me . . . one last . . . sweet memory to take al . . . along." He had one breast now and she twisted around violently while he ducked to avoid a flying elbow.

"Atta girl, Abbie, turn around here where I can get at you." His black moustache came swooping for her mouth, but she clutched a hank of hair at his temple and pulled with all her might.

"Ouch!" he yelped, and she yanked harder until suddenly, unexpectedly, he released her. Sprawled as she was, she went down at a full slide, landing on her knees with her mouth just above his navel. But her elbow caught him precisely in the spot where he'd been shot, and he gasped and stiffened back, arms outflung, as if she'd just crucified him to that chair. His throaty groan told her the battle was over.

She scrambled up out of his thighs, fastening her two neck buttons while his eyes remained closed, the lids flinching. His lips had fallen open, his tongue tip came out to ride the lower edges of his even, upper teeth, then he sucked in a long, pained breath and looked up at the ceiling, with his head still hanging backward. Limply he touched the hair at his temple, massaging it gingerly while she watched, quivering and wary. His arm flopped back down and he finally grunted, pulling himself up by degrees until he was L-shaped again. The silence in the room was rife as he leaned an elbow on either side of his plate and stared down at it as if some piece of food there had moved. She eased to her chair, sat with her hands in her lap, then listlessly picked up a knife that was stuck at a precarious angle into a mound of mashed potatoes. She cleaned it off against the edge of her plate and laid it down very carefully and still neither of them said anything. She tried a bite, but it seemed to stick in her throat. He raised his head and stared past her down the length of the house, out the front door. There was no use pretending to eat, so she carefully wiped her mouth, folded her napkin, laid it down precisely, as if awaiting her penance.

He knew now why he'd done it. It really came as no surprise to him to find that he was jealous, just that he should be so over a woman like her. Yet, never had he been able to make her smile, laugh, or twinkle as that pair of shoes from Melcher had done.

Her chair scraped back into the silence at the same moment he finally decided to speak.

"Abbie, I think—"

"What?" She halted, half up, plate in hand.

He stared out the far front door, not trusting himself to look at her. "I think I'd better get out of here before we do hurt each other."

She stared at the plate in her hand, suddenly very sorry she'd hurt him.

"Yes," she said meekly. "I think you had better."

"Would you get my crutches from the bedroom please?" he asked, very politely.

"Of course," she agreed, equally as polite, and went to get them. She wanted to say she was sorry, but thought he should say it first. He had started it. Silently, she handed him the sticks.

"Thank you," he said, again too politely, pulling himself to his feet, then stumping off toward his room, gingerly favoring the right leg again. There followed a long, deep sigh as he lowered himself to the bedsprings.

Abbie stared out the back door for the longest time, seeing nothing. Finally, she sighed and put the room in order, then crept off to her upstairs room to discard the floral blouse.

But she slumped to the edge of the bed disconsolately, burying her face in her hands. Oh, she was so confused by everything. Nothing seemed simple like it had before the two men had entered her life. She could no longer deny her attraction for Jesse. At times he could be so warm and sympathetic. Like yesterday, when she'd told him things she'd never told another living soul and had begun to trust him, only to have him do what he'd just done. Why couldn't he be like

David? David—so much more like her. David—a gentleman whose values ran parallel to hers. David—who had kissed her so sweetly on the stairs but would never have tried anything like Jesse had just pulled on that chair downstairs. But thinking of it, she felt that odd, forbidden exhilaration that would not be quelled. Why was she unable to resist the dark, foreboding charms that drew her into Jesse's web time and time again?

She tried to imagine her father ever carrying on with her mother in that fashion but simply could not. Why, her mother would have left home. Yet Abbie wondered now why her father and mother never touched or kissed. She had always assumed that their polite way was the way all well-bred married couples acted.

Abbie pressed her hands to her heated face, remembering her mother saying that all men were beasts. She remembered Richard tackling her in the livery stable one time and how she'd slapped him. She remembered Jesse grappling with her on that chair, and that night in the bed with his tongue all over her breasts and belly. She shivered, there in the heat of the upstairs bedroom, assuring herself that what she'd felt that night and today was fear and nothing more. For anything else would be sinful.

She pulled herself up sharply, changed into proper clothing, and made up her mind she must offer him some apology for hurting him and would go down and make lemonade, which would suffice if she could not bring herself to utter the words.

Chapter 13

SHE WAS JUST about ready to pour the lemonade when there was a knock at the front door. There, on the porch, stood a swarthy, well-dressed man of perhaps forty-five years. Everything from his cordoban shoes to his Stetson hat was impeccably crisp, clean, and correct. He doffed his hat with a flawlessly groomed hand and bowed slightly, adjusting a package he held beneath an arm.

"Good day. Miss Abigail McKenzie?"

"Yes."

"I was told in town that you have a Mr. DuFrayne here."

"DuFrayne?" she repeated, confused.

"Jesse DuFrayne," he clarified.

She was momentarily taken aback by the name. Jesse *DuFrayne*? Jesse DuFrayne. It rhymed with train and had a rhythmic, beat-of-the-rails motion to it. Of its own accord, the name repeated itself in her mind, as if steel drivers churned out the message:

> Jesse DuFrayne
> Rode in on a train . . .
> Jesse DuFrayne
> Rode in on a train . . .

Still, somehow she thought the name could not belong to the Jesse she knew. To lend him a genuine surname would be to afford him unwarranted validity.

"Is he here, Miss McKenzie?"

Abruptly she twitched from her musings.

"Oh, I'm sorry, Mr—?"

"Hudson. James Hudson, of the Rocky Mountain Railroad. We have, Miss McKenzie, as you've probably already guessed, a vested interest in Jesse DuFrayne."

So, she thought, Mr. Jesse DuFrayne is no train robber, is he not? This was the moment she had waited for; vengeance was hers. But it somehow lost its savor.

"Come in, Mr. Hudson, please do come in," she said, opening the screen and gesturing him inside. "I believe the man you're looking for is here. He refused to tell—"

But at that moment his voice came from the bedroom. "Hey, Doc, is that you out there? Come on in here."

A smile suddenly covered Mr. Hudson's face, and he made a move toward the voice, then halted—properly if impatiently—asking, "May I?"

She nodded and pointed to the bedroom door. "He's in there."

James Hudson did not conceal the fact that he was in an overjoyed hurry to hit that bedroom doorway. Six or seven long strides across the living room and their voices were booming.

"Jesse, Gol-damnit, how did you end up here?"

"Jim! Am I glad to see you!"

Abbie tiptoed timidly to the door. Jesse'd been shaving, but even through the suds she could tell that he had absolutely no fear of Jim Hudson, was instead elated to see him. To her amazement the two bear-hugged and affably pounded each other's backs.

"Goddamn if you aren't a sight for sore eyes!" DuFrayne exclaimed, pulling back.

"Look at yourself! I could say the same thing. Word came along the line that you'd been shot. What happened? Somebody take your moustache off with a stray bullet? It looks kind of ragged."

DuFrayne's laughter, genuine, spontaneous, filled the room while he glanced in the mirror he held. "I wish that was all a stray bullet had bothered."

"Yeah? What else got hit?"

"My right leg, but it's doing fine, thanks to Miss Abigail here. They hauled me off the R.M.R. coach and plunked me down here and she's been stuck with me ever since."

"Miss McKenzie, how can we thank you?" Jim Hudson asked, but as if to answer his own question lifted the package he'd brought and came to her, extending it. It was wrapped, but even so the shape of a bottle was evident. "This isn't much, but please accept it with my heartfelt thanks."

She stood in startled confusion, reached for his proffered gift with the hands of an automaton, quite stunned by what all this seemed to mean, but Hudson immediately turned back to DuFrayne.

"What happened, Jesse? We were worried as hell. You turned up missing and the boys down at Rockwell found your gear on the train, and no Jesse! Then somebody from the depot in Stuart's Junction wired down a description of an alleged robber they pulled off a train up here and it sounded like you: coal black moustache and tall as a barn door. I said to myself, if that's not Jess I'll eat my fifteen-dollar Stetson."

Jesse laughed again from behind the lather and sank back onto the bed where he'd been when Hudson came in. "Well, you can wear your fifteen-dollar Stetson out of here because I'm all right." He cast a cautious glance at Abbie. "Leg's been acting up a little this afternoon so I thought I'd sit down while I shave is all."

"So . . . what happened? Are you going to keep me in suspense all day?"

"No, not all day, but just a little longer. This shaving soap is drying up and starting to itch. Mind if I finish this first?"

"No, no, go ahead."

"Come on in, Abbie. No need to hover in the door. Jim, this is Abbie. She's done a damn fine job of keeping my carcass from rotting for nearly three weeks now. If it hadn't been for her, I'd be crow bait by this time. Miss Abigail McKenzie, meet Jim Hudson."

"Mr. Hudson and I met at the door. Won't you have a seat, Mr. Hudson?" she invited, pulling the rocker forward. "I'll leave you two alone."

"Wait a minute, will you, Abbie?" Jesse had again taken up razor and hand mirror but was having trouble executing everything at once, needing both hands for the straightedge. "Hold this damn thing, so I can finish." The request was made so amiably that she forgot to take offense and came to do his bidding.

Watching the two of them, Jim Hudson thought this little domestic scene quite unlike his friend Jesse and wondered what had taken place around here during the last few weeks.

"Jess, what in the heck happened to your moustache? Looks like you took the blade to it," he observed. "I never thought I'd live to see the day."

Jesse's and Abbie's eyes met briefly over the mirror before he replied, "Neither did I. I just decided I'd see what I looked like plain-faced. I guess you can tell what I thought of myself. One day without it and I was growing it back as fast as possible. Abbie agrees I look best with a moustache too."

She felt her face flush and was grateful that her back was to Jim Hudson. Jesse swabbed off his face, then his eyes merrily met hers again while she knew a profound confusion at the very different way he always treated her before others, always respectful, hiding any trace of her transgressions, blaming only himself. What manner of man is this, she wondered, while his eyes danced away again.

Shaving done, Jesse stayed on the bed while the men continued talking.

"What's wrong with your hand, Jess?"

"It got jimmied up somehow on that train."

"Come on, I've waited long enough. Tell me what happened here."

"There's nothing much to tell. It was a damn fool mistake is all. I was headed up to Rockwell, as you know . . ." While Jesse told his account of the incident on the train, Abbie leaned over the bed to collect his shaving equipage. As she did, he absently laid a hand on her waist, then gave it a light pat as she straightened and moved away. Jim Hudson noted the touch with interest. The heedless geture was as intimate as a caress might have been, for while he did it, Jess kept right on talking, and Jim was certain he was oblivious of the fact that he'd touched the woman at all. Hudson did a good job of concealing his surprise. Miss McKenzie wasn't Jess's type at all. It hadn't taken more than thirty seconds at her front door for Hudson to recognize that fact. He watched her leave the room, puzzled by what he'd just witnessed.

While Jesse was unconscious of what he'd done, Abbie was not. The spot on her spine where his palm had rested seemed afire. In her entire life no man had ever laid a hand upon Abigail McKenzie in so casual a fashion. It was totally different from the many ways in which Jesse DuFrayne had touched her before: sometimes teasing, sometimes daring, sometimes angry, but always for a reason. No, this touch was different. It was the kind she'd wondered about between her parents, the kind she'd never seen between them, and it raised her bloodbeat by its very offhandedness.

All the while she prepared more lemonade in the kitchen, the thought rang through her mind—Jesse DuFrayne has just touched the small of my back before his friend . . .

In the bedroom, Jim Hudson said, "Now listen, Jess, we'll have all of this straightened out in no time. You know there's no beef with the railroad." He laughed, shook his head good-naturedly, and continued. "Why, hell, we know you weren't robbing any train. But this Melcher fellow is raising a stink. He's up in arms and out to sue us for everything he can get, because of his permanent disability."

"Just what do you think he'll get?"

"We'll find out tomorrow. I've got a meeting set up right here in town for noon and we'll settle it then if we can. Melcher will be coming in, but I'll be there to represent the railroad, so you don't need to come unless you want to, of course, and only if you're feeling up to it. Melcher will have his lawyer present, I'm sure. It'll be best to settle this thing with as little publicity as possible, don't you agree?"

"I agree, Jim, but it still riles me to think what that little shrimp can get by pointing an accusing finger at the railroad and walk away two days later while I lie here with a hole as big as a goose egg blown in me."

"And that's the main thing you should be concerned with. Let me handle the legal stuff. Hell, everybody's more worried about you than about what Melcher plans to ask for as a payoff. He'll probably turn out to be more bluff than threat anyway. But how about you? Just how is that leg healing?"

"Oh, it's stiff as hell, so's the hand, but I couldn't have been luckier if the shot had blown me straight into the arms of Doc Dougherty—he's the local medic. Abbie's got remedies up her sleeve that Doc Dougherty never dreamed of. He fixed me up that first day, but it was Abbie who kept me alive afterward."

"Which reminds me," Hudson put in, "did she get our

message saying we'd compensate her for putting up you and Melcher?''

"She got it . . . and Jim?" He lowered his voice, even though they'd been talking in low tones already. "See that she gets plenty. I've been a regular son of a bitch to her."

In the kitchen Miss Abigail heard a burst of laughter, though she didn't hear what prompted it.

"I take it you're impressed with the lady?" Jim Hudson asked quietly, with one eyebrow raised.

"Have you ever seen a lady that didn't impress me, Jim?"

"Hell, I don't think I've ever seen you with a *lady* before, Jess." There was good humor written all over both of their faces.

"I admit she's something of an oddity for me, but all in all I'm not having a half bad time of it here, other than the fact that she considers me a robber of trains, a defiler of women, a teller of lies, and the blackest of blackguards. And she's doing her damnedest to reform me. I put up with it because I like her cooking—watery broth, slimy eggs, and lethal liver." Jesse laughed, remembering it all.

"Sounds like she's just what you've always avoided, Jess— a straight woman. Maybe she's just what you need."

"What I need, James-Smart-Boy-Hudson, is a train out of here, and the sooner the better. I'll be at that meeting tomorrow whether Doc turns me loose or not. I thought you were Doc when you came in. He's supposed to give me my walking papers, so to speak. I'm already pretty handy on those crutches, though."

"Well, don't rush it, Jess. I'll have to look up this man Dougherty, too, while I'm in town. I expect you ran up a bill with him too, huh?"

"I'm still running it, but I knew you'd come along after me and pick up the bill."

Hudson laughed. "Say, the boys up in Rockwell want to know what to do with your gear."

"Is it okay, Jim?"

"Intact, I assure you. Everything. They stored it all in the line shack up there."

"In the line shack! Hell, those galoots will have every one of my plates shattered. I want them out of there. Are you going up that way?"

"No, I'm headed back to Denver again after the meeting

tomorrow. You know we're listening to every mayor of every mining town in this state beg for a spur line to get their ore out. We can't build 'em fast enough, so hurry and get well."

"I'll trust your judgment on that, Jim. Just let me know what's up because I'm already tired of this leisure life. As soon as Doc even relaxes his grizzled old eyebrows my way, I'll be up and gone from here back to the railhead. I just want to make damn sure my gear is safe in the meantime."

"I could have Stoker bring it down on the supply train," Hudson suggested with a knowing grin.

"God, no! Save me from Stoker!" They both laughed. "He does all right with steel and wood, but I'd just as soon have my gear rolled down the side of the mountain as brought down in Stoker's engine. Just leave it there for the time being. Maybe I'll think of something. I might even make it out of here with you tomorrow. Who knows?"

"Well, rest up, boy. I have this Doc Dougherty to see yet, and as long as I'm up here, I may as well see if the depot agent has any complaints on this new spur. I guess I'd better be going, Jess. One way or another, I'll see you before I leave town."

As Hudson prepared to take his leave, Miss Abigail appeared in the doorway with a tray. "May I offer you a glass of lemonade before you leave, Mr. Hudson?"

"I think we've been enough trouble to you already, Miss McKenzie. I'm the one who must offer you something before I leave. How much do I owe you for your care of the two men?"

Regardless of how many times she had reminded Jesse that she'd taken him in only for the money, when offered payment now she became disconcerted.

Jesse could read her discomfiture over Jim's question, saw her reluctance to put a dollar value on what she'd done. Like many other subjects, money was an indelicate subject for a lady to discuss. "Give the lady a fair price, Jim."

"Just what do you think your hide is worth, DuFrayne?"

The two of them exchanged a look of amused conspiracy before Jess answered, "I don't know what my hide is worth, but a glass of Abbie's lemonade is worth a thousand bucks any day."

"In that case, I'll have to try a glass before I leave," Jim Hudson said, smiling now at Abbie.

"I shall pour one for you then," Abbie offered, uncomfortable before their obvious teasing.

"Where will you take it, Mr. Hudson?" she asked.

"How about on your front porch, Miss McKenzie? Will you join me?"

Why did she glance at Jesse first before answering, as if she needed his permission to sit on the porch with another man?

"Go ahead, Abbie, you deserve a rest," he said, noting the pink in her cheeks. "Jim, you big galoot, thanks a hulluva lot for coming."

Hudson approached the bed and the two shook hands again, Hudson squeezing the back of Jess's as he said, "Get your bones out of here and back on those tracks, do you hear? And don't give the lady any fuss while you're doing it. That's an order!"

"Get the hell out of here before that lemonade evaporates in this heat." Then as the two left the room, he called after them, "See that you use your best manners out on the front porch, Jim. Miss Abigail is a lady of utmost propriety."

The north end of Miss Abigail's porch was in cool shadow now in midafternoon. Hudson saw the slatted wooden swing there but gestured Abbie instead to the opposite end, where the wicker chairs were. His manners showed in everything he did, she thought, even in his choosing separate chairs in the beating sun rather than the more intimate double swing in the inviting shade. He remained on his feet until she was seated. She noted how he pulled his sharply creased trousers up at the knees as he took the opposite chair.

"I take it Jesse has been less than a model patient," he opened.

"He was gravely wounded, Mr. Hudson, hardly expected to live. It would be difficult for anyone to be a model patient under those circumstances." Once said, she didn't know why she had defended Jesse that way, just as he had her.

"I think you're tiptoeing around the mulberry bush, Miss McKenzie, but I know Jess better than that. You've earned every penny you get. I fear he's not one who takes to coddling and being cooped up too gracefully. In his own element he's a damn fine man, the best there is."

"Just what is his element, Mr. Hudson?"

"The railroad, of course."

"So he does work for the railroad?"

"Yes, and a damn fine job he does."

Hearing it, Abbie's senses whirled. So it was true after all. With an effort she kept her hand from fluttering to her throat.

"Your loyalty does him credit, Mr. Hudson, since you yourself seem to be a respectable sort." Taking in his flawless elegance, his politeness, his obvious admiration of Jesse DuFrayne, she felt overcome by the swift shift of her patient's status.

"Men earn respect in different ways, Miss McKenzie. If I'm respected, it's for different reasons than he is. Take my word for it, Jess DuFrayne is a gem in the rough, and there's not a man on the R.M.R. line that'll say different."

"Just what has he done to earn that respect?" She wondered if he could see the glass trembling in her hand.

"I hear rebuttal in your tone, Miss McKenzie, and I'm thinking he's given you little reason to see good in him. I'd do him an injustice to list his merits. You'll only believe them if you discover them yourself. If you ever get a chance to see his photographs, study them well. You'll see more than sepia images . . . you'll see where his heart lies."

Funny, she had never thought of Jesse as having a heart before.

"Yes, I shall, Mr. Hudson, if I ever see them." He *is* a photographer, she was thinking as wings seemed to beat about her temples, he really is!

"Jess was right," Jim Hudson said, placing his empty glass on the wicker table between them. "This lemonade is worth a thousand dollars a glass on a day like today."

"I'm glad you enjoyed it."

"If there's anything you need while he's here, you have only to say the word and it's yours."

"How very gracious of you, sir."

"I'm sure if our graces were held up for comparison, mine should be found sadly lacking beside yours. Good day, Miss McKenzie. Take care of him for me." Jim Hudson looked at the front door as he said it.

That curiously heartfelt remark put the final touch of confusion upon Miss Abigail's already confounded emotions. She had thought Jim Hudson had come to her door to mete out justice, but instead he had vindicated the man she had repeatedly called "robber." Watching Hudson's trouser legs as he walked off down the dusty road, she was shaken anew by the revelations regarding Jesse Cameron-DuFrayne.

Once again, the ironic rhyme came to her out of nowhere:

> Jesse DuFrayne
> Rode in on a train . . .

She could not stand out here on the porch indefinitely. She had to go in and face him. But what could she say? She seemed to be having great difficulty breathing and could feel the blood welled up to her hairline, her pulse clicking off the passing seconds as memories came hurtling back, memories of the countless times she'd taunted him because he was a train robber. She tried to compose herself but found that she was feeling inexplicably feminine, and somehow very vulnerable. How he must have laughed to himself all these days, she thought. And what is he thinking now?

She opened the door silently, stepped before the umbrella stand to check her reflection, but her hand paused before it reached her hair. There on the seat lay a rectangular piece of paper. Something seemed to warn her, for her hand hesitated, then finally picked it up.

There followed an audible gasp.

It was a check boasting the payee's name across the top in block letters: ROCKY MOUNTAIN RAILROAD, DENVER, COLORADO. It was made out to Abigail McKenzie in the amount of one thousand dollars!

Her stomach began to tremble and the paper quivered in her fingers. She looked up at the bedroom doorway, suddenly more afraid than ever to face him again.

One thousand dollars! Why, it would take her two years or more of waiting tables at Louis Culpepper's to earn such a sum. Just what was this Jesse DuFrayne that the railroad would put out money like this for his safekeeping? Utterly befuddled, she gaped at the check, knowing she'd earned not even a quarter of this amount. She remembered the knowing looks exchanged by Jesse and Jim Hudson and the words, "A glass of Abbie's lemonade is worth a thousand bucks any day." More confused than ever, she swallowed back the lump in her throat.

"Abbie, is Jim gone?" he called.

"Yes, he is, Mr.—" But what should she call him now? She could still not connect him with his new name, or with his old.

Everything had suddenly changed. She looked at herself in the mirror, saw her flushed face, the paper in her hand, the confusion in her eyes, and stood rooted, not knowing, suddenly, how to act before the man on the other side of the wall. He had a real name and a very respectable job and a very impressive friend, plus a whole railroad full of cohorts who apparently respected him immensely. But all that seemed secondary to the fact that his being shot had had enough impact to cause the railroad to pay her grandly for his care.

How should she act?

She had called him Mr. Cameron, train robber for so long that it was perplexing to suddenly have to change her opinion, which—she admitted now—had been largely based upon the supposition that he was guilty as accused. But then, how many times had he himself implied he was an outlaw? Why, just yesterday he'd said he wouldn't be around long enough for it to matter what she told him about herself and . . . and Richard. She understood now that he'd been toying with her, implying that it was justice which would come to take him, when he'd known all along it was Jim Hudson.

With a sinking feeling, she recalled all those other things— the fighting and kissing and pulling the gun on each other and the terrible ways they'd goaded and hazed. Was he right about all that? Had she lost her sense of decency thinking he, the train robber, was the indecent one responsible?

Only he was no robber.

But she suddenly came to her senses, realizing she could treat him no differently than she had before James Hudson's visit. He was not instantly exonerated of all he'd put her through! But she held a thousand dollars in her unsteady hand, and deny it though she might, it *did* exonerate him in some way.

Her heart thumped crazily as she approached his room and found Jesse sitting on the floral cushions of the window seat, looking so black and brown against all those yellows and greens, so masculinely out of place in his dungarees and unbuttoned shirt. He was watching Jim Hudson walk back uptown and didn't know she stood there observing him. She swallowed thickly, for he looked too handsome and excusable and she wanted him to look neither. He dropped the curtain, absently scratched his bare chest, and her eyes followed the lean fingers that tracked across his skin. At last she cleared her throat.

He looked up, surprised. "Oh, I probably shouldn't sit here, huh?" He moved as if to rise.

"No, you're fine. It's cool there between the windows, stay where you are."

He settled back down. "Well, come on in. Maybe you're not afraid to now." But all traces of teasing were gone from his voice and eyes, and she suddenly wished they would return and ease this dread fascination she felt for him.

"I . . . I still am," she admitted. But neither of them smiled. "I want to say 'Why didn't you tell me,' only—silly as it seems—you did."

He was gracious enough not to rub it in, and now all she wished was that he would. It would be far preferable to this strained seriousness. All he said was, "I could use a glass of lemonade too, Abbie. Would you mind getting me one, please?"

"How can I mind? After all, it *is* paid for now." She felt his eyes upon her, and her hands shook as she poured the drink. Who are you? her mind cried out. And why? She was totally disturbed by the change she sensed in him since Jim Hudson left. He accepted the glass, thanked her, took a swallow, and leaned forward, bracing his elbows on his knees, staring at her in silence.

"Before I say anything else," she began nervously, "I want to make it explicitly clear that I did not hurt you intentionally in the kitchen before, and . . . and the reason I say so now has nothing whatever to do with whether or not you hold up trains for a living."

"That's nice to know. And of course I believe you. You're a most honorable person, Abbie." His eyes seemed to delve into her very depths.

"And how about yourself?"

"Sit down, Abbie, for God's sake . . . there in your little rocker, where I can talk to you." She hesitated, then sat, but hardly relaxed. "Every damn thing I ever told you about myself is true. I never lied to you."

"Jim Hudson is the friend of whom you spoke? The one who left New Orleans with you when you were twenty?"

He nodded, then stared out the window, disturbed anew by this woman and wishing he were not.

"He's very personable," she admitted, looking down into her glass, then added in the quietest of tones, "and very rich."

He turned his hazel-flecked eyes on her again but said nothing.

"I simply cannot accept a thousand dollars. It's far too much."

"Jim doesn't seem to think so." Her eyes met his directly.

"I don't think Jim alone decided."

"No?" His expression was noncommittal. He raised the glass to his lips as if it really didn't matter to him. She caught herself watching his full mouth upon the rim of the glass, his dark, dark moustache, which he brushed with a forefinger after he drank.

"Who are you?" she asked when she could stand it no longer.

"Jesse DuFrayne at your service, ma'am," he returned, raising the glass as if toasting her in introduction.

"That's not what I meant and you know it."

"I know." He now made a deep study of the lemonade. "But I don't want you to have to reestablish your commitment to me in any way, which may happen if I suddenly become a real person to you."

She drew a deep, ragged breath. "You are a real person to me and you know it, so I may as well have it all."

He continued studying the glass intently, swirling it so the liquid eddied into a whirlpool, leaving transparent bits of lemon meat on its sides. "I don't want to be a real person to you. Let me put it that way then." His disburbing eyes challenged as he at last raised them and looked directly into hers. "But nevertheless, you already know what I am. I'm a photographer, just like I said."

"Hired by James Hudson?"

He took a long pull while looking over the rim of the glass, then dropped his eyes as he swallowed, and said, "Yup."

"Why should the railroad protect you if all you are is a picture taker?"

"I guess they must like my stuff."

"Yes, they certainly must. I'll be anxious to see it, if I'm allowed. Your photos must be something really extraordinary."

"Not at all. They're graphic, but the only thing about them that might be considered extraordinary is the fact that they depict railroad life as it really is."

"That's not what you said the other night."

He smiled for the first time, a little crookedly. "Oh well . . . that's the one time I may have lied just a little. But you can judge for yourself if you ever see them."

"And will I?" she dared, her heart in her throat.

"It's hard to say. Jim and I are going to tie up some loose ends around here tomorrow." He braced a dark arm upon the window frame and studied the road beyond it. "Then I'll be leaving town."

No, not yet! her thoughts cried silently. Already she felt an emptiness, realizing this was unwarranted after all the times she'd wished him gone. Sober eyes still on the road, he added, "If I ever get the chance to drop back in and show you my photographs, I'll be sure to do it."

Sadly she knew he never would. "Are you sure you're well enough to travel?"

He flicked a glance her way. "Well, you want me out of here, don't you?"

"Yes, I do," she lied, then finished truthfully, "but not hurting."

His eyes moved to her face and their expression grew momentarily soft. "Don't worry your head over me, Abbie. You've done all the worrying about me that you'll have to."

"But you've paid me too highly for it," she claimed. He noted her stiff posture on the rocker, the hands clutched around her glass as if still scared to death of him. He supposed she suspected the real truth about him, but leaving would be easier if he never verified it.

"It was the railroad who paid you, not Jim or me," he said convincingly.

"I know. It was just a figure of speech. I only meant it was too much."

"How much would you say my life is worth?" he asked, just to see what she'd say, knowing now how much it mattered that she value him in some way.

Her eyes skimmed the room in a semicircle, ended up studying the glass in his hand. "More than a glass of lemonade . . ." But at last her composure slipped. "Oh, I don't know," she sighed and slumped, resting her forehead on a hand, studying her lap.

"How much would you say it was all worth—all the things you had to do to save my life? I never really did find out for sure everything you did. Some of it I knew that night when I had you—" His eyes went to the bed, then he abruptly looked out the window again. Damn, but the woman did things to his head! Staring out unseeingly at the summer afternoon he said gruffly, "Abbie, I'm damn sorry about it all."

Her head snapped up to study his profile. She saw him swallow, his Adam's apple rising, settling back down. He seemed intrigued by that yard out there, which was fine, for her face was burning and her own mouth and eyes seemed suddenly filled with salt.

"I . . . I'm sorry too, Mr. D . . . DuFrayne," she got out.

Palm braced against the window frame, he turned his head to look across his biceps, resting his lips there against his own skin while studying her. Then he said one last, quiet time, from behind that tan arm, "Jesse . . . the name is Jesse." He wanted somehow to hear her say it, just once, now that she knew he was no criminal.

She lifted her eyes to his face, searching for a trace of humor, finding none this time, finding only that quiet intensity which threatened to undo her. The name hung in the air between them, and she wanted to echo it, but had she done so they'd both have been lost, and in that poignant moment they knew it. Her eyes traveled the length of that muscular arm, lingering at the point where his lips must be. His moustache glanced darkly back at her from behind the arm. It took a perceptive eye by now to tell that it had ever been shaved: Mr. Hudson knew this man very well to discern it. So, must he now know equally as well all those inner qualities he'd hinted at? Abbie wondered.

Minutes ago, studying Jesse from the doorway, it had been obvious that he followed his friend's progress down the street as if anxious to follow him out of here, back to the brawling, tough railroad life the two had shared for many years. She had absolutely no business wishing he didn't have to go quite yet.

The silence grew long and strained, but at last he dropped his arm from the window frame and glanced around the room, surveying it fully as if for the final time. "I want to thank you for the use of your room, Abbie. It's pretty. A real lady's room. I imagine you'll be glad to get back into it again."

"I haven't been uncomfortable upstairs," she said inanely.

"It must be a lot hotter up there these nights than down here.

Sorry I put you out." Then he looked at the small double oval
picture frame. He reached to pick it up. "Are these your
parents?"

"Yes," she answered, following the frame with her eyes,
watching a tan finger curve and tap it thoughtfully.

"You don't look much like her. More like him."

"People always said I looked like him and acted like her." It
was out before she realized what she'd said. The room grew
quiet. Jesse cleared his throat, studied the picture, bounced it
on his palm a time or two, then it hung forgotten in his fingers
as he leaned forward and spoke to the floor between his feet,
his tone as near emotional as she'd ever heard it.

"Abbie, forget what I said about your mother. What the
hell—I mean . . . I didn't even know her."

She stared at the tintype and the familiar hand which held it.
A lump lodged in her throat and tears formed on her lids.
"Yes . . . yes you did. You knew her better than I did, I
think."

He raised his startled eyes while his elbows came off his
knees in slow motion and his muscles seemed to strain toward
her even though he never left the edge of the window seat. For
a heart-stopping moment she thought he would. She saw the
battle going on in him while he sat poised in indecision. He
uttered then the familiar name he'd spoken so often to tease
her, but it came out now with gruff emotion.

"Abbie?"

The way he said it made her want to impress the word into a
solid lump to carry in a locket maybe, or to press between the
pages of a sonnet book. She should correct him, but those days
when she'd chided him seemed part of a misty forever ago, for
light years seemed to have passed during this conversation.
Here, now, with her name fresh on his lips, with his dark
troubled eyes seeming to ask her questions best left unan-
swered, with his black moustache unbroken by smile, she
silently begged him not to look as if he too hurt.

"Abbie?" he said again, soft as before: too beautifully
threatening. And she shivered once, then broke the spell which
should not have been cast in the first place.

"I have at least two more meals to feed you, Mr. DuFrayne,
and not a thing in the house resembling meat. I'd best walk
over town before the butcher shop closes. What would you
like?"

His eyes pored over her face, then slowly, thankfully, the old hint of humor returned to his lips. "Since when have you bothered to ask?"

"Since the buttermilk," she answered, knowing the exact moment.

He laughed lightly, enjoying her immensely, as he so often could. She was a pretty little thing, he had to admit as he scanned her crisp, high collar and swept-back hair. She, in turn, enjoyed his swarthy handsomeness and the imposing breadth of partially exposed muscle before her.

"Ah yes, the buttermilk," he remembered, shaking his head in amusement. They both realized the buttermilk had been a turning point.

"And for your supper?" she asked.

He allowed his warm smile to linger upon her bewitching eyes. His glance, of its own accord, lowered to her breasts, then raised again.

"I'll let you choose," he said, very unlike the Jesse she'd grown used to.

"Very well," she returned, very like the Miss Abigail he'd grown used to.

When she rose, her knees felt curiously watery, as if she'd run a long way. Yet she ran again, though her steps were slow and measured as ever. She ran from the smile in Jesse's eyes . . . to the umbrella stand, to arm herself with a daisy-trimmed hat and a pair of gloves that bore smudges of dirt from leather reins and a creek bank.

Chapter 14

THE TOWN WAS buzzing with the news. Miss Abigail knew it. She sensed eyes peering at her from behind every window of the boardwalk. But she carried herself proudly, flouncing into the meat market as if unaware of all the curious stares following her.

"Why, Mizz Abigail," Gabe Porter plunged right in. "What do you think about that man up to your house turning out not to be a train robber atall? Isn't that something? Whole town's talking about this railroad feller that come in today to pay off your patient's debts. Seems we had him all wrong. Seems he works for the railroad after all. What do you think of that!"

"It's of little interest to me, Mr. Porter. What he is has no bearing on how he is. He is not fully healed and shall be under my care for one more day before he's ready to leave Stuart's Junction."

"You mean you're gonna keep him up there even though he ain't got to stay if he don't want to now?"

Miss Abigail's eyes snapped fire enough to precook the meats hanging on the hooks of the huge tooled iron rack on Gabe's wall. "What exactly are you implying, Mr. Porter? That I was safe with him as long as he was a felon but that I'm not now that he's a photographer?"

That didn't make much sense, even to Gabe Porter. "Why, I didn't mean nothin' by it, Miss Abigail. Just lookin' out for a maiden lady's welfare is all." Gabe Porter couldn't have cut her any deeper had he chopped her a good one with his greasy meat cleaver, but Miss Abigail's face showed no trace of the stark ache his words struck in her heart.

"You may best look after my welfare by cutting two especially thick beef steaks, Mr. Porter," she ordered. "Meat is what builds one up when one has been weakened. We owe that man some good red meat after the blood he lost because of this unfortunate incident, wouldn't you agree?"

Gabe did as ordered, all the while remembering how Bones Binley had said that Gem Perkins had said that Miss Abigail had been out in a trap with that photographer, riding in the hills, and right after young Rob Nelson had seen the man prancing around Miss Abigail's backyard dressed in nothing but pajama pants, mind you. And from the sound of it, he had took to having presents shipped in to her by railroad express from Denver. It had to be from him. Hell, she didn't know nobody else from Denver.

But if Gabe Porter was white-faced at all that, he had the jolt of his life still coming. For on his way home Gabe heard that on her way home Miss Abigail had stopped over to the bank and deposited a check for no less than one thousand dollars, and it drawn against the Rocky Mountain Railroad Company, which, everyone in town knew by that time, the man up at her house took "pitchers" for.

Coming around the corner between the buildings, Miss Abigail was disconcerted to see Jesse waiting for her on the porch swing again. She controlled the urge to glance up and down the street and see if anyone else had seen him there. Ah, at least he has his shirt on, she thought, and coming nearer saw that it was buttoned nearly to the point of decency. But when she mounted the steps she saw that his feet were bare and one of his legs half slung across the swing seat, causing it to go all crooked when he set it on the move.

"Hi," he greeted. "What did you decide on?"

Sheepishly remembering the bugging eyes of Blair Simmons as she slid the check under his cage at the bank only minutes ago, she answered, "I kept it."

Confused, he asked, "What?"

"I kept it," she repeated. "I deposited it at the bank. Thank you."

He laughed and shook his head. "No, that's not what I meant. I meant what did you decide on for supper." The thousand dollars didn't seem to faze him at all. He scarcely seemed to give it a second thought, as if he really thought it was her due, and that was the end of that.

"Steak," she answered, pleased now at how he played down that thousand.

"Goddamn, but that sounds good!" he exclaimed, slapping his stomach, rubbing it, rumpling his shirt and stretching all at once.

All of a sudden she found it impossible to grow peeved with him for his coarse language, and harder yet to keep from smiling. "You are incorrigible, sir. I think that if you stayed around here any longer I might be in danger of failing to note your crassness."

"If I stayed here any longer, you'd either have to convert me or run me out on a rail—probably right beside you, though. I am what I am, Miss Abigail, and steak sounds goddamn good right now."

"If you said it in any other way, I'm not sure I would believe you any more, Mr. Came—Mr. DuFrayne." Her smile was broad now, and charmed him fully.

It was infinitely easier exchanging light badinage with him again. This, she knew, would get them safely through the evening ahead. But just then he swung his foot to the floor, leaned his dark, square palms on the edge of the seat, and with the now familiar grin all over one side of his face, said quietly, "Go fry the steak, woman."

And after all they'd been through, it was the last thing in the world that should have made her blush.

The sun fell behind the mountains while the steak was frying, and the front porch was cool and lavender-shadowed. Jesse DuFrayne sat there listening to the sounds of children playing "Run Sheep Run," drifting in on the wings of twilight. From the shrill babble he could hear occasional childish arguments: "No he didn't! . . . Yes, he did. . . . He din't neither! . . ." Then a swell of argument again before the squabble was apparently settled and the sheep ran again in a peaceful fold. The smell of meat drifted out to him, augmented by an iron clank every now and then and an occasional tinkle of glassware. He got up lazily and limped inside and there she was, coming out of the pantry with a heap of plates and glasses and cups balanced against her midriff. They pulled her blouse tight against her breasts and he admired the sight, then raised his eyes to find she'd caught him at it. He grinned and shrugged.

"Can I help?" he asked.

Oh, he was just full of surprises tonight, she thought. But she handed him the stack of dishes anyway. When he turned toward the kitchen table she surprised him.

"No, not there. Put them in the dining room. That table is never used anymore. I thought we might tonight."

His moustache teased. "Is it going to be a little going-away party then?"

"Rather."

"Whatever you say, Abbie." He moved off toward the dining room.

"Just a minute, I'll get the linen."

"Oh? It's a linen occasion too?"

She came with a spotless, stiff cloth and asked, "Can you pick up those candlesticks too?"

"Sure." He got the pair off the table, along with his other burden, and held everything while she snapped the cloth out in the air. He watched it billow and balloon and fall precisely where she wanted it to.

"Why, that's the damnedest thing I've ever seen!"

"What is?" she asked, leaning over to smooth the already perfect surface of the cloth.

"Well if I tried that, the thing would probably go in the opposite direction and carry me off with it." He cocked his head and hung on to his stack of dishes and watched her little butt as she leaned over the table edge that way, ironing wrinkles with her hands. He snapped back up straight when she turned around.

"Do you want to finish this or stand holding those things all night?"

"I want to see you do that once more," he said.

"What?"

"Flip that thing up and get it to land exactly centered like that. I'll make you a bet that you can't do it again."

"You're insane. And you're going to smash the rest of my dishes if you don't set them down."

"What do you wanna bet?"

"Now you want me to take up gambling on top of everything else?"

"Come on, Abbie, what will you put up? One throw of the cloth."

"I've put up with you, that's enough!" She smiled engagingly.

"How about one photographic portrait against one good home-cooked meal?" he suggested, thinking it would bring him back to Stuart's Junction again with a plausible excuse for coming.

What in the sam scratch got into Abigail McKenzie she couldn't say, but the next thing she knew, she was taking that tablecloth back off the table, flapping it high again while he watched. Of course, the cloth landed crooked this time . . . and the next . . . and the next . . . and by then they were both laughing like loons when it really wasn't *that* hilarious!

The dishes clinked against Jesse's chest as he mirthfully teased, "See, I told you you'd never be able to do it again with one toss. I win."

"But I did it the first time, so it doesn't matter. It was hardly fair after all the air currents were stirred up. Anyway, what am I doing here flapping a tablecloth like a fool?"

"Damned if I know, Abbie," he quipped, and finally set his stack down.

And for the first time in her life she thought, damned if I know either.

"I'd better turn those steaks," she said, and went back to the kitchen.

He followed in a moment with the flat-bottomed glasses she'd given him. "Hey, if this is a party, shouldn't we use champagne glasses and drink the champagne Jim brought?"

"Champagne?"

"I opened the bag while you were gone, and good old Jim brought you champagne. Just in time for my going away party. What do you say we pop it open?"

"I'm afraid I don't drink spirits, and I don't think you—" But things were different now. He was respectable. "You may have champagne if you wish."

"Where are the glasses?"

"Those are all I have."

"Okay, what's the difference?" And he went off to put them back on the table.

He opened the bottle out in the backyard, using a knife blade, and she was sure that the whole blasted town could hear that cork pop—not that too many of them would recognize the sound.

"All set?" he asked, coming back in. She took off her apron, preceded him into the dining room carrying the beef steaks and vegetables on a wide, ivory-colored platter. But all that was there for light were the candles.

"Bring the lantern, too," she said over her shoulder, "it's growing dark." He grabbed if off the kitchen table and came behind her, swinging none too jauntily on his impaired leg, oil sloshing in one container, champagne in the other.

"The matches . . ." she said.

"Coming up."

It struck her that by now he knew where many things were kept in her house and that she liked having him know. She suffered a sudden, wistful pride, watching while he fetched the matches as if he were lord of the manor come to light its fires.

"Sit down, Abbie, I'll do the honors. I'm in charge of the table anyway tonight." He lit not only the lantern but the two candles also, casting the room into blushing rosiness around them. His hand captivated her with its long fingers curled around the match, the dark hairs sweeping down from his forearm and wrist as he blew out the match. The table was twice the size of that in the kitchen, but he had set their two places cozily at right angles. "You'll have to forgive me, Abbie, I'm not dressed for the occasion," he said, checking his buttons as he sat down.

She smiled. "Mr. DuFrayne, for you that *is* dressed."

He patted his ribs and laughed. "I guess you're right."

On his plate she put steak and round, browned potatoes and old gold carrots, and he eyed them all while she served, then began eating with obvious relish, groaning, "God, I'm hungry. Dinner wasn't—" But they weren't going to bring up dinner. He shrugged and went on eating.

"Dinner was interrupted," she finished for him, raising an eyebrow. She'd never in her life seen anyone who enjoyed eating quite like he. Surprisingly, he did it quietly, using the proper moves, using the knife for cutting only, not for stabbing with and eating from. He used his linen napkin instead of his sleeve, relaxed back in his chair when he drank. Abbie could not help comparing this pleasant, polite man to the scoundrel who'd criticized her during those first meals she'd served him. Why couldn't he have been this smiling and amenable right from the first?

"I'll miss this good food when it's not available anymore," he said, as if reading her mind and reinforcing her newly formed opinions of him.

"Like most things, once beyond reach, my cooking will seem better than it truly was."

"Oh, I doubt that, Abbie. Once we stopped fighting at mealtime, I really enjoyed your food."

"I didn't know that before. I thought there was nothing you enjoyed so much as a good . . . or should I say a *bad* fight."

"You're partially right. I do enjoy a good fight. I find it invigorating, good for the emotional system. A good fight purges and leaves you clean to start over again." He peered up impishly at her, adding, "Kind of like liver."

She laughed and had to snatch the napkin to her lips quickly to keep the food from flying out. Ah, she would miss his wit after all. When she could swallow and speak once more, she did so with a bedeviling smile for him.

"But does your emotional system need purging quite so often, Mr. DuFrayne?"

He laughed openly, leaning back in his chair in pure enjoyment. He loved her this way, at her witty best, and took his turn at thinking he would miss this lively banter they'd grown so skilled at tossing back and forth. "Your wry wit is showing, Abbie, but I've come to love it. It has spiced up the days as much as the little fights we had now and then." Behind his glass his eyes looked all black, the night light not bright enough for her to make out those hazel flecks she knew so well by now.

"*Little* fights?" she returned. "*Now and then?*"

He stabbed a chunk of meat, eyeing her amusedly across the table. "I guess you got more than your share of my bad temper . . ." Here he brandished his fork almost under her nose. "But you deserved it, you know, woman."

She leveled him with a look of mock severity and pushed the fork aside with a tiny forefinger. "Quit pointing your meat at me, Jesse."

Too late she realized what she'd said. His expression turned to a suggestive smirk while her face grew scorching. Amused, he watched the blood rise from her chin to her hairline. He hadn't the decency to say something diverting, which would have been the chivalrous thing to do. But when had Jesse ever been chivalrous? He only sat back and used her ill-advised remark to his advantage, his teeth sparkling in a broad smile while she patted the napkin again to her lips and dropped her eyes to her plate, stammering for something to say. "I . . . I . . . did not deserve to . . . to have my best china thrown across my c . . . clean bedroom, and . . . and soup and glass all over everything."

He drew circles on his plate with the chunk of meat which had started all this, finally deciding to let her off the hook. He popped the meat into his mouth, studied the ceiling thoughtfully, and mused, "Now why the hell did I do that again, do you remember?"

This time his ridiculous innocent act caught her unaware. She laughed without warning and spit out a chunk of meat. It sailed clear across the way and landed on her clean linen tablecloth while she clasped her mouth with both palms and laughed until her shoulders shook.

He picked up the errant meat, laughing now too, and scolded, "Why, Miss Abigail McKenzie, you put this right back where it belongs!" Then he held it over her nose. Not quite believing it was herself acting so giddy, she obliged, finding it very hard to open one's mouth when one is laughing so hard.

She listened to a humorous recap of all the indignities he'd suffered at her hands, ending with his accusation that she'd tried to drown him with soup.

"So you grabbed the bowl and slurped like a hog at a trough," she finished.

"Aw, there's a new one—a hog at a trough. I'm a regular menagerie all rolled into one. Do you realize, Miss McKenzie, that you have called me by the names of more animals than Noah had on his ark?"

"I have?" She sounded surprised.

"You have."

"I have not!" But as she smirked, he started naming them.

"Goat, swine, baboon, hog . . . even louse. He held knife

and fork very correctly, feigning a sterling table etiquette. "Now I ask you, Abbie, do I have the manners of a goat?"

"What about the liver?"

"Oh, that. Well, that night, as many others, just when I was ready to make peace with you, you brought that lethal liver. It's true, Ab, every time I made up my mind to be nice to you, you came charging in with some new scheme to make me miserable and mad at you." He wiped his mouth, hiding a smile behind the napkin while she realized how enjoyable it was to laugh at all of it now with him.

"But you know what, Abbie?" he asked, reaching for the champagne bottle. "You were a worthy adversary. I don't know how we put up with each other all this time, but I think we both deserved everything we got." He filled both of their glasses and said, "I propose a toast." He handed her a glass and looked steadily into her pansy-colored eyes. "To Abigail McKenzie, the woman who saved my life and nearly killed me, all at the same time."

His glass touched hers, and the dark knuckle of his second finger grazed her fairer one. She looked away. "I don't drink," she reiterated as the room grew hushed.

"Oh, no, of course you don't. You only try to kill wayward gunslingers." He still held his glass aloft, waiting for her. She felt silly denying him the right to end this all gracefully, which he'd been managing nicely all through their pleasant supper so far. And so she touched his glass and took a small, wicked sip and found it did not hurt her at all, only made her want to sneeze. So she took another, and did sneeze. And they laughed together and he drained his glass and refilled it, and hers.

"You must return a toast of your own," he insisted, leaning back nonchalantly in his chair, "it's the only acceptable way."

Her eyes, meeting his, were violet in the soft light, registering deep thought. He wondered if she was remembering . . . as he was . . . the good times they'd shared since he'd been here. He wished that he could see what images went through her mind, for she looked thoroughly adorable tonight.

Abbie sat with her elbow resting on the table, the unfamiliar champagne bubbling before her eyes.

"Very well," she agreed at last, then sat a moment longer peering at him through the pale gold liquid, puzzling over how to say it. At last she lowered her glass enough to see his face above it and intoned quietly, "To Jesse DuFrayne,, who actually admires my morals all the while he tries to sully them."

But this time after their glasses touched it was he who did not drink from his. Instead his brow furrowed and he scowled slightly.

"What did you say?"

"I said, 'To Jesse DuFrayne who—'"

"I know what you said, Abbie, I want to know why you said it."

Do you, Jesse, she thought. Do you? Or do you understand perfectly, just as I do, that you could have forced yourself on me any one of countless times, yet you always backed off. Must I tell you why? Do you understand so little of yourself? Abbie drew a deep breath and met his eyes.

"Because it's true. Perhaps because I have noted that when others are around you refer to me respectfully as Miss Abigail, no matter what you might call me when we're alone together. Maybe too because you—Oh, never mind." She didn't think she could go through with it and tell him what he couldn't see for himself.

"No, I want to know what you were going to say." He leaned forward now, bracing his forearms against the edge of the table, rolling the glass between his palms, the frown lingering about his eyes.

She considered a moment, sipped a little, then looked away from his mouth: he was chewing somehow on the fringe of his moustache, and she thought it might be a danger sign. "The truth as I see it would sound blatantly conceited were I to say it. I don't want you to leave here thinking of me in that light."

"You of all people are the farthest thing from conceited I've ever met. Self-righteous maybe, but not conceited."

"I'm not sure whether I should say thank you or spit in your eye."

"Neither. Just explain what you meant about me and your morals."

She sipped again for false courage, her eyes picking up some of the champagne bubbles and refracting the lamplight off them. "Very well," she agreed at last, looking into her glass to find it surprisingly empty. He refilled it as she began. "I think that you find me . . . let us say, not totally unattractive. I also, however, think that my feminine gender in itself would serve that purpose for you, because you just plain *like women*.

But that's beside the point. I only mentioned it to point out that I do not say this in a vain way. I think you are attracted to me by the very thing that you seek to change in me. Unless I miss my guess, I am the first woman you've encountered in a good long time who possesses any of the qualities that the old beatitudes praise. And all the time you berate me for my inability to bend, you are hoping I will not do so. In other words, Mr. DuFrayne, I think that for perhaps the first time in your life you have found something besides flesh to admire in a woman, but you've never learned how to handle admiration of that sort, so you resort to breaking down my morals in order to feel at ease in your relationship with me."

He sat there with his shoulders lounging at a slant against the back of his chair, but the scowl on his lips belied the lax attitude of his body. He had an elbow propped on the arm of his chair and ran an index finger repeatedly along the lower fringe of his moustache.

"Perhaps you're right, Abbie." He took a sip, measuring her over the glass. "And if you are, why do you blush like a schoolgirl? Your beatific nature is all intact—everything right where it was when I first found you." Lazily he leaned and reached out that bronze finger that had been stroking his moustache, touched her lightly beneath the chin, and made her look up at him. But she stiffened, drawing her eyes away again, turning her chin aside to avoid the finger that seemed too, too warm and exciting. When she would not look up again he ran the callused finger lightly along her delicate jawbone. That at last made her eyes fly to his.

"Don't!" She jerked back, but something strange happened inside her head. For a moment things looked like they had fuzzy edges.

His eyes traveled over her open lips, noted her quick breath, the distended nostrils, then lazily eased back to the blue threatened depths of her wide eyes.

"All right," he agreed softly, "and this time I won't even ask why."

Panicked by the sudden change in him, she lurched up from her chair, but a tornado seemed to be whirling inside her. She fell forward, hands pressed flat on the tabletop on either side of her plate. Her head reverberated. Her neck felt limp, and a lock of damp hair hung down across her collar.

"You've duped me again, have you, Mr. DuFrayne? This

time with your innocent toasts.'' Her head hung down disgracefully but she couldn't seem to raise it, not even to look daggers at him for doing this to her.

"No I haven't. If so, I didn't mean to. Why, you hardly had enough wine to inebriate a hummingbird.'' He picked up the bottle and tipped it, looking at the lantern light through it. It was still half full.

"Well, this hum . . . hummingbird is in . . . inebriated just the same,'' she said to the slanting tabletop, her head sinking lower between her shoulder blades all the time.

He smiled down at the part in her hair, thinking how appalled she'd be in the morning and how they weren't going to get out of this without another fight after all. Abbie drunk, imagine that, he thought, unable to keep from smiling at her.

"It must be the altitude,'' he said now. "Up this high it doesn't take much, especially if you've never drunk before.'' He came to put an arm around her and lead her toward the back door. "Come on, Abbie, let's get you some fresh air.'' She stumbled. "Be careful, Abbie, the steps are here.'' He took one floppy hand and put it around his waist and it grabbed a handful of shirt obediently. "Come on, Ab, let's walk, or you'll find your bed spinning when you lie down.''

"I'm sure you kn . . . know all about . . . sp . . . spinning b . . . beds,'' she mumbled, then pulled herself up and slapped lamely at his helping hands. "I'm fine. I'm fine,'' she repeated drunkenly, thinking she was regaining a little decorum. But she started humming next and knew perfectly well that she wouldn't be humming if she were truly fine.

"Shhh!'' he whispered, forcing her to walk.

She flung a palm up. "But I'm a . . . a hummingbird, am I not?'' She actually giggled, then swayed around and fell against him, tapping him on the chest. "Am I not a humming-bird, Jesse? Hmm? Hmmm?'' Her forefinger drilled teasingly into his chin, and he lifted it aside.

"Yes, you are. Now shut up and keep walking and breathe deeply, all right?''

She tried to take careful steps, but the ground seemed so far away from her soles, and so evasive and tipsy. They walked and walked, all around the backyard. And once more she giggled. And more than once stumbled so he'd grab her more tightly around the waist to set her aright. "Keep walking,'' he insisted again and again. "Damnit, Abbie, I did *not* do this to you on purpose. I never in my life saw anybody get tight on a thimbleful of champagne. Do you believe me?"

"Who cares if *I* believe *you*. Do *you* believe *me*?"

"Keep walking."

"I said *do you believe me!*" she suddenly demanded, her words ringing out through the still air. "Do you believe what I said in there about you and me!" She got belligerent and tried to yank away, but he steadied her close against his hip and she submitted to his strong, forceful arm.

"Don't raise your voice, Abbie. The neighbors might still be up."

"Ha!" she all but bellowed. "Carve that one on marble! *You* worried about what *my* neighbors might think!" She lurched and grabbed his shirtfront in both fists, shaking it, tugging till it pulled against his neck.

"Shh! You're drunk."

"I'm as sober as a judge now. Why won't you answer me?"

Was she drunk or sober when she reared back and began trumpeting in the most unladylike way, "Jesse DuFrayne loves Abbie Mc—" and he plastered his mouth over hers to shut her up? Her arms came around his neck and he lifted her clean up off the ground, her breasts flattened mercilessly against his rigid chest. But once his mouth covered hers, he forgot he was only trying to shut her up. He took her mouth wholly, and there was nothing dry about it. She had both of her arms folded behind his strong neck, her toes dangling half a foot off the earth, and they stood that way in the silver moonlight, kissing and kissing, and forgetting they had vowed to be enemies, all tongue and tooth and lip and a soft, thick moustache. Her mouth was hot and sweet and tasted of champagne. The smell of roses came from the fabric of her starched blouse and she made a small groaning whimper deep in her throat, her breath coming warm against his cheek. And in no time at all his body grew uncomfortably hard, so he set her down on her feet none too gently, pulled her arms away from his neck, and ordered fiercely, "Get the hell up to bed, Abbie. Do you hear me!"

She stood there drooping, conquered.

"Can you walk by yourself?" His warm hand still gripped her elbow.

"I told you I'm not drunk," she muttered to the earth at her feet.

"Then prove it and get inside where you belong."

"I, Mr. DuFrayne, am as sober as a veritable judge!" she boasted, still to the night earth, for she could not raise her head. He carefully released her elbow, and she swayed a little but remained upright.

"Don't judge me for this, Abbie, just get the hell out of here!"

"Well, you don't have to sound so mad about it," she said childishly, and knew somewhere in her bleary head just how drunk she really was to be talking that way, almost whining. Ashamed now of what she'd done, she turned and weaved her way to the house, gulping deep draughts of the stringent night air. On her way past the dining room table she gulped a whole cup of cold coffee. And by the time she made her way upstairs it was herself she was judging, not him. Champagne was no excuse, none at all. The pure, unadulterated truth was that she'd been wanting him to kiss her all night. Worse, she'd been wanting to kiss him back. Worse yet, she didn't think that was all she wanted anymore.

Upstairs, she flopped backward onto the bed, arms as limp as the excuses she tried to think up. Heavens, that man can kiss! One finger wound around a tendril of hair until she'd curled it all the way to her scalp. She closed her eyes and groaned, then hugged her belly and curled up, suddenly tragically sure her mother had been dead wrong. Here she was, Abigail McKenzie, spinster, thirty-three and heading upward, never to know just what it was that her mother had so warned her against. Certainly it couldn't be kissing. It had been nothing short of a swift, sweet miracle, the way that kiss had felt. It had been so long ago with Richard that it was impossible to recall if it had been this good. And certainly David's kiss had not started such a volcanic throbbing in her. But always before she had held back, afraid of what her mother had said. But when you loosen your reserve and put everything into it, kissing was a different matter entirely. It started such strange and pleasant rippling sensations shimmying downward through one's body.

Lying in the darkness above Jesse, she again pictured his body. Ah, she knew it so well. She knew the shape and hue and texture of each part of it, the valleys of his shoulder blades where strong muscles welled up to leave inviting hollows. His dark arms, long, strong, etched with veins at the inner bend of elbow. His legs and feet, how often she'd seen them, washed them. She knew his hands, large, square, with equal capacity for teasing and gentling. His eyes seemed to seek her out in the darkness, from beneath brows whose outline she traced on her stomach now from memory. Those eyes crinkled at the corners in the instant before his soft, soft moustache lifted with a lazy smile. She knew the spot where the skin grew smooth, down low where the hair of his broad chest narrowed and dove in a thinner line, narrowing, narrowing along his hard belly to his groin.

She rolled onto her stomach because her breasts hurt. She clamped her arms against the swelling sides of those breasts and squeezed her thighs together, locking her ankles, holding them tightly, tightly, trying to forget the image of the naked Jesse. But forgetfulness refused her. She opened her mouth, waiting for the heat of his imaginary kiss. But she touched only the pillow, not warm, soft lips. She rolled to her side clutching a knob of nightgown between her legs, feeling what was happening there, this awful aching need to be filled.

Was this then how it was? How it ought to be? What her mother had known? What her mother had never known? It was fullness and emptiness, acceptance and denial, hot and cold, shiver and sweat, yes and no. It was the coming apart of scruples, ethics, codes, standards, and virtues and not caring in the slightest, because your body spoke louder than your conscience.

Jesse had been right all along, and her mother had been wrong. How could such compulsion be wrong? Senses Abbie had never realized she possessed were now expanded to their fullest. Her body throbbed and beat and begged. How right . . . how utterly right . . . it would be to simply go to him and say, "Show me, for I want to see. Give me, for I deserve. Let me, for I feel the right."

The question no longer was could she do that and live with it afterward. The question now was could she not do that and watch her one chance walk out the door tomorrow to leave her ignorant and unfulfilled.

Chapter 15

―――――――

THE MOON WAS rich cream, high, melting down through the wide bay window, running all over him as he lay, sprawled carelessly, naked on the bed. His head and chin were screwed around at an odd angle, as if trying to see the headboard backward. She had listened to his restless movements for what seemed like hours, working up the courage to creep downstairs. But now he slept, she could tell by his measured breath and the one dark foot that dangled off the end of the bed where he had never fit and never would. She came trembling to the bedroom doorway, afraid to enter, afraid not to. What if he turned her away?

Little tight fists pressed against chin and teeth, she eased closer. Her chest felt as if it were in a vise. How should she awaken him? What should she say? Should she touch him? Maybe say, "Mr. DuFrayne, wake up and make love to me?" How absurd that she didn't even know what to call him anymore. Suddenly she felt awkward and sexless and knew for sure he'd tell her to get back upstairs and she would die of humiliation.

Yet she whispered his name anyway. Or did she whimper it? "J . . . Jesse?"

It might have been the brush of curtain upon sill, so tentative was the sound.

"Jesse?" she asked again of his moon-clad body.

He straightened his head around on the pillow drowsily. Although she couldn't make out his eyes, she saw the moon's reflection on the bolder lines of his face. His moustache made a darker, beckoning shadow. His chin lowered and he looked across his chest and saw her, and pulled a hank of sheet over to cover himself.

"Abbie? What is it?" he asked sleepily, disoriented, braced up on his elbows now.

"J . . . Jesse?" She quavered, suddenly not knowing what else to say. This was awful. This was so awful. It was worse than any of the insults she'd suffered at his hands, yet she stood as she was, her two hands, fisted tight, bound together against her chin.

But he knew. He knew by the tremulous way she spoke his name at last. He sat up, taking more of the sheet across his lap, dropping a single leg over the edge of the bed for equilibrium.

"What are you doing down here?"

"Don't ask . . . please," she pleaded.

The silent night surrounded them and time seemed to cease its coursing until out of the creamy night quiet came his voice, low and knowing.

"I don't need to ask, do I?"

She gulped, shook her head no, unable to speak.

He didn't know what to do; he knew what he must do.

"Go back upstairs, Abbie. For God's sake, go. You don't know what you're doing. I shouldn't have let you have that champagne."

"I'm not drunk, Jesse. I . . . I'm not. And I do not want to go back upstairs."

"You don't need this in your life."

"What life?" she asked chokily, and his heart was clutched with remorse for having made her question the blandness that had always been enough before.

"The life you've always prided yourself on, the one I don't want to ruin for you."

"There have been so many times I thought I knew what would ruin my life. My mother always warned me that men like Richard would ruin it. Then she died and he ran away and I wondered how to exist from one day to the next with all that nothingness. Then a man named David Melcher came into my house and made me hope again, but—"

"Abbie, I tried to apologize for that. I know I shouldn't have done that to you. I'm sorry."

"No, you shouldn't have, but you did, and he's gone and shall never be back. And I need . . . I . . ." She stood as still as a mannequin, the moonlight limning her in ivory, her hands pressed to her throbbing throat.

"Abbie, don't say it. You were right at the supper table tonight. I do value all your old-fashioned morals or I'd have taken you long ago. I don't want to be the one to make them come crashing down now, so just go back upstairs and tomorrow I'll be gone."

"Don't you think I *know* that!" she cried desperately. "You are the one who made me realize the truth about Richard and me. You are the one who accused me of stagnating, so who better shall I ask? Don't change on me now, Jesse, not now that I've come this far. You . . . you are my last chance, Jesse. I want what every other woman has known long before she's thirty-three."

He jumped off the bed, twisting the sheet around him, holding it low against one hip. "Goddamnit, that's not fair! I will not be the one to aid in your undoing!" He tugged the sheet viciously but it was anchored beneath the mattress, tethering him before her. "I lay there thinking about you for hours after I went to bed and I found you were a hundred percent right about my motives. I don't know what it is about you that mixes me up so, but one minute I want to bend you and the next I'm cussing because you're so godalmighty moral that if you bend, I'm the one who breaks. But you know that and you're using it against me!"

She was. She knew it. But she swallowed her pride and spoke in a strained whisper. "You're sending me away then?"

Oh, God, he thought. God, Abbie, don't do this to me when I'm trying to be noble for the first time in my life! "Abbie, I couldn't live with myself afterward. You're not some . . . some two-bit whore following the railroad camps."

"If I were, could I stay?" Her plaintive plea made him ache with want.

Why the hell did I push her so far, he berated himself, wondering how to get them both out of this without lasting hurt to either. This was the moment when her morals and her mother's morals faced off. How ironic that he should now be the spokesman for the mother he had criticized.

"Abbie," he reasoned, "it's because you're not that you can't. Do you understand the difference?" Had she no idea what she did to him, standing there hugging herself, swathed in moonlight and trembles? "You'll hate me afterward, just like you hate Richard. Because I'm going, Abbie. I'm going and you know it."

"The difference is that I know it beforehand."

Sweat broke out across his chest and he tightened the twist of sheet at his hip until it dug into his skin. "But you know what I am, Abbie."

She raised her chin proudly, though her body quaked. "Yes, you are Jesse DuFrayne, photographer, seer of life as it really is. But you are the one running from reality now, not I."

"You're damn right I'm running," His labored breath sounded like he actually had been. "But the reason is you. Tomorrow you'd look at this differently and you'd hate me."

"And would you mind?" she braved, her chin lifting defensively.

"You're damn right I'd mind, or I wouldn't be standing here arguing, wrapped in these sheets like some timid schoolboy!"

"But you know that if you send me back upstairs, I shall hate you anyway."

The moonlight scintillated off their outlined bodies as they strained to see each other's faces. He thought he could smell roses clear across the room. Her shoulders were so small, and she looked all vulnerable and scared with her arms folded up the center of her chest that way. But her hair was loose, lit by moonglow, like a nimbus about her shadowed face.

"Abbie . . ." His voice sounded tortured. "I'm not for you. I've had too damn many quick women." But his conviction somehow faded into appeal and he took a halting step toward her. She too took one tremulous step, then another, until he could make out the quick rise and fall of her breathing.

"All the better that it be you, Jesse, my one and only time— you who know so well." Her words were soft, breathy, and raised the hair along his arms. They were so close that Jesse's shadow blocked the moonlight from her upraised face. Tension tugged at their hovering, unsure bodies. The whisper of curtains in the night breeze was now the only sound in the room. Jesse's nostrils flared while he clutched the sheet tighter,

tighter. He thought of tomorrow and knew she had no idea that David Melcher would be back in town. All he had to do was tell her so and she would turn back upstairs obediently. But the thought of leaving her to Melcher flooded him with livid jealousy. He could take her now, but how she'd hate him afterward, when she found out he'd known all along of Melcher's return.

She knew absolutely nothing about what he could do to her, he was sure. There she stood, imploring him for that of which she was ignorant—his tiny little hummingbird Abbie, who'd fought for his life and defied death right here in this very room. And in return she asked just one thing of him now . . . and he wanted to give it to her so badly that it physically hurt. She was a scant four feet in front of him now. All he had to do was take one step more. Standing there, fighting desire, smelling the aura of roses drifting from her, Jesse floundered, became lost in her. "Abbie," he uttered, the name strained, deep in his throat, "you're so damn small." And the sheet, like a puddle of rippling milk, moved with him as he leaned to whisper in her ear, "Don't hate me, Abbie, promise you won't hate me." His gruff words moved the hair behind her ear and trapped her heart in her throat. A sinewy hand reached through the moonlight to close itself about her upper arm.

Her lips fell open. She raised her face and her nose touched his firm shoulder. His skin smelled of night warmth and sleep and held a faint trace of dampness, not wholly unpleasant. She raised a hesitant hand to brush it with her fingertips. He was so hard, so warm, and she so unsure. He poised, his breath beating upon her ear, and she wondered what he would have her do. She knew so little, only that to kiss as they'd kissed in the yard had turned her body to sweet, shaking jelly. So she raised her lips and asked near his, "Would you kiss me first, like you did in the yard, Jesse?"

His grip on her arm grew painful. "Oh, God, Abbie," he groaned, and let the sheet spill from him as he scooped her up in powerful arms and held her against the heart that hammered wildly in his breast. He buried his face in her hair, knowing he should not do this, but was unable to deny himself any longer.

She rubbed her temple against his lips, eager for the touch of them on her own. Then slowly, timidly, her face turned up, seeking that remembered rapture.

"Abbie, this is wrong," he reiterated one last, useless time.

"Just once, like in the yard," she whispered. "Oh, Jess, please . . . I liked it so much."

Sanity fled. Her childlike plea threw his heart cracking against his ribs. He lowered open lips to her warm, waiting ones. As she met his kiss her arms went twining around his neck, fingers delving the mysteries of thick, black hair at the back of his head. His tongue, once dry with fever, was now wet with fervor, dipping against hers, slipping to explore her mouth greedily. She responded timidly at first, but imitating his actions, her pleasure grew and her tongue became bolder within his mouth. He released her suddenly and her knees and legs went sliding down along his until her feet touched the floor. He cinched powerful arms about her ribs, lifting her untutored body up and in against him. His mouth slanted demandingly across hers and his tongue delved deeper, plying, playing, melting her insides like sugar candy until she felt it drizzle, sweet and warm, far down from the depths of her.

For Abbie it was the wonder of the first kiss magnified a hundred times as her body pressed willingly against his. He made a faint growling sound in his throat, then threaded his long fingers back through the hair at her temples, cradling her head in his palms while he scattered little kisses everywhere. He seemed to be eating her up by nibbles, making her feel delicious as he took a piece of her chin, then her lip, her nose, her eyebrow, ear, neck, settling back upon her mouth again, biting her tongue lightly as if finding it the tastiest. She forgot everything but the slow, sweet yearning inside her body. She let it control her, leaving her with the wonder of this man whom she had so long feared, but whom she wanted now with a desire that shut out all thoughts of wrong. She forgot that his was a practiced kiss, knew only that it was the prelude to all she was so eager to learn from him, of him. He buried his face in her neck, his breath summer warm on her skin.

"Abbie, I have to know, so I don't hurt you," he said in a hoarse, stranger's voice, "did you and Richard ever do this?"

Her hands fell still upon his neck.

"No . . . no!" she answered in a startled whisper, straining away suddenly. "I told you—" She would have turned aside, abashed, but he took her jaw in both of his warm hands, tipping her face up as if it were a chalice from which he would sip, forcing her to look at him.

"Abbie, it doesn't matter," he said low, brushing his thumbs lightly, lightly upon the crests of her cheeks. "I don't want to hurt you is all. I had to ask."

"I . . . I don't understand," she said tremulously, her eyes wide on his, lips fallen open in dismay.

She swallowed hard; he felt it beneath the heels of his hands, and thought, Lord, she's so small, I'll kill her. Yet he brushed her cheek with his lips and hushed, "Shhh . . . it's all right," and lifted her face to meet his kiss again, making them both forget all but the turbulent senses aroused now beyond recall. With his tongue in her mouth, he picked her up again and carried her to the edge of the bed, where he sat with her upon his lap. Silently he vowed to go slow with her, to make it good, right, memorable if he could. He lifted her bashful arms and looped them around his neck. She was ever aware that he was naked, that his skin burned warmly through her wrapper and gown. His lips slid to the warm cay of her collarbone, and he murmured, "You smell like roses . . . so good." She twisted her head sensuously, rubbing a jaw against his temple. He touched her neck with his tongue, and she shuddered with some new, vital want. "Can I take your wrapper off, Abbie?" he asked, trailing brief kisses to a soft spot on the underside of her chin.

"Is that how it's done?" she asked rather dreamily.

"Only if you want."

"I want," she confessed simply, sending his senses thrumming. So he found the twist of belt at her waist and tugged it free and brushed the garment away until it lay tumbling across his bare knees.

He kissed her once more, then said into her mouth, "Abbie, I'm shaking as if it's my first time."

"That's good," she whispered.

Yes, he thought, it's good.

Then she added, "So am I," and he heard the smile in her words. He smiled too, against her cheek, then bit the tip of her ear.

"Remember when we were sitting on the swing? I really wanted to do this then, but I was afraid to put my arm around you all of a sudden."

"You've never been afraid, I don't think. Not of this." But still it pleased her that he said so. His hand slid to her ribs, rubbing sideways, abrading her skin softly through the thin cloth of her nightgown.

"I'm afraid now, Ab, afraid this might melt away beneath my hand."

She held her breath, her skin tingling with anticipation until at last his palm filled itself with her breast, warm and peaked and generous. The pressure of his other hand grew insistent at the back of her neck until she obeyed its command and turned her mouth again to his. But this time his kiss was no heavier than the touch of a moth's wing, more a kiss of breath than of lips. But it made shivers ride outward from every pore of her body. His caresses were loving, gentle, as he took a nipple, hard and expectant, between his thumb and the edge of his palm, squeezing it gently until she sighed against his lips. His hands roamed her shoulders and the nightgown fell down about her hips, letting first the warm fingers of night air ripple over her bare skin . . . then the warm fingers of Jesse DuFrayne. When his hand at last cupped her bare breast, she laid her forehead against his chin, lost in the magic of his touch. He brushed the erect nipple with the backs of his fingers while her wrists went limp, hanging across his shoulders. Drifting in sensation, she unconsciously pulled back to free a space so he could explore further. Finding her other breast as aroused as the first, he made a satisfied sound in his throat. "Ahhh, they're so hard," he said thickly.

She murmured some wordless reply, adrift in pleasure, wanting this to go on forever. She seemed to be floating above herself, looking down at a strange, lucky woman being pleasured by her man. She'd never imagined people talking when they did things like this, yet his soothing tones freed her from the bonds of restraint, and the lover she watched from above answered her consort, "Sometimes all I have to do is think of you and they get that way. Once it even happened in church."

He chuckled softly against her neck, but it was all he could do to keep from tumbling her backward and delving into her, deep and hard and now. He felt like he would burst from his skin! He wanted to taste her, smell her, hear her whimper, feel her flesh surround his. But he restrained himself, knowing it best to make it last long and good for both of them. He plied her with more kisses, running a hand up her back, then low along her spine. His fingers slid to her waist and pulled her bare hip up hard against the erect evidence of his desire, giving her time to learn the newness of a man, teaching her the difference between himself and her. He eased a hand onto her stomach, the other to the base of her spine, and sat as if praying, with her between his folded hands. Then his large palm swallowed up her breast as he took her with him, back, back, onto the softness of rumpled sheets. She fell atop his hard chest, but he rolled her onto her back, dipping his head down to kiss her shoulder, her collarbone, then the warm swell of skin below it. She felt his soft moustache, pictured it vividly as his hot, wet tongue trailed nearer and nearer a nipple until at last he was upon it, receiving the cockled tip beneath his stroking tongue, making her gasp, arch her ribs, and reach blindly for his hair. He tugged and sucked, sending billows of feeling flowing outward, downward from where he taught her skin to crave the moistness of his loving. He left one nipple wet, and she shivered as he moved to the other, her palm now guiding his jaw. With his ardent kiss upon her breast, all of her long-unused senses came to life, sluicing downward in a grand, liquid rush. Her nipples ached sweetly for more, but he stretched out beside her then, bending an arm beneath his ear, tickling her chest with a single playful fingertip. Goose bumps erupted all over her body, then she laughed girlishly and rolled a little bit, pushing the teasing finger away.

"I want to touch you all over," he said. But, curiously, he had removed his touch from her altogether, making her long greedily for its return. They stared into each other's eyes for a long, intense minute, neither of them speaking or moving. She sent him a tacit invitation to come back and try again, unable to say it in words. His hand lay down along his hip. He lifted it slowly and saw her eyelids flinch and widen as he touchéd her stomach lightly with the tip of an index finger, drawing tendrils and grapevines around her navel, up her ribs, around her nipples, up to her throat. Then, still with that single fingertip, he surveyed the line along which the fine hairs of her body met, joined, and pointed like nature's arrows, to the place which wept for want of him. He pressed her stomach, letting his fingertips trail into Spanish moss, lingering there while she lay with the breath caught in her pleasured throat. But as his fingers moved lower she recoiled, instinctively protecting herself against intrusion.

Realizing what she'd done, she felt awkward and stupid, covering herself that way, but she was suddenly, inexplicably afraid. Surely he would get disgusted now and think her utterly childish and realize he'd been wasting his time with her.

But instead, he whispered near her ear, "It's all right, Abbie, it's all right." He looped an arm loosely about her waist and kissed her again, exploring her back, shoulders, and the firm rises at the base of her spine. He lifted his head, looking down into her face. "Abbie, have you changed your mind?" he whispered, husky and strained. Her wide, uncertain eyes looked up at him, but she could not speak. Sensing her last-minute fear, he soothed her with whispered words, running the backs of his knuckles down her shoulder and around the outer perimeter of a breast. "Your skin, Ab, I never felt such skin. It's like warm custard pudding . . . smooth . . . and soft . . . and sweet." And as if to prove it, he leaned to take a taste, just inside her elbow where the soft pulse throbbed. He took the velvety skin gently between his teeth, tugging at it tenderly, then buried his face in the hollow of her abdomen. Her spine went taut, so he eased up to whisper into her mouth, "Don't be afraid, Abbie."

Then gently, insistently, his hand flowed downward, warm, slow, but sure. She squeezed her eyes shut, took a deep breath and held it tightly, envisioning the exact length and strength of his fingers before they sought, found, and entered.

She was sweetly swollen and wholly aroused, all sleek, wet satin. He braced up on an elbow, the better to see her. He moved his finger, watching her face all the while—the eyelids that trembled, the lips that fell open, the cheeks that grew hollow. She arched and gasped at what was happening within her. He plied her with the certain knowledge that she was ripe with the need for this. He teased her knowingly until, in abandon, she flung an arm over her head, eyes hidden now behind her elbow, her breath fast, hot and urgent.

He smiled, watching her go all sensuous and stretching. Then his touched slipped away.

She opened her startled eyes to his smiling face above her. "Jesse . . ." she choked, dying of ned.

"Shhh . . . we have all night." He circled her with a strong arm and turned them onto their sides, pulling her up tightly against his hot length. His knee slid silkily between her legs, rode up high against the place his hand had abandoned. With the sole of his foot he caressed the back of her calf and the softness behind her knee. Even in the vague light he could see the look of longing in her eyes. He kissed her just enough to keep the fever high, then pressed her shoulder blades back against the sheets again. With agonizing slowness he slid his hand along her belly, her ribs, her breast, her armpit, then on up, up, up the length of her loose-flung arm, finally closing over her palm, carrying it down between their two bodies. He felt her tense as she sensed where he was taking that hand.

"No . . ." she uttered before she could stop herself. Her fingers strained against his grip, leaving him doubtful of how to proceed with her. At last he laid her hand upon his ribs, leaving the choice up to her. But to tip the scales in his favor he used ardent words and a timeless language of body to tempt her.

"Touch me, Abbie," he encouraged, "touch me like I just touched you." His voice was a racked whisper, his kisses trailed fire paths across her face, his knees and hips spoke intimate promises against her. The hand remained on his ribs, trembling there, warm and slightly damp. "That's how it's done, Ab, we touch each other first. Did you like it when I touched you?" He heard her swallow convulsively. "It was good, wasn't it? Men like it just as much as women do."

A fearful timidity swelled her throat but the hand would not move. Do it! Do it! she told herself, her heart leaping and lunging within her breast. But nothing had prepared her for this. She had thought to lie passively and let him do what he would with her. The thought of fondling him made her palm burn to know him, but she was afraid once she reached, touched, her mother's spirit would somehow know what she was doing.

"Just a touch, then you'll know." He reached to titillate her again, hinting at bestowing the fire that had driven her wanton before, and she found herself thrusting up in welcome. But his teasing fingers left again, and she understood frustration as she never had before. She swallowed and made her hand move. He fell dead still, waiting. But when at last her fingertips came into contact with his tumescence they retracted into a quick clinch: he was so unexpectedly hot!

He lost all sense of caution then and moved swiftly, capturing her wrist between their bellies. "Just take it, Ab, just touch," he begged in a strident whisper. Fear lodged in her throat. The back of her hand now rested against that soft-hard heat, but timidity crushed her will to do what he asked. She pinched her eyes shut as he relentlessly forced her fingers to close around his engorged flesh and showed her how he would have her please him. A racked sound fell into the night and her eyes flashed open to find him raised on an elbow, his head flung back, mouth open almost as if in the throes of pain. He groaned raggedly and she jerked her hand away guiltily.

"Jesse, what is it! Did I hurt you?"

He swooped over her in a rough, swift enveloping turn, clutching her hand back where it had been.

"Lord . . . no, no, you didn't hurt me. You can do anything you want. . . . Do it . . . please." His lips smothered hers, almost violently, his tongue and hips thrusting rhythmically while his hand slid over her stomach in a frantic search now.

Her senses were torn between the sinuous ebb and flow within her grasp and the warm hand sliding up her thigh, the faint feather strokes with which he again quickened her, his knowing fingertips never faltering. Femininity had lain fallow within her for thirty-three years, planted by nature, nourished by time, until it took now but a kiss-breadth to make it erupt and flower.

She was dimly aware that he roughly jerked her hand off his flesh, but her eyes could no more open than could her body control the volcanic climax which he brought to it so effortlessly. And all the while he chanted murmurously, leaning on an elbow above her, kissing her eyes, stroking her flesh. "Let it come, Ab . . . let yourself fly . . . fly, Abbie . . . fly with me . . ."

His name escaped her throat as spasms of heat pulsated from deep in her stomach downward, downward, and her hips reached high, yearning. When the final seizure gripped her, she was unprepared for its force. She had never, never guessed . . . aaah, the power of it, the rapture . . . Jesse, she thought, ah, Jess, it's so good. . . . Jess, you were right. . . . Mother, why did you warn me against this?

Her nails cut into his arm. A rasping cry of ecstasy was wrenched from her throat and even as she shuddered his body covered hers. He spoke her name as the silken hair of his chest pressed upon her bare breasts, absorbing the faint sheen of moisture there. His tumescent body searched, probed, and found its home. He flanked her narrow shoulders with his hands, bracing away.

"Abbie, it's going to hurt, love, but just once, I promise."

Hot flesh entered her; her own resisted. She started to struggle, pushing against his chest. "Relax, Abbie, relax and it'll be better. Don't fight me, Abbie." But her fists pummeled him, so he captured them and pinned them to the mattress. "I want to make it good for you," he intoned as his weight pressed heavily and he plunged. She gasped and a cry of appeal tore from her throat, but he smothered it with his kiss, then spoke her name in loving apology.

From the ecstasy of a moment ago she was seared by pain. Her shoulders strained up off the mattress, but he held her helpless, moving within her. Delicate membrane tore and sent stabbing anguish through her recently pleasured limbs. She struggled uselessly, for her every resistance was controlled by his awesome strength and size. His breath scraped harshly with each thrust until at last she gave up, throwing her face aside, waiting passively for the torment to end.

As Jesse moved, each stroke brought shards of glassy pain to him, too. The long-unused muscles of his leg flamed as if a hot poker had been thrust into his wound. He gritted his teeth, his hands clinching her wrists like talons, thinking of how small she was, causing himself more misery by shimming his weight high to keep from hurting her. He fought pain in an effort to derive the most from his pleasure, but the faster he moved, the more it hurt. Sweat broke out on his brow as pain slowly but surely got the upper hand. His head sagged down, and his efforts at release grew grim. His arms shook mightily and a deep groan escaped him when finally he collapsed upon her, burning jets of white-hot fire searing his loins. He sighed, but it was not a replete sound, it was filled rather with relief.

He fell half off her, one leg still sprawled across her thighs, and she knew even in the depth of her naiveté that something was wrong. It had not been good for him as it had been earlier for her. He groaned into the pillow beside her ear and rolled himself away, limb by limb. But she could hear him gritting his teeth, and could feel his tensile muscles still shaking. She reviewed it all and knew exactly whose fault it was. His sudden withdrawal could only have been caused by her lack of prowess. Unsure of what she'd done wrong, she knew beyond doubt it was something, for it came back to her how he'd roughly jerked her hand off his body. He lay now with the back of a wrist over his eyes, obviously greatly relieved that it was over. Chagrined, she rolled away, cursing herself for being a stupid virgin of thirty-three, unable to perform even the simplest act to his satisfaction.

"Where are you going?"

"Upstairs." She began to sit up, but a long arm pinned her flat.

"What's the matter?"

"Let me go." She could already feel tears gathering in her throat.

"Not until you tell me what's wrong."

Her eyelids stung. She bit the inside of her lip, disappointment, anger, and guilt settling in with a sudden, deflating whump.

"Thank you, Mr. DuFrayne, for a heartfelt performance," she said stingingly.

"For *what*!" His neck crimped up, his fingers bit into her arm.

"What else shall I call such a sham?"

"What's wrong, Abbie, didn't I do it to suit you?" he asked sarcastically.

"Oh, you suited me fine. I fear I'm the one who did not suit."

He instantly softened. "Hey, it's your first time. It takes time to learn, all right?"

She pried his fingers from her arm and rolled away from him, thoroughly ashamed now of all the moaning and groaning she'd done when he had, in his turn, acted as if he couldn't wait to be done with her. He'd rolled off and out of her as fast as he could, then just lay there like a big, silent lump, saying nothing. All right then! If he had nothing to say, neither did she! She stared at the moonlit window, battling tears, remembering how he hadn't wanted to make love to her in the first place, how she'd practically had to beg him. Mortified, she lurched up as if to leave, but he got her by the shoulders and toppled her back down.

"Oh, no you don't! You're not running out of this bed and leaving this unsettled, because I'm not about to let you! You're going to stay right here until I find out what's got you prickled up, then you're going to give me a chance to put it right!"

"I am not prickled up!"

"Like hell you aren't! Can't we even do *this* without a fight! Not even this!" She bit her lip to keep from bawling out loud.

He went on, "I thought we did rather well, myself, considering it was our first time together. So what's your gripe?"

"Let me up. You're all done with me anyway." Martyrdom felt blessedly sweet. But one hard arm pressed her shoulders relentlessly, allowing no escape.

"I'm *what*!" he barked, growing angrier by the minute at her sudden, unexplained peevishness. "Don't you use that tone of voice on me, as if I'd slung you here against your will and raped you!"

"I didn't mean it that way. I only meant that it was obvious I was nothing."

"Abbie, don't say that." His voice lost its harshness. "This shouldn't happen between a man and a woman and leave them as nothing. It should always leave them as more."

"But I was nothing. You said so."

"I never said any such thing!"

"You said it takes s . . . some time t . . . to learn." The tears were growing plumper on her lids.

"Well, damnit, it does! But that's nothing against you."

"Don't you dare lie there over me, swearing right into my face, Jesse DuFrayne!"

"I'll lie here and do any damn thing I please, Miss Abigail McKenzie! You've got the story all wrong anyway. Look at you! Why, you're half the size of me. Just what do you think would happen if I laid into you with all I've got?" She turned her face aside. He grabbed her cheeks and made her look him in the eyes. "Abbie, I didn't want to hurt you so I held back . . . and there's not as much in it, is all, when a man does that. And yes, you're inexperienced, and no, you don't know all the moves, but I didn't care. By the time we got to the end I knew exactly how painful it was for you—the first time is always like that for a woman. I just wanted to end it quick for you."

"I am not made of china like the soup bowl you shattered once in this room!" she pouted.

"I don't think I know exactly what you're bitching about! Just what is it!"

Her chin trembled and a tear spilled. She looked at the moonlight streaming across the windowseat. "I . . . I don't kn . . . know either. You just . . . you acted like you were glad it was ov . . . over, that's all."

He sighed, tired and disgusted now. "Abbie, my leg hurt

like hell and I was worried about hurting you any more and . . . and . . . *oh, goddamnit!*" he exclaimed, pounding a fist into the mattress and flopping onto his back to stare at the ceiling.

She knew he was done with her for sure then, so sat up. But he touched her arm, gently though. "Stay a minute," he placated. "Will you stay?" There was a new note of sincerity in his voice as he dropped his hand from her arm. She pushed her hair back and wiped her eyes, so sorry now that she'd ever started this. "Don't go, Abbie, not like this," he pleaded, raising up on an elbow.

"I'm just getting the sheet." She found it on the floor and wiped her eyes with it before lying down and flinging it over her. It fell across him too, and they lay there like a pair of scarecrows under the sheet and the silence and the misunderstanding. Finally he rolled onto his side facing her and folded an elbow beneath his ear, studying her stiff profile against the square of milk-white window. His voice came again, soft and disarming. "Abbie, do you think it's always so easy for a man? Well, it's not. A man is expected to lead the way and a woman relies on him to do the right thing. But being the leader doesn't make him either infallible or fearless." She stared at the ceiling, the sheet clinched tightly beneath her armpits as tears dripped down into her ears. He ran an absent finger back and forth along the taut edge of the sheet while he went on quietly. "I took a virgin tonight. Do you know what goes through a man's mind when he does that? Do you think I didn't fear you'd push me away or think I went too fast or too hard or too far? Do you think I didn't know how you recoiled from touching me, Abbie? What was I supposed to do then? Stop, for God's sake?" Back and forth, back and forth went his finger, lightly whisking her skin and the edge of the sheet. "I promised to make it good for you, as good as I could, but the first time is never too good for a woman. Abbie, can you believe that I was afraid after that? Every step of the way I had doubts just like you, just like all lovers do the first time. The farther I went, the more afraid I was that you'd get up and run out of here in the middle of it all. Abbie, look at me."

She did, because he sounded very hurt and sincere.

"Abbie, what did I do wrong?" he asked softly. His hand had stopped toying with the sheet and lay unmoving between her breasts, his elbow resting lightly along the shallows of her ribcage.

"Nothing . . . nothing. It was m . . . me. I was terribly noisy, and afraid to do what I knew you wanted me to do, and I blamed you because it hurt at the end, and . . . and . . . oh, everything." Chagrined, she turned her face against his biceps. Tears were coming fast now. "It . . . it's just easier to get m . . . mad at you than it is t . . . to get mad at mys . . . self."

"Shhh, Abbie," he hushed, "you were fine."

"N . . . no, I was not f . . . fine. I was sc . . . scared and childish, but I d . . . didn't expect—"

A big hand found her cheek, its thumb brushed near a lower eyelid. "I know, Ab, I know. It's all new to you. Don't cry, though, and don't think you didn't give me pleasure, because you did."

She was horrified that she could not stem the flow of tears. His thumb grew sleek upon the hot puddle in the hollow beneath her eye. Her chest felt like it was near bursting from holding the sobs back.

"Th . . . then why were you in such a hurry to have it over with? I even h . . . heard you gritting your t . . . teeth."

"I told you why I hurried. My leg hurt and I thought I'd crush you. Besides, my own performance was none too great at the end either." He lifted his head off its cradling arm to look down into her face and find her eyes tightly jammed shut. In all his life he'd never faced a situation such as this after lovemaking. He too felt inept and wanting, dissatisfied in spite of what had passed. But at the same time he felt singularly protective toward this woman: the first he'd ever encountered who was as much concerned with fulfilling his needs as her own. He leaned to kiss the river of salt that streamed from her eyes, and she suddenly choked and clutched his neck, sobbing pitifully, her arms tenaciously trapping him too close for him to watch her misery. Her chest heaved with wrenching sobs that shook his own and made his stomach cinch tight with the need to comfort her and make things right.

"Abbie, Abbie, don't cry," he whispered throatily against her hair. "We'll try it again and it'll be better." But he understood what she really cried about. He understood how far she'd come from propriety to this. So he held her tenderly, cooing soft endearments as he smoothed the hair up from the

nape of her neck and back from her temples, wondering
miserably how things could have gone so wrong.

"Oh, Jess, I w . . . wanted my memories of this n . . .
night to be good. I didn't w . . . want us to f . . . fight
tonight. I wanted us to pl . . . please each other."

"Shhh, Abbie, there are lots of ways." He dried her cheeks
with the tail of a sheet. "Lots of ways and lots of time."

"Then show me, Jess, show me," she pleaded, desperate
now to see that this night not end in desolation. His hand
stopped moving. He kissed her forehead. She heard him
swallow.

"I can't right now. A man needs time in between, Abbie,
and my leg needs a rest too. But in a while . . . all right?"

But she didn't believe him. She was sure now that he was
only placating her because she'd done such a miserable job the
first time. He rolled to his back again, swallowing the sigh
which formed as he fully rested his leg. She lay very still,
staring at the ceiling, going over it all in her memory,
recateogorizing Jesse DuFrayne once again according to what
this night had taught her about him. No longer could she
consider him a defiler of women, but a tender, considerate
lover instead. Not fearless, as she'd thought, but human, with
misgivings not unlike her own. He'd always seemed so bold
and doubtless in his teasing. What a revelation to think that
there lurked trepidation behind his bravado. Yet even in his
disappointment he eased her with kind, sweet words and
assuaged her feelings of inadequacy by taking the blame upon
himself.

But how could she face him come morning? How could she
awaken here and look into his dark eyes when neither would be
able to deny that their lovemaking had been disastrous? As she
had once before in this room, she lay falsely still, waiting for
sleep to overtake him so she could slip away. But a large,
heavy hand sought and found her hair, smoothed it, then drew
her to his side and pulled her up against his chest. He rested his
chin upon the top of her head and her eyelashes fluttered shut
as she sighed and stayed, unwilling to deny herself the comfort
of being cradled that way. After some minutes his hand moved
lazily against her hair. His brawny chest had a silken texture
beneath her cheek. She told herself she must get up and go—
what would she say to him in the morning? But like a bridling
in its nesting place, she felt secure. His hand grew weighted

upon her skull, then fell still. His other hand, which lay flung across her hip, twitched once spasmodically. His breathing became heavy and buffeted the top of her hair. A lethargy unlike any she'd known before came to lower her lids and sap her limbs. She knew she was falling asleep in the arms of Jesse DuFrayne. She knew he'd been a gentle and considerate lover. She knew she must awaken tomorrow to the fact that he was leaving. But it all ceased to matter.

And they slept, unaware.

The Colorado Rockies spread protective arms about the lovers. The moon pulled the earth around, climbed the clouds, and slid down the other side, to the west. The dawn peepings of birds stirred upon the pinkening air. A sleeping man rolled over and settled his face against a fair, warm arm. A sleeping woman pulled her pillow into the deep curve of her shoulder, bent a bare knee toward her nose. The man snored lightly and shifted onto his stomach, and a lock of hair caught in his moustache, fluttering as he breathed, tickling him distractingly. The edge of a long, dark hand scratched the nose, tried to brush the nuisance away. But his breath fluttered it again, still caught, still tickling. He snuffled, roused, felt something warm covering his fingers, and opened his eyes groggily to see what it was.

Abbie.

He grinned at the sight of a single rose-tipped breast half covering the back of his hand. Her other breast was buried beneath her someplace, for she too was half on her belly, one knee drawn up high, presenting a beautifully turned hip, but hiding her feminine secrets. He smiled crookedly. She likes to hog the bed, he thought. The smile dissolved as he remembered how she'd cried last night. He carefully extracted his hand, rolled onto his side, and braced his jaw on a palm. His eyes leisurely traveled the length of her, several times. Tiny toes, delicate ankles, shapely calves. He remembered glimpsing them before, but never as freely as this. Her hip was as round as the swell of a sea wave, and her waist as sharp as the trough created by tides. The deep crevice carved an enticing angle, buttressed by the knee she'd cast upward toward her chest. Myriad memories flitted through his mind. Abbie, you saved my life. Abbie, I made you cry. Abbie, I must leave soon. He looked at the window where pink-gray light crept over the sill and knew an emptiness unlike any he'd ever faced

upon leaving a woman's bed. No, last night's pleasures, for
him, had been minimal at best, yet his body sprang to life now
at the sight of her. He leaned to dtop a light kiss upon her ribs,
then on that pale hip. He placed a much more lingering one in
the trough of her waist. A small hand came down and swatted
unconsciously at him. Then she flopped over, facing away from
him, with her top leg pulled up high as before.

His heart went crazy and moisture erupted on his brow. She
was small and exquisite and—yes, it was still true—innocent,
for she knew nothing of the ways in which he yet desired her.
He released a pent-up breath and eased down low on the bed,
touched his tongue to the soft place behind her knee, closed his
eyes and breathed against her skin, knowing he was taking
unfair advantage while she slept, yet he was aroused so
ardently that his body felt it would burst its bounds. He tasted
salt and roses and maybe a little of himself. He followed the
contour of her leg, his hair brushing against her thigh, recalling
how very familiar she had long ago become with his own body.

What he did seemed inevitable; the weeks of intimacy they
had shared made it almost preordained. He kissed her
everywhere but the one spot he wanted most to taste, waiting
for her to awaken that he might kiss it, too. He learned the
ridges of her vertebrae, the firmness of her hip, the resilience
of her thighs, buttocks, calves. He memorized even her half-
flattened breast. She awakened when he lightly bit the arch of
her updrawn foot, and with a start she looked back over her
shoulder at the man behind her. Vague, predawn light caught in
his black, aroused eyes as he braced up and searched her face
for permission. Above his open lips his moustache was a dark,
trembling shadow. Her eyes were drawn to it, sensing that it
had just explored her skin. Her startled eyes again fled to his,
and she read in that gaze a kind of ardent agony which she'd
not suspected a man could harbor. It brought her heart and
blood alive with a leap of sensuality and expectation.

"J . . . Jesse?" she stammered croakily. Slowly she eased
her leg down, realizing how immodest her pose had been and
that he'd undoubtedly been awake for some time. "Y . . .
you woke me up."

"I meant to, love," he whispered, holding her captive by
only the strong, sensuous tether of his gaze. She rolled
backward slightly, twisting at the waist, bracing up on an
elbow now and watching his eyes drop to the peak of her other

breast, which curved into view, then return to her face. She felt his warm palm travel from the small of her back, around one buttock, along the back side of her calf, gently tucking her knee back up as it had been before. And all the while his eyes never left hers.

"It's my turn to know your body like you've known mine all these weeks, Abbie." She became aware of all the places where her body was wet, where his tongue had trailed as she slept, where her skin now cooled as it dried. Naiveté vanished as she read his eyes and understood his intention. Involuntarily she shivered, then slowly hid her breast behind her upper arm, not quite knowing how to hide the rest of her. Mesmerized by the hunger in his gaze, she watched in fascination as he dipped his head again to her white hip, his eyes sliding closed while a sound of deep passion rumbled from his throat. He braced up on one hand, twisted now at the waist, and with a warm, caressing palm, pushed her back down onto her stomach. Her cheek grew lost in a pillow and her heart thrust wildly against the mattress as his warm lips brushed up and down her back and he began uttering her name against her skin. "Abbie . . . Abbie . . . Abbie . . ." Over and over, roaming her body with his soft moustache and his softer mouth until everything inside her grew yearning and outreaching. He turned her gently onto her back, moving her limbs where he would have them, trailing wetness and love words as his kisses tracked across her flesh. His gravelly voice whispered that the second time was better, begged her to be still, to let him. "Don't fight me, Abbie, I'll show you . . . Abbie, you're so tiny . . . God, you're beautiful . . . Shhhh, don't hide from me . . . there's more. . . . Trust me, Ab." When she reached instinctively to cover herself, he nudged her hand aside with his nose. Then his teeth gently closed upon the side of her thumb and he carried it to the hollow of her hip.

"Jesse . . ." she rasped once, beseeching him for she knew not what.

"Nothing's going to hurt this time, Abbie, I promise."

No, she thought, people don't do this! But people did, she learned, for his mouth possessed her everywhere, sent her spinning into mindless wonder while she lost all will to resist. He sailed her high and writhing until heat exploded like a skyrocket inside her, sending sparks sizzling from the core of her stomach to the tips of her toes and fingers in a gigantic

burning burst of sensation. She opened her eyes to the sight of
him gazing in undisguised need up her stomach, into her
dazed, glazed eyes. She groaned and rolled a shoulder
languorously away from the mattress, then let it sag back
again. She pulled her senses up from their debilitated depths
and opened her eyes, realizing that he needed fulfillment
equally as much as she had a moment ago. So she raised her
drugged arms in welcome.

He lunged up, rasping instructions in her ear, encompassing
her with powerful brown arms that lifted her, turned her, and set
her on top of his stomach, then brought her down until her
breasts were crushed against the mat of hair on his chest.
Words became unnecessary, for her body and his hands told her
what to do. Innocence, timidity, naiveté all fled as she started
to move, watching his pleasured face as his eyes slid closed
and his head arched back against the jumbled pillows. As his
lips fell open and his breath scraped harshly, she saw in his face
the plenary abandon which he'd earlier brought to her. Her
heart soared. Her eyes stung. This, this, this, is how it should
be for both man and woman, she realized. The one giving to
the other, the one taking from the other, with as much joy
derived from the giving as from the taking. She faltered and his
eyelids flickered opened momentarily, then closed again and
his temple turned sharply against the pillow as she regained the
rhythm. Unbelievably, when he reached his climax he cried
out—was it her name or some mindless profanity or both? It
mattered not, for it made her smile, made her feel skilled and
agile, and bursting with joy.

She collapsed onto his broad chest, her forehead nestling
beneath his jaw. One of his hands fell tiredly onto her shoulder,
rubbed it in a light, caressing circle of satisfaction before
flopping weakly onto the pillow again. Then, surprisingly,
beneath her ear, a slow, quiet, wonderful chuckle began. It
rumbled there like sweet thunder until, puzzled, she raised her
head to study him. But his eyes remained closed while his
chest rose and fell beneath her own, with silent laughter. And
suddenly she understood why he laughed—it was a laugh of
elemental satisfaction. A smile blossomed upon her lips, and a
slow glow began deep down in her belly, in answering
gladness. He slung his tired arms about her, hugged her tightly,
and smiled against her hair as he rolled them both from side to
side several times.

"Ahh, Abbie, you're good," came his lover's hosannah, "you're so damn good."

Nothing he might have said could have pleased Abbie more at that moment. She smiled against his chest. Then his hands flopped back, palms-up, on either side of his head. She sat up, peered at him, but his eyes remained peacefully closed, and while she watched in astonishment, he fell asleep, with her sitting yet astride him—stunned, naked, and new.

Chapter 16

————

WITH HER FIRST rising movement, Abbie knew she'd overdone it. She was thirty-three years old and some of the muscles she'd stretched last night hadn't been stretched for years. Suppressing a groan, she rolled to the edge of the bed.

"Good morning, Miss Abigail," drawled a pleasant, raspy voice behind her. But she couldn't endure the thought of facing him, knowing that in a few short hours he would simply be walking out of her life. Two strong brown hands circled her white hips, and he kissed her down low, almost where she sat, laying behind her, strewn all over the bed hazardly, like the tumbled sheets.

"Where you going?" he inquired lazily, giving her a fond squeeze.

She sucked in her breath and her back went rigid. "Don't do that, it hurts!"

His hands slipped away and he watched her get up slowly with one hand bracing the small of her back. Two or three steps told them both that her back wasn't the only thing that hurt. But she eased her way to the pile of discarded clothing on the floor, bent over painfully to pick up her wrapper.

Ooooo, did he enjoy that!

He'd planned on a little morning morsel of her but could see that was definitely off. She straightened up just fine, but wasn't moving any too spryly. She shuffled out wiltedly while he felt like the first rose of summer—no doubt about it! He flexed, yawned, scratched his chest, and popped up happily to slip into his pants.

Abbie stood looking at the greasy, ivory-colored platter, the bones and hardened fat with dry, curling edges. She surveyed the coffee cups with brown rings and residue in their bottoms, the plain everyday glasses with now-flat champagne lying lifeless in their depths, the spot on the linen where the laughing piece of steak had hit when it flew from her mouth. Miserably she remembered their gay laughter while she'd tried in vain to settle the tablecloth perfectly all those times. She studied it all and it sickened her, standing in the middle of the room, gripping both ends of her tie-belt as if considering pulling, pulling, pulling, until it cut her in half. She told herself she would *not* think of last night as sordid! *She could not*! But eyeing the mess on the table, she wondered sadly which she wanted to wash up first, the dishes or herself.

Behind her, Jesse crossed his brown arms and leaned a shoulder against the doorframe. He could read her as accurately as if the old beatitudes were suddenly running ticker-tape fashion across the back of her sensible, sexless wrapper.

He wondered what to do or say. If he made a joke, it would fall flat. If he tried to take her in his arms, he was sure she'd push him away. If he conferred upon her the right to place the blame on him, it would only make matters worse. Still, he could not let her stand there interminably, being her own censor.

He came up behind her, placed both hands on her shoulders, and decided to simply say the truth. "In the morning sometimes a person needs reassurance, sometimes both people need reassurance." Her neck was very stiff and he slowly rubbed his long thumbs along its taut cords. He felt her swallow and went on soothingly, "It always seems different in the morning, so the best thing to do is wait until later in the day to decide just how you feel about it. In the meantime, it's customary to at least acknowledge one's partner. That is usually done in a very charming and old-fashioned way—like this."

Abbie felt herself being turned by her shoulders. She knew her hair and face were a fright, that this whole situation was frightful. But he made all that seem petty by lowering her

hands when she sought to hide her hair and eyes, by kissing her
ever so lightly while softly kneading her neck. She wanted to
respond, but was afraid and guilty, thus Jesse had to settle for
no reassurance at all, nothing more than the closing of her
eyelids. Yet he understood that self-retribution already had her
in its clutches, so he kissed her tenderly again, touching her
fleetingly on each corner of her mouth.

His kiss was a new surprise, a unique, nice sensation which
threatened her only with gentleness. But in the middle of it,
with his warm lips wishing her the first lover's good morning of
her life, she remembered that before the day wore out he'd be
gone. Stricken, she controlled the urge to cling to him. She bit
her lip as he rested his chin on top of her head. His hands
rubbed her lower spine in heartrending considersation while he
murmured, "The soreness will go away in no time."

And her thoughts cried, Oh, but so will you, Jesse, so will
you!

She was shaken by his sensitivity, his depth of understanding. Both last night and this morning he had been tenderhearted
in his treatment of her, and she now wished this weren't true. It
made his imminent departure too abrupt and harsh to quite
accept. Were he to turn again to his former ways, teasing,
needling, or irritating her in some fashion, it would suit her far
better, for she told herself rigidly that she would not—*would
not!*—beg him to stay.

He patted her then, back there low, and said, "Why don't
you take a nice hot bath and don't worry about breakfast? We
ate late last night anyway."

She turned stiffly from his embrace, his consideration
ripping some new wound in her with each passing moment.
But still it went on, for when she was laying the fire and he saw
her wince as she lifted a heavy chunk of wood, he came to take
it from her, saying, "Here, let me do that. You go gather up
your clothes or those dishes or something while I get a fire
going and bring in some water."

As she turned away, burdened by his sweetness, he stopped
her, calling quietly, "Abbie?"

She craned around, meeting his eyes directly for the first
time across the morning expanse of kitchen. He looked as
engagingly natural as ever: nothing on but his jeans, standing
there barefoot, with that hunk of wood in his long brown

fingers, his hair tousled and dark, his moustache and eyes as unsettlingly attractive as ever.

"What?" she got out.

"You haven't said anything to me yet this morning except 'Don't do that, it hurts.'"

She thought, damn you, Jesse, don't do this to me! I don't deserve it—not all this!

Why did he have to stand there looking so damn handsome and considerate and warm and likeable only now when he was on the very brink of leaving?

"I'm all right," she said evenly, disguising her turmoil. "Don't worry about last night. I can live with it."

"That's better," he said, putting the chunk of wood down, brushing bark bits off his palms. "Abbie, I have to ask you for a favor."

"Yes?"

"Are the stores open in town yet?"

"Yes."

"Well, all my stuff went on the train with my photographic gear. It was all packed together. I want to go buy a set of clothes, but I don't have any money. I never thought to ask Jim for some. If you could lend me some out of that thousand, I'll see that you get it back."

"Don't be silly. You do not need to pay it back. The money was for anything you need, and if you need clothes, of course you may have as much as you wish."

"I thought I'd just wash my face quick and run a comb through my hair and go on up to buy what I need, then come back here and get cleaned up and changed before I leave. Is that all right with you?"

"You're leaving on the morning train, then?"

"No. I'm meeting some people at noon to discuss . . . some business, then I'll take the three-twenty out this afternoon."

"Meeting some people?" she asked, puzzled, but he looked away, busying himself at his firebuilding.

"Yeah, Jim set up a meeting here and told me about it yesterday. He said I don't have to be there, but I want to since it's . . . well, it's railroad business and I'm involved in it."

She couldn't help but wonder what kind of meeting a railroad photographer would be attending in a town as remote and insignificant as Stuart's Junction, but decided it was none

of her business whatsoever. She was acting like a presuming
lover on the basis of a one-night consortion. He had no
obligation to explain his business dealings to her at all.

"Of course," she agreed, watching him poke at the fire. He
looked so natural, bare-chested and barefoot that way. It was
hard to imagine him in a full set of clothes. She'd never
thought to see the day he'd actually buy and wear them,
railroad meeting or not. It struck her that he must be
inordinately eager to leave, for he had memorized the exact
time of the train whistles.

Some minutes later she was sitting at the secretary in the
parlor when he came out of the bedroom, shirt buttoned, all
tucked in neat and proper, boots on, hair combed.

"I hope it's all right if I used your brush, Abbie, since I don't
have one of my own."

She didn't know whether to laugh or cry at that remark after
what the two of them had shared last night. She handed him a
bank draft she'd written out, saying, "Yes, of course it's all
right. Here. I hope this will do. I haven't much cash in the
house."

He reached out slowly, his eyes never leaving her downcast
face while he scissored the check between two lean fingers.

"I'll be back soon." He hesitated, wishing she'd look at
him, but finally swung away, seeing she would not.

As he went out, limping slightly, she called, "It's Holmes's
Dry Goods Store, on the left side of the street about half a
block down."

Her eyes devoured his broad back. But suddenly he stopped,
braced a palm against the porch column, and studied his boots.
Then he slapped the column, muttered, "Damn," and pivoted.

The screen door squeaked like her love-sprung bones, and
her heart careened while she wished desperately that he'd just
go, get out fast. But he came instead to stand dejectedly beside
the desk, his weight slung on one hip, a thumb hanging from
the waist of his denims. He slumped one shoulder, leaning his
half of the way, but she refused to look up from the pigeonholes
of the desk. The thumb left the waistband and came to her
chin, but she jerked aside, snapping, "Don't!" He hesitated a
moment longer, then leaned the rest of the way, and dropped a
kiss on her nose.

"I'll be back." His voice sounded a little shaky, and her chin
quivered. He straightened, touched her lips with the back of a

forefinger, then left the house as fast as he should have the first time. The screen door slammed and she leaned both elbows onto the desktop, then dropped her face into her hands. She sat that way a long time, miserable, knowing she would get far more miserable before she managed to get over him. Yet get over him she must.

At last she rose, bathed, and went upstairs to dress for the day. She donned a black skirt and a pastel blue organdy blouse. She closed the loops over the many buttons of the deep cuffs, then stretched her neck high and smoothed the tight lace up her throat until it nearly grazed her ears. All the evidence of last night's tryst had been erased, but as she studied her reflection in the oval dresser mirror, she looked ten years older than she had yesterday morning. Behind her, reflected in the glass, she saw the red shoes. She raised her own castigating eyes once more, wondering if after last night those red shoes might fit. She turned, picked one up, studied it, closed her eyes, judging herself. Finally she sat down on the bed and drew a red shoe on.

From downstairs she heard the screen door slam, then Jesse, call, "Abbie? I'm back. Hey, where are you?"

"I'm upstairs," she called, casting a baleful look at the shoe.

He came to the foot of the steps and called up, "Is it all right if I take a bath?"

"Yes. There's hot water left in the reservoir, and clean linens in the bureau drawer across from the pantry."

"I know where you keep them." His footsteps moved away.

She closed her eyes against the onslaught of welcome she felt at his returning, calling up the stairs in that familiar way.

Oh, God, God, she didn't want him to go, not so soon.

The red shoe still dangled from her toe, and she leaned to lace it up. She stuck her foot out, rotated the ankle this way and that, admiring the look and feel of David Melcher's gift.

And somehow Miss Abigail felt reassured, so she put on the second shoe.

She examined them again and the red color seemed to fade into a less offensive, less improper shade. She stood up, balanced on the comfortable shoes, and found they had a heavenly fit. They made her feel petite and feminine. It was the first brief wisp of vanity Abigail McKenzie had allowed herself in her entire life. By the time she'd paced off four trial steps, the shoes had lost all garishness and were actually now quite appealing. It did not concern her that this was true only because she wanted it to be. Pacing back and fourth across the bedroom floor, hearing the baby french heels click on the floorboards, there was nothing within Miss Abigail's conscience to suggest that the reason she was going to wear these shoes downstairs was to show Jesse DuFrayne that even though he was about to walk out of her life forever, he could just bear in mind that he wasn't the only fish in the sea.

"Where the hell do you keep the razor anyway?" Jesse called from downstairs, sounding like his old self again. "Abbie? I've got to hurry."

"Just a moment, I'm coming," she answered, hustling down the steps, the red shoes forgotten. She produced the razor from its kitchen hiding place and turned to find Jesse standing behind her in a pair of greenish-blue stovepipe pants—that's all. Her eyes traveled from his waist to his long toes, then back to his face as he reached for the razor.

"Could you fetch me the strop too, Abbie?" he asked, seemingly unaware of anything that might be happening inside of her.

And something was definitely happening.

Here was a bittersweet pang of a new kind. Here was her house filled with the sight and sound and smell of a men's toilette, something she'd long thought it would never again see. Oh, he had shaved and bathed and dressed here before, but now he did it in preparation to desert her. Now she was intimate with the muscle beneath the trouser, the ridges beneath the razor, the texture beneath the comb, the warmth beneath the smell. Now she wanted to call back time, forbid him to beautify his body for any cause other than her. But she had no right.

So she tried to keep from watching his bare shoulders curl toward the mirror, his head angle away, his eyes strain askance as he shaved near an ear. She tried not to dote upon the scent of shaving soap drifting through her old maid's kitchen. She tried to keep her eyes from coveting the rich fabric of the new pants he was wearing. She tried to ignore the whistle of the 9:50 from Denver when it keened through the house, the same train that had brought him here initially. She pretended that there would be no afternoon train to take him away.

"I left the change on the secretary in the parlor," he said, drying his face, leaning to comb his moustache. She'd never seen him do that before. She tore her greedy eyes away and moved into the parlor to sit before the secretary in an effort to appear busy, rummaging through some papers officiously. But all the time her heart grew heavier. He went into the bedroom and from around the doorway came the rustle of clothing, clunk of boot, chink of buckle, soft whistle through teeth, all punctuated by proclamations of silence during which her imagination took fire with images too familiar and forbidden.

And then out he came.

He stepped through the bedroom doorway and it was all she could do to keep from gasping and letting her jaw drop slack. He might have been a stranger, some striking dandy come to call as he paused, smoothing his vest almost self-consciously with a queer look on his face. His bronze skin beneath the slash of moustache was foiled against a high, stiff wing collar of pristine white, its corners turned back to create a 'V' at his Adam's apple. A four-in-hand tie was meticulously knotted and boasted a scarf pin against its bedeviling silken stripes. The rolled collar of a double-breasted waistcoat peeped from beneath impeccable lapels of a faultless cutaway jacket shorter and more contouring than the frock coats she saw in church on Sundays. The sight of him was breath-stopping, especially in this town, where miners trudged in dirt-grimed britches held by weary suspenders over grayed union suits. Jesse's entire suit was made of that startling color that reminded Abbie of the head of a drake mallard.

She suddenly knew a stab of jealousy so great that she dropped her eyes to keep him from reading them, jealousy for a cause which could make him dress like a peacock only as he left her, when all this time she could scarcely get him to don boots or shirt.

She spoke to her desktop. "You found all these . . . *habiliments* in Stuart's Junction?"

He'd thought she'd be pleased to see him dressed civilly at last, but the three-dollar word was definitely irritated and fault-finding.

"You seem surprised, but you shouldn't be." He moved gracefully to the side of the secretary, touched its writing surface lightly with three fingertips. "The railroads bring in everything they have in the East these days. The Yankees no longer have a monopoly on the up-to-date."

"Hmph," she snorted, "I should think you'd have chosen a less obtrusive color at least."

"What's the matter with this? It's called verdigris, I'm told, and it's all the rage in the East and Europe."

"Verdigris indeed?" she disdained, cocking an eyebrow at the fingers that haunted her, no matter how she tried to ignore them. "Peacock would have been more apropos."

"Peacock?" At last he withdrew his hand to tug his new lapels. "Why, this is no more peacock than . . . than the shoes old Melcher sent you."

Reflexively, she tucked her feet behind the gambriole legs of the desk chair while silently admitting the verdigris was not a bit offensive. It was deep, masculine, and utterly proper. But none of that mattered, for it wasn't really the color which riled her, and by now they both knew it.

"Perhaps it is not the suit that is peacock but only its wearer," she said stringently, and could sense Jesse bristling now.

"Why don't you make up your mind what you want out of me, Miss Abigail?" he asked hotly, referring of course to the clothing, but making her color at the memory of last night's request. Her mouth grew pinched.

"It must be a vital assignation you are going to, to bring about such a transformation when I could scarcely get a shirt on you for love or money!" Their eyes at last met in a clash of wills, but her dubious, ill-chosen phrase became poignant with unintended meaning.

"Not for love or money?" he repeated, slowly, precisely. She realized she had employed both in the last ten hours.

"Do not dare take those words figuratively, sir!" she snapped. "Just go! Be off to your *tête-à-tête*—whatever it is—in your *verdigris* suit. But don't forget to take your everyday britches along. You never can tell when you'll get these shot off for you!"

They glared at each other while Jesse wondered how to get out of here gracefully without further recriminations on either side. At last he placed his hands on his hips, his stance wilted, and he shook his head at the floor. "Abbie," he asked entreatingly, "for God's sake, can't we at least say goodbye without all this again?"

"Why? It makes it far more familiar to see you leave with anger in your eyes."

He realized that this was true, that wrapped in the security blanket of anger she needn't make appeals or excuses. He squatted beside her chair as she stared unblinkingly into the pigeonholed depths of the desktop.

"Abbie," he said quietly, taking one of her small, clenched hands, which refused to open, "I don't want to leave you in anger. I want to see you smiling and I want to be smiling myself."

"If you'll pardon me, I don't seem to have a lot to smile about this morning."

He sighed, stared at her hem, and absently rubbed his fingers over her tightly knotted fist that he had placed on his upraised knee.

Damn! Damn! she thought, why does he have to smell so good and be so nice? Why now?

"I knew you'd be bitter this morning," he went on. "I tried to warn you but you wouldn't listen. Abbie, I don't have time to stay here and help you straighten out your conscience. Just believe me. What happened happened, and you have nothing to be ashamed of. Tell me you won't go on feeling guilty."

But she would not say any such thing, or loosen her fist, or even look at him. Had she done any of those things she would end up in his arms again, and already she was bound for a long stint in hell, she was sure. Jesse realized it was getting late, that he must soon leave. "Abbie, there's one thing that's . . . . Listen, Abbie, what we did might not be over yet, you know. If anything happens, I mean if you should be pregnant, will you let me know?"

It had never, never entered her mind. Not before, during, or after making love with him, but his considering the possibility gave her the final, unforgivable cut, for she knew he would never come back and marry her if it did turn out that way.

He was saying, "You can reach me any time by wiring the central R.M.R. office in Denver," when she slowly pivoted toward him and slipped two scarlet kidskin toes from beneath her skirt, right next to that verdigris knee on the floor. He saw the red toes peep slowly from beneath her skirt, like two insolent, protruding tongues, and jumped to his feet, fists clenched at his sides, two small horizontal creases now behind the knee of the very pant leg which he had bent to her with the kindest of intentions.

"Goddammit, Abbie, what do you expect of me! he

shouted. "I told you last night I was going, and I am! Don't think I don't know why you're wearing those . . . those strumpet's shoes! But it's not going to work. You're not going to beat me over the head with the kidskin fact that you are now a scarlet woman, because it takes more than one night in bed with a man to make you one! You wanted what you got and so did I, so don't make me the fall guy. Grow up, Abbie. Grow up and realize that we're both a little right and both a little wrong and that you do not have the corner on guilt in this world!"

She kept her eyes trained on his knee and innocently intoned, "My, my, what a shame, Mr. DuFrayne, to have crimped your faultless peacock pant leg that way."

"All right, Abbie, have it your way, but don't make a fool of yourself by parading down Main Street in those goddamn red shoes!"

At that moment a querulous voice spoke from the front door. "Miss . . . Miss Abigail, are you all right?" David Melcher peered in, suffering the unsettling feeling of *déjà vu*, for it seemed he'd lived through this scene once before.

Miss Abigail shot to her feet, gaping. You could easily have stuffed both red shoes into the cavern of her mouth just then before she gathered her scattered wits enough to stammer, "M . . . Mr. Melcher . . . how . . . how long have you b . . . been standing there?" Frantically she heard the echo of Jesse's comments about scarlet women and pregnancy.

"I only just got here this minute. How long has *he* been here?"

But Jesse DuFrayne would not be talked past as if he were some cigar store Indian. His tone was icy and challenging as he faced the door. "I've been here since before you left, Melcher, so what of it!"

David pierced him with a look of pure hate. "I'll speak with you across a bargaining table at high noon and not a minute before. I am here to see Miss Abigail. I assumed you would have relieved her of your presence long before this, especially since you are obviously well enough to be arranging arbitration discussion these days."

DuFrayne angrily jerked a cuff into place, confirming flatly, "As you say, at noon then." He spun toward the bedroom to get his few things, leaving Abbie to seethe with shock yet unable to show it.

He knew! He knew! All the time he knew! He knew since

Jim Hudson came that David would be returning to Stuart's Junction. He knew because the meeting today was between the two of them, apparently to settle the liability over the shootings on the train. The pompous, conceited bag of arrogance knew that he was not her last chance, yet he stole her virginity anyway, knowing she'd never have given it had she known of Melcher's imminent return. Neither did it take much perception to guess that a man like David Melcher would never accept a soiled bride. Miss Abigail wanted to fly at Jesse DuFrayne and pummel him to a pulp, scream out her rage at how she'd been taken advantage of when he could simply have told her the truth and David might have been hers!

Melcher saw the anger blotch her face, but could not guess at what the foul-mouthed DuFrayne had said this time to place it there. Miss Abigail seemed to gather her equilibrium again, for she turned and invited sweetly, "Please come in, Mr. Melcher," and even opened the screen for him.

"Thank you." He came in bearing her father's cane, but just then Jesse shouldered his way around the bedroom doorway, gripping his wadded-up britches and gun in one hand as he clomped through the parlor.

"Your man has arrived in town then?" Melcher inquired expressionlessly.

"He got here yesterday," DuFrayne answered, the quivers of anger scarcely held in check. "And yours?"

"He's waiting at the depot as the wire stated he should."

DuFrayne nodded once sharply, feeling Abbie's eyes boring into the back of his head in cold, suppressed wrath. He turned, relaxed his jaw long enough to say stiffly, "Goodbye, Miss Abigail."

She was suddenly revisited by all the hate she'd felt for Jesse DuFrayne that other morning when his insinuations had lost David to her. Now it scarcely mattered that it was DuFrayne going and Melcher staying, for the mild-mannered man was again lost to her as surely as if Jesse DuFrayne had raised his gun, pointed, and shot David Melcher square between the eyes.

Jesse read before him the face of woman spurned, and his insides twisted with guilt.

"The same to you . . . *Mister* Dufrayne!"

His eyes bored into hers for a moment before he turned on his heel, banked past David Melcher, and hit for the door. In his wake, Abbie's nostrils were filled with the distressing scent of his shaving soap.

"Well, at least he's learned to address you in terms of respect," David noted stiffly.

Watching Jesse limp away down the street, she murmured, "Yes . . . yes, he has," though she longed to shriek a last dementi at the sarcasm now reflected by the term.

David cleared his throat. "I . . . I've returned your fa . . . father's cane, Miss Abigail." When she did not respond, he repeated, "Miss Abigail?"

She turned absently, forcing her mind away from Jesse DuFrayne. "I'm happy you did, Mr. Melcher, I really am. Not because I wanted it back, but because it gives me a chance to see you again."

He colored slightly, rather surprised by her directness, so different than the last time he'd spoken to her. He thought that he detected a brittle edge to her voice that he didn't remember from before either.

"Yes, well . . . I . . . I had to return to Stuart's Junction to attend a meeting at which we will attempt to ascertain who was to blame for the entire fiasco aboard the train."

"Yes, I only heard of the meeting this morning. How *is* your foot?"

He looked down at it, then back up. "The discomfort is gone. The limp is not."

At last the old solicitude returned to her voice. "Ah, I am so sorry. Perhaps in time it too will disappear." But she recalled how Doc said he would walk with a limp for the rest of his life.

"I see you . . . ahum . . . got the gift I sent," he stammered.

Now it was Miss Abigail's turn to glance at her feet. Gracious! she thought, I would have to have these things on just when he arrived!

"They're even lovelier on your feet than off," Melcher said, completely unaware of the shoe's unacceptability, and she hadn't the heart to crush his pride.

"They're a perfect fit," she said, truthfully enough, raising her skirt a few inches and flexing her toes within the supple kidskin. "I wanted to thank you but I had no address where I might reach you." Looking up then, she saw that David Melcher was embarrassed by how much of her ankle she'd revealed. Quickly she dropped her skirts. How rapidly one forgot propriety before a true gentleman after even a brief sojourn with a rounder like Jesse.

"You must forgive my rude manners, Mr. Melcher. Please sit down," she insisted, indicating the settee and taking a side chair. "I've had a somewhat trying morning and I'm afraid I've allowed my manners to lapse because of it. Please . . . please sit. Enough about me. What about you? Will you be on your way again selling shoes as soon as this meeting today is concluded?"

"I'd hoped . . . that is to say . . . I had considered spending . . . ah well, a couple of days right . . . right here in Stuart's Junction. I've taken a room at the ah, hotel, and deposited my gear there. I have the largest shipment of shoes ever—it was waiting for me in Denver. I thought I would see about finding some new markets for them right here and in the towns close around."

"Well in that case, perhaps you'll be free this evening to pay a call on me and tell me the outcome of today's meeting. I am most interested, of course, since both you and—" she found it difficult to say his name now "—Mr. DuFrayne were both under my care."

"Yes," David said a little breathlessly. "I . . . I'd like that ev . . . ever so much. Of course I realize you'll be anxious for the . . . the news."

"The whole town will be, Mr. Melcher. Nothing quite like this has ever happened in Stuart's Junction before and I'm sure tongues have been wagging fit to kill. When the meeting commences, the townspeople will be even more curious, I'm sure."

He fiddled with his vest buttons nervously before finally asking, with countless clearings of his throat, "Miss . . . Miss Abigail, did . . . agh . . . did you, or rather . . . has your . . . agh . . . has your repu—that is to say, have the townspeople . . . agh, said anything . . ."

She finally took pity on his overstrained sense of delicacy. "No, Mr. Melcher. My reputation has not suffered because of either you or Mr. DuFrayne being here at my house. I believe it's fair to say the people of this town know me better than that."

"Oh, of course," he quickly put in, "I didn't mean—"

"Please," she extended one delicate hand toward him, "let's not speak in parables. It brings only misunderstandings. Let us agree to start over as the best of friends and forget anything which has passed."

Again her directness befuddled him, but he reached out and took the proferred fingertips in his own for a fraction of a second while his raddled face told her again how very, very different this man was from Jesse DuFrayne.

"Until this evening then," she said softly.

"Yes . . . agh . . . until this evening."

He cleared his throat for perhaps the fiftieth time since entering her house, and suddenly it irritated Miss Abigail profoundly.

The inquisitive citizens of Stuart's Junction knew something was up when Max kicked Ernie off his customary bench on the depot porch long before the 3:20 was due, declaring the station was closed for official railroad business until further notice.

All up and down the boardwalk the news spread that that Melcher fellow with the shot off toe had checked in up at Albert's Hotel, along with some dandy in a yellow-checkered suit. They knew, too, that some fancy-dressed railroad bigwig had been in town since yesterday. And it was no secret that the one from up't Miss Abigail's house came uptown this morning and bought that fancy suit they'd all been starin' at in the window of Holmes's Dry Goods Store. When they saw him limp down the street wearing it, speculation grew heavy.

"Well, if he ain't no train robber, what do you reckon he is, and what do you reckon's goin' on up to the depot?"

But all they could get out of Max was that a representative of the R.M.R. had called a meeting here.

Max dusted the runged oak chairs and gathered them around a makeshift conference table made of a couple of raw planks balanced on two nail kegs, since the station was too new to boast a real table yet. Word had it the men were gussied up fit to kill. Max picked a sliver off a raw-edged plank, anxious to please. Yessir, he thought, looks like this is real important, whatever it is. So he rounded up a pitcher and four glasses, and filled it with water from the giant holding tank looming above the tracks outside where the steam engines drank their fill.

The four of them converged on the depot at the same time, the quartet looking altogether like a rainbow trout. There was James Hudson, in a wine-colored business suit. He shook

Max's hand. "Nice clean depot you keep here, Smith."
Instantly he gained Max's sympathy. Jesse DuFrayne appeared
in the teal blue suit which even Max had been eyeballing at
Holmes's Dry Goods. When Hudson introduced Maxwell
Smith, he said, "Smith is our station agent here in Stuart's
Junction."

DuFrayne, extending his hand, noted congenially, "Mr.
Smith, the man who refused to deport me without a release
from Doc Dougherty? I want to thank you for that, sir."

Though Max said, "Aw, think nuthin' of it," he was
enormously pleased and proud.

Hudson seemed to take the lead in all the introductions and
Max kept his ears open, learning that the man in the yellow-
checkered suit was Peter Crowley, Melcher's lawyer. By the
time Hudson suggested, "Gentlemen, shall we all be seated?"
Max was relieved. All this commotion and color during the
hand shaking was getting him dizzy. He'd never seen such a
bunch of dandies in his life!

James Hudson took a seat at the makeshift table as if it were
polished mahogany. There was an air of leadership about him
that stood out among the four. "Now, Crowley," he began, "I
suggest we forego accusations and stick to the straight facts
regarding the circumstances surrounding the shootings. Both
Mr. Melcher and Mr. DuFrayne have obviously undergone
some incapacitation due to the incident on the train."

"Mr. Melcher has come here to discuss liability," Crowley
replied. Melcher nodded. DuFrayane sat like a statue, glowering at him while verdigris arms remained folded tightly across
his chest. Hudson and Crowley went on.

"Do you mean liability on both sides or just one?" Hudson
asked.

"By that I take you to mean that DuFrayne sees Mr. Melcher
as liable in some way?"

"Well, isn't he?"

"He doesn't think so."

"He is the one who precipitated the scuffle in which Mr.
DuFrayne was shot."

"He did not precipitate it. He came in in the middle of it."

"Causing DuFrayne to receive a nearly fatal gunshot."

"From which your client has obviously recovered, according to reports I have here from one . . ." Crowley
examined a sheaf of papers before him ". . . Dr. Cleveland

Dougherty, who states that DuFrayne will, in all likelihood, recover full use of the leg, while Mr. Melcher will undoubtedly walk with a limp for the remainder of his life.''

"For which Mr. Melcher presumably feels he is entitled to a settlement of some sort?"

"Indeed." Crowley leaned back in his chair.

"To the tune of what?" Hudson asked, steepling his fingertips.

"Mr. Melcher was riding aboard an R.M.R. coach when he was shot. Should not the owners of the railway be liable?"

More sharply this time, Hudson asked, "To the tune of what, I asked, Mr. Crowley?"

"Shall we say ten thousand dollars?"

Then all hell broke loose. DuFrayne leaped to his feet like a springing panther, glaring at Melcher with feral eyes. "Shall we *not* say ten thousand, you scheming little parasite!" he shouted.

"Parasite!" the shaken Melcher braved in his angriest tone while Hudson and Crowley tried to settle the pair down. "Just who is the parasite here, I ask!"

"Well, it sure as hell isn't me!" DuFrayne stormed. "You're the one looking for a handout, thinking that the railroad can afford it. After all, railroads are rich, aren't they? Why not milk this one for as much as you can get?"

"Any railroad can well afford that amount, it's true."

"Why, you little—"

"Jess, settle down!" Hudson got him by an arm and pushed him back toward his chair.

"Gentlemen, control yourselves," Crowley interjected.

"DuFrayne obviously doesn't know the meaning of the word. He never has!" Melcher claimed irately.

Crowley took his client in hand. "Mr. Melcher, we're here to discuss liability."

"And so we shall. He is liable, all right, for far more than a physical wound to me. What about the wounds he caused Miss Abigail?"

A fine white line appeared around the entire circumferance of DuFrayne's lips, but hidden on the upper one by his moustache, which outlined his formidable scowl. Rage bubbled in him, spawned by Melcher's accusation, but swelled by his own secret guilt over Abbie. Having Melcher unwittingly remind him of it only increased his hatred of the man.

"You leave Miss Abigail out of this!" DuFrayne barked.

"Yes, you'd like that, I'm sure. You were insufferable to her and would probably like not to be reminded of just exactly how insufferable!"

Confused, James Hudson spoke. "Miss Abigail? Do you mean Miss Abigail McKenzie? I cannot see what possible bearing she could have on any of this."

"Nor I," agreed Crowley. "Mr. Melcher, please—"

"No amount of money can atone for his treatment of her," Melcher said.

"Miss Abigail has already been recompensed for her help," Hudson assured him. "Mr. DuFrayne saw to that."

"Oh, yes, I've seen just how DuFrayne pays her back for everything she does. He forces her—"

Again DuFrayne flew to his feet. "You leave Abbie out of this, you little pipsqueak, or so help me—"

"Damnit, Jess, sit down!" Hudson at last lost patience. But in his anger, Jesse had used the familiar first name of the woman. Max noted it with great interest. When things cooled down a little, Hudson placed ten fingertips on the pine plank and spoke carefully. "It seems you two are picking bones that have nothing to do with the issue at hand. Now, you have asked Mr. Crowley and myself here as your arbiters. Will you allow us to arbitrate or shall we leave the two of you to haggle by yourselves?" A pause, then, "Mr. Crowley, suppose that Mr. DuFrayne agrees to a settlement on Mr. Melcher, what consideration would he receive in return?"

"I'm afraid you confuse me, sir. I didn't think it was DuFrayne's decision. I thought that you spoke for the railroad in this matter."

Hudson cleared the tabletop of his fingers, glanced at Jesse.

"Jess?" he asked quietly. All eyes in the room trained on DuFrayne.

"No."

"It's time, Jess. Do you want to pay out ten thousand for nothing?"

But DuFrayne clamped his lips tightly and brooded while the two arbiters went on discussing. Jesse's dark face was unreadable, although Melcher pierced him with hating eyes. Fraught by guilt over the night before, and by anger that Melcher should be squeezing for every penny he could get, Jesse was plagued by an idea that would not desist. Suppose they settled enough money on the vulture to set him up for life? Suppose they made the damn fool so rich that he could settle down in one place and sell shoes till hell froze over? Suppose they fixed him up comfy and cozy right here where all he'd need next was a woman to settle with? As distasteful as it was, it would at least salve Jesse DuFrayne's conscience over last night. If he could arrange it, Abbie would end up with everything she'd ever need or want—that sheep-faced shoe peddler, the means to set up a substantial business, and enough money to keep the two of them in red kidskin for the rest of their lackluster lives! DuFrayne again pictured Abbie's face as she'd come to him last night, saying, "David Melcher is gone and he shall never return. You're my last chance, Jesse." Glimmers of what had followed painted Jesse's mind. She was a woman with too much fire to be wasted on the likes of Melcher, but she was probably right in assuming that Stuart's Junction offered no better alternatives. Better she should have Melcher to shower a few sparks on than burn for nobody at all. He came out of his ruminations and picked up the thread of argument still going on.

". . . hardly think the sentence of life as a partial cripple would be considered nothing if this were taken to court, do you? You must consider the fact also that Mr. Melcher thought he was *defending* the railroad against what he considered an armed thief." Crowley's tone sounded slightly smug, and at last Hudson lost patience.

"Mr. Crowley," he rebutted testily, "I want to get something straight for the record. I'm tired of DuFrayne's name being bandied about as a train robber when it's the most preposterous accusation in the world! Now I ask you, why would any man want to rob his own train?"

"Jim!" barked DuFrayne, but his friend paid him little mind.

"Yes, you heard me correctly. You see, gentlemen, Jesse DuFrayne is a major shareholder of stock in the R.M.R. In other words, he owns the railroad—which he is accused of robbing."

In his corner, Max sat like a katydid with stilled wings. Crowley looked like he was trying to spit up a goose egg caught in his throat. Melcher looked like he was trying to swallow one. DuFrayne sat like a stone, facing the window, staring at the blue sky beyond, where a tip of the water tank showed. Hudson waited for the spell to take full effect. Melcher was the first to speak.

"If you think that this changes what you own Miss Abigail, it doesn't. Your being a big railroad owner in no way excuses your actions toward her. You may be innocent of robbing that train, but where she is concerned, you are guilty of the most grossly unforgiveable breaches of con—"

"Pay him!" Jesse snapped with agate hardness, attempting to shut the man up, for by now Jess had become aware of the station agent, gawking like a hawk from his corner. The man had ears, and it didn't take much straining to hear everything being said in the room.

"Now wait a minute, Jess—"

"I said pay him, Jim, and I mean it," barked DuFrayne.

Melcher couldn't believe his ears. Only a moment ago he'd have sworn all chance for monetary gain was nil, realizing how thoroughly he'd misjudged DuFrayne's intentions aboard that train. Still, he could not hold his tongue.

"Conscience money is just as sp—"

"And you shut up, little man, if you want so much as a penny out of me!" Jesse spit, jumping to his feet, pointing a finger. "Jim, just do as I say."

"Now wait a minute, Jess, the railroad is partly mine. I want some satisfaction out of this before we just hand him what he wants."

Suddenly DuFrayne lurched around. The scrape of chair legs made Melcher twitch back from the table. "I want to talk to you outside, Jim." DuFrayne was oblivious to the curious stares from across the street. He stood steely, furious, on the depot porch, his thumbs hooked into his waistcoat pockets, eyes narrowed vacantly at the gold pans hanging on display before a store across the way.

"Jess, I had to tell them about your ownership," Hudson reasoned.

"That's all right, Jim, it was bound to come out sooner or later. I just didn't want Abbie to find out about it before I left town, that's all."

"There's something going on here that I don't understand and maybe it's none of my business, but I just want you to think of what you're doing before you make any rash decisions about handing over what that leech wants."

"I've been considering it and my mind is made up."

"You're sure?"

"With several stipulations, and with the understanding that the money paid to Melcher is from my profits only, not yours."

They spoke quietly for several minutes, then reentered the station and took their places at the makeshift table.

"Mr. Crowley," Hudson addressed the man rather than his client, "if the railroad agrees to imburse Mr. Melcher ten thousand for damages, we will in turn demand that certain stipulations be fulfilled by him. First, Melcher will issue a statement to the local newspaper to the effect the railroad was in no way liable for this incident due to the fact that Mr. DuFrayne was carrying a gun, but only to the extent that your client was aboard one of our coaches when he was shot. The statement must in no way denigrate Mr. DuFrayne's name or that of Miss Abigail McKenzie but shall instead make it explicitly clear that Mr. DuFrayne was indeed not robbing the train, but that Mr. Melcher misjudged DuFrayne's intentions at the time. He may indicate that he acted for what he thought was the good of the passengers if he wishes, but that is the only defense he must give for his actions.

"Our second stipulation is that Mr. Melcher invest no less than two-thirds of this settlement money in a business or livelihood based in Stuart's Junction. He may choose whatever type of venture he wishes, but it must be in this town and it cannot be sold within the next five years.

"The third stipulation is that Mr. Melcher, personally, never again ride aboard an R.M.R. train. He may, of course, use the railroad to further his business venture by transporting goods, but he himself shall never again set foot on one of our coaches.

"We shall want these terms validated in writing and notarized, and of course there shall be an inclusion stating that if any of these terms are not fulfilled Mr. Melcher shall be liable to repay the R.M.R. the full amount of ten thousand dollars upon demand."

Crowley raised a silent, inquiring eyebrow at Melcher, who still floundered in the backwash of shock. Not only was DuFrayne vindicated of attempted robbery, he was rich enough and powerful enough to put the final nod to a settlement of ten thousand dollars of what, in retrospect, was his own capital anyway! The fact made Melcher's face flame and his hands shake. He clearly did not understand the man's reasons for stipulating that the money be reinvested in Stuart's Junction,

but he was certainly not about to inquire. It was appalling
enough to be subjected the man's self-satisfied supremacy
without being subjected to his reasoning, which might be as
galling as the fact that he was issuing ultimatums in the first
place.

"I will agree," Melcher stated flatly, "but with one
condition of my own."

"And that?" Hudson asked.

"That DuFrayne pr . . . privately apologize to Miss Mc
. . . McKenzie."

"You go too far, Melcher!" DuFrayne warned stormily, his
face now livid. "Any animosity between Miss McKenzie and
myself has no bearing on this bargaining session and, furthermore, is none of your business!"

"You made it my business, sir, one morning when you took
gross liberties in her bedroom right before my eyes!"

"Enough!" roared DuFrayne, while Max nearly swallowed
his tongue. The big man took to his feet, bumping the table and
nearly upsetting it, sending the water pitcher careening
precariously, glasses teetering. One circled and finally tipped,
sending a splash of water over the table edge onto Melcher's
lap while DeFrayne, with feet aspraddle, glared venomously,
clenching his fists. "Our differences are settled, Abbie's and
mine, so say no more of her, do you hear? You can take your
ten thousand in blood money or toe money or whatever you
choose to call it and live in splendor the rest of your days, or
you can watch me walk out of here with the control of it still in
my pocket and never see me again! Now which will it be?"

Melcher glared at the black moustache, envisioning again
that bold, bare body that had taunted both him and Miss
Abigail, wishing fervently that the bullet had struck Du-
Frayne's anatomy about four inches to the left of where it had!
But were he to voice his thought, he stood to lose ten thousand
dollars of this devil's own lucre. Neither did he doubt that
DuFrayne meant it when he said one more word and David
would see his back but not his money. And so David bit his
tongue, daring not to insist again on the apology he so badly
wanted for Miss Abigail. His Adam's apple bulged where his
pride was stuck in his throat. But he only nodded woodenly.

"Very well. I'll give the newspapers only the answers you
want, but don't you ever come back to Stuart's Junction again,
DuFrayne. You have no reason to." They both knew he eluded

Abigail McKenzie, but DuFrayne carefully thrust one last
oste at Melcher.

"You're forgetting, Melcher, that I own property here, some
which you are standing upon at this very minute. Don't
tate to me where I can and cannot go . . . in business
erests, of course," he finished sarcastically, with one
brow quirked.

udson interjected, "There seems little more to be said
e," attempting to dull the animosity between the two and
w an end to the proceeding before they came to blows. "Mr.
owley, if you will remain, we can draw up the agreement,
ve it verified before I leave town, and we will see about
ting a bank draft to Mr. Melcher within three days at
atever destination he signifies. You understand that Mr.
Frayne will have to free that amount personally from his
counts in Denver."

"Yes, I understand. If that is agreeable to Mr. Melcher, that
agreeable to me."

Melcher stood stiffly.

When things broke up, Hudson and DuFrayne stepped
tside into the arid midday heat, which didn't help Jesse's
nper any.

"What the hell's wrong with you anyway, Jess?" Hudson
ok his friend's elbow as if to cool his temper. "I've never
en you quite this defensive and belligerent over a woman
fore."

"Woman, hell! I just signed over ten thousand of my hard-
rned bucks to that pipsqueak in there! How the hell would
u feel?"

"Now hold on, Jess. You're the one who said give it to him,
d I gathered at the time it was as much to shut him up as for
y other reason. Just what did go on up there at Miss
cKenzie's house anyway?"

Jesse's eyes moved to the gable of Abbie's house, visible
yond the false-fronted saddlery and harness shop. His stare
s mechanical, his lips taut as he replied, "You have an
quisitive mind, Jim, and I have a temper. And that's why you
 the business and I do the field work. Let's just keep it that
ay, only reserve your inquisitions for the likes of Melcher
ere, old buddy, huh?"

"All right . . . as you like it. But if you're after preserving
iss McKenzie's reputation, how about that station agent with

his cocked ear and bulging eyes? I don't know what t⌐
remark meant, about your taking liberties in the bedroom of ⌐
lady in question, but it could come to have all kinds
unexpected ramifications once it rolls off the tongue of o⌐
station agent. Shall I go inside and bribe him or will you⌐

"Goddamnit, Jim, didn't I take enough abuse from Melch⌐
with you adding to it?"

But Hudson understood his friend's frustration, thus ⌐
scolding was taken with a grain of salt. But there w⌐
something eating Jess that he wasn't letting on about. Huds⌐
couldn't help but wonder exactly what it was.

"Just trying to be practical," Hudson added.

"Well, you go on inside and be practical any way you see ⌐
I've already lost enough . . . *practicality* for one day."

They made arrangements to meet back at the hotel ju⌐
before train time, then Hudson went back into the depot wh⌐
DuFrayne made for the local saloon, to be stared at ⌐
everybody in the place except Ernie Turner, who was sou⌐
asleep with his head in a puddle of sweat from his beer glas⌐

Chapter 17

———

FROM THE SECOND-STORY window in his hotel room on Main Street, David Melcher watched Hudson and DuFrayne board the 3:20. He had done as promised, had given the newspaper only the information agreed upon, yet it vexed Melcher mercilessly to have had to gild DuFrayne in any way whatsoever. It would vex him even more to accidentally run into DuFrayne at Miss Abigail's house again, thus he waited until DuFrayne was safely aboard the train and it had ground its way out of town.

Then and only then did David Melcher allow his victory to overwhelm him, to make him smile at its limitless possibilities. The thought of owning ten thousand dollars elated him, and he hummed as he changed clothes and brushed his hair, thinking of the sudden rosy future ahead of him. By the time he arrived at Miss Abigail's doorstep, he was beaming like the headlamp of an R.M.R. engine.

"Why, Mr. Melcher, you're early!" she said when she saw him there. But she was relieved to have his company, for the last five hours had been the longest of her life. Not only had her imagination run rife with scenes from the meeting at the depot, she had had to allow it to run its course with visions of Jesse boarding the 3:20, which she could not see from her

place, and riding out of Stuart's Junction in that stunning sui
with his likable friend, James Hudson, the two of them neve
to return again. When the steam whistle raised its billow o
white above the rooftops and sighed its departing scream, sh
had crossed her arms tightly across her chest and though
Good. He is getting out of my life forever. But when the las
clack of wheels had died away into summer silence, she ha
felt suddenly bereft and lonely.

Having David Melcher arrive, with his cheerful expression
was exactly what she needed to chase away lingering thought
of Jesse DuFrayne. Standing now on her porch step, Davi
wore an almost cherubic look, his pink cheeks blossoming int
a little boy smile, almost as if he wanted to flatten his nos
against the screen in delight. She knew immediately that th
decision at the depot must have gone in his favor.

"And what has brought such a look of jubilation to you
face?" Miss Abigail asked.

For once he forgot himself and asked, "Can I come in?" H
had the door open before she could give him permission o
open it for him. "Yes, I'm early, and yes, I'm jubilant, and ca
you guess why, Miss Abigail?"

She could not help but smile with him. "Well, I guess th
meeting's results met with your approval, but—my goodness
Mr. Melcher—you're almost dancing. Do sit down."

He perched on the edge of the settee, then popped back u
like a jack-in-the-box.

"Miss Abigail, I hope you're still wearing those red shoes
because I want to take you out for supper to celebrate."

"To celebrate? . . . Out to supper? . . . Why . .
why, Mr. Melcher!" She'd never been taken out to supper i
her life.

He forgot himself even further and clasped both of her hand
in his and, looking down into her amazed face, said, "Why
our victory of course. The railroad has agreed to settle te
thousand dollars on me for damages."

For a moment she couldn't speak, she was so stunned. He
jaw dropped down so far that her high collar bit into her neck
"Ten . . . thousand . . . dollars?" she repeated incredu
lously, then dropped off her feet into a side chair.

"Exactly!" He beamed at her a moment longer, then seeme
to remember himself and dropped her hands to take his sea
over on the settee again.

"My, how admirably generous," she said lamely, picturing James Hudson again, and the check for the thousand dollars he'd left on the seat of the umbrella stand.

David Melcher knew he should tell her now about DuFrayne being part-owner of the railroad, but he did not want anything putting a damper on their evening together.

"Do say you'll allow me to take you out this evening to celebrate with me. I consider it our victory, yours and mine together. It seems only right that we should commemorate it with an evening on the town."

"But it's your compensation, not mine."

"Miss Abigail, I don't care to cast shadows over the bright joy of the moment, but considering the circumstances under which we met, I feel—shall we say—rather liable to you for the indignities you suffered at the hands of that vile man DuFrayne. I have felt helpless to make up in any way for all that. Now, coming out the winner in this dispute seems like we've somehow brought him to bay at last. Not only for what he did to me, but what he did to you, too."

She studied the man perched on the edge of her settee. He spoke with such earnestness, wanting to be her champion, that she was suddenly swept by guilt that he should still consider her a flawless lady, worthy of his chivalry. She felt, too, an utter hopelessness, because she could not undo what she and Jesse DuFrayne had done together. How she wished that it had never happened, that she could honestly deserve David Melcher's advocation and admiration. She touched a hand to her high collar and looked away.

"Oh, Mr. Melcher, I'm truly touched, but I think it would be best for me not to celebrate your victory. Let me just congratulate you and keep the shoes as your thank you."

Disappointment covered his face. "You won't even let me buy you dinner?"

But their relationship had no future now. She got up from the side chair and walked over to the secretary and pretended that a cluster of papers there needed straightening. With her back to him, she answered, "I simply think it's best if you don't."

David Melcher swallowed, flushed, then stammered, "Is . . . is it that you c . . . cannot forgive me for what I ac . . . accused you of, that awf . . . f . . . ful morning when I left here?"

"Oh, no!" She swung to face him, an imploring look upon

her face. "That's all forgotten, please believe me, Dav—Mr. Melcher."

But he'd heard her slip. He stood up, gathered his courage, and approached her. Flustered, she turned toward the desk again.

"Then pr . . . pr . . . prove it," he got out finally.

She turned to look over her shoulder at him, one hand still trailing on the desktop.

"Prove it?" she repeated.

"C . . . come to dinner with m . . . me and pr . . . prove that everything up t . . . till now is f . . . f . . . forgotten."

Again she touched the lace at her throat, a winsome expression softening her features. Oh, how she wanted to go to dinner with a fine gentleman like him, for the first time in her life. She wanted the gaiety and carelessness that her youth had never tasted, the charm and companionship of a man at her elbow. She wanted to share the mutual interests which she knew the two of them were capable of sharing.

He still waited for her answer, the invitation alight in his brown eyes.

Recriminations jangled through her mind. If only it were yesterday. If only I had not done what I did with Jesse. If only . . . if only. Anger touched her, too. Damn you, Jesse, why didn't you tell me he was coming back?

She knew she must refuse, but in the end David's invitation was too tempting. What will it hurt if I spent one evening with him—just one? He, too, is here today and gone tomorrow, so what harm can come of a single evening in his company?

"Dinner sounds nice," she understated, already feeling guilty for accepting.

"Then you'll come?" He again looked jubilant.

"I'll come."

"And you'll wear the red shoes?"

Oh, dear! she thought, feeling herself flush. But there was no graceful way to get out of it now, for he was totally unaware of the shoes' flamboyance. But then, as if in answer to her discomfort, came Jesse's belittling voice, as she remembered him warning, "Just don't make a fool of yourself by parading down Main Street in those goddamn red shoes!" And so, diffidently, she left them on, praying all the way that none of the townspeople noticed them on her feet. But she'd have given that thousand-dollar bank deposit if Jesse DuFrayne himself could have seen her wearing them uptown to have dinner with David Melcher, her gloved hand in the crook of his arm as they walked along the boardwalk.

Not a soul in town could find fault with their demeanor.

By the next morning everyone in Stuart's Junction knew exactly how polite David Melcher had been and just how proper and prim Miss Abigail had been. They also knew what the couple had ordered and exactly how long they'd stayed and how many times they'd smiled at each other. But they had it straight from Louis Culpepper's mouth how Miss Abigail showed up wearing *red* shoes, of all things. Red! They must've been a gift from Melcher, 'cause it seemed he was a shoe peddler out of the East somewhere.

Imagine that! they all said, Miss Abigail taking up with a shoe peddler, and an easterner no less. And doing it decked out like December twenty-fifth in red shoes the man had given her after sleeping in her house!

"What a memorable evening," Miss Abigail said as they walked idly back to her house after supper. It was the slowest she had ever walked home from town. "How can I thank you?"

He limped along beside her. With each step he took, she could feel the hitch of his stride pull lightly at the hand with which she held his elbow.

"By not refusing me the next time I ask you."

She controlled the urge to turn her startled eyes up at him. "The next time? Why, aren't you leaving Stuart's Junction soon?"

"No, I'm not. As I said earlier, I have a large stock of shoes to sell and I intend to approach some local merchants in hopes that they'll act as outlets for us. Also, the railroad will be sending my settlement money to Stuart's Junction, so I'll have to wait here till it arrives."

Again she controlled the urge to ask how many days it would take.

He refrained from telling her that he was being forced to invest the major portion of the settlement money right here, for it made him look like DuFrayne's puppet, and the fact that David was galled him. David wanted her to believe that the decision to stay and settle here had been his own, which it probably would have been if it had been left up to him.

"How . . . how many days do you think it will take?" she finally asked.

"Three days maybe."

Three days, she thought. Oh, glorious three days! What harm can come of enjoying his company for three days? They're all I'll have, and then he'll be gone for good.

"In that case, I shall not refuse you anything while you're here," she said, and felt him tighten his elbow around her gloved hand and pull it against his ribs.

"Miss Abigail, you won't be sorry," he promised.

But deep inside Miss Abigail already was, for tonight had been so wonderful. And because her heart had jumped when he pulled her hand against his ribs.

"Tell me what grand things you intend to do with that money once it comes," she said, to distract her thoughts.

"I hadn't thought about it much. It's enough for now just to feel the sense of freedom it brings. I've never been wanting, but I've never had security such as this either."

They were nearly at her house, their steps slower than ever.

"It's strange, isn't it," she asked, "that much the same sort of thing has happened to me because of all this? Did I tell you that the railroad paid me a thousand dollars for my care of you and . . . and Mr. DuFrayne?" It was dreadfully hard to say his name now, and when she did, she felt David's arm tense, but she went on. "It brings me a sense of security too. Temporary, of course, but security nevertheless."

David Melcher certainly did not begrudge her the thousand dollars, only the fact that DuFrayne was the one who'd paid her off and was rich enough to do it so easily.

But he submerged his irritation and asked, "How did that come about?"

"Mr. Hudson came here and left a bank draft for me. He seems to be in a position of authority on the railroad. Is he the owner?"

David swallowed, still reluctant to tell her that DuFrayne was the other owner. "Yes," he answered tightly. "You deserved every penny he paid you, I'm sure."

They reached her porch then, and she asked, "Would you care to sit for a while? Your foot is probably tired."

"No . . . I mean yes . . . I mean, my f . . . foot is f . . . fine, but I'd like to sit awhile anyway."

She glanced at the pair of wicker chairs but led the way to the swing instead, justifying her choice by reiterating silently how little time they had together.

When she had seated herself, David asked politely before sitting, "May I?"

She pulled her skirt aside and made room while he settled quite stiffly and formally beside her, making sure that his coat sleeve did not touch her. There were restless night sounds all around them—insects, the saloon piano, leaves astir in the faint breeze.

He cleared his throat.

She sighed.

"Is something wrong?" he asked.

"Wrong? No . . . no, everything is . . . is wonderful." And indeed it should have been. He had his money, she had hers, he'd taken her to dinner, she was at last rid of Jesse DuFrayne.

He cleared his throat. "You seem . . . dif . . . different some . . . sometimes."

She hadn't realized it showed. She would have to be more careful.

"It's just that I'm not used to everything turning out so well. It all happened so fast. And I'm sure you've guessed that I don't get dinner invitations just every night. I was still thinking about how enjoyable it was."

"It—" He cleared his throat once more. "It was for me, too. I thought of it all the t . . . time after I left St . . . Stuart's Junction, about how I w . . . wanted to come back and take you to dinner." Here he cleared his throat yet again. "And now here we are."

Yes, like two pokers, she thought, surprising herelf, wishing that he would put his arm along the back of the swing like Jesse had done. But he was no Jesse, and she had no business wishing David would act even remotely like him! Still she grew more disappointed as the minutes passed and David sat sticklike beside her. His attitude seemed suddenly puerile. She wondered if she could soften him up somewhat.

"This was where I was when I opened the package with the shoes."

"Right here? On the swing?"

"Yes. Mr. Binley brought them up from the station. Remember Mr. Binley—the one who helped carry you to my house that first morning?"

"Would he be the tall, skinny one they called Bones?"

"The same. He seemed fascinated by the fact that I'd received a package. I'm sure he was hoping I'd open it before him."

"But you didn't?"

"Gracious no. I sat down and took the package here on the swing after he was gone and opened it all alone."

"And what did you . . . ahem!"—that was his throat again—"think?"

"Why, I was amazed, Mr. Melcher, simply amazed. I don't think another woman in this town owns a pair of red shoes." That was the truth!

"Well they will before long, because I have others in my stock. Red is the coming thing, you know."

She simply hadn't the heart to tell him her true feelings about the shoes. He would just have to find out for himself when his stock of reds didn't sell. Out here in the West, the staid, hard-working woman wanted sturdy browns and blacks, but he, like so many people in sales, was convinced that what he sold was the best, and could not see any fault with it.

"Would you have preferred another color?" he asked now.

She lied. "Oh, no! Of course not! I love these!" When had she become so glib at lying?

He once more cleared his throat. He placed his hands over his kneecaps and stared straight ahead. "Miss Abigail, when I approached your door today, I distinctly heard you and DuFrayne arguing about the shoes."

"We were," she admitted candidly.

"Why?" he asked, surprising himself at his own temerity. But where his products were concerned, he had backbone.

"He disliked them."

"Good!" he exclaimed, suddenly feeling very self-satisfied. It was perhaps the most romantic thing he had said that night, but she was too busy worrying about what else he'd overheard this morning to note David's pleased expression.

Her heart thudded as she worked up her courage and asked, "What else did you hear?"

"Nothing. Only his remark about the shoes."

She concealed a sigh but was greatly relieved.

David looked at her entreatingly and said, "He's gone now and we can both forget him."

"Yes," she agreed. But there was a sick feeling in the pit of her stomach and she could not meet David's eyes, knowing that for as long as she lived she would never forget Jesse DuFrayne. She attempted to lighten the atmosphere by suggesting, "Let's talk of more pleasant things. Tell me what it's like in the East."

"Have you never been there?"

"No. I've never been farther than Denver, and I was there only twice, both times as a child."

"The East . . ." He stopped momentarily and ruminated. "Well, the East has absolutely everything one could want to buy. Factories everywhere producing everything, especially since the war is over. The newest innovations and the grandest inventions. Did you know that a man named Lyman Blake in Massachusetts invented a machine for sewing soles onto shoes?"

"No, no I didn't, but I guess I must thank him for his glorious invention." Miss Abigail realized she was bored to death by this conversation.

"The East has all the up-and-coming modern advancements, including women's suffragettes voicing their absurd ideas and encouraging such outlandish activities as the game of tennis for females. Not everything in the East is proper," he finished, making it clear what he thought of women playing tennis.

"I've heard of Mrs. Stanton's Suffrage Association, of course, but what is tennis?"

"Nothing at all for you, Miss Abigail, I assure you," he said distastefully. "Why, it's the most . . . the most unladylike romp that France ever invented! Women actually running and . . . and sweating and swatting at balls with these gut-string rackets."

"It sounds like the Indian game of lacrosse."

"One might expect such behavior out of an uncivilized savage, but the women of the East should know better than to wear shortened hems and shortened sleeves and carry on like . . . well, it's disgraceful! They have lost their sense of decency. Some of them even drink spirits! I much prefer you women out West, who still conform to the old social graces, and for my money I want to see it left that way. Leave the upstart ideas out East where they belong."

He had scarcely stammered at all during that long diatribe.

She realized he was very incensed about the subject. Miss Abigail sat on the porch swing, rocking quietly, and suddenly found herself comparing David Melcher's opinions to those of Jesse DuFrayne on the many occasions he'd encouraged her to set aside her prim and proper ways. She remembered that day up in the hills when he'd taken her hat off for her and teased her about not unbuttoning her wet cuffs. She pictured his dark hand pouring champagne and recalled the loose, easy feeling as it ran through her blood. And then there was that untidy scrap they'd had on that kitchen chair and somehow in the middle of it he'd said he liked her in that old faded shirt . . ."

". . . . don't you agree, Miss Abigail?"

She came out of her reverie to realize David had been expounding upon the virtues of a western woman while she'd been wool-gathering about Jesse, comparing him—and unfavorably yet!—to David.

"Oh, yes," she sat up straight. "I quite agree, I'm sure." But she wasn't even sure what she was agreeing with. Would Jesse's memory always distract her so?

Apparently she had agreed that one o'clock would be a good time for them to meet tomorrow, for he was rising from the swing and making his way across the porch while she followed.

He went down one step, turned, cleared his throat volubly, came back up the same step, fumbled for her hand, and kissed it quickly, then retreated down the step hurriedly.

"Good night, Miss Abigail."

"Thank you for dinner, Mr. Melcher."

For some reason, watching him disappear up the street, she found herself wishing he had not cleared his throat that way or fumbled as he reached for her hand or even kissed *it!* She wished that he might have kissed her mouth instead, and that when he had, she'd have found it preferable to the kisses of Jesse DuFrayne.

Inside, the house was beastly quiet.

She wandered in without even lighting a lamp, listless and dissatisfied. She raised the back of the kissed hand to her lips, trying to draw some feeling from the memory. David Melcher approved of her wholeheartedly, she was sure. She willed that to be enough for now, but the memory of Jesse DuFrayne contraposed every action and mannerism that David had displayed tonight. Why should it be that even though he was gone Jesse had the power to impose himself on her this way? And at the most inopportune times possible? Instead of reveling in David's seeming attraction for her, her joy was blighted by her endless contrasting of the two men in which Jesse invariably came out the winner. With these couple of days so precious, while David remained, she wanted to find him perfect, flawless, incontestable. But Jesse wouldn't let her. Jesse dominated in every way.

Even here in her house, from which he was gone, she found herself listening for his breathing, his yawning, the squeak of the bedsprings as he turned. Perhaps by taking over her old room she could exorcise him. But wandering into it she was smitten by a sense of emptiness for her "gunslinger." The bed was dark and vacant. The pall of silence grew awesome. She dropped down onto the edge of the bed, feeling his absence keenly, knowing a bleakness more complete and sad than that which she had felt at the death of her father.

Twisting at the waist, she suddenly punched one small fist into the pillow he'd occupied so lately, demanding angrily, "Get out of my house, Jesse DuFrayne!"

Only he was out.

She punched the pillow again, her delicate fist creating a thick, muffled sound of loneliness. He's gone, she despaired. He's gone. How could she have grown so used to him that his absence assaulted her by its mere vacuity? She wanted her life back the way it had been before he'd come into it. She wanted to take a man like David Melcher into that old life and forge a relationship of genteel, sensible normalcy, instead she sank both hands into the soft feathers of Jesse's pillow, taking great fistfuls of his absence, her head slung low between her sagging shoulders as she braced there in the gloom.

"Damn you, Jesse!" she shouted at the dark ceiling. "Damn you for ever coming here!"

Then she fell lonely upon his bed, rolling onto her side and hugging his pillow to her stomach while she cried.

Chapter 18

AWAKENING THE FOLLOWING morning, Abbie forgot she was in
the house alone. She stretched and rolled over, wondering what
to fix Jesse for breakfast. Realizing her mistake, she sat up
abruptly and looked around. She was back in her own
bedroom—alone.

She flopped back down, studied the ceiling, closed her eyes
and admonished herself to be sensible. Life must go on. She
could and she would get over Jesse DuFrayne. But she opened
her eyes and felt empty. The day had nothing to inspire her to
get out of bed.

She spent it trying to scrub every last vestige of Jesse from
her bedroom. She washed the smell of him from her sheets,
polished his fingerprints from the brass headboard, and fluffed
his imprint from the cushions of the window seat. But even so,
she could not reclaim the room as her own. He remained
present in its memory, possessing each article he'd touched,
lingering in each place he'd rested, an unwanted reminder of
what he'd been to her.

When her cleaning was done, she had an hour to spare
before David would arrive. But the *Junction County Courier*
arrived before he did. She heard it thwack upon the porch floor

and retrieved it, grateful for any diversion that would keep her mind off Jesse.

Idly, she went back inside, pausing before the umbrella stand and using the folded up newspaper to check the tautness of her chin. But even that longtime, private habit now reminded her of Jesse, standing half-naked in the doorway, teasing, "Is it firm?" Abruptly she turned away from the mirror and snapped the newspaper open, seeking to scatter his memory.

Lotta Crabtree was appearing at the famed Teller Opera House in Central City and would be followed by the great Madjeska.

Another railroad baron had chosen to buld his mansion in the vastly popular Colorado Springs, playground of the rich, who flocked there to soak away their ailments in the famous mineral springs.

Some accused train robber . . .

Miss Abigail's eyes widened and her tongue seemed to grow thick in her throat.

ACCUSED TRAIN ROBBER PROVES TO BE OWNER OF RAILROAD

At a meeting Tuesday afternoon in the Stuart's Junction Depot, arbiters debated . . .

It was all there, including the truth about Jesse DuFrayne, which she should have guessed long ago. Standing in the middle of her proper Victorian parlor, Miss Abigail placed the back of a lacy wrist to her throat. Jesse owns the railroad! The man I called train robber *owns* the railroad! And so he has the last laugh after all. But then, didn't he always?

With a mixture of horror and dismay she recalled the awful things she had done to him—the owner of a railroad!

And suddenly she was laughing, raising her delicate chin high, covering her forehead with a palm. The daft, sad sound cracked pitifully into the silence. And when at last it faded away, she was left staring at the article like a glassy-eyed statue, while its significance sank in, while she absorbed what she should have guessed that day Jim Hudson had come. Maybe she had guessed but simply hadn't wanted to admit it could be true. What she read again pounded home the facts in black and white. The article described the meeting right down to the clothing the four men had worn. It described James Hudson as the business agent-co-owner of the railroad, while Jesse DuFrayne was called the hidden partner who oversaw his enterprise from behind the hood of a photographic camera. The meeting itself was described as a "sometimes placid discussion of terms, sparked at times by fiery clashes of animosity between DuFrayne and Melcher over the seemingly alien subject of one Miss Abigail McKenzie, a longtime resident of Stuart's Junction, who had nursed both DuFrayne and Melcher during their convalescence."

As she finished, she stood mortified! By this time she was in a state of anger that would have delighted Jesse DuFrayne.

David Melcher, however, who happened to the door at that precise moment was dismayed when he stepped inside and she gave him a flat slap across his chest with the folded newspaper.

"Mi . . . Miss Abigail, what's wr . . . wrong?" he stammered.

"What's wrong?" she repeated, barely controlling the volume of her voice. "Read this and then ask me what's wrong! I am a respectable woman who must live in this town after you and Mr. DuFrayne have long left it. I do not care to have my name spewed from the lips of every gossipmonger in Stuart's Junction after the two of you saw to it that I made the front page of the newspaper in the most intriguing way possible!"

Perplexed, he glanced at the article, back at her, then silently started reading, finding more in the paper than he had told the newspaper editor.

"Whatever possessed you to argue about me in a meeting with the press present?"

"There was n . . . no press . . . pre . . . present. It was strictly pr . . . private. I . . . he . . . DuFrayne even made me pr . . . promise that no word would l . . . leak out about you."

That surprised her. "Then how did it?" she demanded.

"I . . . I don't know."

"Just what brought my name into a discussion of liability settlements?"

He'd only meant the best for her yesterday and quavered now at the thought that he'd messed everything up so badly.

"I thought he sh . . . should apologize to you for . . . for all he put you through."

She turned her back on him and plucked at her blouse front. "Had it occurred to you that perhaps he might already have done so?"

"Miss Abigail! Are you defending him against me, when it is I who set out to d . . . defend you against him?"

"I am defending no one. I am simply chagrined at finding myself the object of two men's animosity and having it appear in newsprint. I—What will it look like to the people of this town? And why didn't you tell me last night that he is part owner of the railroad?"

He considered her question a moment, then asked, "Does that change your opinion of him now?"

Realizing that if it did she was nothing but a hypocrite, she turned to show David she was sincere.

"No, it doesn't. I simply think you would have told me that the money was coming from him, that's all."

"It's only right that he should pay me. He's the one who shot me."

"But he was *not* robbing that train when he did it. There lies the difference."

"You *are* defending him!" David Melcher accused.

"I am not! I'm defending myself!" Her voice had risen until she was shouting like a fishwife, and when she realized it she suddenly put her fingertips over her lips. She found she'd been haranguing him in the same way she'd done countless times with Jesse. Angry now at Jesse too, she'd attacked David as if he were both of them. To her horror, she found herself anticipating the exhilaration of the fight, welcoming the kind of verbiage Jesse had taught her to enjoy with him.

But David was no Jesse DuFrayne. In fact, David was stunned by her almost baiting attitude and unladylike shouting. His face grew mottled, and he stared at her as if he'd never seen her before. Indeed he hadn't—not like this. In a calm voice, he said, "We are having a fight."

His words brought her to her senses. Chagrined at what she had just caught herself doing, she felt suddenly small and completely in the wrong. She sat down properly on the edge of the settee, looking at the hands she'd clasped tighty in her lap.

"I'm sorry," she said contritely.

He sat down beside her, pleasantly surprised by her change back to the Miss Abigail he knew.

"So am I."

"No, it was my fault. I don't know what came over me to speak to you in such tones. I . . ." But she stumbled to a halt, for it was a lie. She was not sorry, and she did know what had come over her. The ways of Jesse DuFrayne had come over her, for it was as he'd said, fighting was like an emetic. It felt good. It purged.

David spoke softly beside her. "Maybe we wouldn't fight if we didn't . . ." He was going to say "care for each other," but stopped himself in time. It was too soon to say a thing like that, so he finished, ". . . didn't talk about . . . him."

The tension remained between them, each displeased with the other as they sat silently.

After a moment David said, "You know I would not do or say anything to jeopardize your reputation. Why, it would be as good as ruining my own now, don't you see?"

She looked up at him, perched beside her on the settee.

"No, of course you don't see," he continued. "I haven't told you yet. I was going to tell you when I c . . . came to the door, but you were there with that . . . that newspaper and didn't give me a chance."

"Tell me what?"

He smiled boyishly, the soft, brown eyes locked with hers. "That I am going to stay in Stuart's Junction and open a shoe store right here with the money I have coming from the railroad."

Her heart hit the roof of her mouth. Remorse and fear welled in her throat, then drifted through her veins. His words sieved their way downward and dropped hollowly at last into the womb she had begged Jesse DuFrayne to unseal. She'd been so sure no other man would come along in her lifetime to do it. It was all too, too ironic to think that not only had Jesse done her bidding on the very eve of David's return, but had then given David the fistful of money that would enable him to establish himself right here under her nose and court her, when that was now out of the question. What was she supposed to do? Abet the situation when she knew that under no circumstances must she encourage David Melcher now? Furthermore, it was becoming increasingly obvious that he intended to actively court her.

She had been hazed by Jesse DuFrayne for the final, most

humiliating time of all: he had given David the means for marriage while robbing her of the same.

David Melcher watched myriad expressions drift across Miss Abigail's face. At first she looked surprised, then happy, then perplexed, quizzical, stunned, and lastly, he could have sworn that she looked guilty. At what he had no idea. But after watching that parade of emotions, he certainly did not expect her final reaction, which was the placing of her tiny fingers upon her lips as she whispered, "Oh no!"

He was stricken with disappointment at her words. "I thought you'd be happy, Miss Abigail."

"Oh, I am, I am," she said quickly, touching his sleeve. "Oh, how wonderful for you. I know that you're not a man who likes wandering ways." But she did not look at all happy.

"No, I don't. I've wanted to settle in one spot for the longest time. It's just that I never had the means and I never found the right spot." Timidly he took one of her hands. "Now I think I've found both. Will you come with me this afternoon? You could be such a big help. I must arrange to find a place to rent or find some land to put up a place on. There's a corner at the far end of Main Street that I like. You know who to see and where to find people I'd need to talk to, and of course you could introduce me to those I might need to look up. Oh, Miss Abigail," he implored, "come with me. We'll look them all in the eye and make them take back any gossip the paper might have started."

Sensibly, she withdrew her hand and dropped her eyes. "I'm afraid you don't know the people of this town too well. If we show up arranging business agreements together after what was printed in the paper, they'll take nothing back. I'm afraid we would start more gossip than we'll stop."

"I hadn't thought of that, and of course you're right."

She had quite decided to end any budding relationship with him here and now. It would be the best way. But he looked so depressed at her refusal to help him that she felt mean denying him her help. It was true that she could expedite matters for him, for he was a stranger here.

"On the other hand," she procrastinated, "if we were to face the town and show them we are associating solely on a business basis, we might just put the gossip to rout, mightn't we?"

He looked up hopefully, his face suddenly youthfully attractive, like that first day he'd been carried into her house.

"Then you'll come? You'll help me today?"

She controlled the urge to sigh. Whatever was she doing? "Yes, I'll come. But only as an ambassador, you must understand."

"Oh, of course, of course," he agreed.

David Melcher was a man who left good impressions in his wake. While he and Miss Abigail made business contacts that day, his soft-spoken, likable approach made people realize he was no "slick talker" from the East, as they considered most peddlers to be. Indeed, there were those who said that were it not for Miss Abigail's effrontery Melcher would have gotten nowhere, for he was unpushy and retiring. She, however, opened the way for him in the businesslike manner she always used on the townspeople. If any of them objected to her briskness, they didn't say so. As usual, they treated her—and thus him—with deference. Perhaps it was because they'd grown used to granting her wide berth, perhaps because she had not had an easy life and they all knew it, or perhaps because they were just plain nosy about her relationship to the two men who'd had words over her. For whatever reason, while she and David traversed the town that day they seemed to gain the town's approval and along with it many invitations to attend the following day's Fourth of July celebrations. Indeed, some businessmen seemed more intent upon making sure the two appeared at the morrow's festivities than they were about selling land, leasing property, or discussing lumber prices.

But behind them speculation was rife. That settlement money raised questions they all wished they had answers for. It's no wonder they all said, "Now don't forget to join the fun over in Hake's Meadow tomorrow," or "You're coming, aren't you, Miss Abigail?" or "You're both coming, aren't you?"

Someone else put it more bluntly: "There's to be a basket social and a greased pig contest and log rolling and sack races and what not. Good way for you to get acquainted with all the folks you'll be calling customers afore long, Melcher."

Someone else bid them goodbye by saying, "Bring her over and help us all celebrate. Wagons'll be loading up in front of Avery's store at a quarter to ten or so."

They were also bribed. "It's the only time of the summer you'll find ice cream in Stuart's Junction. You wouldn't want to miss that now, would you?"

But what *they* all really didn't want to miss was a chance to observe Miss Abigail with that new beau she'd apparently taken up with the minute the old one left town. Of course they all knew Melcher was going to be filthy rich on the other guy's money yet. Now who'd've dreamed Miss Abigail would ever become a pants-chaser, and furthermore that she'd make sure those pants had full pockets? 'Course, they all said, it was a fact she was almost clean out of money since her pa died. You couldn't hardly blame the woman. There was that thousand the railroad had paid her, but how long would that last? She was probably just investing in her future, hooking up with Melcher this way. Not a soul in town but couldn't wait to see if the two of them'd show up tomorrow and if she'd seem sweet on him. Nobody could really tell from her businessy attitude today. But tomorrow would be another story!

When he saw her home it was with a mutual feeling of satisfaction. They'd accomplished much in one day. They'd checked out some rental property, found out Nels Nordquist owned the vacant lot next to his saddlery and leather shop, spoken to him about a selling price, checked on the deed at the land office, arranged for blueprints to be drawn up for a simple, single-story frame building with storage at the rear, sales area at the center, and display windows at the fore, and found out whom to see about lumber prices and delivery.

Back at her house now, she led the way to the wicker chairs on the porch.

"I can't thank you enough," he said.

"Nonsense, you were right. I do know everyone in this town and it would have been foolish for you to try to make the necessary contacts alone."

"But you were marvelous. People just seem to . . . to bend to your will."

Before the advent of Jesse DuFrayne in her life she would not have dreamed of replying as she did now. "I tend to cow people and make them afraid of me." She knew it was a graceless, unfeminine admission, and she could see it made David uncomfortable. But she herself felt oddly free after admitting it.

"Nonsense," David said, "a lady like you? Why, you're not . . . pushy."

But she suddenly knew she was and that he did not want to admit it. Pushiness was unfeminine. Ladies should be shyly retiring. But Jesse had taught her much about self-delusion, and she was getting better and better at ridding herself of it.

"It's not nonsense. I'm afraid it's true. However, today it served our purpose, so I shan't complain." Yet it hurt her a little that people opened doors for her because she cowed them while they'd opened doors for David because they instantly liked him.

"There's still so much to be done besides making building decisions. I'll have to take inventory of my stock and put in an order for a much larger number of shoes than I've ever been able to carry with me on the road. And there's the furnishings to order and the awning and the window glass. I'll have to drive out to see about a winter wood supply somewhere—And, oh! I'll need to order a stove from the East and—"

He stopped abruptly, breathlessly, realizing he'd been running on.

But she suddenly looked at him differently and found herself laughing, enjoying his enthusiasm.

"I guess I got carried away by my plans," he admitted sheepishly.

"Yes, you did," she said agreeably, "but you have every right. It's such a big step you're taking. It will take a lot of planning and enthusiasm."

His face suddenly looked worried. "Oh, I didn't mean that I expected you to be running along beside me each step of the way. I wouldn't expect that of you. You've done more than your share today."

But they went on making plans for the store, its furnishing, accoutrements and prospects. He was very animated, but forced himself to sit still and contain his excitement.

Time and again she compared him to Jesse. Jesse with his boundless ego and limited crassness. Never would he sit there like he'd gotten himself caned into that chair seat the way David did. He'd be pacing up and down, probably bellowing, "Goddamnit, Abbie, I know this business can go, and you're going to help it!" Abigail McKenzie! she scolded herself, stop making these unjustifiable comparisons and pay attention to what David is saying!

"It seems we've g . . . gotten ourselves almost . . . ah . . . expected at the fes . . . festivites tomorrow," he stammered. "Do you mind?"

She tried not to be annoyed by his lack of assertiveness, but guilty for having compared him to Jesse all afternoon, she made up for it by answering, "It's almost a matter of good business by now, isn't it? No, I don't mind. I attend the festivities annually anyway. Everybody in town does."

"I . . . ahem . . . we could . . . ah . . . go out together then," he stammered.

It was not at all the way Miss Abigail would like to have been invited. She was reminded that Jesse had once called David a milktoast, then kicked herself mentally for being unfair to him.

"Well . . . if . . . if you'd rather not."

"Oh, I didn't mean— Of course I'll go out with you."

He stood to leave, and she found herself actually quite glad he was going.

"Where is Hake's Meadow?" he asked.

"It's out northeast of town where Rum Creek broadens. As you heard earlier, several wagons leave from Avery Holmes's Dry Goods Store and anyone who wants may ride out from there."

"At qu . . . quarter to ten?"

"Yes."

"Then I'll come. . . . Should I . . . well, come for you a little before then?"

"I'll be ready," she replied, growing irritated by his stammering.

"I'd better be leaving now . . ." His voice had a way of trailing off uncertainly at the end of phrases, which was beginning to make her nerves jangle. It seemed that only the subject of business could wring a positive, assured note from him. Personal subjects made him stutter and stammer. At the steps he did it again.

"I . . . I . . . could I . . ."

But he seemed unable to finish, and only looked down at her with spaniel eyes. She was suddenly very sure that he wanted to kiss her but didn't dare. Even though she had no business thinking it, she wondered, Why doesn't he just grab me and do it? She need not add, like Jesse would. By now she was comparing every action, every inflection, every mannerism of the two men. And unbelievably, in each instance she'd found David lacking. It stunned her to realize, while she watched him walk away, that though David's manners were impeccable, she now preferred Jesse's boorishness.

Chapter 19

———

MISS ABIGAIL DID not approve of everything that went on out at Hake's Meadow on the Fourth of July, but she was always in attendance nevertheless. She had a feeling for patriotism, and this was a patriotic holiday, though somehow it always seemed to turn into one sprawling, noisy beer-soaked melee. Each year it started with the mayor's inept speech while children held flags, but before long the politicians lost ground to beer and the ribaldry that inevitably followed. For the beer flowed as freely as did the baked beans tended by the D.A.R. members, who cooked them in an open fifty-gallon drum. It was, too, a perennial joke that had those D.A.R.s stirred up a few drums of their infamous beans back in 1776 and fed them to the British, they might have cut the war short by seven years. And when those beans merged with beer . . . well, rumor had it that Royal Gorge was no natural wonder; it was ripped out one Fourth of July when the picnic was held down there instead of at Hake's Meadow.

There were battles of every sort imaginable—some scheduled, some not. Rum Creek slid coolly out of the mountains and slithered to a halt above a beaver dam, creating Hake's Pond, where loggers from up mountain whupped the hell out of every aspiring log roller and tree skinner from Stuart's

Junction, who later returned the favor at horseshoes and chasing a greased pig.

Then, too, there was the kissing, which grew more uninhibited as the day wore on and people just seemed to do it whenever and with whomever they could manage. Of course, the darker it got, the easier it was to manage.

The whole affair started at ten A.M. and officially ended with the ten P.M. fireworks display, unofficially when the last roaring drunk was hauled home by his wife, still singing loudly and probably more amorous than he'd been since last Fourth of July.

Miss Abigail had brought a basket for the basket social—her way of joining wholeheartedly in the festivities. She deposited it with all the others under a huge oak tree where the bidding was always done. She wore her daisy-trimmed hat, as usual, and a dove gray dress with matching overjacket of simple lines, which fairly clung to her skin by eleven o'clock. David Melcher, in a brown day suit, white shirt, and string tie, grew equally as hot as the sun rose toward its apex.

The two of them were sitting in the shade sipping sarsaparilla.

"Don't you drink beer?" she asked.

"I never developed a taste for it, I guess."

"Beer, as you've probably already guessed, is the drink of the day here, though I've never been able to understand why these men don't stop at their quota. On the Fourth of July they just don't seem to. Look! Look at Mr. Diggens. He's the one in the blue shirt who is challenging that logger twice his size. Is it the beer that makes him believe he can actually beat that logger at arm wrestling?"

They watched the mismatched contestants across the way as the pair knelt on either side of a stump, and of course the smaller Mr. Diggens lost, though he came up laughing and gamely warned the huge, strapping logger, "A few more beers and I beat you good!"

"Is that so!" the logger bellowed. "Well, let's get 'em into you then!" And before Diggens could protest, the logger lifted him bodily as if he were a bride being carried across a threshhold and carried him to the beer kegs, ballyhooing, "Feed my friend here some beer, Ivan. I want to see him beat me!"

A shout of laughter went up from the crowd and the logger

ook off his shirt, tied it by its sleeves around his waist, and stood like Paul Bunyan himself, drinking beer beside the dwarfed Diggens, as if waiting for him to suddenly sprout up and grow bigger.

Looking on, Miss Abigail and David joined in the laughter.

"As you can see, these little duels enhance the real contest which will all take place this afternoon," Miss Abigail explained.

David's eyes scanned the area. "I've never been much at physical things," he admitted unabashedly.

"Neither has Diggens, I'm afraid."

Then, as their eyes met, they both burst into laughter again.

"I think the speech makers are losing their audience," he noted some time later. Most of the listeners had drifted away from the pondside as soon as the mayor had finished his windy oratory.

"They'd rather listen to the nonsense at the beer kegs."

Another bit of revelry had started up there. Now the hairy-chested logger who'd tied his shirt around his waist was curtseying with that same shirt to Diggens before the two embraced and began a ridiculous impromptu dance while a fiddle scraped in the background. As they spun, beer flew out of their mugs, splattering two young women, who jumped back and shrieked joyously, only to be profusely apologized to by the men. The girls giggled as the logger again made his ridiculous curtsey to them.

"Something just seems to come over people out here on the Fourth of July," Miss Abigail said, unbuttoning her overjacket, which was becoming unbearable in the heat.

"It's a beautiful spot. It makes me happy all over again that I decided to stay in Stuart's Junction. These people . . . they were all so nice to me yesterday. I can't help but feel like I'm welcome here."

"Why shouldn't you be? Don't you think they know that your new business is going to be an asset to this town?"

"Do you think so? Do you really think it will succeed?"

He was very transparent. At times he displayed an almost childish need of her support and encouragement.

"Can you think of a thing more necessary than shoes? Why, just look at all those feet out there." She turned to survey the picnic grounds. A bunch of little boys scuffled under a nearby tree, playing some sort of rugby game they had improvised,

kicking at a stuffed bag with curled-toed boots; a mother
passed by, leading a little girl who was wailing over a stubbed
bare toe; the mother herself wore down-at-the-heel oxfords
long in need of replacing. "Look at the beating all those shoes
are taking. Chances are that later every one of these people will
come directly to your store to buy new ones."

He beamed at the thought, spinning visions of the future, but
at that moment they were approached by a giant of a man
wearing the familiar logger's uniform of loose-slung britches,
black suspenders, and a red plaid shirt.

"Hey there, Melcher, you're the man I'm looking for!" A
huge, hairy, friendly paw was extended. "Michael Morneau's
the name. I hear you'll be needing some timber for a building
you aim to put up. I'm the man's got just what you need. I
brung you a beer so we can talk about it friendly like."

David Melcher found himself pulled to his feet and a beer
slapped into his hand.

To Miss Abigail, the amiable logger said, "Hope you don't
mind, lady, if we mix a little business with pleasure. I'll bring
him right back." A big arm circled David's shoulders and
herded him away. "Come on over here, Melcher. Got some
people I want you to meet."

Miss Abigail saw how David was rather bulldozed into
drinking that beer. It was more than a drink—it was the symbol
of goodwill among those men who swilled together in great
camaraderie. Even from this distance she could tell when they
talked business, from the forgotten way the mugs hung in their
hands. But when some point was agreed upon, up in the air
went the beers before everyone, including David, drank.

She watched his brown shoulders buffeted along among the
mixture of shirts: red plaids, white businesses, even some
yellowed union suits, and into each new group came fresh beer.
Once he caught her eye across the expanse of meadow and
made a gesture of helpless apology for abandoning her, but she
shrugged and smiled and swished her hand to tell him not to
worry. She was fine. She sat contentedly watching all the
commotion around her. David was concluding more business
arrangements and gathering more goodwill among the beer
swillers than he could garner in a fortnight of selling quality
shoes or beating the boardwalks downtown.

So Miss Abigail wandered off to watch the children's sack
races.

Rob Nelson came running past but shied to a halt when he saw her.

"Howdy, Miss Abigail."

"Hello, Robert. Are you entering the sack race?"

"Sure am."

"Well, good luck to you then."

There was something different about Miss Abigail today. She didn't look like she just ate a pickle.

"Thank y', ma'am," the boy said, spinning away only to screech to a halt and return, squinting up at her, scratching his head, something obviously on his mind.

"What is it, Robert?"

"Well, y' know them there straws I brung you that time for that train robber?" He watched for danger signs, but she looked kind of young and pretty and her mouth kind of fell open and she touched her blouse where her heart was.

"Yes?"

"Did they work?"

"Why, yes they did, Robert, and I want to thank you very much for getting them."

"What'd you do with 'em?"

To Rob's surprise, Miss Abigail smiled and leaned down conspiratorially. "I blew soup into him," she whispered near his ear. She straightened then. "Now run along to your race."

But Rob didn't move. Just stood there slack-mouthed, in wonder. "*You* blew soup into a *train robber*, Miss Abigail?" he asked incredulously.

"He wasn't a train robber after all."

"Oh," Robert said shortly, then looked thoughtful before stuffing his hands into his pants pockets and saying, "You know, he really didn't look much like a train robber in those pajama pants."

Now it was Miss Abigail's turn to go slack-jawed. Horrified, she spun Rob about by the shoulders, controlling the urge to paddle his little backside. "Robert Nelson, don't you dare repeat that to a single living soul, do you near? Now git!"

And the impetuous child ran off toward the sack race, trailing a burlap bag as he ran.

But when he was gone she crossed an arm upon her waist, rested her elbow upon it, and lightly covered her smiling mouth. Her shoulders shook mirthfully as she recaptured the picture of Jesse stumping around in pajama pants much too short for him.

"Is something funny, Miss Abigail?"

"Oh, Doctor Dougherty, hello. I was just enjoying the children's sack races."

"I've been meaning to get up to your place and thank you for all you did. You sure helped me out of a pickle."

"I was only too happy to help."

"Did that man behave himself and put that gun away? I sure didn't mean to put you in any ticklish spots by returning it to him."

"Oh, it's all over and done with now, water under the bridge." But she refused to meet his eyes, squinted into the sun instead to watch the races now in full swing.

"Yup!" he agreed, following her eyes to the jumping, writhing boys, some now sprawled out on their stomachs, struggling to regain their feet. "I heard you got paid real well."

Her eyes snapped to him. Only the doc would have the temerity to come right out with a thing like that. "Everybody in this town hears everything," she said.

"Yup," he agreed, "and what they don't hear, they damn well guess at."

"I hear Gertie got back from Fairplay," she said quickly, changing the subject.

"Yeah, she's got my office running slicker'n a greased pig again. And I heard you were all over town yesterday introducing that Melcher around and blazing trails for him to open up a new business."

"That's right. This town owes him that much, I think."

"Why so?"

It was an odd question. She gave him a puzzled look. But Doc had drawn a penknife from his pocket and was calmly cleaning his nails as he went on. "Seems to me we owe Jesse something if we owe anybody. Folks around here were mighty nasty about even letting him off his own train in our midst. If it weren't for you he could've rotted right there on it, for all they cared. And all the time it's his railroad that's brought new prosperity to Stuart's Junction. Just goes to show how wrong about a person you can be."

Doc didn't so much as glance at Miss Abigail, just snapped his penknife shut, tucked it away in a baggy pocket, and glanced out toward the sack races, where a lad lay humped up on the ground clutching his stomach. "Well," Doc murmured, as if ruminating to himself, "guess I'd better go see if I can get the scare out of him and the wind back in." And he shambled off to the rescue, leaving Miss Abigail to wonder just how much he guessed about her relationship with Jesse.

As she watched Doc moving toward the boy, she remembered the night she'd had the wind knocked out of her, and of the things which had followed, and she thought about Doc's words, "Just goes to show how wrong about a person you can be."

"Miss Abigail, I've been looking all over for you," David said, making her jump. She gasped and put a hand to her heart. "I'm sorry, I didn't mean to scare you."

"Oh, I was just daydreaming, that's all."

"Come. They're going to auction off the baskets now. You've been standing here in the sun too long. Your face is all red."

But it was memories of Jesse which had heightened her color, and she was grateful that David could not read her mind. He took her by the arm to where the crowd had gathered under the huge, sprawling oak for the pairing off and picnicking. He continued to hold her elbow as the auctioning began, and she could smell the yeastiness about him from the beer he'd drunk. Now and then he'd weave a bit unsteadily, but he was apparently sober enough to recognize the napkin that matched her kitchen curtains peeking out from under the lid of her picnic basket. When it came up for bids, he raised a looping arm and called out, "Seventy-five cents!"

"Way to go!" Someone slapped him on the back and he barely retained his stance. Then some unseen voice hollered, "That's Miss Abigail's basket, Melcher. Bid 'em up!"

Laughter, good-natured and teasing, went up, and her cheeks grew pinker.

"A dollar!" came the second bid.

"A dollar ten!" called David.

"Hell, that ain't no way to pay back a lady that saved your life! A dollar twenty!"

David rocked back on his heels, grinning quite drunkenly.

From the crowd someone hollered, "Melcher, you ain't too drunk to see Miss Abigail's colors flying from under that there basket lid, are you?"

"A dollar and a quarter!" Melcher thought he shouted, only he hiccuped in the middle and it came out, "A dollar and a quor-horter!" raising a whoop of laughter.

The auctioneer bawled, "Anybody got more'n a dollar and a *quor-horter* for this here basket?" Laughter billowed and so did Miss Abigail's blush.

"Sold!"

The gavel smacked down, and from all around rose catcalls, whistles, and hoots. David just grinned.

"Give 'er hell, David!" someone encouraged as David made his unsteady way forward to get the basket. As he passed Michael Morneau, a hand steered David and steadied him while the lumberman laughed, "We got all that business taken care of. Time for a little fun now, eh, Melcher?"

Miss Abigail thought David would never make it to that basket and back again, but soon he returned, offering an arm, leading her proudly. She was as red as a raspberry by now, moving through the crowd, being watched by the entire town while he plunked the basket down in the shade of a nearby tree. Finally the bidding resumed and drew people's attention away from them for the time being.

She knelt and opened the lid of the basket and began taking food out while he dropped to his knees, bracing his hands onto his thighs.

"Miss Abigail, I have to beg your forgi-hiveness," he hiccuped. "I said I-hime no beer drinker, but the bo-hoys took me in hand. I thought it'd be good business to mingle with the boys a li-hittle."

She was embarrassed by the entire scene, but still there was something unblamable about his tispy state. She remembered all too well how easily she herself had gotten that way on a "thimbleful of champagne." She suddenly couldn't find it in her heart to be angry with him.

He sat with head hung low, hands still grasping thighs—a disconsolate drunk having a staring contest with the ground between his knees. Now and then he would quietly hiccup behind closed lips. She went about calmly laying out their food.

"I'm really sorry. I shouldn't have left you alone like tha-hat."

"Here. If you eat a little something, those hiccups will stop."

He looked at the piece of fried chicken she extended as if trying to identify what it was.

"Here," she repeated, gesturing with the drumstick as if to wake him up. "I'm not angry."

He looked up dumbly. "You're naw-hot?"

"No, but I will be if you don't take this thing and begin eating so people will stop staring at us."

"Oh . . . oh, sure." he said, taking the drumstick very carefully, as if it were porcelain. He bit into it, looked around, then stupidly waved the piece of meat toward a clump of gawking people as if signaling, "Hey there . . . how's it goin'?"

"You know, I really don't like beer," he mumbled to the chicken.

"Yes, so you told me. And as I told you, something just seems to come over people out here on the Fourth of July."

"But I shouldn't have drunk so much."

"Something good seems to have come of it though, hasn't it? I believe you've had your initiation today and now you truly are an accepted member of the community."

"Do you really think so?" He looked up, surprised.

"When you sat down here do you remember what you said? You said something about *the boys* insisting you have another beer."

"Did I say that?"

"Yes you did, just as if you were one of them."

He raised his eyebrows foolishly and grinned. "Well now, maybe I am, maybe I am." Then after a long pause, "Wouldn't that be somethin'?"

"I have a feeling that at first some of the men around here took you for the usual high and mighty easterner . . . and a peddler to boot. That combination doesn't always meet with the approval of Stuart's Junction's businessmen. I wouldn't be surprised if they actually set you up to see if you'd pass their rites."

"Do you think so?" He continued to ask dumb, rhetorical questions but she could not help smiling because he was obviously abashed at his state . . . and it was funny in its own way.

"Oh, I'm only guessing. Don't be alarmed. If they did set you up, it'll be for this once only, and my guess is you already passed muster."

"Do you think so?" he asked again, in the exact dumb tone he'd used all the other times.

"Well, you got some business handled in between beers, didn't you? Or wasn't that what all those raised glasses were all about?"

"Come to think of it, I did." He looked astounded.

"Well then, where's the loss?"

Even in his drunkness he was touched by her magnanimity. "You're being awfully understanding, Miss Abigail, considering how embarrassed you must have been during the bidding."

"Would you like to know a secret?" she asked.

"A secret?"

"Mm-hmm." She tilted her head sideways, a mischievous look in her eye. "Today was nothing compared to the year that Mr. Binley bought my picnic basket."

"Bones Binley?" he asked, amazed. His mouth hung open, displaying a bite of chicken.

"Yes . . . one and the same."

"Bones Binley bought your basket?" The chicken fell out and she hid her laughter behind her hand and came up smiling.

"Aha. It sounds like a tongue twister, doesn't it?" There was no artful coyness in her admission whatsoever. It simply seemed easier for her to erase his discomfiture and have a pleasant day than to hold him responsible for the teasing of the townspeople and the fact that they'd coerced him into getting drunk.

"Bones Binley with the tobacco and the brown teeth at the feedstore all day long spitting?"

It *was* funny, although she'd never seen it as funny before. She rocked forward on her knees, smiling, chuckling as she remembered. "It's funny, isn't it? But it wasn't then. He . . . he bought my basket and nobody teased him at all. It was horrible, just horrible, walking through the crowd with him. And he's looked at me with cow eyes ever since."

"Musta been your fried chicken that did it." He was sobering up a little bit by now, but was still elevated enough to laugh at his joke. Then he sucked at his greasy fingers and they happened to be both laughing when another contingent came past with a basket of their own. Frank Adney waved to David as he passed, calling, "Sounds like she's not too mad after all, eh, David?'' Then he tipped the brim of his hat up briefly at her. "No hard feelings, Miss Abigail?"

"None at all, Mr. Adney." She smiled back. Frank was surprised to see what a pretty woman Miss Abigail actually was with that smile on her face and laughing the way she was. He mentioned so to his wife, and she agreed as they moved away.

Miss Abigail, watching the Adneys move on, felt suddenly more a part of the town than ever before. David, watching her, felt expansive and wonderful. In two short days he'd melded into both the social and business environment of Stuart's Junction with an almost magical smoothness, and it was all due to her support.

"Miss Abigail?"

"Yes?" She looked up.

"I love this chicken, and the deviled eggs too." What he really thought he loved was her.

Suddenly she realized that all of this was simply too, too enjoyable and that she should not be encouraging him with smiles and laughter this way.

"You've lost your suit jacket somewhere," she observed.

Looking down at his chest he acted surprised to find it clad only in shirt and tie. "It's out there somewhere." He waved the chicken at the world at large. "It'll be around when I need it. It's too hot anyway for all that. Don't you want to take your jacket off?"

Informality breeding familiarity, she knew she shouldn't. But it was ghastly hot, and she'd been schooled by Jesse to rid herself of her too-rigid proprieties. She tried not to think of how pleased he'd be if he could see the change in her today. "It is awfully hot," she said, beginning to shrug the garment off.

David quickly used his napkin and walked on his knees, coming to help her out of it.

"Yes, that's much better," she said, laying it across the top of the picnic basket, swiping a hand upward from the nape of her neck to tuck up absolutely nothing; her hair was perfectly in place.

He had finished eating but still felt very mellow from the beer and stretched out on the grass, relaxed. He wondered how it would feel to lay his head in her lap. Instead, he said, "Tomorrow I'm supposed to go up to the logging camp and put in an order with Morneau for some lumber at the mill. But I don't know where it is for sure."

"It's about halfway up that ridge over there," she said, pointing and squinting, conscious of his eyes on her.

He liked the way the shade dappled her forehead when she raised her head to look at the ridge.

"Would you . . ." he began, but stopped. Should he simply invite her out for a ride or tell her he needed her help to find the place? She seemed to shy away from anything personal, but as long as he kept things on a business basis, she was more amenable. "Could you come along and show me where to find it?"

She wanted to say yes, but said instead, "Tomorrow I must do the ironing."

"Oh," he replied flatly. He lay there considering her while she began to pack up the remnants of their meal. Finally he said, "If it didn't take you all day maybe you could make it in the afternoon?"

She was pleased about one thing regarding the beer: since he'd been under its influence he'd stopped stammering. It almost made her break down and say yes, but again she realized she had no right to involve herself with him, not anymore.

"No. I simply can't make it at all," she said crisply, continuing to fuss with the picnic basket.

Rebuffed, he immediately sat up. Her abrupt changes of mood confused him. A minute ago she'd been very amiable, but suddenly she became cold and terse, refusing to look at him.

"I said before that I didn't expect you to follow me hand and foot through this entire opening up of the business, and now here I am, asking you again, the first thing. I shouldn't have asked."

Once again she felt irritated by the way David extended his invitation. Even though she knew better than to encourage him, she wished he would not always dream up an excuse to be with her. Female vanity, she chided herself, remembering the way Jesse had goaded and teased her into taking her for a ride. She put Jesse firmly from her mind, wishing he'd stay away.

As if to make up for his transgression, David asked, "Do you want some ice cream?"

But she was preoccupied, irritated with herself for leading

David on, and at David for not being manly enough to lead her on. It was all very confusing.

"Do you?"

She came out of her maunderings to find him standing beside her. She blinked once, hypnotically. "What?"

"I asked, do you want some ice cream," he repeated. "It's ready." He was handsome and polite and unassuming, and she stared up his body for a moment, confused by the sharp comings and goings of feelings she experienced for him.

"Yes, please," she said, sorry that she'd snapped at him.

The smile was gone from his face as he turned and limped away, only to remind her again of Jesse limping away from her down the street the last time she saw him.

David was thoroughly confused by Miss Abigail since he'd come back to Stuart's Junction. Her quicksilver mood changes were totally different from the steady, sweet woman she had been before. There were times when he swore she liked him— more than liked him—and other times that cold light would come into her gaze, making him sure that she cared nothing at all for him.

But he was reminded again of what she could mean to him when he was served ahead of the children who'd been waiting their turns around the ice cream churn. The whole town seemed to treat him solicitously! Even the fat woman who scooped out ice cream and served him out of turn.

"You tell Mizz Abigail I picked them peaches myself last fall. Tell her Fanny Hastings says she brought a real swell feller here when she brung you," the ingratiating woman said, her dimples disappearing into her plump cheeks.

He thanked the woman and picked his way back to Miss Abigail, wondering what mood she would be in now.

He stood above her, smitten all over again with her cool, calm ladylike demeanor, studying her breasts beneath the high-necked blouse.

"Fanny Hastings says to tell you she picked the peaches for the ice cream herself."

Abbie looked up and reached for his peace offering, knowing by the look in his face that he thought he'd done something wrong, something to upset her, when it was she who continuously upset herself these days. And because he truly had done nothing wrong, and because Jesse DuFrayne refused to free her from the grip of memory, and because there was such a whipped-pup look in David's eyes as he offered her the streaming ice cream, she said, "Mr. Melcher, I believe I'll have time to show you the way to the mill tomorrow after all."

His face was immediately transformed into cherubic radiance. She realized when he smiled so quickly, so joyfully, how little it took for her to make him happy. Gratitude and admiration shone from his eyes at each little bit of attention she showed him.

This man, she realized, could be manipulated by nothing more than a smile. It should have been a heady thought, but it left her inexplicably unexcited. Still, she made up her mind she would be nice to him for the rest of the day, because he did not deserve to suffer the consequences of her constant thoughts of Jessy DuFrayne.

"Let's go watch the tree skinners choose up sides," she suggested, reaching a hand up to him. Like a grateful puppy, he helped her to her feet, his expression one of devotion.

David Melcher's initiation had only begun with the morning draught session and the subsequent bidding on the picnic baskets. Being the subject of much conjecture, he was greeted profusely wherever he and Miss Abigail went. Each greeting was enhanced in cordiality by the offer of a mug of beer, and just like that morning, David found his hand filled with a sweating glass through the entire afternoon, through no wish of his own. It was understood that Miss Abigail would not drink beer, but the mere fact that she accompanied David while he did seemed to make Miss Abigail more human in the eyes of the citizens of Stuart's Junction. At times she was actually seen smiling and laughing, and the townswomen took note of this, poking their elbows into one another's ribs, winking. And hour by hour, David became increasingly inebriated, and more thoroughly accepted.

Before the end of the day, Miss Abigail too felt herself accepted in a way she'd never been before. The women included her in their plans for the next meeting of the Ladies of Diligence Sewing Circle, gave her an apron and a spatula when the pie eating contest took place, kept her in their cheering circle when David participated with their men, and took her by the elbow as they moved to the more rowdy contests. David participated in everything—the sack jousting, pole climbing, Indian wrestling, and even the tobacco spitting contest. And he was a miserable failure at everything he tried. But only if success was measured by the official contest results, for in goodwill he was the greatest achiever of the day. The fact that he tried all the contests, in spite of his lost toe, in spite of his limp, in spite of the fact that he was assured of a loss even before he started, endeared him to the men. And the fact that he had wrought such a change in Miss Abigail endeared both of them to the women.

David was finally forced to desist at the final event of the day, the log rolling contest. It took the nimblest of feet and a perfection of balance to even enter the event—obviously he lacked both. He had been slapped on the back and hugged by more than one of the log rollers, though, as they slogged out of the pond, defeated, dripping, laughing. Thus, by the time he at last returned to Miss Abigail he was as wet as if he'd participated himself. He was roaring drunk too, stained with tobacco and pie, reeking to high heaven of beer—an unequivocal mess. In this deplorable state he was carried to Miss Abigail's side, to where she was working with the women who were putting away pie tins, picking up forks and glasses, and distributing picnic baskets to their rightful owners.

"Miss Abigail," roared Michael Morneau, "this man is the best goddamn sport that every got a toe shot off!"

The women noticed how she didn't so much as bat an eyelash at the word *goddamn*. Instead she turned to find the disheveled David actually borne to her on the shoulders of the well oiled men who were to be his cohorts for as long as he chose to live in this town. They were all laughing, staggering, singing, swaggering, arms around each other so that if one of them leaned to the left, the lot of them leaned. Swaying back to the right, the lot of them swayed.

"Town's got a helluva wunnerful newcomer here, ain't that right, Jim?"

Whomever Jim was, he roared even louder than his companions and drunkenly doubled the motion. "Damn right, and we got Miss Abigail here to thank for bringin' him in! Ain't that right, boys?"

More amiable cussing and approval followed, and Miss Abigail looked up to where David swayed on their shoulders.

"See? We brung him back to you, Miss Abigail." But the inebriated speaker seemed unable to locate David all of a sudden and looked around searchingly. "Didn't we?" he asked, raising another hullabaloo. "Where the hell'd we put 'im?"

"I'm up here!" called a grinning David from his perch on the men's shoulders.

The one who'd been searching looked up. "There you are! Well, how the hell'd you git up there?"

"Why, you dummy, we was bringin' him back to Miss Abigail, remember?" another voice slurred while somebody stumbled and the gleeful band swayed, *en masse*, in the other direction.

"Well, put 'im down then, 'cause here she is!"

She could see it happening even before it actually did. One minute David was up there smiling like a besotted wall-eyed pike, the next minute the shoulders separated almost as if choreographed—half in one direction, half in another. Like the Red Sea they parted, dropping David Melcher, still smiling and waving, down the chasm. Miss Abigail saw him coming and gasped, then lurched futilely to save him. He fell, octuopus-like, a tangle of jellied arms and legs, but just as he plummeted, she gained the cleft in the human sea and David's disappearing shoulder caught her on the side of the neck and down she went with him! She landed flat on top of him, arms and legs splayed in the most unladylike fashion imaginable.

As soon as the crowd realized what had happened, solicitous hands reached toward the pair of casualties piled up in their midst. The men "ooh-ed." The women clucked. But David, with that pikey grin still all over his face, opened his eyes to find Miss Abigail McKenzie's face smack in front of him—and Lord! if she wasn't lying on top of him! Her hair was falling sideways out of its knot, her breasts were smashed against his damp, beery shirtfront, her blue eyes were startled, and her cheeks were a darling pink. He didn't care how she got there, or when. This was just too good a chance to miss.

He threw two very loose-jointed arms around her and kissed her so long and hard he thought he'd throw up for lack of wind and dizziness and the bump his head had just suffered.

Miss Abigail felt his arms tighten and saw his lopsided grin become even more lopsided, and she knew beyond a doubt what he was going to do, but she could not scramble off of him in time to prevent it. She felt her hair go sliding to hang over their two cheeks as he kissed her with the smell of tobacco juice and beer and sweat and cherry pies all around them.

And suddenly she was aware that a great, pulsing roar of applause had burst out. Even the ladies were clapping and cheering. Men whistled through their teeth and kids came scrambling among long legs and petticoats to see what was going on within the circle.

"Atta boy, David, give it to 'er!" somebody yelled.

Miss Abigail pushed and rolled and finally broke free, tumbled to the dirt, and sat beside him. She was positively scorching! But what made the final difference, what everyone could not quite believe they were seeing, was the way she burst out laughing, trying to hide her blushing cheeks behind a small, uncharacteristically grimy hand. Sitting there in the dirt, she reached both hands toward the hovering men and said, "Well, are you going to stand there applauding all day or is somebody going to help me up?"

Everyone was laughing with her as they tugged her to her feet, followed by David. The ladies fussily dusted off her skirts and scolded their foolish husbands. But secretly they were all well pleased. Miss Abigail, it seemed, wasn't the stick-in-the-mud she'd seemed all these years, and David—why, he was perfect for her. Every citizen of the town congratulated himself on what a tidy bit of matchmaking had been accomplished here today. From that moment on David Melcher and Abigail McKenzie were accepted not individually, but as a pair.

She felt it happening all day long, the curious tide of that acceptance. It was a new feeling to her, one that had been denied to Abigail McKenzie all her single life. The subtle change that had started that morning had grown more palpable as the day wore on. If she were to try to define it she could not, in her vast store of words, find just the right ones to describe the exclusion of the single person from the immutable charmed circle of those who live life two by two. Only in retrospect did she feel it fully. Not until the end of this day during which she had felt so much included did she realize how much she had been excluded until now.

Basking in the glow of the feeling she found herself again beside David Melcher, seated on the ground beneath the deep blue night sky of Hake's Meadow. Legs stretched out before them, faces raised, they watched the intermittent bursts of fireworks that illuminated both them and the sky.

From the corner of her eye she could see that David was watching her.

"I ought not to have . . . have kissed you that way," he stammered, sobering for the second time that day, admiring her chin, nose, and cheeks as explosions came and went. She kept her face raised, but said nothing. "I . . . I didn't exactly know . . . what I was doing."

"Didn't you?" she asked.

He looked up as a skyrocket exploded. "I mean, I had too much beer."

"Like everyone else."

He took heart. "You're not . . . you're not angry?"

"No."

The two of them leaned back, elbows stiff, palms on the grass behind them. He edged one hand sideways until his fingers touched hers, and when the next firefall burst, he saw that she was smiling up at the sky.

David's fingers were warm, his eyes upon her admiring. She was filled with a sense of well-being from the day they'd shared and wondered, when they reached the doorstep would he kiss her?

On the ride back to town aboard the crowded wagon, David held her hand as they sat side by side on a bundle of hay, their hands concealed beneath the folds of her skirt. Their hands grew very damp and once he released hers and wiped his palm on his pant leg, then found her fingers again beneath the skirt of dove gray. She thought of Jesse, of his straightforward moves so unlike David's unsure ones. Guiltily, then, as David's hand returned to hers she squeezed it.

He walked her home when the buckboard unloaded, but there were others walking their way so he kept his distance. At her door, with hammering heart, he took her hand once again in his damp one.

"I . . ." he began, but stopped, as usual.

She wished he would simply say what he was thinking, without these false starts. He's not Jesse, she reminded herself, give him time.

"Thank you," he said in the end, and dropped her hand, stepping back as the Nelsons came home next door.

"I didn't do anything deserving thanks," she said quietly, disappointed that he'd dropped her hand.

"Yes you did."

"What?"

"Well . . ." He seemed to search his mind a moment. "How about the picnic?" He spied the basket on the porch floor.

She said nothing.

"You . . . you did more, Miss Abigail, you know you did. You m . . . made . . . m . . . me accepted in Stuart's Junction today."

The night was quiet, contentment seemed to spread around Abbie like a comfortable warm wind. "No, you made me accepted."

"I . . . I . . . what?"

She looked down at her hands and joined them together. "I've lived here all my life and have never felt as much a part of this town as I do right now. You did that for me today, Mr. Melcher."

He suddenly took both of her hands again. "Why, that's what I feel like. Like . . . like I've found my home at last."

"You have," she assured him, "one where you are liked by everyone."

"Everyone?" he swallowed as he asked.

"Yes, everyone."

He stood squeezing her hands a long time and she heard him swallow again. His hands were much smaller than Jesse's. She tried not to compare them. Kiss me, she thought. Kiss me and chase him from my mind.

But he could not gather the courage, sober as he was now. And he knew he was in a sorry state, smelling of beer and tobacco, clothing soiled and damp.

"You'll show me the way to the mill tomorrow?" he asked.

"Certainly. The sooner the building goes up, the sooner you'll be open for business."

"Yes."

He let her hands go, disappointing her immensely, for she knew by the way he did it that he'd rather have continued holding them.

Jesse would have held them.

Damn you, Jesse, leave us alone.

"I had a marvelous day," she urged, finding an almost compulsive need within her to be kissed by this man, although perhaps not solely for the right reasons.

But David only said, "So did I," then wished her good night and turned to go.

Her heart fell. She was doomed to another night of thoughts of Jesse after all. Wearily, she went to the swing and sat there in the dark, listening to the sound of David's irregular footsteps retreating up the gravel street. Soon he moved beyond earshot and the sound of his steps was replaced by the gentle creaking of ropes as she nudged the swing. A cricket answered the ropes. She stared hypnotically up the dark street, saw not dark street but dark moustache instead.

David . . . Jesse . . . David . . . Jesse . . .

David, why didn't you kiss me?

Jesse, why did you?

David, would I have let you?

Jesse, why did I let you?

David, what if you knew about Jesse?

Jesse, if it weren't for you there'd be nothing for David to know. Why didn't you force me to leave your room that night as any gentleman should have? Why did I force my way in as a lady should not have? All it has brought me is pain. No, that's not true, it brought me David, who is all the gentle, refined and likable things I ever wanted in my life. Why must I compare him to you, Jesse DuFrayne? Why should he have to measure up to you, who did everything wrong from start to finish? David, David, I'm sorry . . . believe me. How could I know that you would come back? What would it do to you, with your gentle nature, if you learned the truth about me? Why do I find fault with you for being hesitant and polite and being a gentleman? Jesse was fast and rude and nothing gentlemanly whatsoever and I hated it . . .

Ah, but not at the last . . . not at the last, her disloyal body claimed.

She crossed an arm over her stomach, rested an elbow on it, and cradled her forehead tiredly, trying to forget.

The swing ropes squeaked rhythmically, and memory descended mercilessly. A bare chest showing behind the open buttons of a shirt, an arm slung along the back of a swing, a smile that began slowly at the corner of a moustache, hands upon her skin, lips and tongue upon her skin.

At the instant tears gathered in the corners of her eyes, she realized that her breasts were puckered up like tight little rosebuds.

Get out of my life, Jesse DuFrayne! Do you hear me! Get off my swing and out of my bed so I may go to it in peace again.

Chapter 20

THE TOWNSPEOPLE GREW accustomed to seeing Miss Abigail and David together in the days that followed. The two of them spent long hours making the many decisions necessary for establishing a new business from the ground up. The day after the picnic, when they showed up at Silver Pine Mill, Miss Abigail was right beside David as the arrangements for the sale of lumber were handled. Demonstrating her keen business acumen, she secured his lumber at a better price than he'd have gotten on his own by insisting that they be shown the less desirable knotted pine, which brought the price down. These, she wisely noted, were good enough for building storage shelves at the rear of the building.

The plate glass for the windows, which would be shipped by train from Ohio, would have been one of their most expensive commodities had they purchased plates of the large size he envisioned. She suggested instead that they order numerous small panes that could be shipped at a far smaller price due to the fact that they were far less liable to break in transit. Thus the plan for a flat, cold, indifferent storefront was scrapped in favor of a warm, inviting Cape Cod bow window, the first Main Street was to boast. In the words of Miss Abigail, why not let women ogle the shoes from three directions instead of just one? Perhaps they could sell three times as many that way.

While the store's first studs began rising she marched one day down to the feedstore and presented Bones Binley with a proposition he found impossible to refuse: she would furnish him and his cronies with a picnic basket each day for seven days if during that time they could whittle a set of twenty-eight matched spools of which a railing would be made for the back of the display window. The railing, rather than a wall, would allow the window display items to be seen from inside the store while at the same time creating a warm, inviting atmosphere when viewed from outside.

When it was announced at services one Sunday that pews had finally been ordered for the church, she suggested to David that they see about purchasing the old wooden benches at a fraction of what new chairs would have cost. This done, she next raided Avery Holmes's back room and came up with a dusty bolt of sturdy rep that had been lying there untouched for years simply because it was bright scarlet. She considered scarlet the perfect color to lend the shoe store the interior warmth she was striving for. She talked Avery into selling her the entire bolt at a ridiculously low price and left him feeling only too glad that he'd unloaded it at last. Afterward, she talked the ladies of the sewing circle into experimenting with upholstering, which none of them had ever tried before. They padded and covered the old church benches with the red rep, all the while thanking Miss Abigail for giving them a chance to try their hand at this new craft.

The bolt of rep seemed to have no end. When the benches were completed, there were still yards and yards left. Abbie fashioned simple, flat curtain panels with which to frame the bow window, to be tied back, giving the whole display a stagelike affect. Still she hadn't run out of the red fabric, so the remainder of the bolt she began tearing into strips whenever she found time, to be used later in braided rugs for in front of the door and before the iron stove at the rear of the store.

As August neared and the building took shape, Abbie and David worked together on the massive order that needed placing with the factory in Philadelphia for the first stocking of the shelves. The heat remained intense, the air seeming always to carry its low haze of dust motes. One such late afternoon the two of them were in the coolest spot they could find: on the grass out under the linden tree in Abbie's backyard, with ledgers, lists, and catalogues spread all about them.

"But you have to think about winter coming!" Abbie was insisting. "Be practical, David. If you were to place an order from your company only, for nothing but high-fashion shoes, you'll lose out on the far greater share of your potential business."

"I've always sold fine, up-to-date shoes," he argued. "People can buy boots in a dry goods store—so let them."

"But why lose their business?"

"Because I don't think I'll need it. I'll have all the business I need selling the more fashionable styles I've always handled."

"Maybe in the East you would, and maybe traveling in a circuit like you did in the past, because what you carried was a novelty and those who saw them thought they'd lose the chance to buy such shoes once you moved on. But out here, in one place, you'll need to suit all needs. Work boots would be your best seller of all."

"But how will work boots look in that lovely little Cape Cod window you talked me into?"

"Horrible!"

He blinked at her questioningly. "Well?"

Immediately she was planning: she was always filled with fresh ideas. "Well . . . we'll put them in the back of the store, in a spot more suited to them. We'll display them where the men will feel more comfortable looking at them. That's it!" she exclaimed, the idea suddenly gelling. "We'll make a spot exclusively for the men! Men are so funny that way, they like to have a spot of their own. We'll get a few captain's chairs like the ones out in front of Mitch's feedstore and we'll circle them around the stove and . . . and . . . let's see . . ." She pondered again, placing a finger against her teeth. "We'll make it homey and masculine both at once—a red rug in the middle of the circle of chairs, and maybe we can display the boots in a masculine way that's attractive and takes a little of the dullness away."

"I don't know," David said doubtfully.

She became impatient with him and jumped up, spilling ledgers and scattering notes and papers. "Oh, David, be sensible!"

"I am being sensible. This town already has an outlet for work boots and everyday shoes. I specialize in fashionable shoes and they are what I know how to sell. It's the ladies I want to appeal to. When they see what is in the front window, I want them to run straight home and exclaim to their husbands, 'Guess what I saw today!'"

Abbie stood very still now, hands on her hips, challenging him. "And what exactly will they describe?"

"Well, the window display, of course, filled with the kind of shoes that appeal to their vanity or maybe their husband's vanities. Heavenly shoes the likes of which they've never seen in their lives, straight from the East."

Whether or not it was wise, she asked, "Red shoes?"

"What?" He blinked up at her.

"Red shoes, I said. Will they be describing red shoes?"

"Why . . . why, yes, some of them. Red shoes just like yours."

But they both knew she'd never worn those red shoes since that one and only night when he'd taken her out to dinner.

"You . . . you like the red shoes, d . . . don't you, Abigail?"

She came near him and squatted down, her skirt forming a billowy mushroom about her as she reached to lay an arm upon his sleeve. "Please understand, David. I like them because they are from you, but I . . ."

When she hesitated, he insisted, "Go on."

She looked into his face, then away, then nervously stood up and turned her back on him. "Do you know what . . . what Mr. DuFrayne said when he saw them?"

David instantly bristled at the mention of DuFrayne. "What does DuFrayne have to do with it?"

"He was here the day they arrived, as you know." Resolutely she turned to face David before adding, "He called them strumpet's shoes." David's face burned and his lips pursed.

"Why do you bring him up? What does it matter what he thinks?"

Her tone became imploring. "Because I want your business to succeed. I want you to realize that here in Stuart's Junction people don't wear red shoes, but they wear a lot of work boots and sensible utility shoes. If you are going to succeed, it is imperative that you understand. In the East, where bright colors are all the rage, it is perfectly acceptable to sell them and to wear them. It's different here. You look at those colors from the salesman's point of view. People here, particularly women, are far more conservative. No matter how much they might even secretly admire them, most of these women would not dream of purchasing them. That is the only reason I repeated Mr. DuFrayne's comment, because it symbolizes the views of the town.''

"Abigail." His mouth was pinched, his jaw rigid. He had completely forgotten the reason for her soliloquy. Only one thing now possessed his thoughts. "Are you saying he called you a strumpet?"

Without thinking, she replied, "Oh, no, he was just jealous, that's all."

David jumped to his feet, snapping, "What?"

She tried to make light of it, realizing her mistake. "We're getting off the subject. We were speaking of the most sensible shoes for you to order."

"*You* were speaking of the most sensible shoes for me to order. *I* was speaking of why DuFrayne should have cause to feel jealous. Was there something between you two after all?" David Melcher became strangely self-assured and glib-tongued whenever DuFrayne's name came up. He possessed a firm authority which was missing at other times.

"No!" she exclaimed—too fast—then, calming herself, repeated more quietly, "No . . . there was nothing between us. He was hateful and inconsiderate and insulting whenever he got the chance to be." But she knew that wasn't entirely true, and she could not meet David's eyes.

"Then why should he care one way or another if I sent you a pair of strumpet's shoes? After that scene on the bed the morning I left, I should think he'd be the type to applaud red shoes, if what you say is true and they really are considered inappropriate."

Unwittingly, David had hit on one of those inconsistencies about Jesse DuFrayne that rankled her still, all these weeks after he had left. It was disconcerting to have it put into words by someone else when it was in her thoughts so often, seemingly inexpressible.

"I cannot answer for him," she said, "and I don't think it's your place to upbraid me. After all, you and I are nothing more than—" But she suddenly came up short, chagrined at herself. She dropped her eyes and fidgeted with the button on her cuff. She really did not know what she and David were to each other.

He had been the epitome of politeness in the weeks they'd been working together on plans for the store. The only change—and it was natural—was that they'd begun using each other's first names. He'd made no further attempt to kiss her or even hold her hand. In no other way did he indicate that he was wooing her. She supposed that he thought he'd offended her by getting drunk and kissing her that way before the entire populace of Stuart's Junction on the Fourth of July and was making amends by his extreme politeness since then.

Again with that aura of authority, he said unequivocally, "I don't want that man's name mentioned between us again, Abigail."

Her eyes came up sharply to meet his. By what right did he give her orders? They were not betrothed.

Suddenly David softened. The wind lifted the brown hair from his forehead, and the expression about his eyes grew wistful. He stood with his weight on his good leg—he often did that, perhaps because his other foot gave him discomfort—and it lent him a relaxed look, especially when he had the thumb and forefinger of one hand hidden inside his vest pocket, where he carried his watch.

"Abigail, what were you going to say just then? That you and I are no more than what? You didn't finish."

But how could she finish? It had been a slip of the tongue. He should be the one to finish, to understand what it was she had meant. She had grown so used to being with him, and she enjoyed him most of the time. Now and then she thought of her lost virginity and the fact that she should cease encouraging David, but as time went on she thought of it less and less. Still, he never made any advances toward her or even acted as if he thought about doing so. They shared a platonic relationship at most. And so Abbie thought up a likely answer for him.

"I was going to say business partners, but I guess we're not even that. The business is yours." She could not quite meet his eyes.

"I feel like it's half yours too. You've done as much or m . . . more than I." He began to stammer as soon as the subject broached anything personal. While speaking of the store his enthusiasm kept his voice steady. But now, perilously close to clarifying his relationship with Abigail, he grew timorous again.

"I've done no more than any friend would do," she said humbly, hoping he would deny it.

"No, Abigail, you've done much more. I don't know how I could have done it all without you. You . . . your judgments are m . . . much better than mine."

She waited with her heart in her throat, wondering if he'd go on to more personal things, but she could sense his shyness—for some men it is not easy to be the man in a situation like this. The silence lengthened between them and became uncomfortable and she could see he'd lost his nerve.

"We still haven't agreed on the ordering of the stock," she said, and the moment of discomfort passed.

"Something tells me I should trust your judgment again on this."

"There is room at the rear of the store for boots. I am also very sure that we'll sell more of them if we do it the way I've envisioned it. Come to the store and we'll look around and I'll show you just where we could put the boot section and how we'll plan it."

"Now?"

"Why not?"

"But it's Sunday."

"So it is, and there'll be no noisy hammering and banging and we should be able to talk in peace and study the possibilities."

He smiled, conceding. "You're right. Let's go."

She no longer wore her hat and gloves when the weather was too hot for them. They walked uptown in the late-day sun, nodding hello to an occasional neighbor who now called an amiable greeting to both of them. "Afternoon, David, Miss Abigail. How you doin'?" There were times when Miss Abigail already felt married to him.

The skeleton of the building was up. It had walls and part of a roof, but inside the studs showed. The framework of the bow window lay in wait of panes, and there was no front door yet. The interior walls were to be of tin wainscot above the shelves—the stacks of wainscot lay amid sawhorses and planks.

Abigail picked her way among pails of nails, stacks of shelving, the carved posts Bones and the boys had already completed. "See here?" At the rear of the building she pointed to a spot where a hole had been left for the chimney pipe.

"Now here's where the stove will be. Suppose we cut some giant rounds of oak and leave them, bark and all, just as they come from the woods. We'll put them here near the stove and set the rugged work boots on the wood to add just the right touch of masculinity. A basket of nuts here, the ring of sturdy chairs around the stove, or leaning up against the wall behind it, almost as if reserved for each man. Why, they'll love it! Men love it near a stove. Women get enough of stoves working in their kitchens, so we'll put their shoes up front where it's cool, in the display window surrounded by the spooled railing. And while it might be true that no woman around here might like the color red on her shoes, they will find it cheerful and gay when it is brightening up the store as a background for displays. Imagine it at Christmas with the fire snapping and a hot pot of coffee back here on the stove for the men. We could invite them to leave their mugs right here, hanging on the wall on pegs. We'll sell boots all right, and plenty of them. At the same time the ladies will be up front oohing and aahing over your fancy shoes, and gossiping, away from their husbands."

Abigail didn't know it, but carried away as she was by her plans for the store, her face had taken on the same lovely look that Jesse had discovered upon it the day the red shoes came. Neither did she realize she had said "*we'll* sell boots all right." Her face was animated, bright-eyed and radiant. And just as Jesse DuFrayne had been moved by it weeks ago, David Melcher was moved by it now. The hem of Abigail's skirt had stirred up sawdust in the air, and the sun, glinting down through the chimney hole and half-finished roof, caught it in hovering cantles as she gestured, moved, turned, and spoke. She raised a hand to point at where the coffee pot would be, bubbling away on a winter stove . . . and David forgot the summer heat, imagined her here then, helping the ladies select shoes, bringing her enthusiasm along with her good business sense. He imagined helping the husbands while he told their ladies, "My wife will help you up front."

And suddenly he knew it could not possibly be any other way.

She swung around and he surprised her hand by capturing it in mid-air. For a moment the words stuck in his timid throat. The sawdust drifted around them like summer snow, settling here and there on their shoulders. It was silent and wood-scented and private. And he loved her very much.

"Abigail . . ." he said, then swallowed.

"Yes, David?"

"Abigail, may I . . . k . . . kiss you?" He had made so many blunders with her already that he thought it best to ask first.

She wished he had not asked. Jesse would not have asked. Afraid David might have read the unwanted thought, she lowered her lashes. Instead, he took it for her demure refusal and dropped her hand.

"I'm sorry . . ." he began.

Her eyes flew back up. "How can you be sorry?" she asked quickly. "You haven't done anything." It was unreasonable for her to feel piqued when all he meant to do was be polite, but enough was enough!

"I . . . do . . . don't . . . " he stammered, but her reply had confused him so, he didn't know what to do.

"Yes, you may kiss me, David."

But by now the situation had lost the grace that a spontaneous kiss would have lent. In spite of this, he took both of her hands and leaned toward her. There was a short piece of planking between their feet, but rather than move around it or step over it to take her in his arms, he leaned over the barrier and, with closed eyes, gently placed his lips over hers.

He had fine, soft, warm, shapely lips. And she thought, what a shame he does not know how to use them.

He laid them over hers for a wasting flight of seconds while Abigail felt absolutely nothing. The talk about how they should display the shoes had excited her more than his kiss. He straightened then and remained perfectly silent, as silent as his kiss had been. She gazed down at the sawdust beneath their feet, at the plank which separated them, thinking it might as well have been between their torsos as well as there on the floor for all the contact there'd been during that kiss. A kiss of the lips only, she determined, was a decidedly unsatisfying thing. So she raised her lips to David's again and dared to put her hand behind his neck for a brief moment. But the kiss was brief, and immediately afterward David said the appropriate thing.

"Shall we go?"

She wanted to say, "No, let's try that again without the plank between us. Let's try that again with a little tongue." But he finally came around the plank and took her elbow, leading her

toward the nonexistent door. She could tell, though, that the
kiss had flustered him, for he talked nervously all the way
home, about how she was right and he'd immediately put in an
order for boots so they would arrive in time for the planned
October opening, about how there might even be snow by then
and he'd better get his wood stacked in the back, and how they
would plan a special announcement in the paper, even though
everyone in town knew the store would open and when.

He refused to stay for supper, which he'd done quite often
recently—indeed, suppers together had become the rule rather
than the exception—but collected his materials and left,
insisting that he'd better get started putting the order on paper.

That night she tried to analyze her feelings toward David
Melcher, to sort out her reasons for encouraging him as she had
today. By now she was sure that she was not pregnant, so the
biggest potential obstacle to their relationship had been
removed. Oddly enough, the overwhelming guilt she had once
felt no longer riddled her. She had performed an immoral act,
but she did not think she had to pay for it for the rest of her life.
She did deserve some happiness, and if David Melcher offered
it to her, she no longer believed she'd be deceiving him to take
him up on it.

No, her problem with David was no longer a problem of
morality, it was one of sexuality. She simply was not stimulated
by him. She tried not to think of Jesse . . . oh, she really,
really tried. But it did not work. Being kissed as she had been
by David, it was impossible not to contrast his kisses with that
of the practiced, the fiery, the tempting Jesse. Vivid memories
came flooding back until they swept everything from her mind
except her intimate knowledge of him. She knew every part of
his body as well as she did her own, and it no longer seemed
shameful to admit it. She thought of each part of it, wondering
if the importance of sexual attraction would wane in time if she
married David. Ah, but David had not asked her. Ah, but
David would. It would take a little more time, but she was sure
he would. And when he did, what would she say? No—I won't
marry you because you don't make my blood run high like
Jesse? Or yes—because in every other way we are compatible.
She thought, as she lay awake into the wee hours, that if she
could entice David into displaying more ardor, she might at
least have a larger basis of comparison between him and Jesse
DuFrayne.

* * *

The following evening David accepted her invitation to supper. It was a pleasant meal, shared at her kitchen table in the familiar way they had so often shared such meals. Over coffee, David was hugely complimentary, as he always was.

"What a delicious meal. Everything you make is always delicious. It warms more than a man's stomach."

If she was going to contrast the two men, then let her do it truthfully, and garner for herself an honest choice about them. She let the voice of Jesse echo back, with its infernal teasing, which at the time had so galled her but which now only tempted. "And what are you planning to poison me with this time, Abbie?" She was unaware of the lingering smile the memory brought to her lips.

"Did I say something funny?" David asked, noting it.

"What?" She brought herself back to the present—regretfully.

"You were laughing just then. What were you thinking?"

"I wasn't laughing."

"Well, your shoulders were moving as if you were laughing inside."

She shook her head. "It was nothing. I'm just glad you enjoyed your supper."

Her answer appeased him. He pushed his chair back from the table, suggesting, "I thought maybe we'd read some of your sonnets after supper. That's all it would take to make the evening perfect."

Why all of a sudden did sonnets sound as dry as his kisses had been?

"You always say the nicest things," she said to atone for the errant thought. I really must be more fair to him, she promised herself, for it was not he who had changed. It was she.

They read sonnets, he sitting on the settee and she sitting on a stiff side chair. The lamps were lit, they had nothing to do but enjoy the verses together. But he sensed an impatience, almost a relief, in her when they finally put the book aside. He puzzled once again at the change he sometimes sensed in her, a restlessness that continued to intrude upon the tranquility he loved and sought.

He kissed her good night. A chaste kiss, David thought. A dry kiss, Abbie thought.

Several days later they sat on the swing in the early evening.

September was upon them, the hint of winter not far behind it.

"Something has been . . . bo . . . bothering you, has . . . hasn't it?"

"Bothering me?" But her tone was sharp. She was working on the strips for the rugs, and her hands tore and rolled the rags almost frantically.

"I can tell that I displease you, but I d . . . don't know what it is that br . . . brings it on."

"Don't be silly, David," she said reprovingly. "You don't displease me at all. Quite the contrary."

She ripped a long strip of the cloth, her eyes never leaving it, and the harsh sound scraped on his nerves. He wished that she would stop the rag work while they talked.

"There's no need for you to . . . t . . . try to be kind by disguising it. I would only like t . . . to know what it is that bothers you."

"Nothing, I said!" Her hands were a blur, winding the strips up into a ball. How could she say that everyone in town was expecting the two of them to get married and that she'd give anything if only he would ask her, yet feared more each day that he would? Just how could she explain such a confusion of thoughts to him when she couldn't straighten it out for herself.

Quietly he reached out to lay a hand over hers, which were furiously rolling those rag strips into a tight, tight ball.

"Whatever it is that you call nothing is a very large lump of something. Much larger than I thought. You're winding those rags like you wish they were choking somebody. Is it me?"

She dropped the rag ball into her lap and her forehead onto the heel of her hand, but said not one word.

He sat staring down at the tattered red threads that lay all over her lap like a web. "It started that d . . . day I asked if I could k . . . k . . . kiss you. I could tell you were disgusted w . . . with me. Is that it, Abigail? Are you angry b . . . because I k . . . kissed you?"

She tapped her fingers against her forehead and looked at her lap, not knowing what to say. She didn't know if she wanted him to pursue this subject or not. How could she tell after those two lackluster kisses?

"Oh, David . . ." She sighed heavily and looked away, across the yard.

"What is it? What have I done?" he asked pleadingly.

"You haven't done anything," she said, now wishing

fervently that he would so she could know once and for all what she felt for him.

"Abigail, when I first came here I sensed a . . . a rapport between us. I thought you felt it too. I thought how we were the same k . . . kind of people, but . . . well, since I've been back you seem d . . . different."

It was time she admitted the truth.

"I am," she said tiredly.

"How?" he braved.

The tiredness left her and she jumped to her feet, snapping in irritation, "I don't like sonnets anymore." The rag ball rolled onto the porch floor, untwining, but she paid it not the scantest attention. She crossed her arms over her ribs and left him to contemplate her erect shoulder blades.

He sat staring at them, thoroughly befuddled. In a moment she entered the parlor, slamming the screen door shut behind her. He remained on the swing for some time, wondering just what she wanted out of him, wondering what sonnets had to do with anything. Finally he sighed, rose, and limped to the door. He opened it quietly and entered to find her standing before the monstrous throne-shaped umbrella stand, gazing at her reflection in the mirror. As he watched she did a most curious thing. She raised a hand and pressed the backs of her fingers upward against the skin on her jaw, studying the movement in the glass.

"What are you doing?" he asked.

She did not answer immediately, but continued pressing her chin. At last she dropped the hand as if she were very weary, then turned to him with a sad expression on her face, and answered almost dolefully, "Wishing you might kiss me again."

His lips opened slightly and she could almost see his thoughts drift across his transparent face: he'd been worried for so long that he'd gone too far, kissing her in the store that day. He was relieved yet timid, perhaps a tiny bit shocked that she should ask him. But at last he moved toward her, and she read one last look in his face—awe that she should really, really want him.

This time there was no plank between them, but when he kissed her he still held her undemandingly, fragilely. It was like before, only worse, because now, without hindrance, he could have pulled her flush against him, but he didn't. He held her instead in a wan imitation of an embrace, afraid to believe his lips were on hers at last, and with her full consent.

Suddenly she needed to know about David Melcher, about herself. She lifted her arms and they swirled onto his shoulders as she raised up on tiptoe and offered her lips to him with feigned passion. She pressed her breasts against his vested chest, but rather than accepting her invitation he sucked in his breath, taking himself away from the touch of her, afraid the contact was too intimate yet.

"Abigail, I've thought about this for so long," he said, looking into her eyes. "I thought about you and the house and the store and everything, and it just seemed too good to be true to think that you might feel the same about me as I do about you."

"How do you feel, David?" she asked, trying to force the words from him.

He released her fully, properly, stepping back and holding her only by her upper arms. "I want to marry you and live here in this house and work in the store with you by my side."

She had the sinking feeling that he desired all three equally. She had the even more sinking feeling that she did, too.

"I love you," he said then, and added, "I guess I should have said that first."

What could she say to that? Yes, you should have? Tell me again and kiss me and pull me against you and touch my body here and here and inspire me to love you also? Touch my skin, touch my hair, touch my heart and make it race and touch my breast and make my blood pound and touch me beneath my skirt and show me you're as good at it as another man was before you?

But the cool fact was, none of these things happened. He did not kiss her passionately or pull her against him or touch her hair or heart or breast or any other part of her as Jesse had done. Instead, he drew back, gave her shoulders a loving squeeze, contolling all his body's urges with a will that she suddenly detested. He waited for her reply. She moved to him and kissed him, allowing her lips to grow lax, to be opened by his tongue should he choose. But his soft lips remained together, guarded by discretion.

But discretion was the last thing she yearned for. She longed to be reduced—no, heightened—by the ecstasy she knew could sluice through her body should he wield it in just the right way.

But standing in David's hands she thought, He's not Jesse. He'll never be Jesse.

But might that not cease to matter? Here he was, offering her safe keeping for life. One did not decline an offer of marriage simply because of the way a man kissed or didn't kiss. She ought to be flattered by his courtliness, not be insulted by it. But Jesse had managed to change her sense of values somewhere along the line.

"There's time enough for you to decide," David was saying. "You don't have to answer me tonight. After all, I know this is a bit sudden."

She had the awful urge to laugh aloud. She had known him over three months and her blouse buttons had never touched his vest, yet he thought his chaste kiss and this invitation sudden. What would he think if he knew that in three weeks she'd touched every part of Jesse DuFrayne's body and had pleaded with him to take her to the limits?

"Are you sure you want to marry me?" Abigail asked David, knowing it was not him but herself she should be asking.

"I've been quite sure since the day you threw me out after I accused—" But there he stopped, not wanting to bring DuFrayne's name into it, not realizing it had been in it all the time. "Can you forgive me for what I accused you of? I was very foolish and very jealous myself that morning. I know now that you're not at all that kind of woman. You're pure and fine and good . . . and that's why I love you."

If ever there was a point of no return, it was now. Now, when his words could easily be denied if they were going to be. But deny them she did not. She kept her silence, knowing that even it was a lie.

David gave her shoulders one last squeeze. "Besides," he said in a light attempt at gaiety, "what would my store be without you?"

But again she wondered if he did not value her more because she could help in his store, and because he could live in her house, than he did because she could be his wife.

"David, I'm very proud to have been asked. I'd like to think about it, though, at least overnight."

He nodded understandingly, then pulled her toward him by her shoulders and kissed her on the forehead before leaving. He left her standing next to the umbrella stand. For a long

moment she stared disconsolately at nothing. Finally she
turned her head and confronted her reflection, admitting once
and for all how old she was getting. She sighed deeply, rubbed
the small of her back, and went out onto the porch to collect the
rag ball and rewind it mechanically as she wandered aimlessly
into her bedroom. She stood beside the window seat winding,
winding, remembering Jesse sitting here that afternoon after
Jim Hudson left. She dropped the ball into the sewing basket
on the floor, remembering how Jesse had taken a hank of yarn
from it to tie up that pig bladder with which he had so
mercilessly teased her. She pictured his long-fingered hands,
dark of skin, gentle of touch, flexing on that inflated bladder,
flexing upon her own breast. She thought of David, afraid to
pull her against him as he kissed her on the eve of his marriage
proposal to her.

She sighed, dropped down onto the window seat, leaned her
elbows to her knees, cupped her face in both hands, and cried.

Fortunately, during that night good common sense took over
and made Abigail realize that David Melcher was a decent,
honest man who would treat her decently, honestly for the rest
of her life. She, too, could offer the same, from here on out.
Whether it was scheming or not to consider it, she admitted
that David, in his naiveté, would probably not know whether
or not she was a virgin anyway. If she were mistaken about
that, she would tell him it was Richard, those many years ago.
If her marriage had to begin with that one, last lie, it was a
necessary lie—necessary to prevent David's being hurt any
further. And since there was no chance of her ever falling into
promiscuity again, her decision was made.

David kissed her tenderly, if dryly, when she told him that
she was accepting his proposal. Standing in his light embrace,
she felt a sense of relief that the decision was made. This time
he did hug her to his chest, but his eyes were scanning her front
parlor.

"Abigail, we're going to be so happy here," he said near her
temple. A deep sense of peace overcame him here in her
house.

"You'll have roots at last," she returned.

"Yes, thanks to you."

And to Jesse DuFrayne, she thought, but she said, "And the
itizens of Stuart's Junction."

"I think they were half expecting us to get married."

"I know they were, especially after the Fourth of July."
He released her, smiling his very youngish smile. "When
hall we announce it?"

She looked thoughtful for a moment, then quirked an
yebrow. "How about in Thursday's paper? Mr. Riley started
ll this when he linked my name with yours in June. Shall we
ive him the opportunity to print the ensuing chapter?"

The announcement in Thursday's paper read:

> Miss Abigail McKenzie and Mr. David Melcher
> happily announce their intentions to be married on
> October 20, 1879, in Christ Church, Stuart's Junc-
> tion. Miss McKenzie, a lifetime resident of this
> town, is the daughter of the late Andrew and Martha
> McKenzie. Mr. Melcher, formerly of Philadelphia,
> Pennsylvania, has traveled for several years in this
> area as a circuit salesman for the Hi-Style Shoe
> Company of that city. Upon marriage to Miss
> McKenzie, Melcher will open for business in the
> Melcher Shoe Salon, the edifice currently under
> construction at the south end of Main Street directly
> adjacent to Perkins' Livery Stable. The business is
> slated to open its doors immediately upon the
> couple's return from a two-week honeymoon in
> Colorado Springs.

The first frosts came. The quaking aspens blanketed the hills
vith brilliant splashes of amber. Mornings, even the cart ruts
vere beautiful, trimmed in rime, glistening in the touch of new
ight. Sunsets turned the color of melons and became jaggedly
treaked with purple, presaging the cold breath of winter soon
o follow. The mourning doves left; the nuthatches stayed.
Weather eyes were cast at the mountains as the first leaves
umbled like golden gems to the earth.

A flood of good wishes poured into Miss Abigail's house and
David's store, which was fast nearing completion. Neighbors
nd townsfolk could not resist stopping at one place or the

other when passing by. Their good wishes reaffirmed to Abiga
that she had done the right thing in accepting David's proposal

It was easy and natural now to be with David, and daily the
reaffirmed the fact that they were very much alike in ideals
likes, dislikes, goals. He was a totally adoring suitor, eve
ready with a compliment, a smile, a look which told her h
approved of her in every way. His kisses became more ardent
which pleased her, but his immense respect for her kep
improper advances at bay. He stammered less and less as the
became more familiar with each other. This newfound eas
pleased her immeasurably.

Often as not, David and Abigail could be found at the sho
store, stacking a winter supply of wood at the rear, staining th
lovely spooled rail, building shelves, hanging red draperies i
the bow window, carrying in the huge oak rounds, or unpacking
a partial shipment of stock, which had finally arrived. The
worked together constantly, becoming a fixture of the smal
town's society even before their wedding took place. Thos
who stopped by to say hello or to ask if they needed a han
with anything went their way again thinking they'd never see
a pair more suited to each other; it really was a match made i
heaven. Some chuckled, patting themselves on the back
thinking, well, if not in heaven, then at Hake's Meadow.

Abigail was a mistress of efficiency as the wedding da
neared. Besides helping David make preparations for th
opening of the store, there were countless personal detail
demanding her attention. She had decided to wear her mother
wedding gown of ivory silk, but it needed alterations. The lac
veil was in excellent condition. However, some of the see
pearls had come loose from the headpiece and neede
replacing, thus it had been sent to a jeweler in Denver fo
renovation. David had ordered a special pair of white satin
pumps for her and she anxiously awaited both headpiece an
shoes. Once the entire bridal ensemble was in her possession
she would pose for a photograph—her bridal gift to David. Sh
contracted a Denver photographer, Damon Smith, to come ou
to do the portrait. They'd planned to have a wedding receptio
at the house, and Abbie began baking cookies and *petits fours*
freezing them now that frosts had come to stay. The garden wa
cleaned out until spring. The little iron stove was installed i
the store, and the coffee pot there was already a fixture. Sh
was often happy to have it, for between the store and th

ouse, her duties kept her juggling her precious time and
ttention between wedding and grand opening preparations.

The store was turning out beautifully. There, it seemed, was
where Abigail and David shared their closest intimacies. Times
when they found themselves alone, stocking shelves in the
toreroom, he would steal kisses, making her impatient for
heir wedding day to arrive . . . and, more importantly, their
oneymoon. There were times when she knew he was on the
rink of breaking down his own self-imposed restrictions, but
ither he would back away or they would be interrupted, for
eople came in and out of the store as if it were already open
or business.

The interior was as bright, warm, and cheerful as she'd
magined it, with its red curtains, braided rugs, and uphol-
tered benches. The circle of comfortable chairs wreathed the
ireplace where a cheering blaze beckoned. The smell of fresh
wood and bark permeated the air, combined with coffee,
eather, and the clean smell of shoe wax. People loved it and
here were always friends gathered around the stove. There
vas not a doubt in the world that the business would thrive, or
he marriage either.

Chapter 21

IT WAS ONE of those dark, steely late afternoons when the thought of supper in a toasty kitchen made footsteps hurry homeward. The murky clouds played games with the top of the mountain, gathering, scattering—wind-whipped shreds scudding in a darksome sky, making all mortals feel lowly indeed.

The bell and the pearl headpiece had arrived from Denver. Bones Binley had walked the packages up from the depot after the late train pulled through. Pleased, Abigail now donned her new green coat, wrapped a matching scarf about her head, and flung its tails back over her shoulders. Smiling, she left the house with the small brass bell tucked warmly in her white fur muff.

Snow flecks stung her forehead and the wind sent the scarf tails slapping about her cheeks. She shivered. David would already have the lanterns lit at the store. The stove would be warm, and she pictured David standing with one foot braced on its fender, a cup of coffee in his hand. Oh, he would be pleased that she'd thought of the bell. She skipped once and hurried on.

Coming around the corner of the saloon, she stepped up onto the boardwalk and the wind shifted, hitting her full in the face, driving icy needles of snow against her skin. She glanced down the street at the welcome orange lanternlight spilling from the bow window. A man was standing looking in through the small panes, a big man in a heavy sheepskin jacket with its collar turned up and his hands plunged deep into its pockets. He stood motionless, bareheaded, with his back to her, while for some inexplicable reason her footsteps slowed. Then he hung his head low, stared at his boots a moment before turning toward the livery stable next door and disappearing inside. He was very tall, very broad. From behind he'd reminded her of Jesse, except that he had no limp. Once more she hurried, keeping her eyes on the door of the livery stable, but no one came out as she advanced toward the door of the store, above which hung a fresh, new sign, swinging wildly in the wind.

MELCHER'S SHOE SALON, it said, DAVID AND ABIGAIL MELCHER, PROPS.

It was lusciously warm in the store. As usual, there was a circle of men around the stove, David among them, sipping coffee.

He came forward immediately to greet her. "Hello, Abigail. You should have stayed at the house. There's weather brewing out there."

She raidated toward the stove, removing her coat, scarf, and muff, tossing them onto a red-padded bench along the way.

"I had to come to tell you the good news. My headpiece came back from Denver this afternoon, all repaired at last."

"Good!" David exclaimed, then winking at his cronies around the stove, added, "Now maybe I won't have to listen to her fretting about that photograph anymore." The men chuckled and sipped.

"And look what else came." She held up the tinkling, brass bell. "It's for your door—a good luck charm. Every new store must have a bell to announce its first customer."

David smiled in genuine delight and set his coffee cup down, coming to squeeze and chafe her upper arms affectionately. "It's just the right touch. Thank you, Abigail." The smile on his face made her feel treasured and precious. "Here," he said, "let me hang it."

"Oh, no," she said pertly, lifting the bell out of his reach, "it's my gift. I shall do the hanging."

David laughed, turning back to the men. "Never saw such a nuisance of a woman—always wants her own way."

"Well, David, you just gotta learn to step on 'er a little bit when she gets outta line." Then the men all laughed in easy camaraderie. They could do that now, laugh at Miss Abigail this way—she had changed so much since David Melcher came around.

She got a hammer and tacks from the back room and hauled one of the chairs up near the front door. The bell tinkled as she climbed up, reaching toward the sill above the door to find the perfect spot for the bracket. But even on the chair she couldn't quite reach, so she put one foot up on the spooled railing beside her and stepped onto it.

That was how Jesse DuFrayne saw her when he came out of the livery stable and stopped again before the shop with the sign reading, . . . DAVID AND ABIGAIL MELCHER . . .

She had two tacks in her mouth and was holding the brass bracket against the doorframe, hammer poised, when she saw a man's legs stop outside the Cape Cod window. With her arms raised that way she could not see his face, but she saw cowboy boots, dark-clad legs spraddled wide against the wind, and the bottom half of a thick, old sheepskin jacket. Something made her duck down to peer beneath her sleeve at the face above those wide-braced legs.

Her eyes widened and one of the nails fell from her lips. An agonizing, wonderful, horrible terror filled her heart.

Jesse! My God, no . . . Jesse.

He was gazing up at her with that big sheepskin collar turned high around his jaw while the wind caught at his thick black hair, whipping it like the dark clouds above the mountain. The lantern glow coming through the window illuminated his face and kindled his dark, intense eyes that were raised in an unsmiling study of her. It lit, too, his forehead, cheeks, and chin, making them stand out starkly against the stormy darkness behind him. His moustache was as black as a crow's wing, and as she stared, hammer forgotten in hand, he smiled just a little and lifted one bare hand from his pocket in silent hello. But still she seemed unable to move, to do anything more than gape as if struck dumb, filled with pounding emotions, all at odds with each other.

Then one of the men behind her asked how she was doing up there, and she came back to life, turning to look over her shoulder at the stove and mutter something. When she looked outside again, Jesse had stepped back beyond the circle of window light, but she could still see his boots and knew he

stood there watching her with those jet black eyes and his old
familiar half grin.

She scuttled down to search for the tack on the floor, but
couldn't find it, so clambered back up again and started
hammering the one she had, ever conscious now of the angle
from which he studied her, the way her breasts thrust out
against her dress front and jiggled with each fall of the hammer.

The other tack winked at her from inside the spooled railing
and she climbed down to retrieve it, unable to keep her eyes
from seeking the waiting figure beyond the window. For a
moment she stood framed by red curtains, like a dumbstruck
mannequin on display, quite unable to move her limbs or draw
her eyes away from the dim figure who watched from the
street, frowning as the wind tried to blow him over.

Jesse, go away, she pleaded silently, terrified of his pull on
her.

Somehow her limbs found their ability to move, and she
climbed up on the railing again and pounded in the second nail,
her heart cracking against her ribs in rhythm with the hammer.

David came from the rear of the store then, admiring her
handiwork.

"Should we hang the bell together?" he asked.

"Yes, let's," she choked, hoping he would not note the
hysteria in her voice. "That way it will bring good luck to both
of us." She could see now that Jesse's legs were gone and
wondered if David had spied them out there.

When the bell was on the bracket, David brought her coat
and helped her into it. "You'd better get back home before the
weather gets worse."

"You're coming up for supper, aren't you?" she asked,
trying to keep the desperation from reverberating in her tone.

"What do you think?" he answered, then pulled her scarf
protectively around her neck and turned her by the shoulders
toward the door before he opened it for her and smiled her
away.

The bell tinkled.

Two steps outside she turned, imploring, "Hurry home,
David."

"I will."

She lowered her head to hold the scarf more tightly around
her neck, but the wind lifted its fringed end and threw it back at
her face. She scanned the dark street ahead.

He was gone!

The snow was fine and stinging and had glazed the streets with dangerous ice, which left no tracks for her to either follow or avoid. The wind slashed at her back, buffeting her along the slick boardwalks while her skirts luffed like a mainsail in a gale. She looked into each lighted store as she passed but he was in none of them. Turning at the saloon corner, the wind eddied into a whirlpool and twisted her skirts about her with renewed mastery. She ducked her head, hanging on to her scarf to keep it on her head, pulling her chin down low into her coat collar.

"Hello, Abbie."

Her head snapped up as if the trap door of a gallows had opened beneath her feet. His voice came out of the wild darkness, so near that she realized she'd nearly bumped into him rounding the corner. He stood with feet spread wide, hands in pockets, the swirling wind lifting his white, misty breath up and away.

"Jesse," she got out, "I thought it was you." She had come to a stop and could not help staring.

"It was."

The way they stood, the wind pelted his back but riveted the icy snow into her face, stinging it. She had forgotten how big he was, strapping wide and so tall that she had to look up sharply to see his face.

"What are you doing here?" she asked, but her teeth had begun to chatter, the cold having little to do with it.

"I heard there's going to be a wedding in town," he said, as conversationally as if they were still in her summer garden on a mellow, floral afternoon. Without asking, he withdrew a bare hand from his pocket and turned her by an elbow so that her back was to the wind, his face into it. He moved her nearer the clapboard wall, stood close before her, and jammed his hand back into his pocket again.

"How did you know I was getting married?"

"I figured it before I left, so I kept my eye on the papers."

"Then why didn't you just stay away and leave us in peace?"

His smileless face looked as ominous as the roiling clouds that had brought on the early dark. He scowled, black brows curling together as he ignored her question and asked one of his own.

"Are you pregnant?"

He couldn't have stunned her more had he kicked her in the side of the head with his slant-heeled cowboy boot.

"Why, you insufferable—" But the wind stole the rest of her lashing epithet, muffling her voice as the scarf flapped at her lips.

"Are you pregnant!" he repeated, hard, demanding, standing like a barrier before her. She moved as if to lurch around him, but he blocked her way simply by taking a step sideways, with his hands still buried in his pockets, keeping her between his bulk and the saloon wall.

"Let me past," she said coldly, glaring up at him.

"Like hell I will, woman! I asked you a question and I deserve an answer."

"You deserve nothing and that is precisely what you shall get!"

In an injured tone he went on, "Damnit, Abbie, I left him enough money to set the two of you up in high style for life. All I want in return is to know if the baby is mine."

Rage swooped over her. How dare he sashay into town and imply such a thing—that she had allowed David to make love to her to disguise the mistake she'd made with him, Jesse. At that moment she hated him. She wound up and swung, forgetting that the muff was on her hand. It caught him on the side of the face, doing no damage whatsoever with the soft white rabbit's fur, the pathetic attempt at violence made all the more pitiful by its ineffectuality.

With his hands in his pockets he couldn't block her swing in time, but shrugged and feinted to one side and the muff glanced off his cheek and rolled away onto the icy street behind him.

She made a move toward it, but he caught her by the shoulders, swinging her in a half circle to face him.

"Listen to me, you! I came back here to get the truth out of you and—by God!—I'll have it!"

She skewered him with her eyes and moved again as if to pick up the muff. But he pushed her back against the wall, his eyes warning her not to move, then he knelt and retrieved the muff, but when he handed it to her she had forgotten all about it.

"You despicable goat!" she cried, tears now freezing paths down her cheeks. "If you think I'm going to stand here in the middle of a blizzard and be insulted by you again, you are sadly mistaken!"

"All it takes is a simple yes or no," he argued, holding her in place while the wind threatened to rip them both off their feet. "Are you pregnant, damnit!"

Again she tried to jerk away, but his fingers closed over her coat sleeves like talons. "Are you?" he demanded, giving her a little shake.

"No!" she shouted into his face, stamping her foot and at last spinning free, running away from him. But the ground was glare ice now and a little foot flew sideways, and the next thing she knew she was sprawled at his feet. Immediately he went down on one knee and reached for her elbow, still holding the white muff in his massive, dark hand.

"Abbie, I'm sorry," he said, but she shook his hand off, sat up and whisked at her skirts, fighting back tears of mortification. "Damnit, Abbie, we can't talk here," he said, reaching as if to aid her once more, but she slapped his hand away.

"We cannot talk anywhere!" she exploded, still sitting on the street, glaring up at him. "We never could! All we could ever do was *fight*, and here you are, back for more. Well, what's the matter, Mr. DuFrayne, couldn't you find any other woman to force yourself on?"

All traces of temper left his voice as he looked into her angry eyes, kneeling there on one knee, engulfed in that dreadfully masculine sheepskin jacket, and said simply, "I haven't been looking for one."

God help me, she thought, and gathered her outrage about her like armor, struggling to her feet while he held her elbow solicitously and offered her the muff, which she yanked out of his hand. As she swung away and stalked up the street again, everything in her stomach threatened to erupt.

He watched her retreating back a moment, then called out to it, "Abbie, are you happy?"

Don't! Don't! Don't! she wanted to scream at him. Not again! Instead, she whirled into the banshee wind and yelled, "What do you care! Leave me alone. Do you hear! I've been screaming it to an empty house for three months now, but at last I can scream it to you in person. *Get out of my life, Jesse DuFrayne!*"

Then she spun again toward home, running as best she could on the precarious ice.

For some minutes after she rounded Doc's corner and disappeared, Jesse stared at the empty street, then he stamped the gathering snow off his boots and turned back toward the corner saloon. Inside, he ordered a drink, sat brooding until it arrived, then downed it in a single gulp, his mind made up. He'd damn well go back up to her place and get some answers out of that woman!

The roses were gone now from beside her white pickets, which looked forlorn in the wintry gale. Walking up the path he studied the porch. The wicker furniture was gone now. The swing hung disconsolately, shivering in the wind as if a ghost had just risen from it—maybe two. He took the steps and peered through the long oval window of her front door. He could see her rump and the back of her skirts at the far end of the house. It looked like she was bending over, putting wood into the kitchen range.

Hitching his collar up, he rapped on the door, watching her hurry toward him down the length of the house. He stepped back into the shadows.

As she opened the door, she began, "Supper's not ready yet, David, but it—" The words died upon her lips as Jesse stepped into the light. She lurched to slam the door, but his long fingers curled around the edge of it and a boot wedged it open at the floor.

"Abbie, can we talk a minute?"

Her cheeks made up for the missing roses outside.

"You get off my front porch! Do you hear me, *sir.* That is all I need right now, for you to be seen here." She darted a look beyond him, but the yard and street were empty.

"It won't take a minute, and shouldn't an old friend be allowed to wish the bride well?"

"Go away before David comes and sees you here. He is coming for supper any minute."

"Then I can congratulate the groom too."

Her eyes quickly assessed the hand and boot holding the door open; there was no possible way she could force him to leave.

"Neither David nor I wish anything from you except that you be gone from our lives." The cold air swirled into the house causing the flames to flicker in the lanterns. Jesse's hand was nearly frozen to that door.

"Very well. I'll leave now, but I'll be seeing you again, *Miss Abigail*. I still owe you one photograph and that twenty-three dollars I borrowed from you."

Then, before she could harp once more about wanting absolutely nothing from him, he released the door, bounded down the porch steps, hit the path at a run, and jogged off toward town, kicking up snow behind him.

His limp was completely gone.

When David arrived for supper, Abigail's greeting was far warmer than usual. She took his arm and squeezed his hand, saying, "Oh, David, I'm so glad you're here."

"Where else would I be three days before my wedding?" he asked, smiling.

But she squeezed his arm harder, then helped him out of his coat. "David, you're so good for me," she said, holding his coat in both arms against her body, hoping, hoping, that it was true.

"Why, Abigail, what is it?" he asked, noting the glitter of tears in her eyes, moving to take her in his arms.

"Oh, I don't know," she said chokily. "I guess it's all the plans and jitters and getting everything done in time. I've been so worried about the headpiece not arriving in time for the photograph, and now this storm is starting and what if the photographer can't make it in from Denver?" She backed away, swiped at a single tear which had spilled over, and said to the floor between them, "I guess I'm just having what I've heard most brides have sooner or later—an attack of last-minute nerves."

"You've done too much, that's all," he sympathized. "What with the store and the preparations for the reception and getting all your clothes ready for the ceremony and our trip. It isn't *all* necessary, you know. I've told you that before."

"I know you did," she said plaintively, feeling foolish now at her display of jangling nerves, "but a woman has only one wedding in her lifetime and she wants it perfect, with all the amenities."

He circled her shoulders with an arm and herded her toward the kitchen. "But most women have mothers and sisters and aunts to help carry the load. You're doing too much. Just make sure you don't overdo it, Abigail. I want you well and happy on Saturday."

His concern made her feel somewhat better, but it wa
extremely difficult to forget that somewhere out there Jess
DuFrayne was spending the night, and should David encounte
him between now and Saturday and stir up old animosities
there was no telling what might happen. The results could b
unpleasant, to say the least, disastrous, to say the most. For sh
wouldn't put anything past Jesse.

All through supper she found her thoughts returning tim
and again to one plaguing question: would Jesse stoop so lov
that he'd tell David about what they'd done together?

An instinct for preservation made her broach the subject o
Richard. David was relaxed and lethargic, sitting back on th
settee with his hands laced over his full stomach, fee
outstretched and crossed at the ankle.

"David?"

"Yes, Abigail?" He had never taken to using any shortene
form of her name like Jesse had. It had always disappointed he
just a little.

"Did I ever tell you I was engaged once?" She knev
perfectly well she'd never told him before. He suddenly sat u
and took interest. "It was long ago—when I was twenty."

She could tell by the stunned look on his face that there wer
a hundred questions he wanted to ask, but he just sat ther
waiting for her to go one.

"His name was Richard and he grew up here in Stuart'
Junction. We . . . we used to play hopscotch together. I'n
actually surprised that nobody has mentioned his name to yo
because people around here have long memories."

"No, nobody has," he said, red around the collar.

"I just thought that you should know, David, before we go
married. We've never spoken much about our pasts. We've ha
such a mutual interest in our future, with the store to plan an
everything, that it has rather superseded other topics, hasn'
it?"

"Perhaps it has—you're right. But if you don't want to tel
me about Richard you don't have to. It doesn't matter
Abigail."

"I want to," she said gazing at him directly, "so tha
perhaps you'll understand my sudden jitters." Then she looke
at her lap again as she went on. "There had never been anyone

xcept Richard, and we more or less grew up suspecting that ne day we'd marry. My mother died when I was nineteen, and ithin a short time Richard and I became engaged. I was very oung and naive and believed in such things as destiny then." he paused, creating the effect of the passage of time in her narrative. Then she sighed. "Richard apparently believed ifferently, though, for when my father fell ill and became a tal invalid within a year of my mother's death, it seems ichard found me less desirable as a future wife. I guess you might say he considered my father excess baggage. At any ate, my . . . my fiancé disappeared scarcely a week before he wedding. His family moved too, shortly afterward, and I ave never seen them or him since."

David's face wore a caring expression. He reached for her and. "I'm sorry, Abigail. I truly am."

She looked up at his gentle, unassuming face, knowing at hat instant just what a good, moral man he was and knowing lso that she was very lucky to have found someone like him so ate in her life.

"I understand your jitters now," he said into her eyes, "but I would never leave you like he did. Surely you know that."

"Yes, I do," she assured him. But she felt small and guilty, or she knew he was too good to read into her story the ossibility that she and Richard had been intimate. "David," he said, really meaning what she was about to say, "I do so want everything to be perfect in our lives together, that's all."

"It will be," he promised. But he promised it holding othing more than her hand, and she could not help thinking hat this was the kind of thing which two people in love should e sharing wrapped up tightly in each other's arms. "I'm glad ou told me, Abigail. I could see that something had you upset onight, and now that the story is out, consider it forgotten."

At last he kissed her, and she clung to him with a sudden esperation very much unlike her. Taking his lips away, he aid, "I think it's best if I go now, Abigail."

But she clung harder, willing him to stay a little longer, to eep the threat of Jesse DuFrayne at bay. "Do you have to go o soon?"

He put her firmly away from him. "You can use a good ight's rest, you said so yourself a while ago. I'll see you omorrow evening, like we agreed."

He kissed her at the door before leaving, but he had put
his overcoat first, so all of the warm contact of hugging w
lost in the bulk of woolen coat and muslin skirt.

Chapter 22

IMMEDIATELY AFTER DAVID left, Abbie dressed for bed and retired, wanting to get the lanterns blown out as quickly as possible. The wind buffeted the house, rattling shingles, tapping barren branches against eaves, promising a full night of its wrath. The storm sounds only multiplied her trepidation. Resolutely she closed her eyes and recounted the needs David effectively fulfilled in her life: security, companionship, admiration, love. She spent time analyzing each. He was paving the way to the most secure life she had ever known. Companionship was unquestionable—they had recognized it between themselves from the first. And when it came to admiration—out of all the people she'd known in her entire life none had been more complimentary, appreciative, or admiring. And love—

Her thoughts were hammered to an abrupt halt by the loudest beating her back door had ever suffered. Nobody ever came to her back door. She knew before her feet hit the icy floor who it would be and realized she'd been lying there riddling herself with thoughts of David to keep them off of Jesse DuFrayne.

For a moment she considered letting him bang away until he gave up, but then he shouted at the top of his lungs, and even

above the howling storm, she was afraid someone next do
would hear.

She found her wrapper and hurried to the back do
listening, her toes curled against the drafty floorboards. F
banged and hollered again so she lit a lantern but left the wi
low, almost guttering, still afraid of anyone seeing him throu;
the windows.

"Abbie, open up!"

She did, but only partway, refusing to step back and let hi
in.

He was standing in the wind and snow, hair, eyebrows, a
moustache laced with the stuff, determination boring into h
from eyes as black as the night.

"I told you to keep away from me. Do you realize what tin
of the night it is?"

"I don't give a damn."

"No, you never did."

"Are you going to let me in or not? Nobody saw me, b
they sure as hell will hear me beat the door down if you slam
in my face again." The wind invaded the house while sl
clutched her wrapper together over her breastbone. Her fe
were freezing and the wrapper did little to protect her agair
the shudders that overtook her.

Suddenly he ordered, "Get in there before you freeze
death along with me," and in he came, filling the kitchen wi
ten pounds of sheepskin jacket, three inches of wet moustach
and nearly two hundred pounds of stubbornness.

She lit into him before he even got the door shut. "How da
you come barging in here as if you owned the place! Get out!

He just gave a large, exaggerated shiver, rubbed his palr
together, and exclaimed, "God, but it's cold out there
completely ignoring her order, shrugging out of his jack
without so much as a by-your-leave. "We're going to ne
some wood on that fire to keep us from freezing solid." F
jerked a chair from the kitchen table, clapped it down right
front of the stove, hung his jacket on the back of it, th
opened a stove lid and reached for a log from the woodbox-
all this time he hardly looked at her.

"This is my house and you are not welcome in it. Put th
wood back in my woodbox!"

Again he paid no heed but stuffed the wood into the stov
replaced the lid, then turned and bent over at the wai.

brushing snow curds from his hair. He spied her bare toes peeking from beneath the hem of her wrapper, pointed at them, and said, "You'd better get something on those tootsies, tootsie, because this is going to take a while."

By this time she was livid. "This will take no time at all because you are leaving. And don't call me tootsie!"

"I'm not leaving," he said matter-of-factly.

She knew he meant it. What was she supposed to do with a bull-headed fool like him? She clenched her fists and grunted in exasperation while he took anoher chair and clapped it down beside the first, then stood back with a thumb hooked in his waistband.

"We've got some talking to do, Abbie."

The frost was melting from his moustache now and a drop fell from it as he stood patiently waiting for her to give in and sit down. His nose was red from the cold, hair glistening and tousled from its recent whisking. He looked more like a gunslinger than ever in those boots and denims, dark shirt and rough leather vest. His skin was swarthy, the perfect foil for his black hair, moustache, and swooping sideburns. He might have ridden in from the range just now after rounding up cattle in the blizzard or outrunning a posse. His appearance was totally masculine, from the clothing to the ruddy cheeks, the wind-reddened nose to the untidy hair. Her eyes fell to his hip—no gun.

"You don't have to be afraid of me, Abbie," he assured her, following the direction of her eyes. Then he drew a handkerchief from his hip pocket and blew his nose, all the while studying her above the hankie, his eyes refusing to let her go.

How could her feelings betray her like this? How could she stand here thinking that even the way he blew his nose was attractive? Yet it was. Oh, Lord, Lord, it was because Jesse DuFrayne was undeniably all man. Angry with herself for these thoughts, she lashed out at him.

"Why did you come here again? You know that if David finds out, he'll be terribly angry, but I suppose you're planning on that. You haven't done enough to me, have you?"

He bent forward at the waist, reaching behind to stuff the hankie away in his pocket, and said calmly, "Come on, Abbie, sit down. I'm half-frozen from standing out there waiting for him to leave." Then he sat down himself and held his palms toward the heat.

"You've been standing out in the street watching my house? How dare you!"

He continued leaning toward the stove, not even bothering to turn around as he said, "You're forgetting that I'm financing this setup. I figure that gives me plenty of rights around here."

"Rights!" She came one angry step closer behind him. "You come in here spouting rights to me in my own house and put wood in my stove and . . . and sit on my chair and say you have rights? What about my rights!"

He slowly brought his elbows off his knees, straightened his shoulders almost one muscle at a time, sighed deeply, then got up from the chair with exaggerated patience, and swaggered across the room to her with deliberate, slow clunking boot-steps. His eyes told her he'd put up with no more of her defiance. And he took her upper arm in one hand, the back of her neck in the other, then steered her toward the pair of chairs. This time when he ordered, "Sit down," she did.

But stiffly, on the very edge of the chair, her arms crossed tightly over her chest while she poised like a ramrod. "If David finds out about this and I lose him I'll . . . I'll . . ." But she spluttered to a stop, unable to find harsh enough words, he infuriated her so.

Jesse just stretched his long legs out and leaned back, relaxed, fingers laced over his stomach. "So are you happy with him then?" he asked, studying her stiff profile.

"When you left here that was the last thing on your mind!"

"Don't make assumptions, Abbie. When I left here things were in a jumble and I don't like leaving things in a jumble, so I came back. When I didn't hear from you but I read that you were getting married, I had to know for sure if you might be in a family way."

She pierced him with a malevolent look. "Oh, that's big of you—really big!" she spit. "I suppose I should get all fluttery at your tardy concern."

"I hadn't thought you might, not after the iceberg treatment I got on my way out of here that morning." He grinned crookedly, and out of nowhere there came to Abbie the memory of Jesse in that stunning verdigris suit, bending to her on one knee.

"Well, you deserved it," she said petulantly, but with a little less venom.

"Yes, I guess I did," he admitted good-naturedly, an amiable expression about his eyes.

Behind them the low-burning lantern guttered, sending their shadows dancing on the wall behind the stove. Before them the fire grew, licking against the isinglass window in the cast-iron door of the stove. Outside the wind keened, and for a moment they looked at each other, thinking back.

Then Jesse asked softly, "You're not, are you, Abbie?"

"Not what?"

"Pregnant."

Beleaguered once again by those conflicting emotions that this infernal man could always rouse in her, she turned to stare at the isinglass window. She was so confused. All he had to do was walk in here and start being nice and it started all over again. She pulled her feet up off the drafty floor, hooked her heels over the edge of the chairseat, and hugged her knees up tight, laying her forehead on her arms.

"Oh, Jesse, how could you?" she asked, the words coming muffled into the cacoon of her lap. "Out there in the street you practically accused me of . . . of consorting with David to confuse the issue of . . . of this nonexistent paternity."

"I didn't mean it to sound that way, Abbie." He touched her elbow, but she jerked it away, still keeping her head buried in her arms.

"Don't touch me, Jesse." Now she looked up, accusingly, "Not after that."

"All right . . . all right." He put his hands up as if a gun were pointed at him, then slowly lowered them as he saw the fierce, hurt expression on her face.

"Just why did you have to come back here? Didn't you do enough the first time without coming back to haunt me?"

Their eyes locked, held for a moment, while he asked softly, "Do I haunt you, Abbie?"

She looked away. "No, not in the way you mean."

He looked down at her bare toes curling over the edge of the chair, then sprawled back lazily, studying her while he slung a wrist over the back of her chair. "Well, you haunt me," he admitted. "I guess that's why I came back, to settle all the misunderstandings between us that still haunt me." Without removing his wrist from the chair back, he took a lock of her hair between index and middle fingers, rubbing the silky skein back and forth a couple of times. At the fluttering touch she worked her shoulder muscles in an irritated gesture and pulled her head forward to free the hair.

"I thought we understood each other fully that last day," she said, hugging her knees tighter.

"Not hardly."

Memories of that last day came hurtling back as they sat side by side, warming by the stove, warming to each other again, anger dissipating with the cold. Something unwanted seemed to seep into their pores along with the radiating warmth from the stove. After some time her voice came again, small and injured.

"Why didn't you tell me you knew David was coming back before we . . ." But she was afraid to finish. He was too near to put that into words.

He considered her for a long moment before asking quietly, "Why didn't you go back upstairs when I told you to?"

But neither of them had the answers to these questions that echoed through the windswept night. Abbie lowered her forehead onto her crossed arms again and silently shook her head. She heard Jesse move, sitting forward on the edge of his chair, leaning his elbows on his knees again.

"Is there any coffee in that pot?"

She got up, lifted the blue-speckled pot, found it full, then placed both palms around it. He watched from under lowered brows, reminded of those hands upon him, feeling for fever. She disappeared into the dark pantry.

There, alone, she pressed her hands to her open mouth as if it might help her control this urge to cry when she got back out there where he could see her.

His eyes followed her as she came back out with cups, filled them, then turned to find he had removed his boots and braced his feet up on the fender of the range to warm them. Wordlessly she handed him his cup, their eyes locked while he lowered his feet so she could step past to her chair.

Side by side they sipped, not talking, both of them staring introspectively at the little patch of fire visible through the stove window. He rested his feet once more against the fender while she wound her toes around each other. There was something about sitting barefoot together before a snapping fire that was disconcertingly calming. Animosity ebbed away, leaving them almost at peace with each other.

"Did you think that I knew Melcher was coming back to stay?" he asked without turning to look at her.

"Well, didn't you?" she asked his toes. She remembered what his feet looked like bare and was conscious of how bare her own were right now.

"I know that's what you've been thinking all these months, but it's not true. I knew he was coming for the meeting the next day, but I had no idea he'd end up staying."

She turned to study his profile, following the line of his forehead, nose, moustache, and lips that were lit to a burning, glowing yellow-red. He lifted his cup, took a swallow, and she watched his Adam's apple lift and settle back down. He was, she admitted, a decidedly handsome man.

Almost tiredly she said, "Don't lie to me anymore, Jesse. At least don't lie."

He lifted his eyes to hers, to the firelight dancing away on her smileless face. "I never lied to you. When did I lie?"

"Silence can be a lie."

He knew she was right. He had deceived her by his silence many times, not only about Melcher coming back, but about owning the railroad and being the one who paid her for his keep. She took a drink of coffee, then held the cup carefully in both palms, looking down into it.

"You knew what hopes I'd pinned on him, Jesse, you knew it all the time. How could you not tell me?" She looked perhaps seventeen, and broken-hearted and all golden-skinned in the blush of the dancing firelight. It was all he could do to keep both of his hands around his cup.

"Because if I'd told you he was coming back I couldn't have had you that night, isn't that right?"

Startled, she found his eyes. She didn't know what to say. All this time she had thought . . .

"B . . . but Jesse," she said, eyes gone wide, "it was I who came to you that night. it was I doing the asking."

"No it wasn't." He scanned her face, those wide eyes which looked black in the shadowy kitchen, then forced himself to look away. "Not from the first day it wasn't. It was me, always me, right up to the very end, trying to break you down until I finally succeeded. But you know something, Abbie?" He pulled his stocking feet off the fender, leaned elbows to knees and spoke into the depths of his coffee cup. "When it was over, I didn't like myself for what I'd done."

At that moment the lantern on the table behind them guttered, spluttered, and went out. Shaken, she studied the back of his neck, the hair that grew thick and curling about his ear. "I don't understand you at all."

He glanced back over his shoulder. "I want you to be happy, Abbie. Is that so hard to understand?"

"I just . . . it doesn't . . . well, it doesn't fit the Jesse I know, that's all."

He eyed her over his shoulder for a moment longer, then turned his eyes to the fire again and took a drink of coffee. "What fits me then? The image of a train robber? You're having trouble untangling me from that image. That's part of the reason I came back here. Because I cared what you thought of me afterward, and that's never happened to me before with a woman. You're different. The way we started out was different. We started so . . ." But he stopped, going back to the beginning in his thoughts, enjoying some memories, sorry about some others, but unable to encapsulate his feelings into words.

"How did we start?" she encouraged, wondering what he'd been about to say.

"Oh, all the fighting and baiting and getting even. When I woke up the first time in this house and found out how I got here, you know how mad I was, and you were convenient so I took it out on you. But I just didn't want you to go on thinking that I was still getting even that last night when we made love. That had nothing to do with getting even."

She realized there had been countless times since when she'd thought exactly that. It was part of what haunted her. He looked back over his shoulder, but she was afraid to meet the disturbing eyes of this new, sincere Jesse.

"Is that what you thought, Abbie? That I made love to you so I could hand Melcher the money with one hand and a soiled bride with the other and watch him squirm while he decided what to do with them?" He still sat a little forward of her, coffee cup slung on a single finger, empty, forgotten, looking back, waiting for the answer she was afraid to give. "Did you?" he quietly insisted.

And at last her eyes could not resist. They trembled to find his as she managed to choke out, "I . . . d . . . didn't want to."

Her words were greeted by a long silence before Jesse sat

back in his chair, crossing an ankle over a knee so his stockinged foot brushed her gown, almost touching her knee. One dark hand fell over his anklebone, the other dangled the cup over his upraised knee.

"Abbie, I'm going to tell you the truth, whether you believe it or not. It *was* conscience money I gave Melcher, but not because I'd shot him. It wasn't him I was paying off, it was you, because I felt guilty about the night before. But I swear to you, the idea came to me in the middle of that arbitration meeting. I figured if I gave him that much money he *could* settle here and probably *would*. Oh, I admit I forced his hand a little bit, but I didn't do it to put you on the spot, Abbie. Not at all. I thought if I could fix it so you could have him and a nice cozy marriage and a nice cozy business and a secure financial future, I'd have you off my conscience."

She looked at the side of his face. He was watching the coffee cup as he tapped it on his knee.

"And am I?"

The cup fell still. He looked into her eyes.

"No."

She picked at a thread on her lap. "Are you always so generous with your mistresses?" she asked, seeking to break this spell of madness that was weaving itself about them like some silken, seductive web.

He surprised her by simply answering, "No."

She realized she'd been expecting him to deny the others, and that it suddenly hurt when he didn't. What did it matter that there had been others? Yet she could not look him in the eye for fear he'd understand more about her feelings for him than was prudent at the moment.

"Wouldn't it have been much easier to just turn me away when I came to you?"

His foot came off his knee and hit the floor and he was on his feet, suddenly absorbed in refilling his cup. With his back to her, he answered, "Hardly." Then he took a long pull of coffee while, stunned, she stared at the thick hair on the back of his neck. He stood there for a long time before finally asking, "Did you know you were the first woman who ever said no to me, Abbie?"

Again he had managed to surprise her; what he said made no sense.

"But I—"

He turned to face her suddenly, interrupting. "Don't blame yourself, Abbie, not one more time. It was me who did the asking, no matter who came to whose room, and you know it. But you were different from the rest."

"I should think that in bed one woman is no different from the rest."

His hand shot out, grabbed her by the chin, and lifted her face roughly. He looked for a moment like he might strike her. "You cut it out, Abbie! You know damn well you were different and that it was more than your just being a virgin. It was all we'd been through together that made you different. That and the fact that you'd saved my life."

Suddenly, at his angry touch, at the intensity in his eyes, she felt her own sting with tears. She twisted her chin out of his grip, her eyes never leaving his as at last she unburdened herself.

"Do you know how low I thought you were for using what I didn't know against me? For not telling me David was coming back? For not telling me you owned the railroad? For not telling me it was your money that was . . . was paying me off like . . . like some whore?"

"Abbie—"

"No, let me finish. I've been angry at how you sashayed out of here and thought a little tumble in the hay didn't matter to a woman like me, who—"

"I never thought—" He sat down, putting one hand on the back of her chair again.

"Be quiet!" she ordered. "I want you to know what hell you put me through, Jesse DuFrayne, because you did . . . you did. You made me feel unworthy of David's love, like I had no right to marry him even if he asked. You cannot imagine what that did to me, Jesse. I don't want you to leave here with a clear conscience. I want it to hurt you like it did me, because even after you were gone all I had to do was walk through this house to be reminded of what I'd done with you, or to walk into David's store to be reminded that you'd paid for it all. Even there you seemed to be laughing at me from the very walls you'd financed. I waned to strike back at you, but there was no way, and I'd begun to think I couldn't be free of you."

"Do you want to be?"

"I want it more than anything in the world," she said in utter sincerity.

"Meaning you're not?" He looked up at her hair, down at her trembling lips.

"No, I'm not. Maybe I'll never be, and that's why I'm glad I'm on your conscience. Because all it would have taken was one single statement of fact that night and none of this guilt would have been necessary. Now I face a wedding night of . . ." She looked down at her lap. ". . . . of questionable outcome, to say the least. And you say *you* want a clear conscience?"

"Abbie," he pleaded, moving nearer, turning to face her, with his hand still on the back of her chair. "I told you, I didn't know he'd stay—"

But she cut him off. "You realize, don't you, that I still stand to lose it all. Now, when I am on the very brink of everything I ever hoped for—a husband who thinks the sun rises and sets on me, a business that will mean security for as long as we live." She looked up at him squarely. He was very close, leaning toward her. "Why, I've even acquired an acceptance from this community that I never had before I knew David. As his wife I will at last fit in, where before I was nothing more than 'that . . . that *maiden lady* up the street.'"

It grew quiet, all but for the wind and the fire. He studied her, sitting there in her nightgown and wrapper, looking down at her lap. And he suddenly knew that to stay here was to hurt her further.

"What do you want me to say?" he asked miserably. "That I'm sorry?" His fingers touched the back of her hair again, but she did not flinch away this time. "I am. You know it. I'm sorry, Abbie." She looked up and found his face filled with sincerity, all hint of smile or teasing erased.

"I've gone through hell because of you, Jesse. Maybe sorry isn't enough. I knew from the first day David told me he was going to settle in Stuart's Junction that he was settling here because of me. I knew he had me on a pedestal, but I couldn't tell him differently. He would never, never understand why I did what I did with you. But do you know what my deception is doing to me, inside?"

It was clear to Jesse what it was doing to her. He could see the pain in her face and wished he had not been the cause of it. He moved back a little bit.

"What will you say on your wedding night if he suspects?"

Her eyes moved to the isinglass door. "That it was Richard."

"You've told him about Richard?" he asked, surprised.

"Not all that I've told you, but enough."

"Will he believe you?"

She smiled, somewhat ruefully. "He's not like you, Jesse. He hasn't had every woman who came along the pike."

Repeatedly he lifted the hair from the back of her neck, letting it drop back down. Very quietly he said to her ear, "There've been no women along my pike since I left here."

Shivers tingled up her spine and down her arms. But he was what he was. "I'm going to marry David, Jesse. He's very good for me."

"So was I once."

"Not in that way."

"In lots of ways. We could always talk, and laugh and—"

"And fight?"

His hand stopped toying with her hair for a second. "Yes, and fight," he admitted unabashedly, with a smile in his voice.

"Even after you left I was still fighting you. When I read the truth in that newspaper the day after the meeting I smoldered for days."

He grinned. "You were always good at smoldering," he said, low in his throat.

"Remove your arm from the back of my chair, Mr. DuFrayne, or I shall smolder all over again."

"The name's Jesse," he said, leaving the arm where it was.

"Oh, spare me from all that again. The next thing I know you'll be claiming you're a train robber with a bullet in your hip."

He laughed and squeezed the back of her neck, then gave it a gentle shake and rubbed her earlobe with his thumb. "Let's see you smolder a little bit, huh, Abbie? For old times' sake?" His hand left her neck and he got her by a little piece of hair and yanked it lightly.

But she calmly faced him, repeating, "I'm going to marry David Melcher and until I do you're going to get out of my house and out of my life."

He finally faced the stove again, stretched out with his hands on his stomach, slung down low with the nape of his neck hooked on the chair back.

"Did you really have to scream that to the empty rooms when I was gone?"

"Oh, don't let your ego swell up so," she said testily. "I hated you every time I did it."

He rolled his face her way.

"You never hated me."

"Yes I did."

"You hate me now?"

But instead of answering, she stretched out on her chair too, putting her feet up on the fender beside his.

"Tell me now that you hate me," he challenged, moving his foot to cover the top of hers.

"I will if you don't get your foot off mine and leave here this very minute." He got her foot now between both of his, rubbed it sensuously.

"Make me."

She looked at him to find the old teasing smile back on his lips, certain at that moment that if she could make him believe her, she would at last be free of him. She lounged there on her chair, just as indolently as he, and said without a qualm, "You are still convinced that forcefulness is strength, aren't you? I can't make you go and you know it. But I can repeat what I said long ago, that David Melcher has all the beautiful and gentle strengths which I admire in a man, and I'm going to marry him for them."

Jesse perused her silently for a moment, then reached out and took her hand. Her heart did crazy things, but she watched his thumb stroke hers and kept outward appearances unruffled.

"You know, I think you really mean it."

"I do," she said, letting him have his way with her hand to prove that she was no longer affected by him.

"Is he good to you?" Jesse asked, and she suddenly wanted to lace her fingers with his and pull that hand against her stomach. This was the hardest of all—it always was—when Jesse became concerned and caring and let it show in his voice and his touch.

"Always . . . and in all ways," she answered softly.

The wind moaned about something that hurt.

"And is he good *for* you?"

The snow tittered its secrets against the house.

"Abbie?" he persisted when she didn't answer.

"They're one and the same."

"No they're not."

"Then perhaps the question is, am I good for him."

"That goes without saying," came Jesse's gentle words.

To their joined hands she said, "Don't be kind. It's when you've been kind that we've traditionally made fools of ourselves."

That broke the spell and he released her hand with a light laugh, saying, "Tell me all about your plans. I really want to hear them."

Funny, she thought, but here she was two days away from her wedding and she'd never had a friend with whom to discuss it. How ironic that it should be Jesse who drew her out. But he was right about one thing—they could always talk, and by now she was feeling very comfortable with him. And for some reason she was telling him everything. All about the wedding plans, the reception plans, and about how hard she and David had worked setting up the store. She told him they were going to Colorado Springs on their honeymoon.

He quirked a cute sideways smile at her and teased, "Oh, so I'm paying for a honeymoon too?" But then he told her that the store was nicely done. He could see her hand in it.

And she told how her mother's seed-pearl headpiece had worried her by not arriving until today for the photograph tomorrow. He asked who she'd hired to take it and told her he knew Damon Smith. Smith did good work and she'd be pleased. Then she made him laugh by asking him if he really was a photographer then, and when he smiled at her and said, "You mean you still don't believe me," they ended up laughing together.

They were getting very lazy and woozy-tired by now, and the conversation was becoming a little punchy and lethargic. She told him he looked more like an outlaw than a photographer in those clothes of his, and he asked if she preferred him in that verdigris suit and she admitted no, these clothes suited him better. From time to time during this lazy exchange he'd cast that damnably sleepy grin her way before they'd both stare at the isinglass window again, all natural and relaxed and getting sleepier and looser by the minute. The hour ceased to matter as they talked on into the stormy night.

He told her about how he and Jim had started out surveying on a railroad crew and had gone from there to blasting tunnels, building trestles, and even laying tracks before they'd finally started laying down rails of their own, beginning with one little spur line, because by that time they could see the money was not in laying down rails but in owning them. She'd see, he said, when she got to Colorado Springs where all the railroad barons built their mansions.

"You too?" she asked indolently.

"No," he laughed, he didn't go for that stuff. Besides, his railroad wasn't really that big. But he talked more about how photography had started as a diversion for him, then how he'd come to love it.

By this time he was slung low upon his chair, feet crossed on the fender, contented, half-asleep. Still he asked, "And you believe me now?"

"Yes, I guess I do."

It had taken a long time to hear her say that, a long time and a lot of misunderstandings.

The howling night sounds came and went as they sat, listening in companiable silence now.

"It's very late," Abbie finally said. "I think you should be going or my photograph will be of one very wrinkled looking bride tomorrow."

He chuckled, hands rising and falling on his stomach, remembering. "Just like the first time I ever saw you. God, you were a mess, Abbie."

"You certainly have a way with words." But they were both too lazy to care anymore. They rolled their heads to look at each other.

"Don't let me fool you, though, Abbie," he said quietly.

He'd never change, she realized. He'd always be the same teasing Jesse. But he was not for her.

"I'm glad we talked," he said, sitting up at last, stretching, then yawning widely.

She followed suit, stiff and tired. "So am I. But Jesse?"

"Mmm?" he said, blinking slow at her, his hands hanging limp between his knees.

"Could you sneak back into your room without being seen, or will I have to think up quick excuses for David again?"

"Only a fool would be up this late. I'd be sneaking for nothing."

"You will try not to be seen, though, won't you?"

"Yes, Abbie." And for once he didn't tease.

He tensed every muscle in his body then, grasping the back

of one hand, stretching them both out before him while h
perched on the very edge of his chair in one of those quivering,
shivering, all-over stretches that involves legs, stomach, neck
arms, even head. She'd seen him do it a hundred times before
Memories.

Then he doubled up and began slowly pulling his boots on
Watching, she recalled once when she'd helped him do tha

He stood. He stretched again. He tucked his shirttails in an
she got to her feet, standing uncertainly beside him.

He hooked a thumb in his belt and stood there looking at her
"I guess I'm not invited to the wedding, huh?"

She stilled the wild thrumming of her heart and smiled. "M
DuFrayne, you are incorrigible."

Without taking his eyes off her, he reached for his jack
from the back of the chair and shrugged it on. She stood
watching every movement, hugging her arms.

The jacket was on. But instead of buttoning it up, he use
the front panels to hang his hands on, then just stood there th
way, making no move toward the door.

"Well . . ." he said, relative to nothing. She smile
shakily, then shrugged.

"Well . . ." she repeated stupidly.

Then their eyes met. Neither of them smiled.

"Do I get to kiss the bride before I go?" he asked, but the
was a husky note of emotion in his voice.

"No!" she exclaimed too quickly, and backed a step awa
from him, but tripped on the chair rung behind her. He reach
for her elbow to keep her from falling, then pulled her slow
slowly, inexorably into the deep, fuzzy pile of his jacket from
His eyes slid shut while he cupped the back of her head to ke
her there against him.

Abbie, he thought, my little hummingbird.

And like the heart of the hummingbird, which beats fast
than all others in creation, the heart of Abigail McKenzie fe
as if it would beat its way out of her body.

Standing against Jesse felt nothing whatever like standi
against David earlier. Jesse's coat was more bulky but throu
all these thick, thick layers of sheepskin she could feel t
thrum of his heart.

"Be happy, Abbie," he said against her hair, and kissed
She squeezed her eyes shut tight while a button impress
itself into the soft skin of her cheek.

"I will," she said against the sheepskin and his hammering
heart. The big hand moved in her hair, petting it, smoothing it
down against her neck, tightening almost painfully as he held
her tightly against him for one last second.

Then he stepped back, his hands trailing down her arms until
he captured her hands. With a last searching look into her
startled eyes, he took her palms to his cheeks and placed them
there for a moment, her thumbs resting at the outer corners of
his black moustache. His eyelids slid closed and trembled for
just a moment. Then he opened them again and said so softly
she scarcely heard, " 'Bye, Ab."

Her hands wanted suddenly to linger upon his dark, warm
face, to stroke his moustache, touch his eyes, and move from
there down his well remembered body. But he squeezed them
painfully, and she swallowed and said into his eyes. " 'Bye,
Jess."

Then he backed away and stood looking at her all the while
he slowly buttoned up his jacket and turned the collar up
around his ears.

He turned. The door opened and the snow swirled in about
her feet.

And in the silence after the door closed, slicing off a quick
chunk of cold, she whispered to the emptiness, " 'Bye, Jess."

Chapter 23

————————

WHEN ABBIE AWAKENED the following morning and saw her haggard face in the mirror, she was relieved that David wouldn't have a chance to see her this way. They had agreed she would not go down to the store at all today, so she wouldn't see him until seven this evening, when he came by to walk her over to church for their wedding rehearsal.

Assessing herself in the mirror, she found her face a disaster and her nerves ruined. Both needed immediate help.

The best she could do for her face was to give it the astringent benefits of a freshly sliced lemon. The results were an infinite improvement over the perdition which had shown in every pore when she first woke up. She managed to dim the telltale puffiness and shadows beneath her eyes by using handfuls of snow to soothe and invigorate them. After a bath and hair wash, she began to feel even more human. The visible devastation was repaired.

But what about the invisible?

It certainly didn't help her quivering stomach at all to think about Jesse, but she couldn't help it. She paused in putting the finishing touches to her hair. How different Jesse had seemed last night.

Forget him, Abigail McKenzie!

She forced herself to think of David, of the store, the photograph, the practice tonight, the ceremony tomorrow, the reception. The honeymoon. For a moment her thoughts strayed back to Jesse, but she brought them up short.

Go through the list of things that need doing for the reception! Get out the lace tablecloth, lay out the plates, forks, cups. Frost the tea cakes, slice the breads and set them aside. Press Mama's gown. Worry about the snow.

She glanced out the window but the blizzard had blown itself out toward dawn. Still, snow in the mountains often meant delayed trains, since not all lines had adequate snow sheds so trains were forced to wait while crews cleared the tracks after a blizzard like they'd had last night. Suppose the train was late or never came at all. The photograph was no life and death matter, she told herself one minute. Then the next, watched the clock, listening for the whistle, railing, oh, why did it have to snow!

Jesse—with snow melting off his hair, his moustache . . .

Forget him! Think of David. Get your clothing ready to carry to the hotel.

The 9:50 whistle! At last! That meant Damon Smith had arrived and would be setting up his photographic equipment at the hotel.

Did it mean, too, that Jesse was boarding the train to leave town?

Oh yes, yes, please be gone, Jesse.

Would David find out Jesse had been in town, even for such a short time? Did anyone see Jesse returning to the hotel at three o'clock in the morning?

Don't think about it! Pack the pearl headpiece and veil in tissue, cover the wedding dress on its hanger, get shoes ready to take. Your face looks fine, Abbie, quit looking in the mirror. Your dress is beautiful, everything will turn out fine if you simply forget Jesse DuFrayne.

With fifteen minutes to spare, Miss Abigail McKenzie stood before her umbrella stand beside the front door with its lovely oval window. She glanced outside at the windless, dazzling day, dressed as it was in white, in honor of her wedding. On the seat of the umbrella stand were her garments, stacked all neatly. On top of the stack was a pair of delicate white satin slippers of tapering heel and pointed toe—her wedding gift from David.

In the mirror determined eyes stared back at her, chastising Abbie for her foolish, tremulous misgivings. She watched herself draw arms into a new jade green coat with capelet and hood, purchased for her honeymoon trip. She forced herself to refrain from thinking it was Jesse's money that had bought it. She drew her hands into her muff. He'd bought it, too.

Lifting her eyes, she thought, pick up your wedding garments, Abigail McKenzie, and carry them over town and get this photograph taken and get yourself married to David Melcher and quit being a simpering schoolgirl. She thought of how long it had been since she'd checked the tautness of her chin. She need not do that anymore; she was not old. Yet neither was she young. She was in between, and it was a blessed relief not to have to worry about it anymore. David accepted middle age with total unconcern, which made her do the same. She need not fear life passing her by again. From now on there'd be David.

Edwin Young was behind his front desk when Miss Abigail came into the hotel lobby, lightly stamping snow from her feet as she closed the door behind her.

"Here, let me help you with those things, Miss Abigail," he offered, coming across the lobby.

"Thank you, Edwin, but I've got them in hand."

"These're your wedding things, I suspect."

"They certainly are."

"Too bad the weather had to turn nasty right before your wedding."

"I really don't mind the snow," she said. "I had the thought this morning that it makes the entire mountain look as if it dressed up for David's and my wedding."

Miss Abigail sure has changed, Edwin thought, since David Melcher came to town. She was just as nice and common and friendly as could be. A person felt comfortable around her now. Edwin even dared to touch her chin lightly.

"You just keep that smile on your face, Miss Abigail, and— if you'll pardon my saying so—your photograph will be pretty as a picture."

They laughed and Edwin noted how Miss Abigail had lost her loftiness which used to make him think she considered herself a cut above the others in this town.

"I take it Damon Smith has arrived on the morning train as expected?"

"Oh, he sure did, Miss Abigail. Drug in enough gear to photograph the entire population of Colorado, the way it looked."

"I worried about the snow blocking the tracks. I was relieved to hear the whistle."

"Nope. He's here, all right, and if you'll follow me I'll be happy to show you to his room and help you carry these things."

"You don't need to do that, but thank you anyway. As long as I have everything in hand I'll just go up if you'll tell me what room he's in."

"He's in number eight. You sure I can't help you?"

But she was halfway up the stairs by that time.

The long, narrow upstairs hall dissected the building down the middle, with four rooms on either side. Number eight was the last one on the left, where a long window lit the hall, sun glancing in off brilliant snow, giving life to the faded moss roses on the carpet.

Juggling the garments in one arm and holding the ivory dress folded over the other, she knocked on the door with its centered brass numeral eight. She had never been in a hotel room in her life and was rather discomfited at being here now. She intended to make sure the door remained open during the session.

Footsteps came across the floor on the other side of the door and she wondered what Damon Smith would be like. David had met him and thought highly of his work. The doorknob turned and the door was opened by Jesse DuFrayne.

She gaped at him as if she'd gone snowblind. She blinked exaggeratedly, but, no, it was Jesse all right, gesturing with a sweep of hand for her to enter.

"I must have the wrong room," she said, standing rooted to the spot, the eight on the open door seeming to wink at her.

"No, it's the right one," he said, unperturbed.

"But it's supposed to be Damon Smith's room."

"It is."

"Then where is he?"

"In my room, right there." He pointed to the closed door of number seven. "I persuaded him to trade rooms with me for a while."

"You persuaded him?"

"Yes, rather. A favor between fellow photographers, you might say."

"I don't believe you. What have you done to him?" She turned toward number seven, half expecting Jesse to try to stop her. But he leaned against the doorframe, arms folded, and said—oh so casually, "I paid him off. He won't be taking your photograph. I will."

Angry already, she flung at him, "You are just as pompous as always!"

He grinned charmingly. "Just paying my debts is all. I got that free dinner, but I still owe you one portrait, just like we wagered. I'll take it for you today."

"You will not!" And Abigail rapped soundly at the door of number seven. While she waited for an answer, behind her Jesse said, "I told him you and I are old friends, that you'd even saved my life once and by a lucky coincidence I'm here in town to do you a favor in return."

Just as she raised her knuckles to rap again, the door was opened by a blond, blinking man who was buttoning his vest and suppressing a yawn. It was apparent he'd been sleeping. He ran a hand through his tousled hair, grinned in a friendly manner, and glanced from one to the other. "What's up, Jesse? Is this Miss McKenzie?"

"Yes, this is Miss McKenzie!" snapped Miss McKenzie herself.

"Is something wrong?" he asked, surprised.

"Are you Damon Smith?"

"Yes . . . sorry, I should have intro—"

"And were you commissioned to take a wedding portrait of me?"

"Why, yes, but Jesse explained how he just happened to be in town at the right time to do it instead, and since the two of you are such close friends I have no objection to stepping aside. As long as he paid me for my trouble, there are no hard feelings. No need to apologize, Miss McKenzie."

"I am not knocking on your door to apologize, Mr. Smith. I am knocking to get my photograph taken as we agreed!"

Smith scowled. "Hey, Jesse, what the hell is this anyway?"

"A lover's quarrel," Jesse answered easily, in a stage whisper. "If you'll just bow out, we'll get it settled. See, she's marrying this guy on the rebound." Jesse continued lounging against the doorframe.

Smith grunted while Abbie, outraged, swung first to one man, then to the other, claiming to deaf ears, "He's lying! I hired you to do my picture, not him. Now will you do it or not?"

"Listen, I didn't even set up my equipment, and besides, I don't want anything to do with whatever bones you two are picking. Just leave me out of it. Jesse already paid me twice what you would have, so why should I go through the trouble of setting up my gear? If you want your picture taken, let him do it. He's all set up for it anyway."

And before her astonished eyes, Damon Smith withdrew, mumbling about how in the hell he'd got into the middle of this in the first place, and slammed the door.

Immediately Abbie whirled on Jesse, incensed. "How dare you—" But he came away from that door, propelled her toward number eight, looking back over his shoulder down the hall with a conspiratorial grin.

"Shh," he teased. "If you want to pull your fishwife act, wait until the door is closed or the whole town will know about it."

She balked, outraged, jerking her elbow out of his grasp and taking root.

Rather than force her, he again made a gallant, sweeping gesture, saying politely, "Step into my parlor . . ."

Venomously, she added, ". . . said the spider to the fly!"

"Touché!" he saluted, smiling at her clever riposte. "But all I want to do is take your photograph, and you really don't have much choice in the matter now, do you?"

"I have the choice of having no photograph taken at all."

"Do you?" he asked, quirking one eyebrow.

"Haven't I?"

"Not if you want Melcher to remain blissfully ignorant of your midnight *tête-à-tête* last night with a caller who crept out of your house at three in the morning. Then, too, there's that clerk downstairs who knows perfectly well that you're up here at this very minute, having Damon take your photograph. Just how are you going to explain away your time spent with him if you can't produce a picture?"

She glared at the closed door of number seven and knew the spider had trapped her even before she entered his parlor. She could see that he did indeed have a hooded camera set up on a tripod, but it was little consolation. She thoroughly mistrusted him.

"Having created such a sensation the first time you entered this town," she reasoned, "you're certain not to have been missed this second time. The clerk knows you are up here too. One way or another David is bound to learn that you've been in town."

"But I have a perfectly legitimate business holding in this town, which he probably also knows I came to check on. So far nobody knows that you and I were together last night, or today for that matter, except Smith and he's been taken care of."

The man totally frustrated her. How could he change from the understanding warm person of last night to this conniving sneak?

"Ohhh! You and your railroad and your money! You think you can buy your way into or out of anything, don't you—that you can manipulate people's lives with the flash of your money."

"What good is my money if I don't use it to make me happy?" he asked innocently, once more indicating the open door.

She was licked and she knew it. She entered huffily while he began closing the door.

"Leave it open, if you please," she snapped, thinking, what can he do with the door wide open?

"Whatever you say," he agreed amiably, leaving the door as it happened to be, nearly closed, but unlatched. He advanced toward her, reaching politely for the things she held. She was now so leery of him that when he would have taken the garments, she refused to relinquish them.

Glancing at her hand clutching the ivory satin, he warned, "You'll wrinkle your wedding dress before you pose. What will David say?"

He took the garments and placed them on the bed, then came back to her. "Let me help you with your coat," he said, standing behind her while she unbuttoned it and let him remove it. "Nice coat," he noted as she shrugged it off. "Is it new?" She didn't have to see his face to recognize the knowing gleam in his eye. The coat was obviously part of her trousseau: it was obvious whose money had paid for it.

He laid it on the bed along with the other things, then turned to face her. They said nothing for a moment, and Abbie began to feel uneasy. What was she supposed to do, change clothes now?

"Isn't this where you're supposed to ask me if I'd like to see your etchings?" she asked sarcastically.

He surprised her by exclaiming, "Good idea!" with a single clap of his hands. "They're right over here."

Impossible as it was to believe, he meant it, for he squatted down by three large black cases and began unbuckling the straps on one of them. She knew immediately that these must be his photographs he'd mentioned so often.

"I was being facetious," she said, more mellowly.

"I know. Come and have a look anyway. I've wanted you to see these for a long time and maybe once you do you'll feel better about posing for me."

"You said you don't do portraits."

"I don't," he said, glancing up, sitting on his haunches with his hands resting on his thighs, "just yours."

He opened the first case and began removing layers of velvet padding from around the many heavy glass photographic plates, then the plates themselves.

"Come on, Abbie, don't be so skeptical and stubborn. I'll show you what it takes to build a railroad."

She was curious to see what kind of photographs he took, but still hesitated uncertainly. She'd been disarmed by him many times before.

"C'mon." He reached a hand up as if to pull her down beside him where he sat now, encircled by glass squares. He looked very appealing and even a little proud as he waited for her to join him. She ignored the hand but picked her way to the clear spot on the floor beside him and knelt in a puff of skirts, her eyes moving immediately to the photographs. The first one she saw was not of a train but of a square-sailed windjammer.

"I think this vessel would have a little trouble negotiating the rails," she observed.

He laughed and picked up the photograph, dusted it with his sleeve, and smiled down at it. "She's the *Nantucket*, and she made it around the Cape, from Philadelphia to San Francisco in just one hundred twelve days in eighteen sixty-three. The *Nantucket* brought the first two engines."

"Railroad engines?" she asked, surprised and interested in spite of herself. He gave her a brief smile, but his interest was mainly for the photographs.

"Everything came by ship then and everything rounded the Horn—engines, rails, spikes, fishplates, frogs—everything but wood for the ties and trestles."

Fishplates? Frogs? He sounded like he knew what he was talking about. Furtheremore, while he talked, a delight shone from his eyes like none she'd ever seen there before. Next, he pointed to a picture of a locomotive riding aboard a lithe, graceful river schooner whose stern wheel churned the waters of the Sacramento levee.

"The railroads had to rely on the river steamers," he explained. "Did you know that the levee was built especially to transport supplies for the railroad, only to lose its own lifeblood to the railroads after doing so?"

He studied the picture, and she could not help being touched by the sadness that came into his eyes. He might have forgotten she was in the room, so absorbed was he. He reached to dust the picture with his fingers and she saw things about him she had never seen before.

Without taking his eyes from the picture, he reminisced, "I rode on a riverboat several times when I was a boy. New Orleans will never be the same without them." In his voice, in his touch of fingertips to glass plate, were both passion and compassion, and they moved Abbie deeply.

Next came pictures of trestles, their diamond girders snaking away into the hearts of mountains or the abysses of canyons.

"Sometimes the cinders set them on fire," he ruminated, frowning as if unable to forget a bad memory.

Next was a picture showing hundreds of antlike coolies pushing minute wooden barrows toward those endlessly stretching trestles, ballasting them by hand against the threat of fire. Jesse explained each photo, often smiling, sometimes frowning, but always, always with a concentrated emotion which struck Abbie deeper and deeper.

"That's Chen," he said of a wrinkled, sweating Chinese man.

She looked at the ugly, leathery looking face, then up at Jesse, who smiled down at some good memory.

"Was Chen's skin really yellow like I've heard?" she asked, mystified.

Jesse laughed softly and said, almost as if to himself, "No, more like the color of the earth he carried in his barrow, never

complaining, always smiling." Again he dusted the picture
with his sleeve. "I wonder where old Chen is now."

There were tunnels that stretched into black nothingness,
their domed tops cavernous and foreboding. Even they made
Abbie shiver. There were tent towns Jesse had once described
to her, pictured in sun, in mud, at dinnertime, at fight time,
even at dancing time—men dancing with men at the end of a
dirty day. At these Jesse laughed, as if he remembered those
good times vividly and had shared them. There were faces
seamed with silt, backs bent bare over hammers, pot-bellied
dignitaries in faultless silk suits with gold watch chains
stretched across their bellies, contrasted against the sweat-
streaked stomachs of soiled, tired navvies. There were two
well-groomed hands clasped above the golden spike. There
was a single stiff, gnarled hand sticking out of a mountain of
rubble at which men frantically clawed.

"That was Will Fenton," Jesse said quietly. "He was a good
old boy."

But this picture he did not dust. He just stared at it while
Abbie watched pain drift across his face, and swallowed at a
thick lump in her throat. She had the compulsion to reach out
and lay a hand on his arm, soothe the tight, sad expression
from his brow. Jesse, she thought, what else is inside you that
I've never guessed? She looked at his long fingers resting along
his thighs and again at Will Fenton's hand in the photograph.

What Abbie saw round her was a gallery of contrasts, a
conscientious account of what it had cost to connect America's
two shores with iron rails, of what some had paid while others
profited, a pictorial statement from a man who'd done some of
each—some paying and some profiting—and who knew the
value of both.

James Hudson had been right.

"Well, do I pass muster?" Jesse asked, breaking into her
reverie.

"Impressively," she answered, quite humbled by what lay
around her, no longer sorry he'd tricked her into this room.

"Then why don't you get on all that wedding finery while I
put these away?"

He bent to his task as if forgetting that she was there, and she
glanced at the clothing still lying on the bed, then at the hinged
screen in the far corner of the room and hoped she was doing
the right thing as she went to collect her garments.

Behind the screen, she told herself that although she was very impressed by his photographs, she was not imbecile enough not to realize she'd just been soft-soaped by Jesse.

Step into my parlor, said the spider to the fly . . .

But all the while she was getting into her wedding gown, she kept remembering those photographs and the expression on Jesse's face. She hurried, telling herself to be wary of him, whether he'd won her respect as a photographer or not. He was still the wily Jesse DuFrayne.

He was clattering around out there, putting away his plates, whistling, then it sounded like he was shoving a piece of furniture about. When she stepped from behind the screen, his back was to her. He was kneeling down, taking something from the floor beside his camera. While she watched, he put it beneath the rockers of a chair he'd set before the camera. She caught his eyes while he knelt beside the rocking chair, but he continued that nonchalant whistling, obviously enjoying his trade.

"I need to see in your mirror," she said, noting that he'd rolled his shirtsleeves up as if he meant to do business.

"Fine," he said, rising and stepping aside so she could get between him and his camera to the dresser. He watched out of the corner of his eye while she smoothed back her hair and tightened the hairpins holding the severe french knot pulled back. In the mirror she watched him pull a pedestal table and fern over beside the rocking chair, obviously as a backdrop. Surely he wasn't planning to photograph her sitting in a rocking chair! What about her headpiece and the trailing veil? But she didn't question him yet, just lifted the seed-pearl circle. But when she was about to place it on her head, he ordered, "No, don't put that on!"

"But it's my bridal veil. I want it in the picture."

"It will be. Bring it here," he said, gesturing her toward the rocker.

"Surely you don't intend to have me sitting in a rocking chair in my wedding picture. I'm not *that* old, Jesse."

He laughed, a full-throated, wonderful laugh. He'd never known another woman with her great sense of humor. He stood loose, relaxed, hands on hips, letting his eyes take in the sight of Abbie in her mother's wedding dress. "I'm glad I've taught you that fact anyway, but yes, you're sitting in the rocker."

"Jesse . . ." she started to argue.

"I think I know a little more about this than you, so get over here." When she didn't move, he said, "Trust me."

She thought, look what happened last time I trusted you, but she did as he asked and neared the chair. He had propped it back at a sharp angle, shimming a block of wood beneath the rockers, and she suddenly realize what he was up to.

"This is supposed to be a picture of a bride, not a boudoir," she noted caustically.

"Don't be so suspicious, Ab, I know what I'm doing. David will love it when he sees it."

That made her more suspicious than ever.

"I want you to take my picture standing up."

"I'll be standing up. Don't worry."

"Don't be ridiculous, you know what I mean."

"Yes, of course I do. Just some facetiae of my own. But either we do this my way or David wonders why there's no picture to show for all your time up here today."

He reached out a palm, stood waiting to hand her into the chair. Stymied, she had to do as he wanted. With grave misgivings she let him take her hand and help her into the tilted rocker. His hand was hard and warm and somehow very secure-feeling as he squeezed hers, lending some balance while she lowered herself into the propped-back chair. This rocker was larger than her little sewing one, and had arms and a high back decorated with turned finials on each side of the curved backrest. The way he had the thing listing at such a severe angle, once she fell back into it she was quite helpless to get back out again. She felt positively adrift with her feet dangling free, and tried to hold her head away from the back of the chair.

Jesse took the veil from her hand and moved around behind her to lay it on the bed. He stepped to the back of the chair and looked down at her hair. Laying a hand on her forehead, he pulled her head back against the carved oak which caught her just above the nape of the neck.

"Like this," he said, "relaxed and natural."

At the touch of his hand, her heartbeat became pronounced within the high, tight collar of Mechlin lace. As her french knot touched the back of the chair, she found herself looking at Jesse upside down. They stared at each other for a moment and she wondered frantically what he was going to do to her.

In a velvety voice he began speaking as he slowly moved

around the chair, never taking his eyes off hers. "What we have here is the bride not before the ceremony, but after—the way every groom wants to remember his bride. When her hair is a little less than perfect and she doesn't know it."

He seemed to be moving in slow motion, reaching toward a pocket, producing a small comb while her eyes never left his, but she saw the comb coming toward her temple, where it bit lightly, loosing some strands from their moorings while she failed, for once, to protest. She knew she should put her hands up to stop him from this madness, but he seemed to have hypnotized her with those dark, probing eyes and that low, crooning voice.

"There is a look a man likes about his bride," came that voice again. "Call it tousled maybe . . . less than perfect after all the cheeks that have pressed hers that day and all the arms that have hugged her, all the losers that have danced with her and touched her temple with theirs." He leaned toward her slowly, reaching a dark hand again to hook a wisp of hair in front of the opposite ear, not smiling, but studying, studying. She knew her french knot was being annihilated, but sat entranced while he freed the fine strand, then moved around the rocking chair while she followed him with her eyes.

"He likes tendrils that cling here and there and stick to her damp skin."

No, Jesse, no, she thought, yet sat mesmerized while he wet the tip of his own finger with his tongue, touched it to the crest of her cheek, then stuck the curl onto it. She saw and felt it all as if only an observer at a distance—the tip of his tongue, his long finger, the wet, cold spot of his saliva on her cheek. She tried not to think of how many places on her body he had touched with his tongue, but his finger went to his mouth again and he did the same on her other cheek, then backed away a little, approving, "Oh, much better, Abbie. David will love this."

She gripped the arms of the chair and stared up at him, her errant pulse skipping to every part of her he had touched and many he had not.

"Oh, but you're so tense. No bride should clutch the arms of her chair as if she's scared to death." His hair came very close to her face as he took both of her hands from the arms of the chair and ordered in that same dreamlike voice, "Loosen up," then shook them lightly until her wrists acquiesced and grew

limp. "Just like in your bedroom that night when you fir
laughed," he reminded her. "Remember?" She let him d
what he would with those lacebound wrists. He turned on
over and laid it palm-up on her thigh. "That's right," h
murmured, then ran one of his fingertips from its wrist to th
end of her middle finger, flicking it, finding it relaxed. Shiver
ran across her belly. He rose and disappeared momentarily, an
her wide eyes only waited for the return of his dark face befor
her.

"Now the veil . . ." He brought it, a cloud of white in hi
swarthy, masculine hands, "the symbol of purity, about to b
discarded." Her heart leaped wildly as his arm came towar
her, but he only hung the headpiece on a spooled finial besid
her temple and brought the lace train over one arm to lay in
flowing heap cascading from her lap. "Palm-up, okay, Ab?"
The texture of netting crossed her palm as he placed it there, a
if she had just tiredly removed it from her head. Then he lifte
her other arm and draped its wrist like a willow branch over th
chair arm. He knelt on one knee before her.

"It's the end of the day, right? Far too late for tight shoes an
stiff collars." And before she realized what was happening, h
had swept David's satin gift from her feet, his palm slidin
over her sole in a sensuous fleeting touch. She gazed
awestruck, into silence as he rose and moved behind her again
hypnotizing her with his dark eyes above the slash o
moustache which curved in the direction of a smile as she onc
again viewed it upside down. She knew he was reaching for th
buttons at her throat but was powerless to stop him. His finger
slowly freed the first one, relieving some of the pressure wher
her heartbeat threatened to shut off her breath. He freed
second button, then a third—tiny buttons, close together, hel
by delicate loops that took time, time, time before he ha
finally exposed the hollow of her throat. She stared up into hi
black eyes. His hands slid from her throat to the finials of th
chair and tipped it farther back, holding it as he looked dow
into her tortured eyes and asked throatily, "What man woul
not like to remember his bride this way?"

His eyes, even upside down, burned like firebrands, scorch
ing her cheeks, making her want to cover her face with th
inverted palm that lay instead lax upon her lap. Had she wante
to get up and run from him she could not. She had no recourse
now but to submit to his narcotic voice and eyes.

Looking down at her, Jesse could see a tricky sunshaft emphasize the heartbeat in the hollow of her throat behind the filigreed lace which lay open and inviting. He released the chair slowly until it rested against its shim again, then equally as slowly moved to its side, never taking his eyes from Abbie's face, trailing one hand on the finial very close to her cheek.

"Wet your lips, Abbie," he said softly. "They should be wet when the picture is snapped." But he made no move toward the camera, neither did she wet her lips.

"Wet them," he urged, "as if David has just now kissed them and said . . . I love you, Abbie." Jesse stared down at her soft, parted lips, his eyes roved up to hers, then back down to her mouth again, waiting. The tip of her tongue crept out and slipped across her lips, leaving them glistening, opened yet as the breath came labored between them.

He leaned down, placing one hand on each arm of the chair, his face only inches from hers, his voice like warm honey. "Your eyes are opened too wide, Abbie. When a man tells his wife he loves her, don't her eyelids flutter closed?" She fought for breath, staring at his handsome, handsome face, so near that when he spoke, she felt the words against her skin. "Let's try it once more and see," he whispered, still leaning above her.

"I love you, Abbie." And her eyelids lost their moorings.

"I love you, Abbie," she heard again . . . and they were at half mast.

"I love you, Abbie." And they closed against his cheek as his mouth came hungering. She no longer wanted to get up from the chair, for his open lips claimed hers and his long hands cinched her shoulders, thumbs reaching to stroke the spot where he'd seen her heart fluttering in her throat. He knelt on one knee at the side of the rocker while he kissed her back against it, his tongue dancing and stroking upon hers while everything in her reached and yearned for more.

But suddenly she felt panic rise within, tightening her lungs, her throat, her scalp. "No, I'm being married tomorrow," she choked, turning her head aside from his kiss which taunted her to forget.

"Exactly—tomorrow," he murmured softly into her neck.

Her eyes slid closed, and she turned sharply away from him in a vain attempt to combat the feelings he unleashed in her. "Let me up from this chair," she pleaded, close to tears.

"Not until I get a proper kiss from the bride," he sai
kissing the underside of her jaw. "Ab, you're not his wife ye
but when you are, I won't be here to kiss the bride. Just o
day early, that's all . . ."

When she still refused to turn toward him, he said, "Wh
not, Ab? Let's make you look like a kissed woman for David
photograph. That's how a woman looks on her wedding nigh
isn't it?" Then a strong hand spanned her chin and turned h
mouth to his. But when he swooped to kiss her again, sh
began struggling against him, using arms, hands, and elbow
But he captured her arms effortlessly and lifted them around h
neck, holding them there forcibly until he felt her strugglir
begin to quell.

Those arms had been denied for so long. Now at last the
curled around the dark hair at the back of his neck while sh
arched up and opened the lips she had wet at his command, f
David.

Jesse's mouth twisted hungrily across hers, then sudden
jerked away as he knocked the block of wood from beneath th
rocker with a thrust of his knee. The chair came reelin
forward and he was there to meet her as she came with it. The
mouths met almost desperately and he pulled Abbie from th
chair onto her knees before him. He wrapped a powerful ar
about her waist, forcing her against his hard, bulging loin
which moved in slow, sensuous circles against her sati
wedding dress. His hands moved down to hold her tightl
against him while their tongues spoke messages of want int
each other's mouths and their lips spoke like messages again
flesh that arched and pressed until both ached sweetly.

Tearing his lips from hers, he uttered against her templ
"You can't marry him, Ab. Say you can't." But before sh
could make a sound his impatient mouth sought hers onc
more, delving into its warmth and wetness with his seekin
tongue. "Say it," he demanded in a voice gruff with passion a
he lowered his lips to her jaw, then down, down to the ope
neck of her wedding dress. But she was adrift in splendo
could think of nothing but the pleasured sound which his touc
brought from her throat. She leaned her face into his hai
kissing the top of his head while her hands caressed his face
His mouth moved beneath her palms, opening wide as h
tasted her skin and buttons sprayed like sundrops around them

glancing off his face as he lowered it to the newly cloven garment where her breasts waited for his lips.

She recaptured enough sanity to murmur, "Jess . . . my wedding dress . . ."

Into her breasts he answered, "I'll buy you a new one." Then his head came up and his palms slid within the torn garment, touching a taut nipple, flattening it, then stroking it to an erect, pink peak.

"But it's my mother's," she said senselessly.

"Good," he grunted, running both of his palms upward past her breasts, onto her shoulders, then peeling the garment away with an outward thrust of wrists. He forced it down in back until it lay tight just above her elbows, imprisoning them within the long, lace sleeves but freeing her breasts to his hands, his tongue, his teeth, while her throat arched backward in abandon. He tugged at a nipple, groaned deep in his throat, then released it to rub the soft hair of his moustache back and forth across it as he admitted, "God, Abbie, I couldn't get you out of my mind."

"Please, Jess, we've got to stop."

But he didn't, only moved to her other breast.

"Did you think about me too?" he asked in a choked voice.

She tried halfheartedly to pull his head away from her breasts, but he continued kissing and suckling while her arms remained pinioned by the garment, useless.

"I tried not to. Oh, Jess, I tried."

"I did too . . ."

"Stop, Jess . . ."

"I love it when you call me Jess that way. What do you call him when he does this to you?" He knelt up straight again and held the back of her head in his two wide hands, searching her eyes before pulling her to him to kiss her with an almost savage anguish. Breaking away, he touched her very deliberately in her most sensitive spots—breast, belly, down her ivory skirts that remained between his hand and the warm, weeping female flesh within. "Can David make you quiver like this, want like this? Can he make your breasts get hard and your body go dewy like I can?"

And he knew from the tortured look upon her face what the answer was before she touched his face and kissed his chin, moving close.

"No . . . not like you, Jess, never like you . . ."

And she knew if she lived with David a thousand years the answer would remain the same.

Chapter 24

————

THE BELL TINKLED and David looked up to find Bones Binley shambling toward him between the red benches. Now that the cold weather was here, Bones had taken to loitering in the store, which was far more comfortable than Mitch's veranda, and where the coffee was hot. Then, too, it gave him a chance to eye Mizz Abigail now and again.

She wasn't here today . . . but Bones knew that before he came in.

"Howdy, Bones," David greeted the gangly stalk, experiencing the peculiar momentary twinge of ego he always felt in Bones's presence ever since he'd heard Bones had eyes for his woman. As Abbie's "chosen one," David often patronized Bones just the smallest bit. As the "non-chosen," Bones sensed this and bridled inwardly. He couldn't figure out what Mizz Abigail saw in Melcher anyway.

"What say, David?" Bones returned.

"Thanks for taking Abigail's packages up from the depot yesterday. She was really happy to see them. She'd been waiting for the headpiece for days and was worried it might not get here in time."

Bones nodded at the floor. "Yup."

"She said to thank you again when I saw you."

"Yup."

"She's up at the hotel having her picture taken."

"Yup."

David laughed. "I don't know why I bother telling you anything. There's not a thing happens in this town you don't know about before it does."

Bones again laughed at the floor—a soundless shake of shoulders.

"Yup, that's a fact. Now y' take like yesterday, with that blizzard brewin', I musta been the only one out when the two-twenty come in and that DuFrayne feller gits off carryin' all that pitcher-takin' gear and checks in up at Edwin's." Bones found his twist of tobacco and bit off a good-size chew.

David went white as the new snow.

"D . . . D . . . DuFrayne?"

"Yup."

"Y . . . you . . . m . . . must be mistaken, Bones. That wasn't D . . . DuFrayne, it was D . . . Damon Smith with the picture-taking gear."

"Him? He the blond one? Short? About so-high? Naw, he din't come in till the nine-fifty this morning. No, that other one, he come in on the late train yesterday and checks in at Edwin's just like I said. Far as I know he's still right there." Bones lifted the lid off the pot-bellied stove, took deadly aim, and let fly with a brown streak of tobacco juice that sizzled into the lull that had suddenly fallen. Then he wiped the side of his mouth with the edge of his hand, keeping the corner of his eye on David.

"I . . . I see it's time for me to go m . . . meet Abigail, Bones. I t . . . told her I w . . . would, after she was d . . . done with the ph . . . photograph. If you'll excuse me . . ."

"Sure thing, sure thing," returned the pleased Bones as David hurried to the back room for his coat.

Three and a half minutes later, David entered the hotel lobby.

"Well, David, my man, how's business?"

"All s . . . set to go, right af . . . after the w . . . wedding."

Edwin chuckled amiably, noting David's nervousness. He gave David a conspiratorial grin. "Last twenty-four hours before a wedding are the toughest, eh, David?"

David swallowed.

"Don't you worry now, with that store and that wife, you're gonna be as happy as a hog in slop."

Normally David would have laughed heartily with Edwin, but he only asked now, with a worried look upon his face, "Is she here, Ed?"

"Sure is." Ed thumbed toward the ceiling. "Been up there an hour already. Should have a dandy photograph by this time."

"I . . . I n . . . need to talk to her a m . . . minute."

"Sure thing, go right on up. Smith's in number eight, end o' the hall on your left."

"Thanks, Ed. I'll find it."

Upstairs the sunlight streamed through sheer lace on the long, narrow window at the end of the hall as David strode silently upon the long runner strewn with faded moss roses. His toe had begun to hurt, and his heart felt swollen, as if it were choking him. An hour? She had been here an hour? Did it take an hour to have a photograph made? But it *was* Damon Smith she was with, It was! Yes, it surely must take at least an hour for the posing and the developing, which was done on the spot.

As he approached number eight, he saw that the door was closed but not latched.

A murmur of voices came from inside—a man's, husky and low, a woman's, strained and throaty. David felt suddenly weak and placed his palm against the wall for support. The voices were muffled, and David strained to hear.

"Stop, Jess . . ."

Oh, God, that was Abigail's voice. David's eyes slid closed. He willed his feet to move, to take him away, but it felt as if those moss roses had suddenly sent up tendrils to hold his ankles to the carpet. Tortured, he listened to the husky words that followed.

"I love it when you call me Jess that way. What do you call him when he does this to you?"

David's mind filled with terrible moving pictures as a long, long silence followed and sweat broke out on his brow. Move! he told himself. Get out! But before he could, DuFrayne's voice, fierce, passionate, asked, "Can David make you quiver like this, want like this? Can he make your breasts get hard and your body go dewy like I can?"

And Abigail's shaken reply, "No . . . not like you, Jess, never like you . . ."

David hesitated a moment longer, nausea and fear plummeting through him while from within the room came the sounds of lovers who forget themselves, and the temptation became too great.

Stepping to the door, he pushed it open, then gulped down the gorge that threatened to erupt from his throat.

Abigail knelt on the floor, eyes closed, head slung back as hair tumbled in wanton disarray down her bared back. The bodice of her wedding gown was lowered, pinning her elbows to her sides, baring her breasts to Jesse DuFrayne, who knelt on one knee before her, his mouth upon her skin. Abigail's bridal veil was crushed beneath their knees, its headpiece lay in a misshapen gnarl under the rocking chair behind her. Pearl buttons lay ascatter amid hairpins, a comb, the satin shoes he'd given Abigail as a weeding gift. Sickened yet unable to tear his eyes away, David watched as the woman he was supposed to marry tomorrow reached blindly to cup the jaw of the dark man before her, guiding his mouth from one breast to the other as a soft moan escaped her lips.

The shamed blood came suring to David's face as he bleated out a single word. "Abigail!"

She jerked back. "David! Oh, my God!"

"Well, you certainly had me fooled!"

The blood drained from her face, but as quickly as she pulled back, Jesse instinctively pulled her against his chest, shielding her bare breasts from intruding eyes, cupping the back of her head protectively, even his raised knee tightening against her hip as he settled her safely against the lee of his loins.

"You'd better watch what you say, Melcher, because this time it will be me who answers, not her," Jesse warned, his voice resounding mightily against Abigial's ear which lay against his chest.

"You . . . you scum!" David hissed. "I was right all along. You're two of a kind!"

"It seems we are, which makes me wonder why in the living hell she'd want to marry you."

"She won't be! You can have her!"

"Sold!" barked Jesse, piercing Melcher with an ominous

glare while he reached blindly to pull the shoulders of Abigail's dress back up.

"An apt word, I'd say, considering the money she's already taken from you, you son of a bitch!"

Abigail felt Jesse's muscles tense as he put her away from him and made as if to rise.

"Stop it! Stop it, both of you!" Abbie cried, clutching her dress front and struggling to her feet, followed by Jesse, who kept a shoulder between her and the door. The torn garment, their compromising pose, and what David had overheard made denial impossible. She felt as if she were freefalling through endless space into the horrifying noplace of *déjà vu*. She lurched around to move toward David, but he backed away in distaste.

"David, I'm sorry . . . I'm sorry, David, please forgive me. I didn't intend for this to happen." She reached a supplicating hand toward him even as the other continued to hold her bodice together. But apologies and excuses were so pitifully inadequate they only added to her shame.

"You lying harlot," he ground out venomously, all signs of stammering somehow surprisingly gone from his voice. "Did you think I wouldn't find out? Just one more time before you married me, is that it? Just one more time with this son of a bitch you'd rather have than me? Well, fine—keep him!"

Today was the first time she'd ever heard David swear. She reached to clutch his sleeve, horrified at what he'd witnessed, at herself for having fallen so low.

"David, please . . ."

But he jerked free, as if her touch were poison.

"Don't touch me. Don't you ever touch me again," he said in cold, hard hate. Then he tugged his coat squarely onto his shoulders, turned on his good foot, and limped away without a backward glance.

Standing there staring at the empty doorway the enormity of her offense washed over her. Tears formed in her eyes and her hands came to cover her open mouth, from which no sound issued for a long time. She felt sickened by herself and her eyes slid shut as she started quaking uncontrollably.

"He'll never marry me now. Oh God, the whole town will know within an hour. What am I going to do?" She covered her temples with her fingertips and rubbed them, then clutched her arms tightly and rocked back and forth as if nearing hysteria.

Jesse stood several feet behind her, did not approach or try to touch her as he said quitely, "It's simple. . . . Marry me."

"What!" She spun to face him, staring for a moment as if he'd gone mad. But she was the one suddenly laughing, crying, shaking all at once in a queer fit tinged by frenzy. "Oh, wouldn't that be jolly. Marry you and we could spend the rest of our lives screaming and biting and scratching and trying to get the better of each other. Oh . . ." She laughed again hysterically, "Oh, that's very funny, Mr. DuFrayne," she ended, tears streaming down her face.

But Jesse was not laughing. He was stone serious, his face an unmoving mask as he said intensely. "Yes, sometimes it is very funny, Miss McKenzie—funny and exhilarating and wonderful, because that's our way of courting each other. I found I missed it so much when I was away from you that I had to come back here to see if you were as good as I remembered."

"You purposely came back to cause trouble between David and me, don't deny it."

"I'm not denying it. But I changed my mind last night while we talked. What happened here today was not planned. It just happened."

"But you . . . you tricked me into this room, into . . . into sitting in that rocking chair and . . . and . . ."

"But you wanted it just as bad as I did."

The truth was still too frightening for her to face, and she was, as always, confounded by his changeability. She could not help wondering what his motives were today. She swung around him and swooped toward the screen in the corner, accusing, "It's all a big game to you, manipulating people so th—"

"This is not a game, Abbie," he argued, following her right around the screen, talking to her shoulder as she turned her back on him. "I'm asking you to marry me."

She unbuttoned her cuffs as if they were made of itchweed. "Oh, wouldn't we be the laughingstock of Stuart's Junction—Miss Abigail and her train robber!" She turned to him, yanking at the sleeves, affecting the sugary tone of a gossip. "Oh, you remember, don't you? The couple who were caught in the act the day before her impending marriage to another man?" She yanked the bodice down, fuming. He moved up close behind her.

"That in itself should tell you that we're right for each other. You know damn well you enjoy it more with me than with him or you never would have let me get as far as I did today."

She whirled on him, holding some garment over her breasts. "How dare you insinuate that I did anything with David! We did nothing—absolutely nothing! We were as pure as the driven snow and this town knew it!"

They stood nose to nose, each of them glaring.

"Who gives a damn about what this town thinks? What has this town ever done for you besides label you a spinster when you were only twenty years old?"

"Get out of here when I'm changing my clothes!" she shouted, and presented her back to step out of the wedding dress, bending forward and giving him a rear view of white pantalets more ruffled than any he'd seen on her clothesline. His eyes traveled down her skin, down the shadowed hollow that receded into the white cotton waistband.

"When I get out of here, it will be with you on my arm, wearing that expensive green coat I paid for, telling this town to kiss off as we board my train!"

She yanked a camisole over her head and he watched the fine hair at the back of her neck as she looked down and tied the string at her waist.

"You're still not done flaunting your money, are you?" She threw a brief, disparaging look over her shoulder. "Well, you've come up against the one thing you can't buy!" She pulled a petticoat and skirt on and buttoned them at her waist.

"Buy you!" he shouted, "I don't want to buy you. I want you free! You have to give yourself to me freely if we get married, because you want to."

"You planned this seduction today, don't tell me you didn't." She pulled a blouse off the top of the screen and slipped her arms into it.

He reached out and got her from behind by both breasts, pulling her back against his hardness. She purposely remained aloof, acting as if his touch went thoroughly unnoticed except when she had to push his hands aside to close the buttons of her blouse.

"So we're even then, aren't we, Ab?" he asked, pressing the side of his mouth against the hair behind her ear. "Didn't you plan my seduction once? Only you succeeded where I haven't . . . so far." As he nuzzled her rose-scented neck, he fervently began caressing her breasts, at last awakening the fight in her. She fought his hands, but he only held her tighter, slipping his palm inside her partially opened blouse, leaning to kiss the nape of her neck, sliding his other hand down her stomach, then lower. They grappled together, elbows flying, sending the screen crashing to the floor.

"You have the most unscrupulous courting methods I've ever seen!" she bawled, pulling at his wrists, but just then he got one powerful arm cinched around her stomach, his other hand once more finding its way to her breast and forcing her back against his tumescent body.

"Feel that. Tell me you don't want it. Tell me I don't know what's best for you."

For a moment she wilted and his grip slackened, giving her enough advantage to break free and spin to face him.

"How can you know what's best for me when I don't even know myself?"

Her eyes flicked to the door David had left open.

"Then I think it's time I showed you again," he threatened with honey in his voice, taking a step nearer.

Her heart was hammering wildly now, confused by the mixture of emotions Jesse could always stir up in her. They eyed each other like a pair of cats at howling time, beginning slowly, slowly to circle until she gained the side of the room closest to the hall. Suddenly she turned and hit for the door, but he had it slammed so fast the wind dried her eyeballs. She backed away, big-eyed, panting, feeling the throb of her pulse in every wary nerve of her body.

He leaned back casually, holding the doorknob behind his back. One foot was flat on the floor, the other crossed in front of it with only the toe of his boot on the floor. He wasn't even breathing heavily. He lounged there as if he had all the time in the world, the ghost of a grin crawling up one side of his mouth while those hazel-flecked eyes assessed her with a tinge of knowing mirth. His voice was soft, cajoling, seductive.

"You know we're doing it again, don't you? The old courting dance we both love so much. This is the way we always start out, Abbie—me pursuing, you fighting me off. But this is no fight and you know it, because in the end we both win." He brought his shoulders away from the door in slow motion. "So come here you little hell-cat," he ended with a hoarse whisper, "because I'll only stalk you so long before I pounce."

She loved it, she'd missed it, she wanted it, this hammering of the senses that exhilarated like nothing else she'd ever experienced as she waited, waited, knowing what he'd do. Her breasts were heaving and her eyes sparkled, but like a true hell-cat she spit one more time. "Come here! Do this! Do that! Marry me! And then what? Go through this for the rest of our lives!"

His grin grew bolder. "You're goddamn right," he said, low.

"Oh, you . . . you . . ."

But he was done waiting.

"Damn . . ." he muttered, and sprang! He grabbed her wrists and swung her adeptly until her back slammed flat against the closed door. His hands grasped her beneath the armpits and she felt her feet leave the floor as he lifted her bodily, holding her plastered against the mahogany panel, kissing her. His wide palms bracketed the sides of her breasts while his lips, too, held her prisoner, controlling hers, sending spasms of desire rippling through her body, directed each to its own nerve by his mastering tongue. Emotions stormed her senses while Jesse stormed her body, breathing now like a hurricane while he besieged her with deep kisses, his tongue fierce and probing, impaling her against the door.

At last he freed her mouth, gazing with dark, tempestuous eyes into hers.

"Damnit, Abbie, I love you. It was me saying I love you before, for myself, not for David."

She seemed unable to speak, and they both suddenly realized he still had her up against that door. He let her slide slowly down, a last hairpin dropping unnoticed from her hair. When her toes touched the floor, he continued holding her lightly by both breasts, searching her eyes for some sign of entente.

"What do you say, Abbie?"

Her eyes, kindled yet confused, sparkled within the shock of loosened hair framing her face.

"How can I marry a man I'm afraid of half the time, who just flung me against a door?"

A pained expression crossed his face and he dropped his hands from her breasts to her ribs, touching her gently, caringly.

"Oh, God, did I hurt you, Abbie? I didn't mean to hurt you." He kissed one of her eyelids, then the other, then backed away to look into her blue eyes, his voice as close to tortured as she'd ever heard it. "Are you really afraid of me, Abbie? You don't ever have to be afraid of me. All I want to do is make you happy, make you laugh, maybe moan . . . but not from hurt. From this . . ."

He closed her eyes once again with his lips, then trailed them down her nose to her cheek, along her delicate jaw to her chin, then finally up to her lips, which had fallen open by the time he reached them. His hands went to the shoulders of her unbuttoned blouse, squeezing until she thought her bones would crack. But his mouth upon hers was a direct contrast to the pressure of his hands—soft, gentle, convincing, while his warm tongue skimmed lightly, lightly over her lips, then over her teeth before he moved to her ear and said into it. "Admit it, Abbie, it's what you want too. Be honest with me and with yourself."

"How can I be honest when you've got a hold on me this way? Jesse, I can't think."

He cautiously dropped his hands, but only to her ribs, riding them lightly as if afraid she might escape him yet. And there they lay, warm, large, spanning her torso, one of his thumbs reaching up to brush the underside of her breast while he searched her face.

"Abbie, you said you had to shout to the empty rooms when I was gone, trying to be free of me. Doesn't that tell you something?"

Her eyes pleaded but he did not relinquish his hold on her. Instead, the warmth from his palms seeped through the layer of cotton over her skin, his hands now inside the blouse, on her ribs, that long thumb still arousing her to shivery sensuality as it slid slowly back and forth.

"I'm so mixed up," she said in a trembling voice, eyes sliding closed, head resting back wearily against the door.

"You have a right to be. I'm exactly the opposite of what you've been told all your life was right for you. But I am right, Ab, I am."

She rolled her head from side to side, swallowing. "I don't know . . . I don't know."

"Yes, you do, Abbie. You know what kind of life we'll have. We're good together at everything we do. Talking

guing, making love, making sense . . . and nonsense.
hat are you afraid of, Abbie, that you'll get hurt again? Or of
hat this town will say? Or what David will say?"

She opened her eyes but looked over his shoulder at the lacy
indow curtain and the snow beyond.

"I've hurt David so badly." Her nostrils flared and her eyes
id shut.

"Maybe you had to, for your own salvation."

"No, nobody deserves to be hurt like that."

"Did you, thirteen years ago?"

She looked into his eyes again.

"I refuse to appease my conscience by saying two wrongs
ake a right."

"Then let me share part of the blame for hurting him. Hell,
l even march up the street and apologize to him if that's what
takes to win you. Is that what you want me to do, Abbie?"

Tears suddenly stung her nose, for the loss of David, for this
an's devotion. She somehow believed Jesse meant it and
ould actually face David and apologize. After all, Jesse was a
an who'd go to any lengths to get what he wanted. It struck
er just how badly he wanted her. Still, she leaned against that
oor and let him go on convincing her, for it was heavenly
anding there with his dark face so close to hers as he leaned
oth forearms now on either side of her head.

"There's a whole country out there, Abbie. You can pick
ny city you want to live in. I'll take you anyplace. You want
 live like the wife of a railroad baron in some mansion in
olorado Springs, all right. It's yours. You name the place and
e'll go. How about starting in New Orleans? I'll take you to
e the ocean, Abbie, and to meet my family. You've always
anted to see the ocean, you told me so. You even tried to
ring a little of it here by designing that Cape Cod window in
at shoe store, but I'll take you to Cape Cod to see the real
ing if you want." His eyes were filled with sincerity as he
ent on. "Abbie, I don't want to buy you, but I would if I had
. I'm rich, Abbie, so what's wrong with that? What's wrong
ith me wanting to spend my money making you happy? I owe
ou my life, Abbie, let me give it to you . . ."

This, this, this, she thought, was what she had always
reamed of, the Jesse she'd always dreamed of, whispering
ve words in her ear, making her blood pound and her senses
oar. Her eyes drifted open and found his, dark, intense,

promising her the world. She floated in the warm security
the knowledge of his love for her, quite unable to speak at
moment.

Is this me, she thought, Abigail McKenzie? Is this rea
happening? This startlingly handsome man, with his elbo
leanings beside my ears, convincing me with utter sincerity
his every word that he loves me? Her heart felt ready
explode.

He leaned to nuzzle her neck, to nip her earlobe, then to
the inside of it with the tip of his damp tongue.

"That's what I want, Ab, but what about what you w
right now?"

She felt his breath—warm, fast—beating upon her ear, th
his voice came again, strangled and strange, making thi
melt within her body. "Don't discount it as unimportant. I
slipped my hand beneath your skirt and touched your body
know what I'd find. Don't deny that it's important, Ab. I
felt it there before because you wanted me, and I know
there again."

And deep inside Abbie felt a welcome liquid rush
femininity, accompanied by the sensual swelling of that part
her which no man except Jesse had ever touched.

Her eyes slid closed. Her chest tightened. Her breath ca
jerky. Even the hair at the back of her neck felt like it h
nerves, each of them aroused, ready for response.

Across the fullest part of her stomach, she felt him press
aroused body, lightly, lightly brushing from left to right, ri
to left, making circles on her while his palms remained press
flat against the door above her head. Her own palms tingl
eager to be released and to touch him, yet she kept the
pressed flat against the door behind her hips, drawing out t
sensual mating dance to its fullest, wanting it to build slow
slowly, slowly in tempo and heat while he rubbed against h
his shirt buttons now lightly grazing the tips of her nippl
which were drawn up tight like tiny, hard bells beneath t
flimsy cotton camisole.

She trembled with sensation. Jesse, Jesse, she thought, y
are so good at this . . . so good . . .

He looked down to find a faint smile upon her lips, her ey
still closed, her breasts now straining as far forward as s
could manage and still keep her shoulder blades against t
door. He smiled slowly, understanding her well, letting

ɔws slide several inches lower, bringing his midsection
ɩy from hers, then flicking his tongue out to touch the very
ɪer of her eye.

ɪe's had so little love, he thought, I will drown her in it for
ɩ rest of her life.

Jo word was said. Her hands came from behind her to
ɩdly find his hips and pull them back against her, bringing
ɩ heat and hardness where she wanted them, making him
ɩe against her hair and slip one arm between her shoulder
ɩes and the door, down to her waist. His other hand grasped
ɩ doorknob for leverage as he ground himself against her, a
ɩ clapped tight now upon the seat of her petticoats, quite
ɩble to feel much more through all those layers.

Ier hips began to move with his, while her palms remained
ɩ below his belt as if she must know fully his every
ɩion—she must, she must, she had waited so long. She
ɩned her eyes as if drugged, pleading silently until his mouth
ɩe down to find hers open, waiting, yearning. And together
ɩr tongues dove deep while their flesh pressed so tightly
ɩether that pulses seemed inseparable.

ɩhe writhed between him and the door and he moved his
ɩuth to her ear, whispering hoarsely, "Abbie, I'm going to
ɩ you to that bed and make love to you like you never
ɩgined you'd be made love to again."

ɩe felt her shudder and understood what was happening
ɩde her. His own body was straining against the confines of
ɩthing. Still, he leaned low and lightly bit one of her
ɩples—as if in passing—through the cloth and all, making
ɩ twist and suck her breath in sharply and open her eyes.
ɩe slipped an arm around her shoulder, the other beneath her
ɩes, and lifted her effortlessly from her feet, her arms
ɩning up and about his broad shoulders, fingers twining into
ɩ hair at the back of his neck while he turned slowly, slowly
ɩvard the bed.

"And I'm going to keep it up . . . and keep it up
ɩ . and keep it up . . . until you admit that you love me
ɩ say you'll marry me," he said throatily.

They stared into each other's eyes as he strode toward the
ɩd, the muscles of his chest hard and warm against her breast.
ɩhe heard the springs sing out as he knelt with one knee and
ɩned to lay her down. With a hand on either side of her head,
ɩ hung above her, and said into her eyes, "And I don't intend

to be hindered by the petticoats you chose to wear for
wedding to another man—whether I paid for them or n
Then without watching what he was doing, he found
buttons at her waist and she felt them come free. Ti
shafted through her and she smiled, a glitter of eagerness
playing up at him from behind fringed lashes.

"But, Jesse, you paid so dearly to arrange that weddi
she said softly, seductively.

"Well, I'm unarranging it," he said gruffly, and he stri
the petticoats away down her calves, then grabbed her
and pulled her to a sitting position.

"And neither will I contend with Victorian collars
signify nothing."

With agonizing slowness he removed her blouse.
obediently complied, but when his dark head dipped near
as he slid the garment away she informed him, "Whetl
marry you or not, I will dress as I see fit—like a lady.

"Fine," he returned as the blouse came off. "You do tha
our parlor when you have the ladies of the other railroad ba
to tea." He tossed the blouse over his shoulder. "In
bedroom you leave them hanging in the chiffonier along
your camisole and these." He inserted a single finger into
waistband of her pantaloons, tugging.

She fell back languidly, arms flung loosely above her h
and lay there in wait, loving him more with each passing we

"You paid for these too. I suppose that gives you the rig
do what you will with them."

He knelt beside her and without taking his eyes from
face, removed his vest and shirt, flinging them over
shoulder to join her petticoat and skirt on the floor.

"Exactly. Just like I paid for that green coat you were g
to wear on your honeymoon. And if you weren't proud of
fact that I'm rich you wouldn't keep pointing it out time
again." And off came his belt.

"I would have been content to run a simple shoe store,"
purred, reaching out to brush the backs of her fingers aga
the part of him she'd first seen when he was dying upon
bed, making his eyes burn bright before her fingers tra
away from his trousers.

Then slowly, tantalizingly, he freed the buttons up the f
of his pants, while his voice poured over her like liquid s

"When I'm done here, I'm going to shoot down

oddamn sign that's got your name on it with his." The ardor
his tone made the word *goddamn* almost an endearment.
en his pants, too, were gone.

"Signifying nothing," she murmured with a slow smile.

"Like hell," he said gruffly, reaching to untie the string at
e waist of her camisole, then sliding a hand inside, up, up,
er her ribs as he sat on the bed and stretched his long, dark
nbs toward Abbie.

Her nostrils widened and her breath came jagged.

"You don't think it's significant that I'm taking back what I
nce gave away so foolishly?" he asked possessively, pushing
e camisole up by increments, leaning his dark head to kiss
e hollow between her ribs, then that beneath her left breast.

Eyes closing, she whispered, "This whole town probably
nows what we're doing right now," caring not the least,
oving it anyway.

He moved his tongue to the hollow beneath her other breast,
nuckling deep in his throat, his lips nuzzling against her skin.

"And they'll probably run home and do a little of it
nemselves, just at the thought."

"Not everyone's like you, Jess," she said, smiling behind
osed lids, wishing he would hurry up.

But he moved like a seductive snail, unbuttoning the waist
f her pantaloons and slipping them only to her hips, exposing
neir hollows provocatively.

"No, but you are, and that's all that counts." Again his
nouth found her hollows, these just inside her hipbones, while
ne stirred sinuously. And after some moments the last
arment moved slowly, slowly downward while he kissed a
ath in its wake and she lay with a wrist across her forehead,
ll resistance gone, her lips parted as his tongue danced upon
er.

"I remember this best," he whispered hoarsely before
elving into her, following as she arched, stroking until she
noaned and fell back, shuddering beneath him.

"I did too . . . I did too," came her strangled voice.

He knew her well, he loved her well, he drew his head back
nst at her breaking point, moving up her body to thread his
ngers back through her hair and lay his hot, hard length upon
er, not in her.

"Say it, Abbie," he begged, kissing her beneath the jaw as
er head arched back. "Say it now while I come into you."

She opened her eyes and found his filled with love as t
probed hers. His elbows quivered beside her as he bra
away, waiting to hear the words.

She reached between them and found him, guided I
home, her eyes never leaving his as he came into her, mov
strong and sure to the rhythm of her repeated words,

"I love you, Jesse . . . love you . . . love you .
love you . . ." over and over again in accompaniment to
long, slow strokes. He saw tears well and slip from the corn
of her eyes as her lips formed and reformed the words, fa
and faster, until her lips fell open. And shortly, he followed
way she had gone, through that plunging ride of ecstasy

The room grew quiet, the afternoon light reflecting in off
snow as her hand lay on the damp nape of his neck. She to
with his hair absently. Then, closing her eyes tightly,
suddenly grasped him to her, holding him, possessing h
lying perfectly still for that moment, recording it in
memory to carry with her into the length of their days togeth

"Jesse . . . oh, Jesse."

Lost in love, he rocked her, rolling wordlessly from side
side, and finally falling still beside her, looking into her ser
face.

"The train is coming," he said softly.

She smiled and touched his lower lip, then trailed a finge
from the center of his moustache to its outer tip. "Even
train schedule accommodates you, doesn't it?"

"And what about Miss Abigail McKenzie?" he ask
holding his breath.

She gazed into his beloved eyes. "She too," she said so
"she too."

His eyes slid shut and he sighed, content.

But she made them open again when she asked, "But w
shall she do with her houseful of wedding cakes
sandwiches?"

"Leave them to the mice. They'll like them better th
oatmeal."

"Leave them?" she asked, puzzled.

He braced up on one elbow, all trace of smile gone from
face as he gazed at her intently.

"I'm asking you to get up off this bed and put on y
clothes and walk to the train depot with me, holding my a
never looking back. Everything starts with now."

"Leave my house, my possessions, everything—just like that?"

"Just like that."

"But the whole town is probably out there waiting for us to come out of this hotel. If we go straight to the depot, they'll know."

"Yes, they will. Won't we create a sensation walking out right under their noses, boarding the executive coach—Miss Abigail and her train robber?"

She eyed him, considering it.

"Why, Jesse, you want to shock them, don't you?"

"I think we already have, so why not finish it off with aplomb?"

She couldn't help lauhing. At least she tried to, but he hugged her again, pressing his chest across hers, and he was very, very heavy. All that came out was a soundless bouncing, which made him relieve her of some of his weight, but not quite all—not until she said yes.

"We are so very different, Jesse," she said, serious again, touching him upon his temples. "In spite of what we have in common, we are still opposites. I could not change for you."

"I don't want you to. Do you want me to?" For a moment he was afraid of what she might answer. Instead she said nothing, so he sat up on the edge of the bed, turning his back on her.

But she knew him well enough by now to recognize the tensing of his jaw muscle for what it was. She sat up behind him and ran a hand over one of his shoulders, then kissed his back.

"No," she said quietly against his skin, "just as you are, Jess. I love you just as you are."

He turned to her with a smile aslant his lips, the bedeviling moustache inviting as he reached out a single hand, palm-up.

"Then let's go."

She placed her hand in his and let him tug her off the bed, almost catapulting into his arms, laughing.

He hugged her naked body long against his, running his hand down her spine while her bare toes dangled above the floor.

"Back off, woman," he warned with a chuckle, "or we're going to miss that three-twenty to Denver."

Then he let her slip down and slapped her lightly on her naked rump.

* * *

They dressed, their eyes on each other instead of what they were doing. But when she began gathering up the torn wedding gown and the buttons and satin shoes, he ordered gently, "Leave them."

"But—"

"Leave them."

She looked down at the dress. The touch of its satin beneath her fingers reminded her again of David, and she knew what she must do. "Jesse, I can leave everything else, but I must . . ." She looked up entreatingly. "I must not leave David—not this way." Jesse did not move a muscle or smile. "Not hurting him as I have. May I just go back to the store and try to make him understand I never meant to hurt him?"

Jesse's eyes were dark, unscrutable, as he knelt before her, buckling the straps on one of his photograph cases.

"Yes. If it'll mean not having him between us for the rest of our lives, yes." They were the hardest words Jesse Dufrayne had ever spoken.

A few moments later he held the new green coat as she slipped her arms into it. Then they turned at the door to survey the room for a moment—the overturned screen still lying on its side, wedding gown in a heap, torn and wrinkled, its buttons strewn around the room along with her crushed veil and the discarded satin pumps.

Hoping he'd understand, she went back in and retrieved the shoes, tucking them into her coat as they left the hotel and stepped into the cold, sparkling sunlit afternoon.

He held her arm as they walked along the boardwalks to the shoe store at the end of the street, and he stood outside stoically, his hands buried in his pockets, waiting, while she went inside to return the white satin pumps to David Melcher. It seemed to take forever, though it was a matter of only several minutes.

The bell tinkled and Jesse looked up, searching her face as she came back out and took his arm to walk back toward the depot.

There was an odd, sick feeling in the pit of his stomach. He looked down at her gravely.

She smiled up at him. "I love you, Jesse."

And he breathed again.

They walked the length of Main Street, feeling eyes upon

them every step of the way. At the station the train waited, chugging and puffing impatiently, its breath white upon the cold Colorado air.

On the side of the second to the last car glittered an ornate crest bearing an R.M.R. insignia done in gold leaf, intertwined with a design of dogwood petals.

Puzzled, Abbie looked at it, then up at Jesse, but before she could ask, he scooped her up in his arms and mounted the steps of the executive coach.

But suddenly he stopped, turned, looked thoughtfully out at the deserted street, deposited her on her feet again, and said, "Just a minute. Don't go away." Then he swung down the steps again.

And cool as you please, Jesse DuFrayne drew a gun, took a bead on the sign down the street that bore the names of David and Abigail Melcher, and popped off two shots that brought every person out of the shops from one end of Main Street to the other to see what in tarnation was going on.

But all they saw was that sign lying in the snow down there in front of the shoe store and the back of Jesse DuFrayne disappearing up the steps into the train.

Inside, he again scooped Abbie into his arms, closing her surprised lips with his own.

"There's no place like home," he said when he had kissed her thoroughly, kicking the door shut behind them.

"Home?" she repeated, glancing around at the lush emerald green velvet interior of the car. "What is this?"

She strained to see around his head. As she turned this way and that he nuzzled her neck, for she was still in his arms and he had no intention of putting her down just yet.

"This, my darling Ab, is your honeymoon suite, especially ordered for the occasion."

What Abbie saw was no common steerage. She had never seen such luxury in her life—a massive bed covered in green velvet, an intimate dinner table set for two, a magnum of champagne in a loving cup, an ornate copper tub off to one side near an ornate pot-bellied stove, where a fire crackled, deep chairs, thick rugs.

"Jesse DuFrayne, you conniving devil! How did you get this coach to Stuart's Junction at the exact time we needed it? And quit kissing my neck as if you don't hear a word of what I'm accusing you of." But in spite of her scolding, she was giggling.

"It'll be a cold day in hell before I quit kissing your neck, Miss Abigail McKenzie, just because you order me to."

"But this *is* an executive coach. You ordered this car to be here. You *did* plan my seduction right down to the last minute!"

"Shut your precious mouth," he said, shutting it for her as the train started moving, and he strode to the oversized bed at the far end of the car, the kiss actually becoming quite slippery and misguided as the coach rocked and gained speed.

They laughed into each other's mouths, then he tossed her onto the bed, stood back, and asked, "What's first? A bath, dinner, champagne . . . or me?"

"How much time do we have?" she asked, already undoing her coat buttons.

"We can go all the way to New Orleans without coming up for air," he replied, that roguish grin tempting her while his eyes danced wickedly.

Taking her coat off she eyed the copper tub, the magnum of champagne, the table set for two, the window beside it where the world raced past. And the man . . . unbuttoning his cuffs.

"Well then, how about all four at once?" Abigail McKenzie suggested.

His eyebrows flew up, and his hands fell still momentarily before starting down the buttons on his chest.

"Well, goddamn . . ." muttered Jesse DuFrayne deliciously, his moustache coming at her in the most tantalizingly menacing way.

Bestsellers you've been hearing about—and want to read

____	**GOD EMPEROR OF DUNE** Frank Herbert	08003-X-$3.95
____	**HERS THE KINGDOM** Shirley Streshinsky	08109-5-$3.95
____	**FOR SPECIAL SERVICES** John Gardner	05860-3-$3.50
____	**THE CASE OF LUCY BENDING** Lawrence Sanders	07640-7-$3.95
____	**THE NEW ROGET'S THESAURUS** **IN DICTIONARY FORM** ed. by Norman Lewis	07269-X-$2.95
____	**FLOATING DRAGON** Peter Straub	06285-6-$3.95
____	**STEPHEN KING'S DANSE MACABRE** Stephen King	08110-9-$4.50
____	**SAVANNAH** Eugenia Price	06829-3-$3.95
____	**THE LAZARUS EFFECT** Frank Herbert and Bill Ransom	07129-4-$3.50
____	**ICEBREAKER** John Gardner	06764-5-$3.50
____	**DANCEHALL** Bernard F. Connors	07062-X-$3.50
____	**THE SEDUCTION OF PETER S.** Lawrence Sanders	07019-0-$3.95
____	**A SHIELD OF ROSES** Mary Pershall	07020-4-$3.95
____	**THE AUERBACH WILL** Stephen Birmingham	07101-4-$3.95
____	**RED SQUARE** Edward Topol and Fridrikh Neznansky	08158-3-$3.95

Prices may be slightly higher in Canada.

Available at your local bookstore or return this form to:

BERKLEY
Book Mailing Service
P.O. Box 690, Rockville Centre, NY 11571

Please send me the titles checked above. I enclose _____. Include 75¢ for postage and handling if one book is ordered; 25¢ per book for two or more not to exceed $1.75. California, Illinois, New York and Tennessee residents please add sales tax.

NAME_____

ADDRESS_____

CITY_____STATE/ZIP_____

(allow six weeks for delivery)

Turn back the pages of history...
and discover

Romance

as it once was!